The Flower Girl

The *Flower* Girl

Gilda O'NEILL

CANELO

First published in the United Kingdom in 1996 by Headline Book
Publishing

This edition published in the United Kingdom in 2019 by

Canelo Digital Publishing Limited
57 Shepherds Lane
Beaconsfield, Bucks HP9 2DU
United Kingdom

A CIP catalogue record for this book is available from the British Library.

Print ISBN 978 1 78863 565 3
Ebook ISBN 978 1 78863 456 4

Look for more great books at www.canelo.co

Printed and bound in Great Britain by Clays Ltd, Elcograf S.p.A.

For Anne Williams with my sincere thanks

Chapter 1

April 1933

The crowd gawped openly. Some actually gossiped animatedly amongst themselves, not even bothering with the nicety of hiding their loud whispers behind the shield of raised hands.

But it would have been a high-minded person who would have blamed them too harshly for their behaviour because, in truth, no one had seen anything like it. Not in Linman Street, Poplar, anyway. As Cissie Flowers' elderly neighbour, Ethel Bennett, said to Dick, her husband, the turnout for Davy Flowers' funeral was more suited to a king than to an East End barrow boy. And, for once, Dick didn't find himself disagreeing with the old bat.

Ethel, her elbows stuck out in defence of the prime spot she had established for herself at the front of the crowd, was going to get to the bottom of this if it was the last thing she did. For a start, where had all those wreaths come from? That's what she wanted to know. But it wasn't only nosiness that drove her curiosity, Ethel believed she had the *right* to know. After all, hadn't she been Cissie Flowers' next-door neighbour since the day the girl had moved in six years ago? A full two weeks before her wedding day, as Ethel Bennett never tired of telling people. And another thing: who were all those well-off looking blokes standing around like they owned the place? It was all driving Ethel barmy.

Even the pong from the Cut, growing riper by the minute in the baking morning sun, didn't stand a chance of driving her back indoors – the nearby crossing over Limehouse Cut, where Upper North Street became Bow Common Lane, hadn't been nicknamed Stink House Bridge for nothing – because if she dared turn her back for a moment, Ethel was worried that she might just miss an important clue. But the smell really was bad. Although it was only the middle of April, it felt as hot as any summer's day and the stench from the water was at its most choice, the vapours rising from its oily surface and wafting along the cobbled sidestreets like steam coming from a pan of rancid soup. The stink had grown so powerful, in fact, that some of Ethel's less strong-stomached neighbours had gone scurrying back inside to watch the proceedings from the safety of the other side of their window panes.

But what they saw next had even the most odour-sensitive amongst them popping back out of their street doors like rabbits from their burrows at twilight.

Ethel and the others watched, open-mouthed, as a procession, led by a tall, top-hatted man, turned off Bow Common Lane and entered their narrow little street, the cobbles of which were being strewn with barley straw by a young boy trotting ahead of them, to ensure that any sounds were deadened to a dull, deferential thud.

The soberly dressed man moved slowly forward; his measured strides setting the pace for the four glossy jet horses pulling the glittering glass-sided hearse, which bore a brass-handled mahogany coffin and the mortal remains of Davy Flowers. The animals' carefully oiled hooves were bound and muffled in leather pads, which had been buffed until they shone almost as brightly as the gleaming patent harness and the blue-black plumes which nodded between their brushed and clipped ears. As if that wasn't impressive enough, next came the cars, a whole polished line of them – too many of them even to fit into the street.

Ethel Bennett shook her head in wonder and dug her husband, Dick, in the ribs at the sight of them. There looked to be at least half a dozen cars queuing back to Upper North Street, just to ferry the mourners to Bow Cemetery – a walk of surely no more than thirty minutes for even the most infirm amongst them – and that was without all the private cars that had been parked halfway along Bow Common Lane since first thing. And as for the wreaths, they were bringing even more of the things. Strapped to the roofs, boots and bonnets, the floral tributes made the vehicles look more like mobile flower stalls than cars.

Admittedly, Davy had been a florist, his house at number seven was always full of fresh blooms, everyone knew that, but there were more flowers piled on to those cars than anyone in the neighbourhood would ever have believed unless they had seen them for themselves.

As word got round and people heard the whisper about what was going on in Linman Street, the crowds of sight-seers grew by the minute, as did the general opinion that this turnout made even the publican Charlie Brown's funeral last year seem mean by comparison. And that had been an East End event of such grandeur that it had been reported in all the newspapers. And so now it wasn't only Ethel and Cissie Flowers' other neighbours from Linman

Street who were curious, the crowd was buzzing with unanswered questions.

Why was the funeral of an ordinary street trader so elaborate? That's what they all wanted to know. And, more intriguing, where had that pretty young widow of his got the money from to pay for it all? Although the East End of the 1930s wasn't exactly awash with spare cash, the Flowers family had always done all right for themselves, everyone knew that, as well as they knew most of the rumours about how they managed it, but, even if the rumours were true, this funeral was more than a case of just doing all right. This was big-time stuff. And surely even the best of penny policies wouldn't have stumped up for this little lot. And if it wasn't the insurance company paying, then who was?

There was another, more discreetly asked question going around the crowd: what were so many 'faces' – the well-known hard men, familiar to most people by sight and reputation if not personally – doing with their fancy, bleached and painted girlfriends amongst the mourners at a bloke like Davy Flowers' funeral?

As Ethel Bennett said to those around her, Davy Flowers' laying-to-rest would be the talk of the East End for a long time to come or she was a monkey's uncle.

Suddenly all speculation was momentarily forgotten.

The whispering stopped and was replaced by gasps – of both admiration and contempt – as Cissie Flowers herself appeared in the doorway of number seven. Even in mourning she looked lovely. Small and slim, and, as always, smartly turned out. Her thick black fringe, cut in exactly the way that Davy loved, rested just above her blue eyes, showing discreetly beneath the brim of her hat.

She looked straight ahead, apparently neither seeing nor hearing anyone or anything around her.

Gladys Mills from number four, shook her head sadly. 'Just look at her will you, Em, God love her,' she sniffled into her handkerchief. 'That girl don't know what's hit her. She looks like she's been pole-axed, poor little mare. She's too young to be a widow. Too young. It ain't right.'

'The grief ain't too terrible to stop her wearing a new hat though, I see,' Ethel Bennett hissed at her husband through tightly pursed lips, nudging him savagely in the side for being stupid enough to dare look at their pretty young neighbour without sneering.

Dick, as usual, ignored her, cocking a well-practised deaf ear to his wife's moaning. But that didn't deter Ethel from carrying on.

'Someone's paying for this little lot, you mark my words.' She nodded meaningfully towards the group of prosperous-looking men standing smoking on the corner of the street outside Clarke's general shop. 'And there'll be plenty of 'em sniffing around that little madam before that old man of hers is even cold in the ground, you just see if there ain't.'

'Mind out, Ett.' Gladys Mills straightened her worn felt hat, and stepped forward, pushing Ethel firmly to one side. 'Me and Ernie wanna get past, if you've finished your criticising and gossip-mongering, of course. Cos some of us,' she added curtly, 'know how to show respect.'

Gladys turned to her husband. 'Come on, love. Now Cissie's out here, we'll be getting ourselves in the cars soon, I reckon.'

Ernie Mills exchanged a brief half-smile of sympathy with Dick Bennett at his misfortune to be married to the likes of Ethel, then, taking Gladys by the elbow, he guided his wife along the road towards the end of the line of cars.

'Pretending they ain't interested,' Ethel snorted. 'They don't fool me. Everyone wants to know where that little madam got all this dough from. Everyone. And you ain't telling me them pair are any different.'

She folded her arms across her coarse-aproned chest, and tapped her foot belligerently. Gradually, a look of realisation spread over her wrinkled features. 'Here, I bet them Millses know already. I bet they know who's stumping up for this little lot and that cocky cow Gladys is sodding keeping it to herself.' She tutted, furious that others might be in the know when she wasn't. 'There's more to this than meets the eye, Dick Bennett, you just see if there ain't. I'd lay money on it.'

Not knowing all the inside business really was driving Ethel to distraction. It wasn't as though she hadn't done her best to find out what was going on. Since the day of Davy Flowers' accident, Ethel had pulled every single stroke she could think of to glean information. She had spent hours on end hanging around the corner shop, but neither Sammy Clarke, the pink-cheeked grocer, nor his customers knew a thing, or at least they said they didn't. She had haunted the stalls of Chrisp Street market until she was sick of the sight of potatoes and greens – but again to no avail. And she had sat on her front window ledge until her backside was numb keeping a watch on the comings and goings at number seven. She had even tried slipping inside the Flowers' street door a couple of times, when visitors or well-wishers had called to pay their respects. But despite all her efforts and all her attention to every whisper and rumour of the past few days, she had had no luck whatsoever.

But probably the most annoying thing for Ethel Bennett was that since Davy Flowers' sudden death, his widow, Cissie – Ethel's very own next-door neighbour! – had said nothing to her. Not a single, solitary word. She had appeared now and again at the street door to let someone in, her face as white as a ghost's, her eyes hollow, but her mouth had remained tightly shut whenever and whatever Ethel had called out to her.

It had all so infuriated her that Ethel had even speculated to Myrtle Payne from number nine, whose nosiness almost equalled her own, that Cissie Flowers had lost her mind, because she certainly didn't seem to hear or see anything when Ethel spoke to her. Cissie hadn't even thanked her, Ethel told Myrtle by way of proof of the girl's insanity, when she'd pointed out to her that, if she didn't want to show herself up, her street doorstep could do with a bloody good scrub before the funeral.

Myrtle Payne had tutted and shaken her head in appropriate disapproval of such typical bad manners, because, being Cissie's other immediate neighbour, Myrtle felt just as put out that she and her Arthur weren't privy to the full strength of what was going on. Although she too had made every effort to find out, and had even almost managed an unwitting coup when she had asked a stranger banging on the Flowers' street door who he was and what he wanted. He had just had time to reply that he was a friend of Davy's from the wholesale flower market at Covent Garden and had come with bad news about an accident, when Lil, Davy's mum, had come to the door, shouting the odds at the bloke about how she didn't appreciate being woken up from her afternoon kip. Myrtle had told Ethel later that even though she was only trying to be neighbourly, asking the stranger what he wanted and whether Lil wanted her to come in to help in any little way she could, Lil had just glared at her, had pulled the man into the passage and then slammed the street door right in her face.

That definitely hadn't pleased Myrtle, especially as she was sure that Ethel, no matter how often she denied it, had been watching the scene of her humiliation through her net curtains. As Myrtle had said to her Arthur, while he was making her the cup of tea she had insisted she needed in order to recover from the shame of being treated so badly, those Flowers were getting just a bit too big for their boots.

And now there was this turnout, with all the wreaths and horses and cars. All right, so the feller was dead, but Myrtle couldn't see that that was any excuse for showing off.

–

When the sombre-paced cortege eventually reached the cemetery gates, it was just after eleven o'clock.

Cissie stepped from the car and shivered.

As she walked along behind the priest, her gaze fixed on his dusty, swishing skirts, the sun beat down on her neck, sending trickles of sweat running down her back and making her dark clothes cling to her body. Yet she felt icy cold, chilled through to her very bones.

Matty and Joyce toddled along wordlessly beside her. At just four and a half and three years old, Cissie had decided that her children were too young to know the details of what had happened to their father, and she hoped and prayed that they were also too young to understand what was going on today. But still she squeezed their hands tightly, drawing them closer to her, as they came to a halt on the mat of lurid artificial grass edging the bare earth of the open grave.

Cissie closed her eyes and swallowed hard. This was it, they were really going to bury him, were going to sink him deep and alone into the cold, dank ground. She screwed her eyes tighter as the pain of remembering his touch flooded through her body.

Suddenly, a lark's beautiful, warbling trills sounded high above the mourners' heads. Cissie's legs trembled, threatened to give way under her. She couldn't bear it. It wasn't right. Instead of standing there beside her with the sound of bird song filling his ears and the sunshine warming his skin, her darling Davy was being slowly lowered into the ground by dark-suited men she didn't even know.

Cold, grey, hopeless fear overcame her.

Up until then, Cissie hadn't cried. She had promised herself to remain at least outwardly composed, to do everything she could to protect her children from the hurt that was tearing her apart, but she could hold back the tears no longer.

Why, she asked herself over and over again, as her tears flowed unchecked down her cheeks, had this happened to them? Everything had been so good. They had been so happy together. Their life had been so special. They hadn't been like those people who moaned and went on about the bad times they were having. They had laughter, fun, good times. And she and the kids had wanted for nothing. Davy had always seen to that. He had never had a day without work, had always grafted to make sure they had everything they needed.

In her mind, she was no longer standing by the graveside with the vicar droning on meaninglessly about a man he had never met, instead she was sitting at their kitchen table watching Davy as he listened to the news on the wireless while he was eating his tea.

She almost smiled as she remembered how angry he would become and how he would start jabbing his fork in the air, as he explained to Cissie how, if only they'd all get off their arses and make a bit of effort as he had done, then all the bellyachers and moaners who reckoned they couldn't find work could do as well by their families as he had done by his; and how the lazy so-and-sos would then be able to make sure that their kids not only had shoes on their feet, but that they had a good pair for Sundays too, just like his little Matty and Joyce had.

Davy.

Cissie let go of Matty and lifted her gloved hand to her face. Brushing her damp, black fringe from her forehead and tucking it away under the snap brim of her velvet hat, she stared down at the brass plate screwed to the top of the coffin.

Her poor, poor Davy. Twenty-eight years old. Such a pointless, stupid way to die. She screwed her eyes tight. Why hadn't he seen the crates? Why hadn't he realised they were going to fall on him? Why? How many times had she asked herself that during the past few days?

'And so, as we commit the mortal remains of David Prentice—'

Cissie's eyes flicked open and she met the rheumy, bloodshot gaze of the ancient-looking clergyman. What was he saying? What was he talking about?

'No!' she gasped. 'No!'

All eyes were now on Cissie.

'He wasn't David Prentice. Don't call him that. He was Davy, Davy Flowers. That's what everyone knew him as, and that's who he was, Davy Flowers. And me, I'm Cissie Flowers, Davy's wife.'

Matty and Joyce, scared by their mother's uncharacteristic outburst, stared at her. Her cheeks were trailed with tears. They didn't understand. Their mummy was crying. As one, the children began crying too, in pitiful, frightened, gulping sobs.

Lil, ignoring her grandchildren's distress, stepped forward and gripped her daughter-in-law's arm. 'All right,' she hissed into Cissie's ear, 'don't go showing yerself up in front of everyone. Just pull yerself together. People's watching.'

From the anxious look on his face, Lil might have been speaking those words to the vicar. He was glancing nervously about him, seeming more than a little worried about how one particular man was reacting to his performance.

But Cissie was far too upset to notice the vicar's discomfort. 'You know nothing about my Davy, nothing,' she sobbed at him.

The vicar reached out and patted Cissie paternally on the arm. 'What do we know about anyone, my dear?'

Cissie pulled away from his touch. 'Leave me alone, just leave me alone.'

He withdrew his hand hurriedly and flashed another worried look at the powerfully built man who, despite the heat, was swathed in a voluminous black overcoat and a full-brimmed fedora. The vicar hesitated, waiting uneasily for the man to nod his approval, before concluding what he had to say as hastily as he dared. He then bobbed down and scooped up a handful of soil.

With Lil's fingers digging into her flesh, Cissie stood there and watched as the mourners filed past the grave, each taking some of the earth from the vicar's shaking hand and scattering it over the coffin.

Despite her grief, Cissie was still aware enough to take note of just how many people there were politely awaiting their turn to take her hand and to offer their sympathy at her time of loss. Her husband had been a popular man – there were always visitors popping in and out of number seven – but she really hadn't expected quite so many to be at his funeral. She was proud that there were all these people who cared for him. She recognised neighbours and men from the market, of course, but that by no means explained all of them.

She frowned. She was confused by her grief, yes, but she was also puzzled by the affluent-looking men and their expensively, if showily, dressed female companions who stopped briefly, touched her hand or her arm and paid their mumbled respects. They didn't look like the type of people Davy would know. And she certainly didn't recognise any of them. So what were they doing here?

Next in line came a tall, broad-shouldered man in a black overcoat, the man whose approval the vicar had so anxiously sought. As he took her hand in a grip that was surprisingly gentle considering the size of him, Cissie lifted her eyes to meet his.

She recognised him immediately. It was the infamous Big Bill Turner, a man known by sight and reputation if not personally to practically everyone in the East End.

He took off his hat and inclined his head deferentially. 'I'm sorry for your trouble, Mrs Flowers,' he said.

Cissie watched him walk away towards the cars. What was *he* doing here? But she wasn't distracted by him for very long. Her gaze was inevitably drawn back to the dreadful hole in the ground before her.

What did it matter how many people surrounded her, who they were, and why they were there? All that mattered was that she felt completely and terribly alone. None of them could make up for the absence of the two people who, apart from her darling Davy, Cissie wanted to be there with her more than anyone else in the world.

Cissie wanted Ellen and Frank, her mum and dad.

Her parents hadn't liked Davy for some reason, and even though it wasn't their way to run anybody down, where Davy Flowers was concerned they had made an exception. They were determined that Cissie should change her mind about marrying Davy and did everything they could to get her away from him. But she wouldn't listen. Even when they had resorted to pleading with her at least to consider what she was doing before she married him and wait for a few more months before she said yes, Cissie would have none of it.

It wasn't as though they had anything specific to say against the handsome young man who had come wooing their daughter with his arms full of flowers and a continual round of good times and fun. All they would say was that they didn't think he was right for their Cissie. She was only nineteen and, if only she would take her time and think, she would get over him and find herself someone else. Someone decent.

In what had seemed to their neighbours almost insane desperation, Ellen and Frank had, just two weeks before their daughter's wedding, packed up all their possessions and left their cosy little house in Devons Road, where they had lived since their own wedding day, and had moved into a couple of rooms in Charles Street, Stepney – a real bug hole by all accounts, but all they could get at such short notice according to Ethel Bennett. Ethel had also told everyone that they had thought Cissie would go with them, when they had got her away from the area she'd meet new people. A new boyfriend even. But they had been wrong. The day they moved to Stepney was the last time Cissie had said a single word to either of them. She had moved into number seven, unmarried, as bold as brass, and in broad daylight. Not giving a damn about who saw her or what they thought.

During the next six years, Cissie had made no attempt at reconciliation with her mum and dad. She was in love with Davy, swept off her feet, and wouldn't listen to anybody who questioned or even doubted anything about him. She loved him totally.

Just once, four years ago, the day Matty had been born, she had almost sent Davy to fetch them, wanting them to see their first grandchild, but the flash of memory of her dad calling Davy – what was it? – a bad lot who would bring her nothing but unhappiness and trouble, had stopped her and, as time had passed, she had become all the more determined that Davy was all she needed.

But now, as she stood alone with her children, she wished with all her heart that things could have been different.

She looked down at Matty and Joyce. They looked so small, so lost. The way she herself felt. She thought about how much she and the children had missed by not seeing her mum and dad. If only things could be different. Maybe she could send them a note? Maybe. But it was probably too late now. She'd made her bed...

'Are you coming or what?' snapped Lil. 'They'll all be halfway back to the Sabberton Arms by now and you're standing here like a bleed'n statue.'

Cissie said nothing; she just stood there, rooted to the spot, staring at the two men who were now filling in the grave, shovelling heavy spades of crumbling earth on to her Davy.

The words came back into her head: *If only things could be different.* If only. One moment everything had been wonderful then, with no warning, everything had been lost.

'Cis?' Gladys Mills placed a hand tenderly on her shoulder. 'Shall I take the kids with me, love?'

Slowly, Cissie lifted her head and looked at her blankly. 'What?'

'Look, Cis, you take it from me, honest, things'll get better, darling.'

Gladys slipped her arm around Cissie's shoulder. 'You won't think so now, but you're young. You'll be happy again one day, you just see if you ain't. And I'll be here for yer until then, I promise. Whenever yer need me, girl.'

Lil shoved forward, pushing her grandchildren and Gladys out of the way. She grabbed hold of Cissie's arm again. 'You should watch that mouth o' your'n, Gladys Mills,' she snapped. 'Marriage is the last thing on Cissie's mind on a day like this.'

Gladys looked mortified. 'But, Lil, I never meant—' she began.

But Lil had no interest in what Gladys meant. 'What the hell does the likes of you know about anything anyway? Don't you listen to her, Cissie, or yer'll wind up in the same state as she is. And a right shit life she's got, ain't she? Getting up at half past four every morning to go bloody scrubbing steps up the City, while that useless old man of hers lays about all day. He ain't had a day's work in two years to my knowledge. So yer wanna listen to *her*, I don't think.' Lil gripped Cissie's arm even tighter. 'Now, if yer don't mind, Gladys, just get out of our way and let us get back to that motor.'

Gladys stepped aside without saying a word. Everyone knew Lil was a spiteful old cow, but that didn't stop her words from stinging. Lil always knew exactly how to hurt people. Although her Ernie certainly wasn't a lazy man, his failure to find work was really getting to both of them. Not just because it was making it increasingly difficult to feed and keep their five children and Nipper, Ernie's elderly granddad who lived with them – never mind finding money to feed and clothe themselves – but Ernie was coming to see the situation as a personal failure. A failure to be a good husband, father and grandson. The physical strain of doing the badly paid, early morning cleaning was nothing to Gladys compared to the pain she felt watching her dear Ernie suffering.

But actually, for once, Lil was no longer interested in being cruel to Gladys, Ernie, or anyone else for that matter. The reason she wanted to hurry Cissie away from the graveside, to join the crowd of mourners who were making their way to the pub, was because she had spotted Ellen and Frank, Cissie's parents. They were standing by themselves at a tactful distance from the graveside, so as not to cause a scene, partly hidden by the elaborate Gothic monuments and headstones.

Lil had no intention of letting them even talk to their daughter, let alone try to make their peace with her, because, despite her disparaging remarks about Ernie's supposed idleness, doing nothing was a way of life that Lil herself treasured. She hadn't willingly done a day's work since she'd been born and didn't intend to start now. Davy's dad, up until his death, and then Davy himself, had, in turn, been her meal ticket and, now they were both gone, Lil had decided that her good-looking daughter-in-law was going to have to fill that role. There'd soon be another bloke on the firm, she was confident of that. Lil might have been lazy, but she wasn't stupid, and she also knew that if she allowed Cissie to start getting all pally with her mum and dad again, she might also get all sentimental and daughterly and start giving the old buggers some of her money. And Lil didn't much fancy that, she didn't much fancy that at all, because whatever there was, Lil intended to have it all.

Chapter 2

Cissie sat in the Sabberton Arms, oblivious of her surroundings, which was probably not a bad thing, as most of the people there were acting more like guests at a wedding breakfast than at her husband's funeral. They were eating, drinking, chattering loudly, even singing and laughing at one another's feeble jokes. It was as though they were intent on marking and celebrating their own good fortune at being alive, at not being planted six feet under as Davy Flowers had just been.

But although they were acting that way with one another, most of those present seemed far more reluctant to include Cissie in their antics, or even to go over and speak to her. It wasn't that they were deliberately ignoring her, or even trying to escape the embarrassment of not knowing what to say in such a situation, no, it was more to do with them getting the message that it wasn't their place to do so. It was being made very clear, what with the interest Big Bill Turner was so obviously showing in Cissie from the other side of the pub, that they were not important enough to intrude on the young widow. Turner, everyone knew, always took precedence in such a situation.

But sitting there alone with her two little ones didn't seem to bother Cissie Flowers. In fact, she hadn't even noticed. Apart from a peremptory nod in recognition of each brief paying of respect from her neighbours before they hurried back to the bar for another free glass of whatever took their fancy – an opportunity definitely not to be missed, even if they didn't have a clue as to how Cissie would be footing the bill – she seemed to be a million miles away. She just held on to her children's hands, apparently feeling, hearing and seeing nothing, the shock of burying her husband having sent the usually laughing, outgoing Cissie into a hollow-eyed trance.

Lil, on the other hand, was taking the whole thing in a different way entirely. Either she wasn't shocked in the least at having just buried her son, or, if she was, she was certainly making a very good job of hiding the fact.

'I don't mind if I do,' Lil twittered as she took a cigarette from the broad-shouldered man with a scar across his cheek who had been standing beside Big Bill Turner at the graveside. 'I'll just have a little pinch of me snuff for now, and I'll have this later on,' she added, tucking the Player's Navy Cut behind her ear.

On the other side of the lounge bar, Matty was gently peeling Cissie's icy fingers from around his hand. He kissed her warily on the cheek and said softly, 'I'm just gonna see Nanna a minute, Mum.'

He might have been only four and a half years old, but Matty was as bright as a button; he was desperate for the lavatory but understood that he shouldn't disturb his mum.

He wasn't sure why or what, but he just knew that something was wrong, more wrong even than when his puppy had got knocked down in St Paul's Road and the man had taken it away to make it better, but had never brought it back to him.

Cissie nodded blankly as Matty scrambled down from the bench that ran along the length of the pub wall. The roughly patterned upholstery scratched the back of his bare legs as he slid to the ground, making him wince, but he said nothing. Instead, he smiled reassuringly at his little sister, who was sitting tucked into her mother's side, anxiously sucking her thumb, then, quietly, he began struggling to make his way through the sea of adult legs in his effort to try to find Lil in the crowded pub. All the time he repeated over and over in his head, 'Nan'll know where to go. Nan'll know where to go.'

Matty eventually found his grandmother wreathed in a fug of smoke and whisky fumes. She was leaning across the polished wooden counter complaining to the barmaid about Ethel and Dick Bennett, two of her next-door neighbours from Linman Street.

Lil wiped her mouth with the back of her hand. 'Typical of that pair,' she sneered. 'Couldn't manage to find their sodding way to the cemetery to see my boy buried, could they? No, course they couldn't. But the Sabberton Arms? Well, that's a different matter, ain't it? They could find this place all right. Find it in the bleed'n dark with their eyes shut and a bag over their heads. Crafty rotten bleeders.'

The barmaid, brought in especially for the funeral, had had Davy's family all pointed out to her by the landlord so she knew who Lil was, but she wasn't sure who this Ethel and Dick Bennett were that Lil was going on about. 'Elderly couple, are they?' she asked without looking up from the glass she was drying, her voice professionally friendly.

Lil gulped down another mouthful of scotch and rolled her eyes. 'Not that much older than me if yer must know.'

'Well, p'raps it was too far for 'em then, eh?' the barmaid suggested with a recklessness that came from not knowing Lil's reputation. 'I mean,' she went on, 'it's a fair old trot down to Southern Grove for someone of your age, ain't it, dear?'

'You cheeky bloody mare!' Lil began, but the barmaid was saved from the full benefit of one of Lil's famous tongue-lashings by Matty arriving on the scene.

The little boy tugged warily at the skirt of his grand-mother's black dress. He had never been inside anywhere like the Sabberton Arms before, and especially not on a confusing day like this. It was bad enough being desperate for the lav, but the smell and the press of so many bodies all towering above him was making him feel sick as well.

'Nan,' he whispered, 'please, I really wanna wee. Can yer take me? I wanted to go when we was at that other place before. I told Mum, but she must've forgot.' He wriggled with discomfort. 'I think she's a bit sad. But I've really gotta go, Nan.'

'Don't bother me now, boy,' Lil snapped without looking down at him. 'Can't yer see yer nanna's busy?'

Lil held out her glass to the barmaid for a refill, still without even bothering to meet her grandson's anxious stare. Her glass replenished, Lil disappeared into the smoky throng leaving Matty to get on with it.

Matty squirmed, he was going to wet himself, he just knew it, and in front of all these people. His face crumpled. He would die of shame.

Shaking her head in disgust at Lil's callousness, the barmaid wiped her hands on the glass cloth, lifted the flap in the counter, and stepped round to where Matty was standing sniffling quietly to himself.

'Come on, love,' she said kindly, 'you come with me eh? I'll take yer to the one out the back.' She dabbed at Matty's cheeks with the hem of her apron and looked into his sad blue eyes. 'You've got smashing eyes, yer know, little 'un. Just like yer mum's. Cissie Flowers is yer mum, ain't she?'

Matty nodded miserably as the barmaid ushered him behind the bar.

'Yer mustn't take no notice of yer nan,' she said without much conviction, leading him by the hand through to the back kitchen. 'She's upset, see. It's one of them days when people get themselves all worked up and don't know what they're saying. But she'll be all right later on, you just see if she ain't.'

'I wish me dad was here,' Matty whispered, as much to himself as to the barmaid, as he closed the lavatory door modestly behind him.

The barmaid was glad the poor little kid had shut himself in the dingy, cramped cubicle. Maybe the door would muffle the sound of his grandmother's raucous shouts and laughter that were now echoing through from the bar.

'My Davy was a right little bugger, Gawd rest his soul,' Lil was yelling at Ted Johnson, another one of her neighbours from Linman Street, the whisky making her even louder and more aggressive than usual.

'I might have gone mutton when I was in the trenches, Lilly Prentice, but yer don't need a sodding foghorn,' Ted replied, leaning as far back from her as the crush would allow. 'The whole of bleed'n Poplar must be able to hear yer, the way yer hollering and hooting. Now why don't yer get yerself over to that table, get a bit of grub down yer to sober yourself up, then go and sit with that daughter-in-law of your'n? She looks in a right old state, poor little thing.' With a sneer of contempt at this man who was daring to tell her what to do, Lil went off to bother someone else.

She was just squeezing by the door when it burst open and a scabby-kneed boy of about nine years old launched himself past her into the bar. He was waving the strips of printed paper carrying the latest dog-racing results that he touted around the local pubs.

'Dog-inner! Dog-inner!' came his familiar abbreviated yell. And, just as familiar, came the reply from one of the wags propping up the bar: 'No, son, there ain't no *dog in 'ere.*' He looked around, making sure he had an audience. 'He's outside having a piss, ain't he!'

'Blimey, I ain't never heard that one before, mister,' the boy snapped back sarcastically, backing away just in time to avoid the empty cigarette packet the man had aimed at his head. Peals of drunken laughter reverberated around the room. The boy felt humiliated. It was bad enough putting up with abuse from the usual afternoon gaggle of old men and miserable-looking victims of the slump, nursing their warm half-pints of mild, but being confronted by a pub full of rich-looking blokes and fancy women, all laughing at him as though he was some sort of sideshow was too big a price to pay for the few coppers he earned from his round. They could stuff the results if that was their attitude.

He turned away and started back towards the door, but a hand on his shoulder stopped him in his tracks. He spun round to see what further shame the man wanted to heap on him. But it wasn't the man, it was Cissie. She was standing behind him with young Joyce still gripping her hand.

'Why don't you all leave the kid alone?' she said flatly, her eyes fixed on the surprised-looking boy. 'Yer know the poor little bugger's only doing it to earn a few shillings to help out his mum since his dad…' Cissie's words were barely audible as she continued. '…since his dad got killed down the docks.'

Cissie ushered the boy back towards the bar, lifted her chin and stared about her. 'What, don't no one wanna know how the dogs done today?'

Big Bill Turner stepped forward from the crowd at the bar. He sank his hand deep into his pocket and pulled out a fistful of coins.

'Here y'are, kiddo,' he said loudly, picking out a shiny half-crown. 'Here's a tosheroon for yer, and I'm sure there's plenty of other fellers in here what'll be only too glad to buy all the rest of them results off yer.' He looked about him, watching as men rummaged through their pockets for loose change. 'And,' he added meaningfully, 'I reckon they'll give you a couple of bob extra for yer to take home to yer mum and all.'

Without a word, wallets were taken from inside pockets as, to a man, Turner's friends and colleagues hurriedly made sure they didn't look cheap in front of him. The man who had thrown the cigarette carton being particularly careful to make sure that Turner saw him hand over a crisp ten-shilling note.

The delighted, if astonished, child hastily stuffed his loot into the pockets of his ragged jacket and made a run for it before they all came to their senses and demanded their money back, only pausing at the door to call a hurried thank you to Turner. Just wait till he told his mum and his little brother; there'd be fish and chips all round tonight.

Cissie also wanted to express her gratitude to Turner. 'Thanks, Mr Turner. That was kind of yer,' she said, averting her eyes as she sat back down and settled Joyce next to her on the bench.

'It's Bill. Call me Bill,' Ethel Bennett, her ears practically, flapping with amazement, heard Turner reply before he went back to the counter to speak to the barmaid.

Ethel watched his progress with open-mouthed fascination as he finished his business at the bar then returned to where Cissie was sitting.

'Like I said before, I'm sorry for your trouble, Mrs Flowers,' Turner said as the barmaid appeared at his side.

'Here's the drinks you ordered, Mr Turner.'

'All right if she puts 'em down there on the table?' Turner asked Cissie.

Cissie nodded distractedly.

The barmaid put the tray in front of Cissie and disappeared back to the bar.

'That's what me old Irish granny used to say at times like these, yer know, Mrs Flowers. "I'm sorry for your trouble," she'd say. And I wanted to say it too, cos what else can yer say at a time like this?'

'Thanks,' she said quietly.

'Mind if I join yer for a bit?'

Cissie said nothing, she just lifted Joyce on to her lap, making space for him on the bench next to her.

Matty, who had just fought his way back from the lavatory in the barmaid's wake, stood watchfully by his mum's side, wondering what new turn of events this could be. He had never seen this big, red-faced man before, and he didn't know if he liked him being so friendly with his mum. But he knew he wasn't allowed to interrupt when grown-ups were talking, so he said nothing.

'I hope I got the right drinks for the kids,' Turner said, handing Matty and Joyce each a green bottle with a straw poking from the top. He smiled, making his face crease into deep folds. 'Mind you, all little chavvies like a drop of lemonade, don't they?'

'Say ta,' Cissie said automatically.

Cautiously, Matty drew his bottle towards him. He looked at his mum to make sure it was OK to start, but she wasn't even looking at him, so he just thanked the man, as he had been told, and then clamped the straw between his lips.

'That's all right, son, yer don't have to thank me.'

Matty pulled away as Turner reached out to ruffle his hair.

'I'd have killed for a bottle of lemonade when I was a nipper,' Turner said, not seeming to notice, or maybe to mind, Matty's wariness.

'Did yer see that, Myrtle?' Ethel gasped, jerking her head towards Cissie's table. 'Did yer? Bold as bleed'n brass, if yer don't mind.'

'Disgusting,' Myrtle agreed. 'And at her husband's funeral.'

The two women, glasses of stout gripped firmly in front of them, shook their heads disapprovingly at the sight of the young widow and her two children barefacedly accepting hospitality from the likes of Big Bill Turner.

'What, jealous because the man's decent enough to show his respects to me daughter-in-law, are yer?' Lil hissed into Ethel's ear as she made her unsteady way past them towards where Cissie and Turner were sitting. She turned her head and looked her neighbours up and down. 'Or is it cos yer know he wouldn't look twice at anyone in your sodding ugly crew of a family?'

With a final sneering appraisal of her two elderly neighbours, Lil turned her back on them and concentrated on her goal.

'Hello, Mr Turner,' she simpered, shoving Matty out of the way and plonking herself unceremoniously on to the bench. 'We're right chuffed yer found time to come.' She dropped her chin and added pitifully, 'It helps to know that people are around at sad times like this.'

Feeling unable to bear the company of her mother-in-law, who always found a way to upset or annoy her at the best of times, Cissie tried to stand up but, with Joyce on her lap, she could hardly move let alone escape from Lil's whining voice. She could have got out if Turner had moved, but he appeared to have no intention of shifting himself. To make matters worse, Ethel and Myrtle, who had been hovering close by, had now made their way right over to the table and were standing there, gawping at her with undisguised interest.

Cissie rubbed her face with her hands. What on earth did those two old cows want with her?

Ethel smiled, a rare and not very pleasant sight, showing her uneven brown teeth. 'Hello, Mr Turner,' she began, 'me and me old mate Myrtle here was just saying what an honour it is for young Cissie to have you at her husband's funeral like this.'

Matty, the straw still firmly clenched between his lips, frowned to himself. A funeral? Wasn't that when people were dead? He'd have to remember to ask his mum about it later on. He'd have asked her now but his nan didn't look very happy, and he knew better than to do anything that might upset her such as asking questions.

Lil, in fact, wasn't so much unhappy as furious. She was scowling, scowling horribly at Ethel, narrowing her eyes at the woman's effrontery for daring to interrupt when she was speaking to Turner. But Lil would have her back later on all right, she was sure of that. She'd find a way to get the old bag. Pasting a grieving look on her face, Lil dabbed at her bone-dry cheeks with her handkerchief and whispered in a cracked little voice, 'Yes, she's right, Mr Turner, it's a real honour to have yer here.'

'And yer do know, Cis,' Ethel went on, reaching across the table and patting Cissie's hand, 'if there's anything you ever need, love, anything at all, you've only gotta ask me or my Dick and it's as good as done, darling. Good as done.'

'That's right neighbourly of yer, Ethel,' Lil sighed pathetically. 'We'll bear that in mind, won't we, Cissie?' Lil would have smacked the stupid grin off the old trout's gob if Turner hadn't been there.

'Being good to yer neighbours,' Turner said with an approving nod. 'I like that. I like to see people looking after their own.' He raised his hand in the air and gestured with an almost imperceptible flick of his fingers. A tall broad-shouldered man immediately appeared by his side.

'Yes, boss?'

'Take these two ladies,' he said, indicating Ethel and Myrtle with a lift of his chin, 'over to the bar, Bernie, and make sure they have whatever they fancy.'

The two delighted women followed their new-found benefactor with much proud fluttering of their eyes and hands, making sure that everyone in the pub got a good look at them being treated by a friend of Big Bill Turner's.

Turner took a swallow from his glass and shook his head. 'I reckoned you didn't need them pair giving you earache on a day like this, Mrs Flowers.'

Cissie slowly raised her eyes and looked levelly at Turner. 'I can look after meself, ta. I don't need no one sorting me out.'

Lil slid her hand under the table and squeezed hard on the soft flesh of Cissie's inner thigh. She smiled winningly at Turner. 'Yer don't wanna mind me daughter-in-law, Mr Turner. Only she's upset like, ain't she?'

'If yer don't mind, Lil,' Cissie said evenly, 'I'd like you to get yer hand off my leg and stop pinching me. Now.'

Lil flashed Turner another smile. 'Upset,' she mouthed silently.

Turner appeared totally unperturbed by the obviously uneasy relationship between Cissie and Lil, and made no effort to move away from the table and leave them to it. 'Looks like there's a few people wanna speak to you, Mrs Flowers,' he said smoothly, indicating the group of people lurking around the table with his now almost empty glass.

Lil gave another simpering smile. 'That'll be you treating Ethel and Myrtle like that. They'll all be offering my Cissie all kinds of help just to impress you, Mr Turner.'

Cissie closed her eyes and buried her face in her hands. Why was she sitting here listening to Lil carrying on like this when all she wanted to do was go home and go to bed? She wanted to get away from all of this.

She turned to ask Turner to move when a woman's voice said softly, 'Cis, I don't wanna disturb yer, or nothing.'

'Not much,' sniped Lil sarcastically, glaring up at Gladys Mills.

Gladys wouldn't let Lil get to her. Instead of responding to her nastiness, she just kept on speaking to Cissie. 'I only wondered, Cis, you know, if there's anything, anything at all I can do for yer.'

Cissie looked up, pleased to see her friend from number four. 'Yer all right, Glad. Thanks for asking, but I'll be fine.'

Gladys tipped her head towards Matty. 'How about the little ones?'

Cissie looked at her children as though only just registering that they were still there with her.

'Let me take them and get 'em a bite to eat eh?' Gladys flashed a look at Turner as she held out her hands to Matty and Joyce. 'There's loads of food over there, but I'll bet neither of 'em has had a thing past their lips 'cept that lemonade, have they? They must be starving.'

Turner leant back in his seat and watched, eyebrows raised, as the children clambered down from the bench to go with Gladys. He wasn't used to being treated like that. He didn't like it. But now wasn't the time to react.

The kids seemed only too pleased to be going off with their mum's friend, so he wasn't going to cause trouble and risk having them bawling their heads off. Lil, he noted with interest, obviously wasn't so impressed by the woman as her grandchildren had been. She'd stood up and was hissing something into Gladys's ear. He couldn't make out the words but it was obvious that she was wild about something.

'Don't worry about *me* having no grub, will yer, Gladys Mills?' she was sniping spitefully. 'I mean, I'm only Davy's bloody mother, ain't I?'

Gladys didn't rise to it, she just led the children away, chattering encouragingly to them about all the tasty bits of food they could have.

Turner smiled inwardly as Lil sat down. She was defeated for the moment, but she had a look on her face that he recognised all too well. He knew, as plain as night followed day, that Gladys had been marked down for future reference by Davy's vindictive old cow of a mother. She was a woman after his own heart.

'She seems a decent sort of a person,' Turner said to Lil without a trace of irony, before swallowing the last of his drink. 'I always approve of people looking out for one another. Good to see it. Very good.' He sat back to see what his bait attracted. He didn't have to wait long.

'*Looking out for one another*?' Lil gasped incredulously, forgetting for the moment her poor grieving mother act. 'Do me a favour. What could she do to help anyone? Ernie, that old man of her'n, ain't done a stroke of work in bleed'n years, and she's having to work her fingers to the bone, sodding early morning cleaning. Can't even help herself, that one, let alone no other bugger!'

'It ain't Ernie's fault there's no work about,' Cissie said quietly. 'And Gladys has been a good friend to me over the years.'

'Fat lot of good friendship is when there's no money coming in,' Lil snorted.

'I've always appreciated friendship and loyalty, as a matter of fact,' Turner said.

'Aw yeah,' agreed Lil hurriedly, coming back to her senses and realising what she'd said. 'Me too, Mr Turner. I mean, there's nothing like friendship, is there now? I've always said that, you ask Cissie if I ain't. Ain't that right, Cissie? I've always said it.'

'Have yer? I dunno about that.' Cissie shook her head in wonder at her mother-in-law's gall. 'But I know something. That girl ain't got a pot, but she'd still give anyone the last slice of bread off her table if they asked for it.'

Cissie picked up her bag and pushed the table away from her to make room so that she could stand up. 'Now, if you don't mind…'

'Something wrong?' asked Turner, reaching out his arm to block her way. He wasn't used to people leaving until he decided it was time for them to go.

'No, nothing's wrong. Apart from me husband being dead and buried.' Cissie had had enough of this farce.

'Don't be like that, sweetheart. I only wondered if something was up.'

'And if something was up, why would I tell you, a complete stranger? Now, like I said, if you don't mind, I'd like to get out.'

'Why?'

'If you must know, I'm gonna thank everyone for coming, and tell them that I'm sure they're all very kind

32

but, before anyone else starts offering me any help, I want 'em all to know that me and my kids can manage just fine.'

'Don't be so hasty, Cis,' Lil said, lowering her voice and grabbing Cissie by the arm. 'You don't *know* yet how we're gonna manage, do you? How we're gonna get by.'

Cissie shook off Lil's grip and again tried to get past Turner.

'Hello there.' A bleary-eyed, brassy-looking woman in her late thirties, with unnaturally orange-red hair, stuck her hand across the table at Cissie. 'I was sorry to hear about Davy.'

Frowning, Cissie took the offered hand and nodded her thanks. Who was this woman who knew her husband? She stank of booze and stale perfume, and her nails looked like scarlet painted talons. 'I don't think I know yer, do I?'

'Sorry. Course yer don't. I'm Eileen, Eileen Clayton. I'm a friend of Bill's. Ain't that right, Bill?'

Without warning, Turner slipped his arm along the bench, took Cissie's hand from Eileen's, and jerked Cissie roughly back down on to the seat.

Furious at such presumption, Cissie tried to pull her hand away, but Turner wouldn't let go. He held her hand – and her gaze – for a long, tense moment.

Cissie's mouth went dry. What the hell did this man think he was doing?

Then, just as unexpectedly, Turner let her go.

He stood up and leant across the table towards Eileen. In a menacingly low voice he said, 'If you know what's good for you, sweetheart, I reckon you should keep that trap o' your'n shut. Now why don't yer just clear off and leave Mrs Flowers in peace? Go on, there's a good girl.'

Eileen opened her mouth as if to speak, then, thinking better of it, she shrugged defeatedly and, with a falsely carefree laugh, she stepped away from the table. But she didn't move far, she just leant back against the wall close to Cissie and sullenly sipped at her drink.

Turner didn't sit back down, he just stared at Eileen, his curled lip showing his distaste. 'That's it, yer silly cow, pour more of that gear down yer gullet. You'll only need a few more and you'll be flat on yer back, then we can all get a bit of peace.' Ignoring Lil completely, Turner pushed past her and made his way over to the bar without a word of apology or explanation to any of them.

Looking nervously about her to see if anyone had witnessed the way Turner had treated her, Lil made a great show of patting her hair into place. 'I'm just gonna go to the lavvy, Cis. You can fetch me a nice little drink while I'm gone. Something to steady me poor old nerves.'

Cissie didn't even bother to reply. She just sat there feeling angry; and lonelier and sadder than ever.

With both Turner and Lil out of the way, Eileen sidled back to the bench. She looked Cissie up and down. 'Yer not a bad-looking girl,' she slurred, leaning unsteadily against the table. 'Nice black hair. Dyed is it?'

'No. It's not.' Cissie wouldn't meet the woman's gaze, she just stared into her still-full glass of port and lemon. Why couldn't all these people just leave her alone? Why, if they felt they *had* to do something, couldn't they be like Gladys and just do things that would actually help? Why did they all keep pestering her? Going on at her? Why?

Either Eileen wasn't very sensitive to other people's moods, or she was simply choosing to ignore Cissie's patently obvious wish to be left alone. She sat down and pressed herself close to Cissie, as though she were about to tell her a secret. She went to open her mouth to speak, but then changed her mind and looked nervously over her shoulder at Turner. Being a good six inches taller than everyone around him, Eileen could see him clearly as he stood at the crowded bar, surrounded by a mob of grovelling hangers-on. She hesitated for just a moment, then, with a shrug of resignation, she returned her attention to Cissie.

'If you ever need to talk or anything,' she muttered, her voice thick with drink, 'I'd be only too pleased to listen. I've been through it all myself, see.' Eileen dug into her battered crocodile handbag and pulled out a dainty gold-covered note-pad. 'He bought me this,' she said, slipping a slim, gold propelling pencil from a slot in the side. She scribbled something down and tore the sheet of paper from the pad. 'This is where I live,' she said handing it to Cissie. 'Remember what I said: any time. I've been through it all.'

'What would I wanna talk to you for?' Cissie wasn't being rude, she honestly didn't understand what she and this whorey-looking woman could possibly have in common.

Eileen checked over her shoulder again. She saw Turner was still looking at her. 'Like I said,' she breathed, her eyes fixed on Turner. 'I've been through it all meself.'

Cissie too was now looking at Turner. His face was like a mask as he stared back at them. She couldn't understand what this woman was going on about? And how did she know Davy? 'What, you're a widow, yer mean?' she asked, trying to make sense of it all. 'Is that what yer've been through?'

'Not exactly,' Eileen replied with a sardonic laugh. 'Now,' she insisted, 'stick that bit of paper in yer bag a bit lively. We don't want no one knowing our business, now do we?'

With that, Eileen stood up and moved off into the crowd without another word.

Cissie wasn't left alone for long to muse over the curious exchange; Lil, wiping her hands down the front of her black dress, had reappeared from the lavatory. 'I saw that old tart with the red hair – what was her name? Eileen? – back talking to yer again. What did she want?'

'Nothing.' Cissie tucked Eileen Clayton's address into her pocket. She wasn't sure why exactly, but she didn't want her mother-in-law to know she had it.

'Well, that Big Bill Turner don't like her. That's obvious. So you'd better not let him see yer talking to her no more.'

Cissie gasped at her audacity. 'I don't think I heard you right, did I, Lil? D'you mind repeating that?'

'Ssshhh,' Lil hissed, flapping her hand about in Cissie's face. 'Look sharp, he's gonna say something.'

Cissie twisted round to see that a space had been cleared around Turner so that everyone had a good view of him.

Tapping the ash from his cigar on to the floor, Turner pulled himself up to his full height and began speaking. 'I wanna start off by saying what a very sad occasion this is.' Murmurs of agreement buzzed around the bar.

'And I wanna say how nice, how very nice, it's been to see all Mrs Flowers' friends and neighbours showing their respect and concern by turning up here today, and by the generous offers to help the little lady at such a difficult time.'

A sense of smug pleasure at being congratulated by someone as important as Big Bill Turner replaced the murmuring.

'But I know these are hard times for everyone.' Turner paused, waiting for the edgy, unsure laughter to begin at his joke. Satisfied with the response, he raised his hand immediately to crush it. He grinned. 'Well, hard times for *some*, I should say.' More uneasy laughter rippled around the bar.

'So I don't want no one worrying about Mrs Flowers and her young 'uns as far as money for this little lot is concerned. *I'm* footing the bill for this funeral.' He jerked his head in the direction of the landlord. 'Including all the booze. So you can swallow pints till yer boots are overflowing.'

This time the laughter came easier.

He continued. 'I'm gonna show everyone that we know how to look after our own in the East End. And that's why I also wanna say that there'll be no worry about Mrs Flowers wanting for anything in the future neither. I'm gonna see to that personally. Now, come on, drink up to Davy Flowers.'

He raised his glass in salute and then downed his drink in a single gulp. 'And there's plenty more where that come from!'

Under cover of the loud clapping and shouts of approval, Cissie turned to her mother-in-law. 'What do you know about this, Lil?' she demanded.

Lil rolled her eyes. 'Don't start, girl. Yer wanna show yer appreciation, not start bleed'n moaning. Turner's a powerful bloke. Rich and all.' She took a swig of scotch, and giggled happily to herself. 'He's a bloke what could make my old age very comfortable. Very comfortable indeed.'

Cissie was too stunned by her mother-in-law's cold-blooded greed to even think of a reply. She just sat there as a series of men and women, most of whom Cissie had never met before, but who all seemed very keen that Turner should see their generosity, came over to her table and pledged their ostentatious offers of help. Every single one of them made sure that she realised they weren't treading on Mr Turner's toes – his help took precedence, of course, that went without saying – but they wanted her to know that they were there if ever she needed them. And these weren't the empty gestures made by Ethel and Myrtle, these were offers supported by bulging wallets.

Lil beamed with pleasure at her son's widow being paid court by such well-to-do people, especially as it was so obviously driving Ethel and Myrtle to distraction to see her receiving so much attention. They were livid at being relegated to the role of poor relations, and began sharpening their knives.

Ethel stabbed her thumb in Turner's direction. 'Yer do know who that is, don't yer?' she asked Myrtle quite unnecessarily. 'Only the biggest crook this side of the West End.'

'Yeah, that's right,' concurred Myrtle. 'And I know who his old woman is and all.' She sniggered nastily. 'I wonder what Moe Turner would have to say if she could see him now, hanging around with the bleed'n merry widow?'

'I dunno about what she'd say to *him*,' Ethel sneered, 'but I reckon Moe would have that Cissie's head right off her shoulders. No shame, some women. No shame at all.' She held up her empty glass. 'Come on,' she urged Myrtle, 'drink up for Gawd sake. You don't get free booze every day of the week.'

But when Ethel reached the counter she was disappointed. She was just about to order another gin, when Turner slapped his hand on the counter and called loudly, 'Right then everybody, Mrs Flowers'll be wanting to get off home, so I reckon it's about time all you good people did the same.'

With that, he set his wide-brimmed hat on his slicked-back greying hair, threw his topcoat over his arm and strode over to the door. He waited for someone to open it for him, then turned round, looked in Cissie's direction and raised his hat. 'I'll be seeing you, Mrs Flowers.'

Outside, the pavement was soon as crowded as the pub had been, full of people milling around, talking and, having got the taste, making arrangements to move on elsewhere to another pub.

The man who had kept Lil supplied with cigarettes was talking to Turner.

'Shall I get back to the office, boss,' he asked, 'or is there anything you want me to do first?'

Turner took a silver case from his inside pocket and snapped it open. The other man had a match lit and at the ready before Turner had even put the cigarette in his mouth.

'No, don't go back to the office just yet, Bernie. I've got a little errand I want yer to run for me first.' Turner took in a lungful of smoke then blew it in a lavender stream from his nostrils. 'I wanna know what that slag Plains is up to. And I wanna know what we're gonna do about Flowers' pitch.'

'Shall I take a few of the lads with me, Bill?'

'No.' Turner narrowed his eyes as he took another drag, then exhaled slowly. 'Let's just see what the bastard does first.' He jabbed the cigarette at Bernie, using it to emphasise the importance of what he was saying. 'I don't want nothing upsetting that little widow lady, right?'

Bernie nodded to show he understood.

'I'm gonna let her get over the shock first, see? *Then* I'm gonna make me move.'

'You was always the gentleman, Bill,' Bernie laughed. 'But maybe I should take a set of knuckles with me. Just in case, eh?'

It was Turner who laughed this time. 'And a razor and all if yer've got any sense. I mean, we don't want yer going out naked or nothing, now do we?'

'Excuse me.' Gladys Mills, holding Matty and Joyce's hands, was easing her way through the throng. She pushed past Bernie but paused next to Turner.

Leaning close so that only he could hear, she said to him, 'We don't need the likes of you round here, Turner. You don't impress me, or Cissie, yer know. She's disgusted with that little performance in there. She's sitting there, crying her eyes out. So just leave her alone and don't waste your time.' Gladys then smiled down at the children. 'Come on, darlings, let's get home and put the kettle on for Mummy. She'll be gasping for a nice cup o' tea.'

She stared at Turner for a long, calm moment. 'She'll need to get the nasty taste out of her mouth.'

With that, Gladys marched forward with the children beside her.

'Who the hell does she—'

'Leave it, Bern.' Turner put a steadying hand on the man's arm and ground out his cigarette beneath his heel. 'Give 'em a few weeks,' he grinned, 'and they'll be begging me for help. Now, I thought you had a job to do.'

Chapter 3

'Mummy.' Joyce tugged miserably at the hem of Cissie's skirt. 'Mummy.'

Cissie reached out and stroked her daughter's hair, the hair that was as black as her own. 'Sorry, darling,' she said wearily, 'Mummy's tired, and I've gotta get this done. Play with Matty, eh?'

Joyce's bottom lip began to tremble.

Cissie hooked her hands gently under Joyce's arms and lifted her on to her lap. 'I know you're fed up, baby, but Mummy's gotta do this. Honest.'

She brushed her lips across Joyce's forehead as she stared down at the pile of bills that seemed to be growing in front of her eyes; and at the rent book with its two weeks owing; and at her almost empty purse. There they were, all laid out on the kitchen table in front of her, all accusing her of being a bad mother and a useless manager and provider.

Cissie sighed loudly. 'I really have gotta do something with all this, babe. I ain't sure how, but I know I've got to. We'll play later eh?' She picked up one of the bills and frowned at it. She never even knew that they hadn't paid the man who had mended the cracked window in Davy's truck.

'Mummy,' Joyce whimpered again.

'Tell yer what,' Cissie said, trying to make herself sound enthusiastic – none of this was Joyce's fault, 'I'll make up a really good story for yer when I've finished. How about that? Now you just let me get on with this, eh?'

Matty, who, up until then, had been busily playing under the table with the army of lead soldiers his dad had bought him in the Chrisp Street Woolworth's, was suddenly far more interested in his mother and sister than in the battle he had been organising.

'I'll help yer do that, Mum,' he said, his eyes wide with anxiety.

He hated his mum sounding so sad and tired, it really scared him. Ever since they'd been to those horrible places – the cemetery and the pub – she'd been like this. He'd hated both those places right away, but he'd hated them even more when his mum had explained why she'd had to take them there.

They had buried his dad, because he had had to go and live in Heaven with the angels, and he would never be coming home. Not ever again, no matter how hard Matty wished or even prayed. That was it. He was gone. And now Matty was terrified that his mum would get so sad without him that she would leave him and Joyce as well, and go to Heaven to be with their dad.

'I *can* help, Mum,' he insisted. Matty wasn't sure what he would be helping with, but he knew he had to do something. He'd be going to school in the autumn, when- ever that was – his mum had told him that too – so he had to do what he could now, to make her happy while he was still around. It was no good him expecting Joyce to be any use, even though she was three years old, Matty knew that she was still a baby. So, it was up to him.

He crawled out from under the table and wrapped his arms around Cissie's legs. 'Don't cry, Mum. Please. I'll help yer.'

Cissie leant forward and hugged him and Joyce close to her, feeling their vulnerability as sure as she could feel the warmth of their little bodies.

'What's going on in here? What's all this wailing about?' Lil screeched from the kitchen doorway.

Lil Prentice wasn't a big woman, just an average sort of build for a woman in her late fifties, but she had a voice on her that Davy had always said could carry as far as the Aldgate Pump. 'It's like a flipping graveyard in here,' she bellowed, grasping hold of the door-frame for support.

Cissie wiped her eyes on the back of her hand and shook her head disbelievingly. She'd been drinking again, Cissie was sure of it. But that was no excuse for her spite-fulness; Cissie would never get used to Lil's nasty, uncaring ways. It was hard to believe she was Davy's mum. But she was, and that was why Cissie, as much as she couldn't stand the woman, had never objected when Davy had brought her to live with them when they'd moved into Linman Street.

'Well?' Lil persisted.

'I've been trying to work out things. You know.' Cissie nodded towards the children, hoping that, for once, Lil would take the hint and keep her mouth shut in front of them. They had enough to fret about without their nanna adding to their fears.

Lil walked unsteadily across the narrow room and plonked herself down opposite Cissie. Almost tipping the chair over, she had to grab hold of the edge of the table to steady herself. 'I need all this, I reckon,' she said, pushing the pile of bills away from her with a careless flick. 'I wish I'd have stayed down the bloody Sabberton instead of coming home to your sodding moaning.'

'You've been down the pub again. I knew it.'

'What? I need your permission to go for a drink now, do I? Yer cheeky mare!'

Matty and Joyce clung to their mother, scared by their nanna's drunken shouting.

'Come on you two.' Cissie was doing her best to sound calm, but the thought of her mother-in-law pouring what could have been their rent money down her throat in the Sabberton Arms made her blood boil. 'Time I was getting you little 'uns up to bed.'

As Cissie led her two bewildered children from the kitchen and along the passage, Lil shouted after them, 'I've been thinking about upstairs,' she hollered. 'I reckon now it's just you up there, Cissie, yer don't need all that space. So I'll have that front bedroom o' your'n and you can move your stuff down here into the parlour and have my bed.' She paused before adding slyly, 'I reckon it's what my poor Davy would have wanted, me having that upstairs room, away from all the noise in the street.'

Cissie smiled down at the children. 'See how fast you two can run up them stairs and get your jimjams on, eh? I won't be a minute, I'm just gonna talk to Nanna for a bit.' Cissie waited at the foot of the stairs until the children had disappeared into the back bedroom, then she took a deep breath and strode back into the kitchen.

Lil was ready for her; she started immediately. 'I'm entitled to that room. Entitled.'

'Aw, right, I see. You wanna take my room from me, do yer? And d'yer wanna take over with the kids and all? Yer don't mind jumping in and out of bed all night, settling the poor little loves down after all their bad dreams? That right, is it? That what yer wanna do?'

Lil folded her arms belligerently. 'What, can't be bothered to walk up a flight of stairs to see to yer own kids? Davy'd be very proud, I don't think.'

Cissie ran her fingers distractedly through her hair; her hands were shaking. 'Look, just leave it, eh, Lil. Just leave it. We're both tired. This ain't the time.'

Lil snorted derisively. 'I ain't just tired, I'm *sick* and tired. Sick and tired of *you*. Why don't you use yer loaf for once? That Turner made you an offer that most women'd jump at. He's just waiting to make our lives right comfortable for us. Just waiting for you to be nice to him. But you, Lady Muck, that's beneath you, ain't it? Being *nice* to someone.'

Cissie summoned every bit of strength she had in her to stop herself wrapping her hands around Lil's throat. She turned on her heel and walked back out into the passage. 'If it wasn't for the kids being here,' she muttered to herself as she hauled herself up the stairs, 'I'd bloody kill that woman.'

—

By the time Cissie had settled the children, reassuring Matty yet again that she wouldn't be going away and leaving him and Joyce, she had calmed down enough to be able to face Lil without wanting to smack her hard round her miserable face.

She gripped the banister rail firmly, confident that she wouldn't let her mother-in-law upset her again. The children were her priority, not Lil and her drunken rantings about Big Bill Turner. She would go on the streets before she had anything to do with the likes of him, and that was why she would sort things out – somehow or other. She straightened her back and urged herself forward; with all those bills to pay, she couldn't afford the luxury of feeling sorry for herself. Things had to be done.

But, as she stepped back into the kitchen and saw what Lil was up to, Cissie was, once again, shaking with rage.

'What the hell have you got there?' she demanded.

'What, begrudge an old girl a drop o' something to comfort her after her boy's death would yer?' Lil was sitting at the table draining the remains of a half-bottle of scotch into her glass. 'My Davy wouldn't have let you treat me like this.' She knocked back the whisky in a single gulp. 'Been dead just six weeks he has, Gawd rest him, and it's like yer've forgotten him already.'

Cissie snatched the empty glass from her hand and took it over to the sink. 'The drink's making yer talk rubbish,' she said, running the tap at full force and soaking the front of her dress. 'Now look what yer've made me do.'

'You ain't even wearing black,' whined Lil pitifully.

Cissie spun round and walked slowly back to the table, jabbing her finger at herself as she spoke. 'This navy frock,' she said, her chest rising and falling with the effort of keeping her anger under control and her voice down so that the children weren't disturbed, 'is the darkest thing I've got apart from me black costume. What d'yer want me to do? Go up West and buy meself a load o' new gear?'

Lil looked up at her, her eyes swivelling drunkenly in and out of focus. 'When my Davy was here, you always looked a picture.'

47

'And I still do me best to look nice.' Cissie dragged the chair roughly from under the table and sat down opposite Lil. 'And I still want Davy to be proud of me and all, even though he's not here no more. Proud of me, just like he always was.' Cissie's head fell forward and she began to cry softly. 'He never liked me in dark things. That's why I've only got this and me costume.'

Lil sneered disgustedly. 'Davy'd love all this carrying on.'

'But he ain't here now, is he?' Cissie buried her face in her hands. 'He was killed down that bastard market.' Her shoulders shook with her sobs. 'Why did it have to be my Davy them crates fell on? Why?'

'What a flaming way to carry on.' Lil, who never showed any emotion except rage, shuddered at such a distasteful display. 'I've had enough of all this, I'm gonna nip back down the Sabberton. See if someone'll buy a tot or two of something for a grieving mother.'

With that, Lil staggered to her feet, wove her way out of the kitchen, went crashing along the passage and out of the street door.

Cissie was glad to see the back of her. With a bit of luck she'd be sound asleep in bed by the time Lil eventually got thrown out of the pub. But now she had to get stuck in and sort out the bloody bills.

Cissie blew her nose, went over to the sink and threw water over her face, then sat back down at the table to try to figure out a way to somehow make ends meet.

–

Cissie scratched her head with the end of her pencil and then, listlessly, she let it fall on to the table.

It just hadn't occurred to her that the roll of money Davy had left in the dresser drawer – the only money apart from the few pounds Lil had got, and spent almost immediately, from Davy's single insurance policy – would run out quite so soon. She would never have believed how much a family needed just to survive, let alone to lead the kind of life they had been used to when Davy was alive: having smart, decent clothes to wear; always plenty of food on the table; being able to buy things for Joyce and Matty whenever they needed, or wanted, them; and not having to worry about the cost of having the doctor round if Lil felt a bit under the weather.

Cissie rubbed her hands over her face, kneading her knuckles into her tired and bloodshot eyes. She felt worn out with the effort of it all. It was no good, no matter how many lists she wrote, juggling one bill against the other, nor how she tried to cut back on things, there just wasn't enough to go round. There was nothing else for it – she would have to sell something.

She picked up the pencil and launched it angrily across the room. Selling things; things that Davy had bought. The thought sickened her. Unlike so many of her neighbours, Cissie wasn't used to hard times; she wouldn't even go with Gladys when she paid one of her regular visits to the pawn shop. For Cissie had always felt, although, of course, she would never have said so to her friend, that poverty was like some sort of contagious disease – risk making contact with it and you were contaminated for ever.

Yet what other choice did she have but to sell something? She certainly had no intention of doing what Lil wanted her to do. Go running to Big Bill Turner. The thought of him and his offer of 'help' sickened her even more than the prospect of going to the pawnbroker's.

She held her left hand up and looked at the deep-blue stones of her engagement ring, the ring that Davy had bought her because he said it matched her eyes.

Cissie dismissed the idea immediately. No, she couldn't. Not her engagement ring. Tears began to fill her eyes yet again.

'Davy,' she moaned, 'why did you have to leave me? I need you.'

As soon as the words left her mouth, Cissie felt ashamed. Her children needed *her*, and what was she doing? Sitting there crying. She had to pull herself together, and if it wasn't going to be the ring that she sold, she would just have to think of something else. Something that would see them through for a good while. Something that would give her enough time to think what to do next.

She picked up the stack of bills and stared fixedly at them as though they would tell her what to do, how to pay them. A faint smile twitched around her lips. The bill for the truck window... That was it! She would sell Davy's truck. That would be bound to bring in a fair few pounds, more than enough to give her breathing space.

Excited by the idea of at last having a solution, albeit a temporary one, to their problems, Cissie wiped her eyes roughly on her sleeve, sorted out the sheet of paper with the least lists of bills written on it, snatched up the pencil from the floor, grabbed the truck keys off the dresser, and rushed outside.

As Cissie opened the street door, she felt the still warm air on her face; it was a lovely late May evening, a perfect match for her newly optimistic mood.

She pulled the door to behind her, trying not to make too much noise. The children would be all right, she told herself, she'd only be a minute; the truck was parked just along the street, on the bit of waste ground next to number nine, where Myrtle and Arthur Payne lived. She could stick a 'For Sale' notice on the windscreen and be back indoors without them even knowing she'd been out.

But before she had taken a single step along the street, the sound of someone pushing open the front bedroom window made her look up.

It was Matty. He was looking down at her, his fair hair tousled from tossing and turning on his pillow.

'Where you going, Mum?' His little face was taut with anxiety.

'I'm just going to have a look at Daddy's truck, darling. I'll be two ticks.'

'You sure you ain't going out for a drive without me and Joyce, Mum?'

'Course I ain't. I wouldn't go for a drive without you, daft. Now get back in your own room and into bed and I'll tuck you up all nice and cosy as soon as I get back.'

Matty didn't look completely convinced, but he did as he was told.

'Good boy,' Cissie called up to him as he disappeared inside. She waited until she was satisfied that the window was safely closed again, then she returned to her task.

To get to the waste ground she had to pass Ethel Bennett and Myrtle Payne, who were sitting outside number nine, Myrtle's place, on kitchen chairs, making the most of the pleasant evening air as they gossiped and rumour-mongered and got on with causing their usual mischief.

As Cissie walked by with a nod and a brisk 'Good evening', the women, as one, turned their heads to stare at her. Ethel said something to Myrtle in a harsh, cackling whisper. But she hadn't lowered her voice quite enough to prevent Cissie hearing her.

Cissie stopped in her tracks, spun round and confronted them.

'Would you like to say that again, Ethel Bennett?'

Ethel smiled, or rather, she pulled her lips across her brown and crumbling teeth, making a shape that, for her, had to pass as a smile. 'Say what again?' she asked with an innocent shrug.

'That what you just said. That bit about me being – what was it – "getting me comeuppance", wasn't that what yer said?'

Myrtle stuck her hands inside her crossover apron and looked Cissie up and down. 'You don't have to answer to the likes of her, Ett.'

'I don't bleed'n intend to, Myrt.'

'Come on, tell me to me face if yer've got something to say. Or are yer too scared?'

'Scared o' you?' Ethel raised her eyebrows in disbelief. 'I don't think so, darling.'

Cissie went to say something but thought better of it. It was as pointless trying to get those two to behave decently as it was rowing with Lil, and anyway, she had better things to do with her time. So, with a final, disgusted shake of her head, Cissie stuck her chin in the air and walked along to the waste ground, leaving them to it.

As she stood there, by the truck, she could hear them still talking about her. The pair of them were going on about how she was being paid back for all her fancy ways, and how it served her right, and maybe she'd know now what it was like for other women trying to get by. But Cissie ignored them, she was far more interested in how she should word the 'For Sale' notice, than what those two vicious, tittle-tattling old busybodies had to say about her.

She tipped her head to one side and ran her finger through the thick dust on the truck's red bonnet. When Davy had been alive, it had gleamed with polish, now in the fading rays of the last of the evening sunshine, it looked dull and uncared for. Davy would have hated to see it being neglected, he had been so proud of it.

Her eyes misted over, and she smiled sadly to herself as she remembered the day that Davy had brought it home and parked it outside number seven, honking the bulbous horn, bringing everyone out to see the first vehicle owned by someone in Linman Street. Davy had taken her out, that very night, to begin teaching her to drive it. How he'd shouted at her! – something he never did – when she had got the pedals muddled up and almost crashed it into a wall.

The mist in her eyes turned to water, and the first, fat tear fell on to her cheek.

'Penny for 'em, Cis?'

Cissie lifted her gaze away from the grimy paintwork. 'Hello, Glad,' she sniffed. 'Sorry. I was miles away.'

'I know that, girl.' Gladys rolled her eyes. 'D'you know I was hollering at you at the top of me voice when your Matty was hanging out of the window just now? Shouting from just up the road as I come out of Clarke's, I was. And yer didn't even see me. Yer in a right bloody dream.' She paused. 'So, how's things?'

'Fine. Fine,' she said hurriedly.

'That why you've been crying then?' Gladys asked, narrowing her eyes suspiciously. 'Cos everything's fine?' Cissie flapped her hand in the direction of Ethel and Myrtle. 'It's them old bags next door,' she sighed, 'they've been having a go at me again.'

'Come on, Cis, this is me, Gladys Mills, yer talking to. I know they drive yer barmy, they drive us all sodding barmy, but they ain't got what it takes to make yer cry. Not even when they're playing their flaming double act.'

Gladys lifted her chin at the paper and pencil Cissie was carrying and gently touched her friend on the arm. 'Anything to do with that?'

'What d'yer mean?'

'I dunno, to tell yer the truth, Cis. It just ain't what yer expect to see though, is it? Seeing yer mate on the waste ground writing letters.'

'I ain't writing a letter, Glad. I'm doing a "For Sale" sign. For Davy's truck.'

Gladys looked confused. 'Why on earth would you do that? That truck was your Davy's pride and joy.'

'Don't yer think I know.' Cissie said it so quietly that Gladys could barely hear the words.

With a sudden look of realisation, Gladys leant closer to Cissie so that Ethel and Myrtle couldn't eavesdrop. 'Look, Cis, tell me to mind me own business, but you ain't short o' money or nothing, are you, girl?'

Cissie smiled weakly through her tears. 'Daft! Course I ain't.'

'Well, if you ever are – any other time, like – you know I'll always help, however I can. Like I promised before, I'll always be here for yer, Cis. I know I ain't got no money, but I can always put a word in for yer up the City. They need new cleaners all the time up there.' She laughed mirthlessly. 'Cos they keep wearing out all the old ones, don't they.'

'I told yer, Glad,' Cissie snapped. 'I'm fine. I ain't broke and I don't need no help from no one. Right?'

'Yeah, right. But there's no need to bite me head off is there.'

Cissie shoved the paper and pencil into her dress pocket and examined her tear-stained face in the truck's smeary wing mirror. 'Time I was off home.'

Gladys stepped aside as Cissie brushed briskly past her and strode off in the direction of number seven.

'But how about the "For Sale" sign?' Gladys asked as loudly as she dared with Ethel and Myrtle sitting just a few yards away.

'I've changed me mind,' Cissie answered boldly, stopping in front of the two gawping old hens. 'Got that, did yer, you two? Davy's truck *ain't* for sale.'

–

The shiny black car pulled up outside Aldgate station. In the back, sat Big Bill Turner with Bernie, one of his burly henchmen.

'So, how's this Richie bloke doing on Flowers' old pitch then, Bernie?'

Bernie stuck out his bottom lip and waggled his head up and down. 'A very fair job, guv. Very fair. The takings are almost up to what they were before, you know—' He paused and considered his words. 'Before Flowers had his accident.'

'Good, but this Richie bloke had better not make himself too comfortable.' Turner dropped his chin and stared out of the car window at the pavement where Davy Flowers had once run his stall. 'I've got other plans for that pitch.'

The driver, Jack, looked in the rear-view mirror and caught Bernie's eye. Bernie shook his head, a signal that he should keep his trap shut, but Jack couldn't resist asking, 'You mean you're still gonna—'

'Are you questioning me?'

'No, Course not, boss,' the driver assured him.

'Good. Now, turn the engine off, I wanna go and have a word with Fat Stan over on the paper stall.'

Jack did as he was told without a murmur.

Turner sat there and waited for Bernie to get out and open the door for him. Then he indicated with a stab of his thumb that Bernie should wait in the car.

'Private business,' he said, putting on his hat.

Bernie immediately climbed back in the car. He and Jack watched as Turner strolled, with a slow, confident gait, over to the newspaper vendor, a massive cigar in one hand and an envelope in the other.

'I can't believe he's still banking on Flowers' missus being interested in him,' Jack said in a voice so quiet that Bernie had to lean over the seat to hear him.

'Always has thought through his trousers, that one,' Bernie replied, with a partly cynical, partly admiring laugh. 'Do anything to pull a bit of skirt he's set his sights on.'

'Mind you, who can blame him where she's concerned, eh, Bern? What a looker that girl is. I wouldn't say no to a bit of that on the side meself.' Jack sniggered coarsely.

'Specially if I had to get into bed with Moe Turner every night.'

'That Moe's a big old bird, all right,' agreed Bernie with a nod. 'I'll bet she's got a right hand on her when she gets her wild up.'

Jack looked out of the window to make sure that Turner was still out of earshot, then he twisted round, sticking his hand across the seat to Bernie in the back.

'Tenner says Flowers' missus is in Turner's bed before the end of the summer.'

Bernie blew noisily through his pursed lips. 'Leave off, Jack! What d'you think I am, straight off the bleed'n boat?' He leant back in the soft leather seat and grinned. 'The way Davy's old mum's been boozing all their dough away down the Sabberton Arms, that young girl's gonna be buzzing round Big Bill Turner before this sodding month's out, ne'mind no summer.'

Chapter 4

As she opened her eyes, Cissie smiled contentedly: it was wonderfully warm and cosy in the big feather bed, and the sun coming through the yellow curtains was flooding the room with bright, joyful colour.

She stretched slowly and, turning lazily on to her side, she reached out for Davy.

Davy…

She rolled back on to the pillow.

When would it finally sink in that her Davy was dead? When would she ever really believe that he was no longer with her; that he wouldn't ever again appear in the bedroom doorway with a cup of tea and a saucy wink, just as he used to? How could she have wiped it from her mind, yet again, that he was gone?

It was only last night that she was lying there, staring up at the ceiling, promising herself – and Davy, because she prayed that he could hear her wherever he was, and that he was watching over her – that she would do everything she could to look after Matty and Joyce and, God help her, Lil. No matter what, she swore she would do it. Now, just a few short hours later, her mind was playing its cruel tricks on her all over again.

Cissie raked her fingers roughly through her hair, threw off the bedcovers and willed herself to get up and get going. She glanced at the clock on the bedside cabinet — a pretty little walnut pot cupboard that Davy had brought home for her as one of his surprises.

She couldn't believe it. It was half past nine. She felt just like a slut. She really would have to get herself back into some sort of routine. The trouble was, she was having so much trouble getting to sleep at night, and then, when she finally dropped off, she would wake up every hour or so, either to see to the kids or just to lie there thinking, that she was exhausted by the morning and it was really hard for her to get up. But, hard or not, it wouldn't do when Matty started school in September. She had just over three months until then, so she'd have to do something to sort herself out. She really would. Everything was down to her now. Everything.

Sighing loudly to herself, Cissie pulled her dressing-gown around her shoulders and went downstairs to the kitchen, without so much as a glimpse at herself in the dressing-table mirrors.

'Matty?' Cissie was shocked to find her son, dressed in his little striped winceyette pyjamas, balancing on one of the bentwood kitchen chairs, just about to open the corner cupboard.

Wobbling, with the effort of looking over his shoulder at his mum, Matty had to grab hold of the cupboard door to steady himself, but he wasn't quite quick enough. The chair toppled over and Matty went crashing on to the hard, lino-covered floor, his head missing the stone butler sink by inches.

'Matty!' Cissie yelled.

As she rushed over to him, with her legs catching in the flapping hem of her dressing-gown, she almost finished up on the ground beside him.

Struggling to sit up, Matty clutched his leg. 'I'm all right,' he insisted, warily examining his grazed knee. 'I didn't wanna wake you up until I'd made the breakfast for us all.' He bowed his little fair head in shame at his failure. 'I was gonna help you cos you've been sad.'

'Aw, darling!' Cissie clasped him to her.

'Joyce's still asleep,' he said into her shoulder, 'but I think she's wet the bed again.'

Cissie let go of her son and straightened up. 'We'll leave her for the minute, eh? I'll see to her later on, make her nice and dry. But first,' she said hauling Matty to his feet, 'I'm gonna make us both something nice to eat.' She bent forward and whispered conspiratorially, 'Just for us two, eh? Cos if that chair falling over didn't wake her up, it looks like Nanna's out for the count and all.'

She picked up the chair and set it by the table for Matty to sit on.

'No, I don't think Nanna's asleep,' he said matter-of-factly, as he clambered up to the table. 'She came in just now. She was looking for her medicine, but she said the bottle was empty. So she went back to bed.'

Cissie smiled encouragingly at Matty then went over to the cupboard, thinking as she did so that she'd like to break Lil's empty 'medicine' bottle right over her head for her. 'She's probably not feeling very well, Matt. So we'll leave her in bed a bit longer and all.'

'Mum.'

'Yes, love?'

Matty picked distractedly at the shiny oilcloth that covered the kitchen table. 'Is Nanna Lil gonna die like Daddy?'

Cissie felt the lump rise in her throat. She grasped the cupboard handle as though it could rescue her from her pain. It was bad enough having to go through all this herself, but seeing the way it was affecting Matty was almost more than she could bear.

She turned and looked at her son, doing her best to smile. 'Remember what I told yer, Matt? About how sometimes people—'

'Die,' he interrupted her, his voice small and scared.

'Matty...' Cissie went over to him. She knelt down on the hard floor and hugged him to her. She had to find a way to make it all right for him and Joyce again. She had to.

'Someone's knocking.'

'Is there?' Cissie leant back on her heels and listened. 'Aw yeah, they're knocking all right. Just listen to 'em bashing on that knocker.' She stood up and wagged her finger at him with a smile. 'Now, no more trying to do no breakfasts while I'm seeing who it is. All right?'

He nodded.

Cissie dragged her dressing-gown tighter round her and went to see who was so impatient for an answer.

As she opened the door, she immediately wished she hadn't. 'Aw, Mr Brownlow,' she said flatly. 'It's you.'

'Morning, Mrs Flowers.' Mr Brownlow raised his bowler hat and treated her to the horrible spectacle of his famously leering grin. 'You seem surprised to see me.'

'I wasn't expecting yer,' she stammered. 'I didn't realise it was so late, did I?'

'It's late all right,' Cissie heard Ethel call from next door – she was out on her step nosing, as usual. 'Too bleed'n late to still be in yer night things, if you ask me.'

Mr Brownlow waggled his bushy eyebrows at Cissie and flashed her a suggestive smirk. 'I thought that meself.'

'Disgraceful,' pronounced Ethel. 'In my day, we'd have been up and dressed hours ago. Our washing would've been in soak, our pots scoured, *and* our steps would have been scrubbed clean and all.'

Cissie would have loved to have given Ethel Bennett a piece of her mind, but she knew how the old cow could twist and turn anything anybody said and make them look bad for having even opened their mouth, and she definitely didn't need that at the moment. And especially not in front of Brownlow, because she was about to put a proposition to him – one that she badly needed him to agree to.

'Look, Mr Brownlow,' Cissie said quietly, 'I've got something private like to say to yer. Could yer step inside for a minute, d'yer think?'

The landlord looked delighted at the prospect.

As she pulled the door to, Cissie caught a glimpse of Ethel Bennett clasping her pudgy cheek between the sausagey fingers of one hand, and scratching her head between her ever-present curlers with the other. Cissie didn't have to be a genius to know that her nosy old trout of a next-door neighbour was in a real quandary: should she heave her fat carcass along to the end of the turning, so she could report events to Myrtle Payne at number nine? Or, should she stagger across the street to number eight and tell her daughter, Lena Dunn, that she had just seen a man – Mr Brownlow the landlord of all people! – being invited, bold as brass, into the young widow Flowers' house?

Whichever of them Ethel decided to tell, Cissie knew that both were equally capable of exaggerating the truth, spreading lies, and causing mischief. So, in the end, it was all the same to her.

'Now, Mrs Flowers,' said Brownlow, leaning towards her, his clipped grey moustache bristling like a shaving brush. 'What's all this about then, you inviting me in like this?' The passageway of number seven was dark and narrow, as in all the other houses in the street, and Cissie had to press herself flat against the wall to create even a little bit of space between herself and her ogling landlord.

'It's like this, Mr Brownlow,' she began, increasingly and unpleasantly aware that all she was wearing were her night things and that his hot breath was burning her cheek. 'I'm gonna have to ask yer for a little bit of a favour.' She tried a smile; she could feel it, tight on her lips.

'And what sort of favour would that be then?'

'I'd appreciate yer keeping your voice down, Mr Brownlow.' She inclined her head towards the closed front parlour door. 'Me mother-in-law's having a lie in. She's feeling a bit poorly.'

'What, the ale gone off down the Sabberton, has it? Give her gippy guts?'

Cissie's smile set even more rigidly; her jaws ached with the effort of keeping it there. 'She's been very down since... since Davy... you know.'

'She must miss him.' Brownlow's voice had become a menacing, rasping whisper. 'And so must you,' he added, making the words sound disgusting.

Clasping her dressing-gown to her throat, Cissie nodded. 'Yes. Yes, I do. Course I do. And it's not been easy to manage without him these past weeks. That's why I need a favour.'

She turned her head away from him, took a deep gulp of air and then blurted out: 'I'm gonna need a bit more time to get the rent, Mr Brownlow.'

Brownlow's piggy eyes blinked waterily behind the thick lenses of his round tortoiseshell specs. He coughed, spluttering all over her, before running his sharp pink tongue around his lips. 'Why worry yourself about the rent, Mrs Flowers? I mean, we could come to some sort of an...' He paused, and then, laying revolting emphasis on each syllable, he continued, '...*an arrangement*.'

As the full significance of what the landlord was suggesting dawned on Cissie, she immediately sprang into incensed action. 'Yes, Lil,' she shouted at the closed front-room door, replying to her mother-in-law's non-existent question, 'it is Mr Brownlow. Ain't it nice of him? He just popped in to pass on his *wife's* condolences to us.' Cissie jabbed her finger at his chest. 'You will remember to thank *Mrs* Brownlow for me, won't you?' she asked between clenched teeth. 'Cos we all know how funny she can turn when she gets upset, don't we?'

The landlord's eyes goggled with suppressed rage, his mouth opening and closing like a dying cod's on a fish-monger's slab.

'Now,' Cissie reached across him to open the street door again, trying not to flinch as her bare wrist brushed against the shiny brown material of his well-worn suit, 'if you don't mind, Mr Brownlow, I'll be getting me kids their breakfasts. And I'm sure you've got plenty to do, and all.'

Cissie flung the door back on its hinges to find Ethel, Myrtle and Lena – Ethel having obviously gone for the full set – all waiting eagerly by her street doorstep for developments.

'Thanks for calling by with your *wife's* kind thoughts, Mr Brownlow,' Cissie emphasised loudly.

With her chin stuck defiantly in the air, Cissie treated her three trouble-raking neighbours to a stare that challenged them to say a single word out of place. 'And we right appreciate yer being so understanding about waiting until next week for the rent and all.'

As Brownlow stepped past her to make his escape into the street, Cissie caught hold of his sleeve and hissed into his ear, 'You'll get your money, Brownlow, don't you worry yourself about that. But that's all yer'll be getting, you dirty old bugger.'

With that, Cissie gave him a discreet yet determined shove, ejecting him out of the house with such force that, if he hadn't swerved so neatly, he would have landed right in Ethel Bennett's arms. And there were some women, although not that many, at which even Mr Brownlow drew the line.

'I'll say good-morning to yer then, Mr Brownlow.' Cissie smiled, wide-eyed, at her audience. 'And keep yer hand on your money satchel, won't yer. There's some funny people round here. Bloody funny.' With that she slammed the door firmly behind him.

Leaning against the passage wall, Cissie caught up her hair between her hands and pulled it back off her face. She could feel her usually pale skin flaming scarlet with anger and shame. What had she been thinking of, inviting that pig into her home? She must have been off her head. She had to pull herself together, get on and make Matty's breakfast, act as though everything was normal. *Something* had to stay normal in the poor little devil's life.

But she should have known from the way her luck was running lately, that it wasn't going to be as easy as that.

Back in the kitchen Matty was sitting at the table, tears streaming down his cheeks. 'I know yer told me not to do nothing, Mum,' he gasped between sobs, 'but you was such a long time, and I was hungry. So I...' He bowed his head. 'So I went and looked in the cupboard.'

Slowly, he lifted his chin, his face was puffy from weeping. 'There ain't nothing in there, Mum. We're gonna starve, ain't we? And then we'll all be dead like Dad, won't we?'

Cissie took Matty's face gently in her hands and kissed the top of his head. 'It's all right, darling. I'll sort it out. Just a couple more minutes, I promise, and yer'll have a lovely big breakfast, with all yer favourite things. All piled up on yer plate.' She kissed him again and then walked over to the kitchen door. 'I'm just gonna have a word with Nanna.'

'Lil!' Cissie shouted, striding along the passage. 'I wanna word with you!'

Cissie ran upstairs to get dressed, feeling murderous. How could Lil do that? Even if she had had too much to drink last night, fancy not thinking to leave something, anything, in the cupboard for the kids. She was so bloody selfish.

As she stepped into the front bedroom, the first thing she saw — the first thing she always saw — was the wooden-framed photograph of her, Davy and Matty. They'd had it taken at Southend when they'd gone there for a day trip on a paddle steamer along the Thames. Matty hadn't even been Joyce's age then, not much more than a baby really, but he already had the look of Davy about him with his fair hair and his cheeky grin.

She looked at the happy image of herself smiling out from the picture, and compared it with what she saw looking back at her from the dressing-table mirrors.

Davy had always been so proud of her, the way she looked and the way she dressed. He'd loved being seen with her on his arm as they walked along the street together with the kids, all done up in their Sunday best. He'd brought home the swagger coat she had on in the photo as a surprise – he'd got it off some feller he knew in the market. Typical Davy. She was so pleased with it, she'd worn it all that day, even though it was really hot and sunny. She hadn't even taken it off when, after they'd gorged themselves on skate and chips and cups of steaming, dark brown tea, they had gone down to the beach for a paddle.

She pressed the picture to her lips. She had been so lucky, so happy; but had she taken it all for granted? The thought that maybe she hadn't shown Davy how much she loved and appreciated him, while he was still with her, tormented her. She could only pray that she had.

She dipped her head and looked in the dressing-table mirrors. Dark smudges spread like faint mauve bruises across the pale skin under her tear-reddened eyes, and her hair hung lank and unwashed around her face. What would Davy think of her now? She couldn't let herself go around in this state for much longer.

She snatched up her hairbrush and ran it harshly through her hair. After she'd got herself over to the corner shop and made something for the children's breakfast, she would wash her hair and make herself look decent.

She pulled her nightie over her head and dropped it on the ground at her feet, then dragged on some underwear and the navy cotton dress she'd left on the dressing-table stool the night before. Looking around for a pair of stockings, she could find only one, and that was snagged from where it had been draped over an open drawer of the tallboy.

The room was in a real mess. It didn't take much working out to realise that it was going to take more than getting dressed and a hair wash to sort things out. She felt like weeping. It was all so difficult, there was so much to do, so much to remember.

Davy, she was beginning to realise, had done a lot more than just bring home the housekeeping every Friday night. He had kept her world together, had given her a reason to laugh, a reason to make sure she looked nice, a reason to live.

She dropped down on to the unmade bed. Was it really only six weeks since her life had been turned upside down?

'Cissie! You still upstairs?' Lil's foghorn of a voice shattered its way into Cissie's thoughts.

'Yes, Lil,' she answered, closing her eyes with exhaustion at just the idea of dealing with her mother-in-law.

'Ain't yer been over that sodding shop yet? I'm bleed'n starving down here.'

Wearily, Cissie rose to her feet. She wanted to shout back that if Lil hadn't stuffed her greedy self last night there would have been at least some eggs and toast for them all. But it was too much effort to even think about starting a row that, on previous form, Cissie knew Lil could continue for hours, or even days, on end if the fancy took her.

Cissie trudged downstairs as though she were wading through a river of treacle. She stood in the kitchen doorway and looked at Lil sitting at the table with Matty. Lil was staring moodily at the teapot.

'Not even a few lousy grouts to make meself a cuppa,' she moaned without even raising her eyes to meet Cissie's.

Matty looked from his mum to his nanna, and back again. 'I ain't that hungry no more,' he said quietly.

Biting the inside of her cheek to stop herself from breaking down into tears, Cissie smiled weakly at her sad-eyed child. Slipping a floral crossover apron over her dress, she went over to the hearth and took down the old silver-coloured tea caddy from the overmantel.

'Let's see what we've got in the rainy day pot, eh Matt?' Cissie said as cheerfully as she could manage.

She lifted the lid and looked inside. A single half-crown? Surely she wasn't seeing straight? She was positive there'd been at least twenty-five shillings the last time she'd looked.

Cissie thought for a moment. Yes, she was right, only yesterday she'd thought about getting it ready to give to Brownlow when he called this morning. But she'd thought better of it. Davy had always said it was only to be used in a real emergency, an emergency such as not having any food to put on the table for the kids. She could see herself back then, laughing at Davy for even suggesting that such a ridiculous thing might ever happen.

'Lil,' Cissie began.

'What?'

'You ain't borrowed no money or anything out of here, have yer?'

'That money was my Davy's,' Lil snapped shirtily. 'He wouldn't have begrudged his old mum a few coppers.'

'But there's twenty-two and six missing.' Seeing the frightened look clouding Matty's face, Cissie lowered her voice. 'What have you done with it?'

'I don't have to answer to *you*.' Lil shoved back her chair and stomped out of the back door into the yard. She snatched open the wooden lavatory door and shut herself in the little outdoor cubicle. 'I'll be in here for a while,' she hollered. 'I'll be ready for me breakfast when I come out.'

'What we gonna do if we ain't got no money, Mum? Yer can't get things without money, can yer?'

Cissie ruffled his hair. 'We've got money, daft,' she said light-heartedly. 'Now you wash them hands o' your'n, then go upstairs and wake up yer little sister for me, while I nip over Clarke's and get all the bits and pieces for a great big fry-up.'

As Cissie opened her street door she saw Ethel, Myrtle and Lena still in a gossiping huddle by her step.

'Nice not to have no jobs to do,' Cissie said, avoiding their eyes as she pulled the street door shut behind her.

'I see mourning don't mean nothing nowadays,' Myrtle sneered as she eyed Cissie's floral apron.

Cissie didn't bother to answer, she just strode purposefully across the street.

She was intending to go straight to Sammy Clarke's corner shop to see how far the half-crown would stretch, but as she passed number four, Gladys's house that stood next door to Clarke's, Cissie stopped. She took her purse from the pocket of her apron and opened it. Two and six. Some chance of feeding the four of them even a decent bit of breakfast, dinner and tea today, let alone affording anything for tomorrow.

Gladys's street door was, as usual, wide open. From where she was standing, Cissie could hear the sound of laughter coming from the kitchen. It was the younger Mills children and their dad, Ernie. It sounded so happy, so normal in there, that Cissie didn't think twice.

'All right, Ern,' she called in greeting as she walked down the narrow passageway. She poked her head round the kitchen door. 'It's only me.'

Ernie was sitting in a carver chair by the stove, supposedly reading the paper, but, in reality, acting as a monkey climb for his three youngest who weren't yet school-age.

'Hello, Cis,' he said with his usual friendly grin. 'Come on in, girl.' He lifted the kids on to the floor with one sweep of his big, labourer's arms. 'I was just minding these little monsters.' He shrugged apologetically. 'While Gladys is out, like.'

Cissie smiled, knowing Ernie was embarrassed to be at home while his wife was out working. 'Right handful at that age, ain't they?'

'Yeah.' Ernie nodded self-consciously. 'Here,' he said standing up, 'I'm forgetting me manners. Let me stick the kettle on the hob and I'll make us a cuppa. Yer've got the time, ain't yer?'

'That's something I've got too much of lately, Ern.'

Cissie sat at the table and watched as Ernie moved around the cramped little room, filling the kettle, getting

71

the cups off the shelf over the sink, and warming the pot. He did it so naturally; Davy, as far as Cissie was aware, hadn't even known where she kept the milk.

But then Davy had always been the breadwinner.

Cissie rubbed her hands over her face.

'You all right, girl?' Ernie asked putting the pot down on the table in front of her, and then slipping the worn, knitted cosy on top.

'Yeah, I'm all right. I was just, you know, thinking about things.' Cissie dropped her chin to hide the tears that were threatening to flow again.

Gently, Ernie patted her shoulder with his dinner-plate-sized hand. 'I know it ain't easy, love.'

'Oi!' a woman's voice demanded cheerfully from the kitchen doorway. 'You leave my old man alone, if yer don't mind, Cissie Flowers.'

Cissie looked up. 'Glad,' she sniffed miserably. 'Aw, Glad, I just dunno what to do.'

Gladys held her arms out to her friend. 'Come here,' she said, signalling with a jerk of her head for Ernie to make himself and the kids scarce. 'Come and tell me all about it.'

-

'No thanks, Glad,' Cissie said, putting down her empty cup. 'I won't have no more. Lil'll be wondering where I've got to with their breakfasts.' She sighed distractedly. 'And I don't need her going on at me. I can't help it, just the sound of her voice gets on me nerves.'

'Lil'd get on a bloody saint's nerves, Cis. So yer don't wanna go blaming yerself, and getting yerself all worked up over that.'

'But it ain't only that.' Cissie hesitated. She had never been in the position of having no money, not since the day she married Davy. And she hated it.

'So what is it? Yer can tell me, Cis, yer know that. And it won't go no further than these four walls, I promise yer.'

'I know, Glad. It's just, well, to tell yer the truth, I'm skint.'

'You?' Gladys asked incredulously. 'But I thought yer said yer was all right for money. When I asked yer about selling the truck——'

'I was lying.'

Cissie turned her empty cup slowly round and round in her hands. 'See, Davy did leave a bit of money, well, more than a bit really, just laying there in the dresser drawer it was. But during these past weeks, I've just sort of spent it.'

'What, all of it?'

Cissie nodded wretchedly. 'Every brass farthing of it. I've never had to worry about where the next few quid was coming from before, see. So I didn't sort of realise how quick it goes.'

'It's all right for some,' said Gladys more wistfully than unkindly.

'And anyway, I always thought there was the emergency money to fall back on.' Cissie leant back and reached into her apron pocket for her purse. She opened it and tipped the single half-crown spinning on to the table.

Both women watched the coin turn round until it stopped and fell flat on its side.

'Me emergency money,' said Cissie flatly.

'Is that it?'

'That's it. Everything there is.' Cissie shrugged, angry and ashamed at herself for being such a fool. 'Lil's poured the rest down her gullet in the Sabberton.'

Gladys reached out and took Cissie's hand. 'I'm sorry yer in this state, darling.'

'Me and all.' Cissie stared down at the single silver coin. 'Glad,' she said quietly, 'will you help me?'

Gladys squeezed her hand. 'Course I will, daft.'

Cissie looked up at her friend, her big blue eyes full of hope and tears. 'How much can yer lend me?'

Gladys let go of Cissie's hand. 'No, love, sorry. I don't mean I can help yer with money. Yer know Ernie ain't worked for months on end now, and I've got him, Nipper and the five kids all to feed and clothe out of the miserable few bob I bring in each week.'

Cissie lowered her eyes again. 'Aw,' she said, her voice now so quiet, it was barely audible. 'So how can you help me then?'

'I could put a word in for yer up the City. Like I said before, even in times like these, there's always work for cleaners. It might not be much to start with, just a few hours, say from four till eight of a morning, but once they see you're a willing grafter, the word soon gets round and you can pick up a good few extra hours a day.'

Gladys topped up her cup, giving Cissie a chance to speak, but Cissie said nothing.

'So, what d'yer reckon?' Gladys prompted her.

'Look, Glad,' said Cissie eventually, picking up the half-crown and putting it back in her purse. 'I don't wanna sound ungrateful or nothing, but I don't think I'm that desperate yet.'

'Thanks very much!'

'Look, Glad, I didn't mean—'

'No, I know. It *is* a poxy, rotten job, but, like they say, beggars can't be choosers, can they?'

Cissie stood up and slipped her purse into her pocket. 'I'd better be getting on. Lil and the kids, you know.'

'Don't forget, Cis, if you change your mind about the cleaning...'

'I won't, but thanks for the tea.'

'Any time.'

—

As Cissie walked the few steps from Gladys's door to the shop, she wished with all her heart that she hadn't set foot in her friend's kitchen. How could she have been so stupid as to think that Gladys would have had money to lend her? It made her feel that she'd been as selfish as Lil at her very worst.

And now Gladys knew she was broke. It was all so humiliating.

Clutching the purse in her pocket, and without even a glance at the piles of goods on offer on the pavement outside the shop, Cissie pushed open the door of Clarke's General Store. The half-crown would have to do.

The bell tinkled its familiar welcome and Sammy Clarke, the young, fresh-faced owner, who had run the shop single-handed since the death of his parents, smiled warmly at her from behind the counter.

'Morning, Cissie,' Sammy greeted her, his pink cheeks shining.

Ignoring Lena, who had just followed her into the shop and was now standing between her and a drum of chicken food, arms folded, watching her every move, Cissie returned Sammy's smile. 'Morning, Sam.'

'Let her go first,' Lena cut in.

Momentarily surprised by such uncharacteristic generosity from Ethel's daughter who, although she was barely out of her thirties, looked almost as old and sour as her mother, Cissie turned to thank her. But when she saw the predatory look in Lena's eyes, Cissie didn't bother. Lena had obviously pounced on the opportunity for picking up a bit of gossip. With a woman like Lena Dunn, even the contents of a neighbour's shopping bag could give her ammunition for spite. Someone could as easily be condemned for profligacy if they dared spend more than Lena approved of, or of meanness if they didn't. Lena had them either way.

But today Lena was actually interested in something far more intriguing than the items on Cissie's grocery list. She, like everyone else in the neighbourhood, knew that Sammy Clarke fancied the young widow Flowers something rotten, and had done so ever since they were both kids playing Knock Down Ginger and High Jimmy Knacker up and down St Paul's Road where they had both gone to school.

Everyone knew he fancied her that is, except Cissie herself, but then she had only ever had eyes for Davy. Still, the idea that boring, chubby, pink-faced Sammy could ever compete with Davy Flowers had given a lot of them a good laugh. But now Cissie was by herself, who knew what developments might occur. Yes, it was definitely worth Lena hanging around to see what unfolded.

Cissie stepped back from the counter. 'You're all right,' she said lightly. 'You go first.'

'I insist,' Lena barked rather than said, and hauled her basket further up her arm to indicate that that was an end of the matter.

Cissie tried again. 'But—'

'Look, me boys are both at school. Reg is at work. I ain't got nothing to rush home for. Not like you with them poor little kiddies o' your'n.'

Having decided that she had fired her winning shot, Lena sat herself down on the chair by the counter, tucked her hands inside her apron front in the way the older women like her mother did, and prepared herself to take mental note of the proceedings.

Sammy raised his eyebrows in incomprehension, baffled by the apparent brainstorm that had transformed Lena into this caring, considerate neighbour. He might have served women in the shop every day of the week except Sundays for all his adult life, but, being single, the opposite sex and their doings were as much a mystery to Sammy Clarke as what went on in Timbuktu – wherever that might be.

'Now,' he said, smiling until his pink cheeks shone, 'what can I get for yer, Cis?'

Having never had to consider the price of her shopping before, Cissie hadn't worked out what she could afford, so she looked about her and thought for a moment. From the chalked signs on the little blackboards stuck into the sacks and piles of goods, she soon realised that she couldn't afford very much at all. And she had promised Matty a fry-up of all his favourite things.

'Sam,' she said quietly, beckoning him closer.

Sam leant across the counter towards her. 'Yeah?'

'It's like this,' she breathed, her neck and face burning. 'I'm a bit short at the minute, see. But there's quite a few bits I need and...'

Cissie might have thought that she and Sammy were speaking in whispered confidence, but, as he filled her basket and insisted that she pay him whenever she was ready, Lena's acute meddler's hearing picked up every single, gossip-worthy word. She could hardly suppress her glee at such a tasty titbit.

By the time Cissie had finished cooking, it was nearly half past twelve, a bit late for breakfast, but she didn't care; she was just relieved to be able to put the half-crown back in the tea caddy on the overmantel, and to fill her cupboard with the food Sammy had let her have on the slate.

Lil wasn't so impressed by her daughter-in-law's efforts to provide for them.

'This it?' she demanded. With a sneer of disbelieving contempt, Lil glared at the fried eggs, streaky bacon and buttered toast that Cissie had put in front of her.

Matty, his toast soldier inches from his mouth, stopped eating and looked up at his mum. 'I like it,' he said.

Joyce banged her hands on the tray of her high chair in happy agreement, and opened wide for Cissie to spoon in another mouthful of runny yolk.

'You should be feeding yourself, young lady,' Cissie teased her daughter, deliberately ignoring Lil's complaints. 'And you get on with your food, Matt, there's a good boy for Mummy.'

Lil didn't take kindly to being ignored, especially not by her clueless daughter-in-law. 'When my Davy was alive, we had decent grub on this table. Grub that could line your stomach and build you up. Not this muck.'

She shoved the untouched plate away in disgust. 'What have we got for our dinner then? More o' these bacon scraps and some rotten veg? And how about our teas? What do we get then? Dry bread and water?'

'Have you finished?'

'If yer mean have I finished with that shit,' Lil said, curling her lip at the slowly congealing breakfast, 'then yes I have. But, if yer mean have I finished with *you*, then you ain't so lucky, my girl, cos I ain't finished with you by a long chalk.'

Very calmly, Cissie smiled reassuringly at her children, then she stood up, walked around the table to where Lil was sitting and, bending down so that only Lil could hear her, Cissie began speaking.

'You might not reckon yer finished with me, you vicious old bag, but you wanna watch yourself, Lil. Cos I might just be finished with you. And you wouldn't wanna lose yer meal ticket, now would yer? Even if it is only – what did you call it? Shit?'

Cissie straightened up and, smiling happily for the benefit of the kids, she reached across to the overmantel and took down the tea caddy.

'Here, Lil, here's half a crown. The Sabberton'll be open by now.' She thrust the coin into her astonished mother-in-law's hand and hissed under her breath, 'And if you've got any brain at all in that thick head o' your'n, you'll keep well out of my sight until I figure out how I'm gonna get us out of this mess.'

Matty sat in watchful silence as Lil, the money clasped tightly in her hand, stomped out of the kitchen and, by the sound of the street door slamming, left the house. Only then did he speak.

'Mum,' he began slowly.

'Yes, love?' Cissie replied, the relief at Lil's absence obvious in her voice.

'You know it's me birthday soon?'

'Course I do,' she said, ruffling his hair.

'Well, now we're poor, does it mean I can't have that football yer promised me? Cos I told the Godwin kids they could play with me when I got it. And they'll think I'm a right little liar.'

Cissie managed to reach her bedroom before she started crying.

She threw herself on to the bed and sobbed into the pillows. She couldn't let Matty down. There was nothing else for it. Keeping the truck was a luxury; she would have to sell it, whether it had been Davy's pride and joy or not.

She rolled on to her back and stared up at the ceiling. It made sense to sell it, she told herself. And it wouldn't be a problem, there had to be plenty of flower sellers or market traders who'd be only too pleased to pay a fair price for an almost brand-new vehicle.

She'd be able to pay Sammy back what she owed him, wipe her slate clean, and still have enough to live off while she worked out what to do next. She was stupid not to do it yesterday, when she'd first thought of it. The market would be closed over the weekend, but she would drive the truck to the flower market first thing on Monday morning.

She smiled sadly at the memory of Davy panicking every time she crashed the gear lever because she'd forgotten about the double declutching. He'd always wince in pain as the cogs and wheels groaned and squealed in mechanical protest.

Cissie suddenly pushed herself up on her elbows.

The flower market…

She blew her nose noisily and brushed her greasy hair away from her face.

Slowly, a much broader smile appeared on her lips. Why hadn't she thought of it before? *She* would run the flower stall. She would take over where Davy had left off. It was such an obvious solution.

A kaleidoscope of ideas danced in her mind.

Admittedly, she hadn't been near the stall for years, not since their courting days, in fact. And even then she and Gladys had only paraded up and down the street, passing back and forth past the old factory building near Aldgate station where Davy had his regular pitch, so that Cissie could flutter her eyelashes to try to catch his attention – and it had worked, she thought to herself with something almost like a laugh of pleasure.

She *could* do it. She *could* run the stall. She wasn't stupid, what she didn't know she could learn. Anyway, there couldn't be that much involved in it. Much as Cissie loved Davy, she'd be the first to admit that he was no genius, even he always acknowledged that she was the clever one in the family, yet he'd always made more than a good living for them all, even during times that everyone else seemed to agree were the worst they could remember.

She'd have to make arrangements for the children, of course, but she was sure that Gladys and Ernie would help her out. Anyway, Matty would be starting school before long, and if the worse came to the worst – and it would be the worst as far as Cissie was concerned – she would blackmail Lil into getting off her lazy arse to keep an eye on them while she went out to earn their living.

For the first time in weeks, Cissie felt genuinely hopeful. Davy would have been proud to see her back to her old self.

She jumped off the bed and raced downstairs to the kitchen to wash her hair. She was young, strong and single-minded, and the mother of two kids she would die to protect. And if Matty wanted a football for his birthday, then he would bloody well have one.

And, if it made him happy, she'd even let him take it along the street to play with the dookie Godwin kids from number one.

Chapter 5

Cissie did her best to keep an expression of careless ease on her face as she stood by Ernie Mills's side while he energetically worked at turning the truck's starting handle.

'I really appreciate this, Ern,' she said to the back of his head. 'I could've kicked meself, struggling with the bloody thing like that in front of Ethel and Myrtle. I felt a right idiot knowing they was lapping it all up.'

'That's all right, girl. It's just a knack, that's all,' Ernie said, wiping the back of his hand across his sweating brow. 'Any time, you know that. Whatever I can do to help. Anyway this ain't women's work. You should've come over and asked me earlier.'

The engine suddenly burst into noisy life.

'There y'are, Cis.' He straightened up and rubbed his aching back. It was hard for him to acknowledge how quickly he'd grown soft, sitting at home all day – starting a truck would hardly have taken his breath away in the old days. 'Now, are you sure you don't wanna wait till Gladys gets back and I'll come with yer?'

'I'm sure, Ern,' Cissie shouted over the engine noise, reassuring him for what seemed like the hundredth time that she could manage alone. She clambered up into the cab. 'You're doing me a much bigger favour keeping an eye on the kids.' She smiled sheepishly. 'Yer know how Lil would've carried on.'

With that, Cissie slammed the cab door shut, released the handbrake with surprisingly little effort, and pulled off the waste ground, taking her eyes off the cobbled surface of Linman Street only to flash a quick, triumphant grin at herself in the rear-view mirror before turning at a cautious crawl into Upper North Street. She could just imagine what Ethel and Myrtle were saying about young women driving trucks by themselves.

She felt so pleased with herself, that it wasn't until she came to a shuddering halt at the junction with East India Dock Road that Cissie even thought about whether she could remember how to get to the lock-up where Davy kept the stall.

When she eventually pulled into the narrow turning off Middlesex Street, where the Petticoat Lane and other local street traders kept their stalls and stock, Cissie was hot, sticky and more than a little angry with herself. She had driven around in circles for almost an hour before she had recognised the street she wanted. If she was going to make a success of being the breadwinner, and be able to keep herself and the kids out of the workhouse, she really would have to do better than this.

With a weary sigh, and her dress clinging stickily around her thighs, Cissie dropped down on to the hot tarry blocks of the roadway. Raucous shouts and appreciative whistles greeted her from across the street before she could even begin to restore her modesty.

Mortified, Cissie hurriedly averted her eyes. She *knew* she should have worn her black costume, they'd have shown respect to a widow. But it was so hot, and she *had* to be strong and determined if she was going to carry on, so why shouldn't she wear a summer's dress on a flaming hot day?

'Had a good eyeful have yer?' she snapped at them. 'Why don't you just sod off and get on with what yer meant to be doing? Or is that yer job, shouting at women?'

Her indignation only had the effect of sending the two men, who she now saw were supposedly repairing the wheel of a stall, into loud, impertinent laughter.

Furiously she dragged her handbag out of the cab and began frantically digging around in it for Davy's keys. The keys she had definitely put in there before she left. She could even remember taking them off the hook inside the cupboard door. If only her hands weren't trembling so much.

Cissie eventually did manage to find the keys, and then, after more struggling, to find the right key on the bunch, and finally to get it into the padlock, and to fold the high doors back on their hinges.

She stepped inside the lock-up. After being outside in the bright late morning sunshine, it took Cissie a moment to focus in the gloom, but then, there it was, the stall.

She bit her lip, still vaguely aware of the men's raucously crude remarks coming from behind her, but they no longer had any effect on her, not now. Compared to this, they meant nothing. It might have been just a few pieces of wood and wheels covered in a dusty tarpaulin throwover, but to Cissie the stall was as potent as a dried rose petal falling from between the leaves of a book of love poetry.

Slowly, she reached out and lifted the edge of the cover and ran her finger along the red and green painted surfaces. The colour stood out fresh and bright as jewels in the dim light of the lock-up. It was as though Davy had parked it there just the night before.

But he hadn't.

She pulled her hand away.

Davy hadn't been there for six whole long, agony-filled weeks. Weeks that had passed in a hateful blur of disbelief, pain and denial.

'Oi!' one of the men called out. Angry that Cissie hadn't succumbed to his charms, he had become hostile instead. 'What you up to over there? Who give you permission to poke about?'

Cissie spun around to face him. 'Not that it's anything to do with you, moosh,' she hollered back across the road, 'but this lock-up was me husband's, and now...' She hesitated, the words were almost choking her.

'And now *what*?' the man sneered.

'And now,' she managed to go on, 'it's mine. All right? And you can keep yer dirty mouths shut and yer filthy talk to yourselves and all, you dirty pair of buggers.'

With that, Cissie turned back to the stall, and with energy that surprised her, she ripped off the heavy sheet, threw it to the ground, and set about dragging the stall outside.

By the time she had finally manoeuvred it out on to the road, and had checked that the lock-up and truck were secure, Cissie felt worn out, but she was damned if she'd let the two now sniggering men see what an effort she was finding it all.

'Right,' she said loudly, grasping the handles firmly and shoving the unwieldy contraption forward. 'That's me organised. I'd better be on me way. Got lots to do. Unlike some people I could mention.' She treated them both to a brief sneer of contempt. 'See you then. *Gentlemen.*'

'I think yer'll find, darling,' one of them retorted gleefully, 'that yer meant to pull the bleed'n thing, not push it!'

–

The journey to Davy's pitch was even worse than the drive to the lock-up from Linman Street, even though she had, as soon as she was out of sight of her sarcastic adviser, actually followed his suggestion and had started pulling the stall.

By the time she reached her destination, Davy's old pitch, Cissie's hands, unused to such punishment, were blistered and sore, and her dress felt damp and horrible. But at least she had made it. She positioned the stall between St Botolph's church and the entrance to Aldgate station, close by the door of the old factory building – just where Davy had always put it – then she leant back against the rough brick wall to recover.

She gave herself a few moments, then, summoning more strength than she thought she possessed, she set about getting the vases, jars and buckets from the compartment under the stall and setting them out in neat rows on the banked painted shelving. Cissie found it oddly soothing, arranging the containers. She had always had a flair for that sort of thing, an eye for making things look nice – putting a lacy doily here, a little mirror there. It was one of the things that Davy had always admired in her.

When she was satisfied with her display, she ran along to the cigarette kiosk by the station and asked the man inside the little glass-fronted booth where she could get some water to fill them up.

The man seemed surprised by her request, and when Cissie insisted that she had every right to be there with the stall, he called across to a shady-looking group of men who were sitting on old orange boxes by the newspaper stall in the station forecourt playing a disorderly game of chase the lady.

The toughest-looking of the group rose slowly to his feet and stared at her. Despite the weather, he was wearing a dark, heavy suit and a snap-brimmed hat which cast shadows across his face. There was something about him that made Cissie uneasy, and something vaguely familiar too, but as soon as he spoke, it was what he had to say rather than his identity that was of most interest to Cissie.

'You ain't got no flowers,' he growled, inclining his head towards the stall. 'So you might as well piss off out of it. Anyway,' he added, jerking his thumb over his shoulder to a stall on the other side of the station, 'Richie there's selling all the flowers they need in these parts.'

'Do what?' Cissie gasped, taking in the presence of the rival stall for the first time. She'd been so preoccupied with setting up, she hadn't thought of looking along the street to check out whether she had any opposition.

'You heard,' he said, his tone uncompromising. 'The pitch's taken.'

Cissie shook her head, not in disagreement, but in realisation of her stupidity. 'Flowers,' she said, dropping her chin in a picture of complete misery. 'I never thought to bring none. And I never thought no one'd take our pitch neither.'

'*Our* pitch? How d'yer mean?' the man asked with a frown. 'Here, you in this with someone? Has someone sent yer?'

Cissie shook her head dejectedly. 'No. No one sent me. It used to be me husband's pitch.'

'Right,' he said, as though something had just occurred to him. 'You're Davy's old woman, ain't yer?'

'I'm his widow if that's what yer mean,' she answered bleakly.

'That's different, darling,' the man said, suddenly friendly.

'Is it?' she asked hopefully.

'Yeah. Course it is.' He said something to a bulky, older man in a flat cap who was leaning against the paper stall and then sat back down on his orange box. The older man nodded and, levering himself away from the stand, he made his way over to Cissie.

'He was a regular fixture here, your Davy,' the man said to Cissie.

'You knew him?'

'Yeah, I knew him,' he said with a nod that made his chins quiver. 'Now you come back tomorrow – with some stock this time – and there won't be no other flower stalls for four hundred yards around. You can guarantee that.'

'But how—'

'You just take my word for it.' He held out his great rough paw to her. 'Fat Stan,' he said. 'I'm at yer service, Mrs Flowers.'

–

'Flowers!' Cissie shouted at herself yet again as she parked the truck on the waste ground. 'Flaming flowers! I'm so bloody, sodding stupid!' She smacked her hand hard on the steering wheel. 'All that effort for nothing.' She felt so worn out that all she wanted to do was go home and put her feet up, but she knew she had to go into Gladys's first.

She was so tired that she didn't even have the energy to stop Matty screaming up and down the street with three of Gladys's kids while one of the grimy-looking Godwin boys sprayed them from a length of hose that was snaking out of his house and along the pavement.

'Glad? It's only me,' she called as she willed herself along the passageway of number four. 'I've come for Joycie.'

'Blimey!' Gladys exclaimed. 'You look like you've been out bleed'n labouring.' She was sitting at the table with Joyce on her lap, somehow managing to hold the lively toddler still with her arm while she was peeling her way through a mountain of mud-covered potatoes. She dropped her knife into the saucepan of water and put Joyce down so that she could get to her mother. 'Sit yourself, girl, and I'll put the kettle on.'

'I could certainly do with a cup o' tea.' Cissie sat down and hauled Joyce on to her lap. She planted a kiss on her daughter's dark, shiny hair and then put her back, protesting, on the floor.

'Here, Joyce,' Gladys said over her shoulder as she lit the gas stove. 'Let yer mummy have a rest, eh? While you play with them bricks what Auntie Glad showed yer.'

Joyce thought for a moment, working out which option she preferred, her mummy or the bricks. Her decision made, she let out a wailing yell of 'Mummy!'

and held her arms out to Cissie with a pathetic tremble of her bottom lip.

Without saying a word Cissie lifted her on to her lap again, in fact, she didn't say another thing until Gladys had made the tea and had sat herself down opposite her.

'I'm stopping yer from getting on,' Cissie said, inclining her head towards the pile of unpeeled vegetables.

'Don't you worry yourself, girl,' Gladys reassured her good-naturedly. 'There's no rush. Nipper's over with Ted Johnson – they're talking about their old army days as usual – and Ernie won't be in for a while yet. He had to pop out, see.' Gladys leant forward and smiled conspiratorially. 'Yer know that new girl up the road? That skinny little thing. The one who's got the upstairs rooms in old Ruby's house.' Gladys was wide-eyed, trying to encourage Cissie to join in with her enthusiasm. 'You know, Tilly Mason.'

Cissie nodded lethargically. 'Tilly, yeah.'

'That's her. Well, she come round earlier. Come to say that her Bob told her to tip my Ernie the wink that they're looking for men down the brewery. That's where he works like. Her Bob, I mean. So Ernie went straight down there, didn't he.' She took a gulp of tea. 'Mind you,' she added, not wanting to push her luck, 'I don't suppose nothing'll come of it. Never does, nowadays, does it?'

Cissie's only response was a vague lift of her chin.

'It was right nice of her though, that young woman bothering herself like that. I mean, she don't know us from Adam, does she? Only been in the street for five minutes.' She laughed happily to herself. 'And only been married for that long and all, I reckon, the way her and that husband of hers look so soppy at one another. Good to old Ruby she is though. Well, so Sammy told me. Did all her shopping for her and that when she was poorly.'

Still Cissie said nothing.

Gladys tried another tack. 'So, ain't yer gonna tell me all about it then? Come on. Tell us. How'd you get on?' Cissie lowered her eyes and began slowly stroking Joyce's hair. 'Terrible.'

'What? Didn't sell many?'

'I didn't sell none.' She raised her head and looked directly at Gladys. 'I forgot to get any flowers, didn't I?'

'You what? A flower stall with no flowers?' Gladys failed completely to suppress her laughter. 'You silly mare!'

'And there were all these horrible men, all looking at me and saying all these things,' she added sulkily. 'And I don't think it's very funny.'

'I do,' Gladys grinned.

Cissie shook her head. 'No, Glad, it ain't funny at all. I've had a rotten, stinking day. A stupid waste of time with nothing to show for it. *And* there was another stall on the other side of the station. So, take my word for it, it ain't funny at all.'

'Whatever's got into you, Cis? Where's your sense of humour?'

'I've lost it. Can you blame me? Lost it, just like I've lost me husband.'

She stared down at the worn lino. 'Yer wouldn't believe my luck. There was this bloke, Fat Stan he called himself, promised he'd sort out the pitch for me, he did. Get rid of the other stall, like, so I'd have a free run.'

'I don't understand. That's good ain't it?'

'It would be if I had any money to buy stock.'

Gladys reached out and laid her hand over Cissie's. 'Getting yerself all upset over it won't help, now will it, love?'

'What d'you want me to do? Burst into song?'

'I'm sorry, Cis, I didn't mean to upset yer.' Gladys sighed loudly as she topped up their cups.

'I still can't believe he's gone, yer know,' Cissie said as much to herself as to Gladys.

Gladys put the cosy back on the pot and shifted it out of Joyce's reach, then she took Cissie's hand in hers. 'I honestly don't know what to say.'

'There's nothing no one can say. Nothing.' Cissie picked up her cup and sipped mechanically at the hot tea. Tears ran unchecked down her cheeks.

'Don't, love, don't cry.' Gladys saw the anxiety clouding Joyce's face. She reached out and took the toddler back on to her lap. 'You'll upset the little one.'

Cissie bent forward and swiped at her tears with the hem of her crumpled dress. 'It's her and Matty I'm really worried about, Glad. How am I gonna manage? How? Tell me that. I might as well sell the stall for firewood, much good it'll do me.' She began weeping noisily. 'How am I gonna manage?' she wailed.

Gladys's look of concern was replaced by a frown. 'I'd say you'll manage like a lot of other people manage. By struggling from day to day, doing yer best to survive on handouts from them bastards from the RO. And having to put up with 'em treating yer like rubbish just so's yer can put a bit of bread and marge on the table for yer kids. That's how. But you won't have to go through all that, will yer? No. Cos if you use yer brains, and yer've got plenty of them, and yer pull yourself together, stop moaning and stop and think about it, you'll realise that yer can do it. Yer've got a good little business you can run there.'

'But yer don't understand.' Cissie sobbed into her hands. 'No one understands.'

Gladys held Joyce, who was now also crying, tightly to her chest. 'I know something I don't understand, girl, how you can say you're worried about yer kids, and then you go frightening this little love with all this carrying on. You wanna stop feeling so sorry for yourself.'

The anger in her usually placid, easy-going friend's voice shocked Cissie into stopping crying as instantly as a tap being closed. 'You meant that,' she gasped through her fingers.

'Yeah, I did,' snapped Gladys, drying Joyce's tears on her apron. 'Now you just listen to me, Cissie Flowers. We've been mates me and you, good mates, since before you ever knew Davy. And I've always liked yer. Liked you a lot. But I reckon you should know, for yer own good, that there's plenty around here what don't. And they're just waiting for you to be knocked down a peg or two.'

'How d'yer mean?' Cissie was now listening attentively. She was mystified by what she was hearing. 'I ain't done nothing to no one. Why wouldn't people like me?'

'Well, for a start, just listen to yerself. Since yer've come into this house, it's all been about you. *Your* trouble. Horrible blokes looking at *you*. Going on and on. Well, how about me? Have you even thought to ask how I am, how I'm managing?' Gladys hesitated a moment, then added, 'And you used to be able to laugh at yourself.'

'If you'd just lost your husband—'

'God forbid,' Gladys interrupted, flicking her eyes towards the ceiling. 'But that's not what I'm getting

94

at, Cissie. I ain't talking about what I feel about yer.'
She rattled her spoon absent-mindedly on the edge of
her saucer. 'Look, I might as well be blunt. You've got
a terrible name for yerself round here. The name of
thinking that you're better than everyone else in this street.
What with all yer nice clothes, and your driving, and the
way you look.'

'The way I look?' Cissie sounded baffled.

'Use your loaf, Cis, it was bad enough when you was
a married woman, but with a pretty face like your'n…
Well, now you're a widow, some women just don't like it,
do they? You being available like.'

'Gladys! How can you even say that?'

'*I'm* not saying it, am I? I told you, I'm just telling you
what other people are saying. I mean, just think how they
talk about her next door.'

'Elsie Collier?' Now Cissie was really confused. 'What's
all this gotta do with Elsie bloody Collier?'

'Are you stupid or something?'

'I reckon I must be. There's no harm in Elsie. She's a
nice sort of a woman.'

'That don't stop 'em, does it?'

'I ain't got a clue what you're on about, Gladys.'

'You know what I mean. Her *gentlemen*. The old bags
round here love it, don't they? All their nasty little hints
and whispers. You'd think she was running a bloody
knocking shop in there instead of having a few lodgers.'
Gladys shrugged. 'And even if she is, which she might be,
I suppose, she don't interfere with none of us, now does
she?'

'So what's that gotta do with me?'

'Blimey, have I really gotta spell it out for yer?' As Gladys spoke she tapped her finger on the table to emphasise her point. 'They're jealous of you, Cissie Flowers. You're a good-looking young woman who, up until now, has had things a whole lot easier than most round here. And who ain't really seemed to care what happened to no one else. So, if you let yerself go under, they'll all be ready to have yer. To jump on yer like a pack of starving dogs after a bone. So yer wanna pick yerself up, pull yerself together and get yerself going again, before it's too late.'

'Why're you saying these things to me, Glad?'

'Cos yer me friend, that's why.'

Cissie stood up. 'It don't sound much like a friend talking to me.' She reached out and took Joyce from Gladys's lap and stood her on the floor. 'It sounds more like yer just wanna have a go.'

'Hello, girls.' They both turned round to see Ernie standing in the kitchen doorway. 'Them kids're having a right old game out there with that hose. Wonder who them Godwins nicked it off, eh?' He winked at Joyce who was smiling up at him from behind her mum's skirts. 'Bloody soaking they are. Little buggers!'

Gladys was now also on her feet. She went over to Ernie and looked into his eyes. 'Yer didn't get it, did yer?' She wrapped her arms around him. 'I'm sorry, love.'

'Me and all, girl,' Ernie said with a shrug. 'Me and all.'

'I'd better be going,' Cissie said flatly.

Ernie reached out and chucked Joyce under the chin. 'Don't let me drive yer away. Sit down and finish your cuppa.'

'Thanks all the same, Ern, but I've gotta be off.' She turned round to face Gladys. 'Me and Glad've been having a little talk, and she's said a few things I wanna think about.'

'Honest, Cis, drink your tea. I was gonna pop over to fetch Nipper from over old Ted Johnson's anyway.' He laughed. 'I put a bet on for Ted yesterday on me way back from the Labour Exchange. And I wanna slip him his winnings before that girl of his gets home.'

Gladys smiled fondly at her husband. 'You'd better hurry, that Sarah's got a right sharp tongue on her. I think she's got a bit of a screw loose at times, the way she shouts at her old dad.'

Cissie couldn't stop herself: 'What d'you expect?' she snapped. 'Having yer fiancé killed in the trenches, it's enough to drive anyone mad, losing the bloke yer love.'

'Yer right, girl,' Gladys admitted. 'Sarah would probably have been a different woman now if her Jimmy hadn't have copped it. And who knows, if he had lived, Myrtle and Arthur might not be the miserable bleeders they are now either. I mean, it must be as bad losing a son as losing a fiancé.'

'What would you know about it?' Cissie demanded so loudly that Joyce started crying again. 'What would you know about anything?'

With that, Cissie scooped Joyce into her arms and ran from the kitchen.

'I'm sorry,' Gladys and Ernie heard her call from the street door. 'It's just that I miss him so much.'

Gladys went to follow her but Ernie held her back.

'No, love,' he said firmly. 'Yer'd better—'

Gladys didn't let him finish, she pulled herself away from him and ran along the passage.

She caught up with Cissie just as she was about to cross the street.

'Look, Cis, I didn't mean to row with yer,' she said catching hold of Cissie's arm. 'I know you've had a right basinful, but if yer don't do something soon, people are gonna start getting right fed up with yer.'

'Why should I care what anyone thinks of me?' she yelled, shaking off her friend's hand.

'Don't you care what I think?' Gladys asked her quietly.

'No,' Cissie said with a brisk shake of her head. 'I don't give a bugger what you think.'

Gladys stood and watched as Cissie dashed across the road to number seven without so much as a wave to young Matty, who had stopped playing with his mates and the hose to watch the unprecedented spectacle of his mum and Auntie Glad rowing.

Chapter 6

The next morning, Cissie woke at the first ring from the alarm. Despite having had an exhausting night of disturbed sleep and terrible dreams, she was filled with a determination so strong that she felt she could tackle anything.

When she had left Gladys standing in the street after their row the previous evening, she had gone indoors and cooked tea for Lil, Matty and Joyce; had taken the children up to bed; and then had sat down in the kitchen to spell out very clearly to her mother-in-law that for the next few weeks at least – until she sorted out something more permanent and suitable – that she, Lil, would be responsible for the children during the day whilst Cissie was working on the stall.

She hated having to depend on Lil, but she had no choice as she could hardly have asked Gladys to mind them after what had happened. And so, for once, when Lil had demanded to know why she had to put herself out, Cissie had not crumbled under her mother-in-law's barrage of moans and complaints, and, rather than giving in to her for the sake of an easy life, she had remained resolute. Lil would have to pull her weight and that was final. There was too much at stake for Cissie to let Lil's whingeing stand in her way.

Cissie was washed, dressed and ready within minutes. The bed was made, the curtains drawn and her room tidied, not very thoroughly maybe, but she'd made a start, just as she had planned. And she was ready to face the world.

Before she went downstairs, she peeped into the children's room and was comforted to see that they were still sleeping soundly. After all the ructions they had witnessed yesterday they had both had as much trouble settling down as she had done. Only Lil had gone straight off to sleep. The several pints of stout she'd cadged in the pub had seen to that. The role of the grieving mother was still standing Lil in good stead when it came to mumping free drinks from boozily sentimental drinkers in the Sabberton Arms.

As she skipped lightly down the stairs, Cissie ticked off the next job on the mental list she had written and rewritten in her head as she lay alone and lonely in the darkness of the early hours – she was off to the corner shop to see Sammy Clarke.

'Hello, Sam,' she said, relieved that no one else was in there yet.

'Morning, Cissie. Don't usually see you about at this time o' the morning.'

She blushed at her deserved reputation for not being an especially early riser – something that made her not far off being a streetwalker according to some of the more elderly residents of Linman Street. 'P'raps I'm turning over a new leaf, eh?'

'Don't get me wrong, Cis,' Sammy hurriedly reassured her. 'If I didn't have to sort out the stock, set this little lot out, and then be open and ready for me customers, I'd have a nice lie-in of a morning and all.' He noted the doubting look on Cissie's face and decided he'd said enough on that particular subject. 'Anyway,' he went on, 'this won't do, will it? Me rambling on about meself. Now, what can I get for you?'

'I'm gonna ask you a favour, Sam,' Cissie replied warily. 'A right big one.'

'Anything I can do, Cis, you know that. I've told you enough times.'

'I need to put some more gear on the slate,' she said bluntly. 'But I promise it won't be for long, and I promise I'll pay yer back every single penny what I owe yer as soon as I get meself straight again. I'll pay interest on it and all, if yer like. Whatever you say.'

She ran her fingers nervously through her thick black fringe. 'See,' she went on, 'I've been thinking, thinking really hard, and I've realised that if I'm gonna sort meself out, I'm gonna need help. It ain't easy asking, but I've gotta do it for Matty and Joyce. They're more important than my pride.'

Sammy lifted the flap in the counter and stepped through to the customers' side of the shop. He wiped his hands down the front of his white apron, then reached out and touched Cissie gently on the arm. 'You just let me know what you want, Cis, and I'll get it all packed up in a box for you. And I'll bring it over to the house as soon as I get a minute. And don't even think about no daft ideas about interest. You can have as much credit as you like, for as long as you like.'

Cissie dropped her chin until it was almost touching her chest. 'Ta, Sam,' she said quietly. 'I really appreciate it.' She pulled a piece of paper from her pocket and held it out to him. 'If it's all right with you, I wrote down a few things.'

She looked up and met his gaze. 'I've put the ones I really need at the top, and then the rest are bits that I could, you know, sort of use, if it wouldn't be taking too much of a liberty, like. But I'd understand if yer thought I was stronging it.'

Sammy took the note and held it up high between them. 'There ain't nothing in this whole shop you and the kids couldn't have if you wanted it, Cis. Nothing.'

Suddenly aware that not only had he overstepped the mark but, worse still, that Myrtle Payne had just appeared in the shop doorway, Sammy sprang back from Cissie and hastily returned to his place behind the counter.

'That looked cosy,' Myrtle said nastily, positioning herself between Cissie and Sam. 'Offering a bit of sympathy to the young widow woman, was yer, Sammy Clarke?' Ignoring her insinuations, Sammy looked straight past Myrtle. 'You just leave this with me, Cissie. All right?'

'All right, Sammy. Ta.'

As Cissie left the shop she heard Myrtle sneering. 'Unbelievable. Just look at her, her and her flowery frock. Disgraceful, I call it. Young women nowadays. I was in black for a full twelvemonth when my boy Jimmy was taken away from me, God rest his soul. But I suppose you think she can do no wrong, just cos she's got a pretty face.'

Cissie didn't hang around to hear Sammy's reply; she had things to do.

–

By the time Lil eventually roused herself, Cissie had given the children their breakfast; had swept and dusted the whole house – apart from Lil's room – from top to bottom; had pegged out the hand-washing she had had in soak since she got back from Sammy's; and had put on a sausage stew with onions and boiled potatoes for dinner time. All Lil had to do was keep an eye on the little ones, take in the washing if it looked like clouding over, which it didn't, and add a bit of flour and water thickening to the saucepan of stew ten minutes or so before they were ready to eat.

But despite all Cissie's efforts, Lil still found reason to moan.

'What d'yer mean, you've gotta go out *on a bit of business*? What business? And why ain't Gladys minding the kids for yer?'

Cissie flashed a warning look at Lil and nodded towards the children who were playing on the floor in their favourite place under the kitchen table.

Lil either didn't understand Cissie's signal or wasn't bothered by her daughter-in-law's concern that they shouldn't be discussing such things in front of the children, because she carried on questioning her regardless. 'I said, what business? And why should I be minding 'em?'

'Don't you ever listen, Lil? I explained all that last night. Gladys and me have had words,' Cissie said levelly. 'And, as for the business I'm going on, it's about the stall.'

'You ain't still on about that, are yer? Yer'll never be able to run that stall.'

'Yes I will,' Cissie said determinedly. 'I've decided that I'm gonna make a right go of it. I'm gonna have to find out how to do it proper. All right, there's more to it than I thought. But I'm gonna go and see Davy's friends. Get a bit of advice, like.'

Lil immediately brightened. 'Now that is a good idea. You can go and see Big Bill Turner. He knows anyone who's anyone, that bloke. He'll be able to give yer all the advice yer need. And, with a bit o' luck yer'll be able to forget all this nonsense about selling flowers. I mean, you heard him yerself,' she winked knowingly at her daughter-in-law, 'he said he'd be only too pleased to help yer.'

'I said I was gonna ask Davy's friends,' said Cissie, with a derisive sneer. 'Turner was hardly that.'

'Aw wasn't he now? So why d'yer think he was at the funeral?'

'There was plenty of people at the funeral. Plenty. People who probably only ever met Davy when they bought flowers off him.'

Cissie turned away from Lil and ducked her head to catch her reflection in the overmantel mirror. She fiddled around unnecessarily with her hat which was already set perfectly straight. 'Davy must have known hundreds of people,' she added as she slipped her black swagger coat around her shoulders.

The linen coat was part of the costume Cissie had worn to the funeral. As much as she would have hated to admit the fact, Myrtle's words about mourning had stung her to the quick.

'Hundreds and hundreds of people,' she went on. 'Friends and businessmen and all sorts.'

'But Turner's—' Lil began.

'Look, Lil, I ain't got no time to argue with yer,' Cissie said, bending down to kiss the children. 'Now you both be good for Nanna, and we'll go over and see if we can get some sweeties off o' Sammy later on. All right?'

'Sammy Clarke!' snorted Lil. 'Yer over there talking to that bloke a bit too often if you ask me.'

'Do what?' Cissie asked, disbelievingly. 'He runs the flipping corner shop. Why shouldn't I go over there?'

'D'yer really need me to tell yer?'

Cissie stuck her fists into her waist. 'I reckon I do.'

'Yer know how he gets all smarmy with yer.' Lil shuddered. 'I can't understand why yer bother with the likes of him when Turner's interested. He's a waste of space, the great soft sod.'

Cissie wanted to say that Lil was out of her mind and that Sammy was just a friend, and a very good friend at that. And that Lil was happy enough to eat the food he'd let them have on tick. And that was before she even started on putting her straight about Turner. Again. But, even if she wasn't in a hurry to get out and get on with her plans, and even if there had been any point trying to make her mother-in-law see sense, Cissie was fed up with rowing. And, apart from that, she needed Lil's help with the children. So rather than giving her a piece of her mind, she just bit her tongue instead.

But one day she'd really tell Lil her fortune...

–

Cissie took a deep breath and then pushed open the heavy wood-and-etched-glass door. Going into a pub by yourself wasn't what a respectable woman did, even if it was the local her late husband had always used. But the Sabberton Arms was the place where Cissie reckoned she had to begin if she was to find Davy's friends, so, that's where she was going.

'Morning, Mac,' she said. She had intended to sound bright and cheerful, but her voice cracked with anxiety as she made her way across the bar towards the counter.

It was only half past eleven but the place was already busy and full of smoke. It was so warm in there, she wished she had the courage to slip off her coat, but she was embarrassed enough as it was walking through the room full of men, without showing them her bare forearms into the bargain.

'Hello, darling,' the landlord said with a surprised smile. 'Don't usually see you in here.' Then it occurred to him. 'If yer looking for Lil, Cis, we ain't seen her yet today.'

Cissie shook her head; her cheeks were burning with embarrassment. 'No, Lil's back home with the kids. It was Davy's friends I was looking for.'

'Aw yeah?' Mac took down a wine glass from the rack above the bar. He held it out to her. 'Drop o' port and lemon, love?'

'No, not for me, thanks, Mac.'

'It's on me, darling,' he added enticingly. 'Go on, have a drop, on the house. It'll do yer good.'

'No, honest, thanks all the same, I won't, but it's that warm out there, I'd love a glass o' lemonade.'

'Then lemonade it shall be.' The landlord poured her drink, passed it across to her and then rested his arms on the counter. 'Now, these friends yer looking for.'

'I need to find 'em to see about the stall, Mac. See, I've decided to give it a go. To see if I can run it meself, like.'

'Have yer now?' He sounded impressed, if a little dubious, with the idea.

'Yeah. I have.' She smiled, pleased with the effect she was having. At least he hadn't laughed at her. 'But I'll need some advice. So, can yer tell me how to find 'em? Davy's friends, I mean.'

'Well, I will if I can, but it depends on what friends yer mean exactly.' Mac rubbed his hand over his chin. 'From round this way, are they?'

'I don't think so, cos I don't even know their names. That's the trouble. But I reckon they're definitely the fellers Davy used to knock around with down the flower market.'

'That could be a lot of people. Nothing more?'

'Well, I know they seemed ever so kind. Cos all of 'em promised to help me, even though I'd never met none of 'em before.'

Mac shrugged helplessly. 'It ain't a lot to go on, girl.'

She thought for a moment. 'You *do* know who I mean, Mac, they was the ones what came to the funeral.'

He immediately straightened up from his relaxed position against the bar. 'I don't know 'em. And I don't know their names neither,' he said stiffly. 'Sorry, love.' He snatched up a glass cloth from one of the pumps. 'Look, I can't stand chatting, I've got a queue of customers waiting to be served.'

Cissie looked around her. There was nobody waiting; she was being dismissed, but she didn't understand why. She swallowed the last of the sweet, tangy drink and shoved the glass back across the counter. 'Thanks, Mac,' she said flatly, then she turned on her heel and left the pub without another word to him.

It was bad enough having to ask for help, without being treated like that. And it was so unlike the usually easy-going landlord of the Sabberton Arms. But if he couldn't, or, she suspected, wouldn't for some reason, tell her who

Davy's friends were, then she'd just have to find someone who could. But who?

She slumped dejectedly against the pub wall. Why was everything so rotten complicated?

'I heard what you was saying in there.'

Cissie looked round; a seedy-looking man had appeared beside her. He reeked of booze and it wasn't even dinnertime yet.

'Did yer?' she asked warily.

'Yeah. Waste of time asking him for help. He wouldn't do a good turn for man nor beast, that one. Tight as a bleed'n tick. A man could be dying of thirst and he wouldn't give him the drippings off his nose let alone a bit o' credit.'

Cissie didn't agree; Mac was usually a kind, generous man, and if he hadn't helped her, he must have had his reasons, although, for the life of her, she couldn't think what they might be. Maybe he owed one of the men money or something. As anyone who knew him would have vouched, that wouldn't have been anything unusual; Mac was known for his big spending and his big borrowing, as he was a gambler of the hardened kind, a man prepared to lay a bet on anyone or anything. But Cissie wasn't about to argue the odds with a drunk, so she said none of what she was thinking.

'I could give yer a few names, if yer like,' the man slurred, grabbing at the pub window ledge to steady himself.

'I won't be able to pay yer nothing,' she said backing away.

The man grinned wonkily. 'I don't want no money off yer. I just like the idea of having one over on that old bastard, that's all. I'll teach him to refuse me a drink.'

Cissie wasn't really listening, she just wanted to get away from him, but it was too late, he had hold of her arm.

'You know the Still and Star? Up Aldgate Pump way?' He leaned closer to her. 'I could take yer there if yer don't.'

Cissie nodded hurriedly, and gestured with her hand to show that she knew exactly where he meant. She didn't actually know where the pub was at all, even though it was quite close to Davy's pitch by the sound of it, but she wasn't about to ask the man for directions; she just knew that, standing this close to him, if she opened her mouth to speak she would be able to taste the sour stench of his breath. Even the idea of it made her feel sick. She would soon find someone who did know the place.

'Right, so you know the Still and Star.' He paused as though he were trying to remember something, then, letting go of Cissie's arm, he slapped his hands together in triumph. 'I know what I was gonna tell yer. You go in there. That's it. That's what yer do. Go in the Still and that's where you'll find 'em. The Still and Star. You ask for Bernie Denham, or any of his mates. That'll do it.' His message for Cissie apparently at an end, the man staggered away, mumbling and laughing to himself about how that'd serve that bastard Mac right for daring to refuse him a bit of tick.

–

When she eventually found the pub, Cissie was surprised by how nice a place the Still and Star seemed to be. It was bustling with lunch-time drinkers but wasn't claustrophobic in the way that the Sabberton Arms had felt. And whereas the Sabberton's trade was a fairly rough mixture – stall holders from the market who nipped in for a few quick glasses of something; dockers who'd been unsuccessful on the stones that morning; and an ever-increasing number of victims of the slump who had nothing better to do with their time than nurse the single pint they'd scraped around to buy themselves – most of the customers in the Still and Star appeared to be workers from the nearby offices in the City. They were all wearing posh-looking suits and were sipping at half-pints rather than knocking back the pint after pint that most of the men in the Sabberton would have swallowed if given half the chance.

The Still and Star was also different from the Sabberton in that there were women in there, not that many, but a surprising number. Cissie still felt awkward walking into a pub by herself, but she definitely found it an easier atmosphere in which to find herself alone. The barmaid didn't even blink when she gave the name the drunk had passed on to her, she just carried on pouring drinks and, with a lift of her chin, pointed out a group of five men sitting in the corner.

'Over there, ducks,' she said to Cissie without even looking at her.

Cissie went over to the table and coughed politely. The men, who were playing cards, ignored her.

'Excuse me,' she said softly.

'Look,' one of them began, angry at being disturbed, 'yer don't disturb someone's game, right?' He slapped down his hand and looked up, ready to give her a mouthful, but, when he saw Cissie, the scowl on his face disappeared. 'Hello, doll, what can I do for you then?'

Hearing the appreciative tone in his voice, the other four looked up to check out the talent.

Cissie noticed, with a second nature which came from having been the object of men's approval since she was barely thirteen years old, that three of them obviously shared the first man's opinion of her, but the other one looked more suspicious than impressed.

'Yer do know who this is, chaps, don't yer?' the suspicious one stated rather than asked. 'You're Davy Flowers' missus, ain't yer?'

All their smiles vanished.

'That's right.' Cissie was confused. If these *were* the men at the funeral, and she couldn't be sure that they were – she'd been in too much of a state that day to take notice of people's faces – but if they were, they were meant to be Davy's friends. So what was wrong with them?

'Look, I don't wanna be a nuisance or nothing. I mean, I don't wanna spoil yer game. I just want a bit of advice about running the stall, that's all. See—'

'If you really want advice, darling, then I'll give it to yer.' The man who had started off by being so friendly was speaking. 'You get yerself back home to yer washing and yer cooking and leave running stalls to the fellers.'

Cissie bristled. 'I wish I could. Believe me. I wish everything was the way it was, and that I could sit at home with everything back to how it was. But that ain't gonna happen, now is it? So, please, help me. All I wanna know is who should I go to, to get me flowers at the right price. I just wanna earn a living to keep me and the kids. That's all.'

'You finished?' he asked.

Cissie nodded.

'Good, cos we wanna get on with our game, all right?'

'Thanks for nothing.' Tears of anger and frustration filled Cissie's eyes. 'Good mates you lot turned out to be.' The man seemed to soften. He stood up and spread his hands in a gesture of helplessness. 'Look, sweetheart, I'd love to help yer if I could. But it ain't as simple as that.'

One of the other men grabbed his arm. 'George,' he said, the warning clear in his voice.

George shook him off. 'I ain't stupid,' he said to him over his shoulder, then turned back to Cissie. 'See, it's like this. Your old man, your Davy, he used to earn his living—'

'That's enough, mouthy.' The other man was now also on his feet. He forced George back on to his chair and then spoke to Cissie in a low, menacing voice. 'It's nothing personal, darling, but yer've gotta understand yer can't go around asking questions, right. So just clear off and forget all about ever coming here.'

'But—'

'Look, I'd hate to see something happen to that pretty little face of your'n.' With that, the man sat down and picked up his cards. 'Right,' he said as though Cissie no longer existed. 'Whose go?'

–

Cissie stood outside on the pavement by the pub doorway in the hot midday sun, her chest rising and falling as her breath came in short, frightened bursts. All she'd wanted was a bit of help but, instead of the kindness she'd expected, Mac had turned his back on her, and now this man had really scared her. She wasn't used to being threatened. And this time there wasn't even a smelly drunk around to come to her aid.

But maybe there was somebody else who could.

With a dry mouth and shaking hands, Cissie took a piece of paper from her coat pocket. It was the last thing she had wanted to do, but she'd come this far and, if she was going to get the stall going, she had to carry on, and, as far as she could see, she had no other choice. She was going to have to visit Eileen, the brassy redhead who had given Cissie her address at the funeral.

Eileen wasn't the sort of woman Cissie would even look at normally, let alone associate with, but there wasn't much that *was* normal about all this. Something strange was going on and Cissie wasn't sure how or why but she was sure she had to find out more if she was going to run the stall, and Eileen had seemed to know plenty. And, unlike everyone else she had gone to, Eileen also seemed more than keen to talk.

Cissie found the place on the paper at last; it was the upstairs of a pokey little terraced house in a narrow turning off the Whitechapel Road. The downstairs street door had been propped open, presumably to let in some fresh air in an attempt to blow away the stink of stale boiled cabbage and of something else that Cissie didn't even want to think about.

She climbed the stairs, careful not to touch the banister which she knew just by looking at it would be sticky with accumulated layers of ancient dirt and grease, and found herself on a little upstairs landing. The small space was almost entirely taken up by a filthy gas stove and a rickety pot cupboard with a cracked jug and basin balanced precariously on its top. In front of her stood a single, splintered door with the sign '15a' chalked on it in a childish scrawl.

Cissie peered in the gloomy light at the address on the paper, hoping she'd made a mistake, but, unfortunately, this really was the place. She dug around in her handbag and pulled out her handkerchief. Wrapping it around her hand, she knocked on the door – the thought of actually touching its grimy surface revolted her.

Looking around her, Cissie couldn't believe the way some people lived. It was as bad as the Godwins in Linman Street. Violet and Norman and their brood of filthy kids seemed happy enough, but they lived just like pigs. Her Davy would never have put up with that sort of thing. Never.

Cissie's thoughts were interrupted by the door being opened. A woman, bleary-eyed and with make-up smudged all over her face, was standing there. When her grubby wrapper fell open, showing her tatty but surprisingly expensive-looking underwear, she made no move to pull it around her. Her hair hung about her shoulders in matted waves. It was the unnaturally vibrant red of the hair that made Cissie recognise her as being the right woman.

'Yeah?' Eileen asked. From the disappointment in her voice, it was obvious that she had been hoping it was someone else calling to see her.

'I'm Cissie Flowers. Davy's wife.'

Eileen frowned, slowly appraising Cissie from head to toe. 'So you are,' she said pulling her wrapper around her in a parody of modesty. 'What d'yer want then?'

'You said you'd help me.'

'Did I?' Eileen sounded distant, as though trying to recall some long past event rather than something that had happened a matter of weeks ago. It was as though she was a machine operating at half-speed.

She went to speak, changed her mind, then sighed resignedly. 'Yer'd better come in.' She stepped aside, flapping her hand in careless invitation, then closed the door and followed Cissie into the room.

She started on a futile attempt to clear a space amongst the discarded clothing piled high on the single overstuffed armchair, so that Cissie could sit down, but soon gave up and pointed at the unmade double bed that took up more than half of the crowded little room. Cissie did her best to produce a grateful smile as she sat herself gingerly on the very edge of the sagging mattress.

Eileen noted Cissie's obvious distaste at being in such surroundings, and gave a little, involuntary shudder. It was as though she was seeing her room for the first time, seeing her room as Cissie saw it: an unkempt slum with pathetic bits of lace and frills dotted around, which only added to the air of desolation and failure.

'This is only temporary, yer know,' she said perching on the edge of a narrow drop-leaf table that was stacked with toppling drifts of used cups, plates and glasses. 'While I look around for something more suitable like.'

Cissie again tried to smile convincingly. Why on earth had she ever thought that this woman could help her? She might as well have gone off with the drunk from outside the Sabberton. He probably would have made more sense, and he definitely wouldn't have stunk so much.

'What was it yer wanted again?' Eileen asked.

With a resignation born of despair, Cissie told her. 'I'm asking around to find out where Davy used to get his flowers.'

'Flowers?'

'Yeah. I ain't stupid, see, I know the wholesalers'll realise I ain't got a clue about buying, and I ain't got no money either, so I can't afford to have no liberties taken with me.'

'No, course yer can't.' Eileen looked as bewildered as she sounded.

Cissie took a packet of cigarettes from her bag, put one in her own mouth, gave one to Eileen, then lit them both with what Eileen, despite her hangover and her confusion, immediately recognised as a solid gold lighter.

'So I want some proper advice see, from the blokes my Davy used to trade with. Trouble is, I ain't sure who they are.'

Eileen said nothing, she just stared into the middle distance.

Cissie drew deeply on her cigarette, giving Sammy a silent thank you for thinking to slip the twenty Craven A into her box of groceries, and wondered if she should just get up and leave. But she was grasping at the idea of Eileen being able to help her, like a drowning woman clinging to a branch. Throwing caution to the wind, she decided to continue.

'I asked these blokes in the Still and Star, you know, the boozer up Aldgate Pump way, and they just took the piss. Thought someone like me wouldn't know how to do a day's graft, I reckon. Said it was man's work. But they're wrong.' She was speaking earnestly, meaning every word.

'I've got two kids to think about. I'll work every hour God sends if needs be.'

'You'd have to work bloody twenty-five hours a day to earn a living selling flowers,' said Eileen, squinting at Cissie through the plume of smoke she'd just exhaled. 'I mean, who's got money for that sort o' thing these days?'

'My Davy never had no trouble providing for us.' Before Eileen could reply, there was a loud knocking at the door.

Eileen leapt to her feet. 'Sorry, but yer'll have to go. That's me friend what I'm expecting.'

Seeing the disappointment on Cissie's face, Eileen relented a little. 'Look, you go and find a cafe somewhere. Come back in a while and I'll see if I can come up with some names for yer. How'd that be?'

'Ta,' Cissie said, stubbing out her cigarette in the already overspilling ash-tray. 'I appreciate this, Eileen. I won't forget it, yer know.'

'Too nice for me own good. That's always been my trouble.'

The knocking grew more impatient.

'All right, all right,' Eileen yelled as she opened the door. 'Keep yer bleed'n trousers on.'

Over Eileen's shoulder, Cissie saw a dishevelled-looking, middle-aged man leaning against the jamb. At the sight of Cissie, his face lit up.

'Who's this little lady then? New girl is she?' He leered horribly. 'Do a double act do yer?'

'Out o' your price range, darling,' said Eileen, grabbing the gawping man by the arm and hauling him into the room in a single movement. Just as speedily, she ushered Cissie past him and out on to the landing.

'When shall I, you know, come back?' Cissie asked, both shocked and fascinated by what was going on.

Eileen looked the man up and down. 'About five minutes'd do, if I was honest,' she said with a world-weary sigh. 'But yer'd better give us half an hour to be on the safe side.'

Chapter 7

Cissie didn't go to a cafe as Eileen had suggested. For one thing, she couldn't afford to – just as she had decided she couldn't afford to use the truck unless she had to – and for another, she welcomed the chance to be out in the fresh air, or rather, what passed for fresh air on a hot June day in the East End. So instead she wandered around the streets, smoking one cigarette after another. She walked around for well over an hour; the thought of accidentally interrupting Eileen and her 'friend' so horrified Cissie, that she couldn't even think of returning any earlier.

But when she eventually did return to the flat, Cissie was pleasantly surprised. Not only was the room a lot tidier, but Eileen herself was also looking a good deal more presentable than before.

She was wearing a fitted barathea dress, probably more suited to an evening on the town than to sitting around in a shabby bedsit, but at least it was clean. She had also wiped off her old coating of make-up and had applied a new brighter layer of powder and paint. It was still far too heavy for Cissie's taste but at least it looked better than the streaks and smudges Eileen had sported earlier. And her hair actually looked quite nice. She had caught it back and tied it with a scarf in a big loose bow with the ends trailing over one shoulder.

She'd probably been quite a looker in her day, mused Cissie as she warily took up her seat on the now tidily made-up bed.

Eileen also seemed happier, more relaxed. Watching her pick up a lipstick-stained glass and a half-bottle of gin from the bedside table, before settling down contentedly on the now cleared single armchair, Cissie thought she could guess why.

'I like all my callers to bring me little presents,' Eileen explained, filling the glass to its brim and then knocking back the contents in a single gulp.

Cissie fumbled around, clumsily retrieving her bag from by her feet, and then stood up. 'Look, I'm sorry, I told yer before, I'm broke.'

Eileen threw back her head and laughed, an unexpectedly girlish and attractive sound. 'Hark at you! I didn't mean *lady* callers, did I? Sit yerself back down. Go on.'

She reached out and gently patted Cissie's arm encouragingly. 'Anyway, even if I did mean lady callers, I wouldn't take nothing off you, now would I? I like you. You remind me of meself when I was a few years younger.'

Cissie did as she was told and sat down, nervously joining in with the laughter.

'Drink?' asked Eileen.

Cissie declined.

'Suit yourself.' Eileen shrugged and carefully refilled her own glass with straight gin. 'Now, you wanted names, that right?'

Cissie leant forward eagerly, her reservations about Eileen vanishing rapidly. Here was what she was after. 'Yeah, that's right. I need to know who to buy flowers from, so I can stock the stall without getting conned.'

Eileen took two cigarettes from the packet on the arm of her chair and handed one to Cissie, but she didn't offer a match, she waited until Cissie took out her lighter.

Her cigarette lit, Eileen inhaled deeply, then, jabbing it in the air to emphasise her words, she began speaking with surprising solemnity. 'I'm gonna tell you something, Cissie Flowers, and I don't want you blabbing yer mouth off to no one that it was me what told yer. I want you to keep shtum. Understand?'

Cissie nodded in ready agreement, although, in truth, she didn't understand why on earth Eileen should think that telling her the name of a decent wholesaler should be such a big secret. Apart from the fact, of course, that Eileen was getting herself well and truly plastered again, and was talking the same nonsense spouted by any street-corner drunk at closing time.

She could have kicked herself for not having returned earlier, before Eileen had the chance to start hitting the bottle again. It would have been worth taking the chance that she would still be with her 'friend'. But how was she to know Eileen's drinking habits? And anyway, it was too late for regrets, Eileen had already swallowed a good third of the bottle and was pouring herself yet another measure.

'Right, that's all right then,' Eileen continued. 'Now, like I said, I like the look of you, Cissie. That's why I'm gonna help yer.' She smiled happily and raised her glass in an exaggerated toast. 'Trouble is, darling,' she sighed, 'I ain't got a sodding clue about no flower markets, or who could tell you where yer should buy yer flowers neither for that matter.'

Cissie dropped her chin and stared down miserably at the ragged bedside rug. Another waste of time. It wasn't fair, all she wanted to know was where she could buy a few bloody flowers. Mind you, at the moment she would have settled for just getting out of there. But she wasn't that stupid, she knew she'd have to be careful about taking her leave. Cissie might have had an easy, protected life being married to Davy, but she'd been brought up in a tough enough neighbourhood. She'd learnt from an early age that drunks could turn from smiling sentimentality to aggressive fury in the time it took to unscrew the top off another bottle of light ale.

'It don't matter,' Cissie muttered.

'Yes it does,' Eileen said matter-of-factly. 'That's why I'm gonna tell yer what yer can do to sort yerself out.'

'Yeah?' Cissie, suddenly alert, looked up hopefully. 'What's that then?'

Eileen kicked off her shoes and draped her bare legs over the arm of her chair. 'You just get yourself down that market, wherever it is, and you mention Big Bill Turner, darling. No one'll dare try and have you over then.'

The disappointment stung so badly that Eileen might just as well have slapped Cissie's face for her. She stood up, not caring any longer whether she offended Eileen or not. 'Thanks for your time,' she snapped briskly. 'You've been a real help.'

Eileen, who was considerably taller and heavier than Cissie, was now also standing.

'Gawd help us, you're worse than a bleed'n Jack-in-the-box. I ain't even *started* helping you yet. Sit yerself back on that bed,' she insisted. 'Go on.'

Feeling she had very little option, Cissie sat back down again, but she paid no attention to what Eileen was saying – she was too busy wondering why she had ever thought

Eileen could help her in the first place, and what had then possessed her to return to this filthy little room and become trapped into listening to the irrational rantings of a raddled old tom.

But then something she said made Cissie sit up and listen. Eileen might have been rambling, but what she was saying infuriated Cissie. She couldn't let her get away with this, drunk or not.

'Are you suggesting that my Davy was involved with Turner in some way?' she demanded. 'Cos if you are—'

Eileen winked and flashed Cissie a lopsided grin. 'Calm yerself down, girl. I never actually said that in so many words, now did I? I only sort of said how it's interesting how much money your Davy managed to make from running that flower stall of his.' She pointed to Cissie's hand and smirked. 'Look at that bleed'n lighter for a start.'

Cissie turned the lighter over and over in her hands, examining it as though she had never seen it before. 'What about it?' she asked suspiciously.

'Let's just say it ain't exactly made out o' brass, now is it?'

'I don't understand.'

'No,' Eileen said with an ironic laugh, 'I don't think you do. But there's something you'd better understand.'

'What's that?'

'As far as Turner's concerned, and I ain't talking about no business now—'

'I dunno what you're talking about,' Cissie interrupted her angrily. 'And I don't reckon you do neither.'

'There's no need to take that tone.' Eileen sounded menacing.

'Sorry.' Cissie was quick to apologise.

Eileen had not only finished off the gin, but was steadily drinking her way through a bottle of vicious-looking green stuff that she'd dug out from the pile of dirty laundry stuffed behind her chair.

'So you should be sorry and all. Now, I want you to listen to me, Cissie Flowers. I'm gonna mark yer card for yer about Big Bill Turner. And I don't want you to breathe a word of it to no one.'

Cissie sat and listened; she had very little choice.

'When I was a kid down Hoxton way, we was poor. Really poor. Not that it mattered really, cos we wasn't no different from any other family round there. Being that poor was ordinary, see, dead ordinary. And we was just another ordinary family.'

Eileen took out another cigarette and tossed the packet to Cissie for her to help herself.

'Then, one day, I must have been, what, sixteen? Well, that was when everything changed. See I heard my mum, my usually miserable, down-trodden mum, giggling away like a young girl. She was upstairs with the bloke next door. She'd told me he'd come in to help her "mend the bed", while me dad was out down the boozer. He was always down there – when he wasn't indoors fighting and rowing with me mum. So hearing her sound so happy was a bit of a red-letter day for me. I wanted to see what was going on up there, didn't I?'

Cissie, drawn into the story despite herself, had to ask: 'You was sixteen and you didn't know, you know, nothing about—'

Eileen flashed her eyebrows. 'Funny innit? I didn't have a clue. I wasn't very grown up for me age, still a kid really. And my mum and me were never close enough to talk

124

about things like that.' She paused, lost for the moment in her distant past.

'Anyway, so up I goes after 'em, with this great big stupid grin on me face, ready to join in. Well, when I threw open her bedroom door and...' Eileen shrugged, dismissing the memory. 'She beat me black and blue, didn't she. I ran away from home that night. Started a new life on the streets.'

'How did you manage?'

'Not very well at first. Yer know, when I think back, it's a miracle I never got done in. The chances I took!' She laughed mirthlessly, shaking her head in wonder. 'But I learnt. I had to. And there was plenty of other girls around to put me straight.'

Slowly and carefully, Eileen tapped the ash from her cigarette, using the tip to make a little mound with it in the ash-tray. She concentrated intently, as though it were of great importance that she got it right. When she was satisfied with her efforts, she continued speaking.

'Then I met Bill. I was hanging around a pub up West, seeing if I could get anyone to treat me without wanting too much in return. Cos, believe it or not, I was still a virgin. I ain't sure how I managed it, but I was. Well, he came in with this crowd of blokes. I went up to one of them and tried to cadge a drink. But all I got was a right mouthful. He started hollering and hooting, calling me a little whore. Wanted to look clever in front of the others, I suppose, but Bill wasn't impressed,' she said proudly. 'He stuck up for me. And that was that, really.'

'How d'yer mean?'

'He took me in.' She looked away, avoiding Cissie's gaze. 'Or should I say he took me on?' she added under her breath.

'To his house?'

Eileen shook her head. 'No. He was married to Moe even then. She might have started out as just a chorus girl in one of his clubs, but once she had her fat legs under Bill's table she thought she was a sodding princess. Rules that man she does. But he told me he loved *me* not her. And I believed him. I had to. I had to believe someone loved me. It was just a shame I wasn't clever enough to realise I was one of many. One in a very long line. Maybe if when me mum had hit me I'd have gone to a friend, who knows what might have happened. It might all have died down and everything have been all right again. I've often wondered. Still, perhaps it was just meant to be, eh? Me and Bill.' She stared into the middle distance, remembering. 'Anyway,' she said, returning to the present, 'I had that thing he wanted most, I was young.'

'But you was only sixteen. He must have been years older.' Cissie was obviously appalled by the idea.

'Look, don't get the wrong idea about him. These girls I'd met, they'd shown me how to do meself up a bit. Look older so I didn't get no trouble from the law. I passed easily for nineteen, twenty. So he didn't reckon I was that young. I mean, he ain't the sort what likes kids or nothing funny like that. Not like some of 'em yer meet.'

Eileen poured herself another drink. Again Cissie refused the offer of one for herself.

'Strange innit?' Eileen mused. 'When yer a kid, yer spend all yer time trying to look older, then when yer get to my age… Still, although I might not be that fresh now, I was back then all right. When yer think of it! All fresh and beautiful I was, but scared and all. Scared of what would become of me on the streets. Shame I never realised then what I should really have been scared of. Then I could've used me loaf, sold a few bits and pieces on the quiet like, to have a few quid to put by for harder times. You can't imagine what it's like having nothing put by when you've been used to a good life.'

Cissie shifted uncomfortably – yes she could imagine it. 'Getting old, that's what I should really have been scared of. Losing me looks. After all, what's the point of someone having you as their bit o' stuff if you ain't got the looks no more? I got used to men being nice to me because of the way I looked. Then it all changed. I know I ain't ugly, well, not yet I ain't, but the turps and the late nights ain't helping me beauty routine much. I mean, look at me, I'm wearing more and more bloody slap every day.' She laughed, mocking herself. 'It'd scare the bleed'n life out of yer if yer saw me without me warpaint.'

For a brief moment Cissie felt she should protest in some way, insist that Eileen was still a good-looking woman, but, in truth, she couldn't bring herself to say anything. It would only make things worse.

'That's why I didn't blame Bill when he got tired of me,' Eileen continued in a matter-of-fact tone which couldn't conceal her pain. 'Told me I had to start "earning me own way", didn't he? So that's when I got into this business.' Eileen lifted her hands and began studying her nails again, anything to avoid Cissie's gaze. 'While he was keeping me, I never ever went with no other men, yer know. Not that I ever wanted to, but he would never have allowed it if I had. I kidded meself he was jealous at the time, but I knew he was just scared of me getting a dose and passing it on to him. But once he'd finished with me, I could have gone with a whole bloody regiment and then their mascot goat for good measure and all, for all he cared.'

She leant back in the armchair, closed her eyes and sighed. 'I had a nice little flat all of me own once. Lovely it was. I had a char coming in, the lot. Now look at me.'

'Didn't you do something?' Cissie could hardly believe what she was hearing. 'Tell him no?'

Slowly, Eileen opened her eyes and made a clumsy attempt to refill her glass, spilling most of her effort around her feet on to the grubby mat. 'How could I? Trouble was, I still loved him. Still do. So now I drink to try and forget all about it.'

'Yer mum or dad never tried to find yer?'

Eileen wrinkled her nose and shook her head. 'No. Not really. At first, when they knew I had a few quid, they was interested for a while. Came sniffing round. But when they found out that Turner used to pay me bills and buy me things, but didn't give me no money – that would've made me too independent see – they sort of gave up. I ain't seen 'em in years. I think about 'em though. Especially when I'm a bit down like.'

Cissie swallowed hard; this was getting a bit too close to home. 'You ever have any kids?' she asked, changing the subject.

'No. One visit too many to granny and her knitting needle put paid to that.'

Eileen's voice was increasingly slurred, her movements more erratic. 'I never knew he was married, yer know. I swear on my life. Well, not at first I didn't. And then I thought he was unhappy with the old cow.'

'You loved him and he lied to you,' Cissie said gently. 'That wasn't fair.'

'No, no he never lied. He never told me he was unhappy. I just sort of wanted him to be. It was as easy and as stupid as that. What more can I tell yer?'

Cissie fiddled nervously with her hair. If she didn't ask her now, she would soon be too drunk to answer. 'You can tell me how yer know Davy,' she breathed.

Eileen laughed coarsely, the girlish sounds made harsh by the drink. 'Sorry, darling, I ain't being rude, but you've got the wrong idea there. I'd be the first to admit that your Davy was a fine-looking man, but no one involved with Turner would ever dare come near me. Even now.'

Cissie was now on the very edge of the bed. 'There, you've said it again. What d'you mean, "involved with Turner"?'

'It ain't my place to say, girl. Sorry.'

'You're making all this up, ain't yer?' Cissie snatched her bag from the floor and stood up. 'I don't know why, but you are.'

'All right. All right. Don't get yerself excited. Let's just say Davy had business interests linked to Bill's. Satisfied?'

'No. No I'm not bloody satisfied.' Cissie could barely spit out the words. 'How d'you know Davy? I want to know.'

Eileen shrugged innocently. 'He was a friend.'

'Well he never mentioned you. And I hope you ain't trying to suggest he was a "friend" like that dirty pig in here earlier.'

'No. I ain't. And don't look at me like that. Cos I could be a friend to you, Cissie Flowers. And if you had any sense, yer'd know how important it is to have friends. Especially in your position, a young widow with kids.'

Cissie shook her head in disgust, turned her back on Eileen and started towards the door.

'One more thing, darling,' Eileen called after her, her voice thick with sarcasm. 'Big Bill Turner ain't changed, yer know. He eats pretty little things like you for breakfast.'

Forgetting her earlier qualms about touching the door with her bare hands, Cissie grabbed hold of the filthy handle, ripped it back on its hinges and left without saying another word.

As she walked back towards Poplar through the dusty streets – not having the money for the tram fare – Cissie was oblivious of the early evening crowds making their way home from work. She was far too wrapped up in what Eileen had said even to notice the elbows and bags that dug into her sides and bashed her legs. With her worries, how could she be concerned with something as trivial as getting a few bumps and bruises?

First she had lost Davy, and now this new madness had come into her life. Davy involved with Turner? He couldn't have been. He just couldn't.

But she genuinely didn't know what to think or believe any more. On the one hand, Eileen was obviously unreliable – a pathetic, drunken whore – but how else had she known Davy apart from her connections with Turner? That Davy might have been one of her 'friends', a client, was more than Cissie could even contemplate.

She hated Eileen for what she had done to her: making her doubt everything she had ever believed in. But had she honestly never thought, she asked herself, even for a moment, that her parents might have been right, that there was something about Davy — a bloke with a little flower stall having so much money in his pocket — that didn't quite ring true?

No, she hadn't, not until now. She had never doubted her Davy. Not once. And she refused to let an old brass ruin the reputation of the man she loved, and would love for ever.

She knew what it was, she decided, Turner had been a customer of Davy's. That was it. With all those women he knocked about with he was bound to have bought flowers — if only to keep his wife quiet, when he'd been out until all hours with his latest tart on his arm. And Eileen had, no doubt, been with Turner on more than one occasion when he was buying the poor, deluded woman a bunch of roses as a way of easing his conscience. If he had one.

And, knowing Davy, he'd probably flashed Eileen one of his smiles and spoken to her as though she was a decent woman. He had such a way with him, he could make anyone think he was their friend.

That was it. That was the answer.

Cissie smiled through her tears, as she pictured him, standing by the stall, a bunch of roses in his hand, smiling back at her. If only she could talk to him, he'd make it all better, just like he always did. She missed him so much and, hard as it was to admit it, she was really missing her parents as well.

Bloody Eileen. When she'd talked about how she'd suffered at home, Cissie couldn't help thinking how lucky she'd been to have a mum and dad who had cared about her. All right, they'd never had much, but Cissie had always known the security of their love.

She'd thought once, when she'd first married Davy, that Lil might take her parents' place in her heart, that she would come to love and respect her as she had loved and respected them, but instead, Cissie had soon come to see Lil for what she was: a grasping, hard-headed woman who cared for no one but herself.

Eileen had a lot to answer for. She had made Cissie think about too many uncomfortable truths concerning her parents. And also about friendship...

Cissie felt her cheeks flare with shame as she thought about the way she had treated Gladys. How could she have been so selfish, ignoring her struggles and problems, taking her for granted just because she'd always managed so good- naturedly, and not whined and moaned about every little thing as Cissie had done lately?

Eileen had made Cissie take a long hard look at herself, and she didn't much like what she saw: a thoughtless, misguided young woman who'd kidded herself for far too long that the world would always be on her side. She had reason to be thankful to Eileen. Even though what she said was a load of self-pitying, drunken rubbish, she had made Cissie realise that no one owed her anything.

She would still need advice, and help, but she was going to have to learn to roll up her sleeves and stop expecting favours just because she was pretty little Cissie Flowers.

Chapter 8

By the time Cissie eventually turned into Linman Street, footsore and tired out after her long walk in the exceptionally hot June weather, it was almost six o'clock. Even though it was much later than she'd told Lil to expect her back, she still didn't go straight home, instead she stopped first at the corner shop.

Sammy was just turning over the 'open' sign on the door to read 'closed'.

'Hello, Sam,' she said looking over her shoulder for signs of nosy neighbours. 'You're locking up early.'

'Yeah,' he replied, stepping to one side to let Cissie inside the shop. 'Nice day like this, everyone goes down Chris Street to the market. I've hardly seen a soul all day.'

'It looks different in here with the blinds down. And with all the gear from outside piled up everywhere.'

Sammy folded his arms and smiled. 'You ain't come over to see what I do with me potatoes and greens when I lock up of a night, now have you, Cis? Cos I know it don't even interest me very much, so I'm sure you couldn't give a bugger about it.'

'No, yer right.' Cissie tugged nervously at her fringe. 'See, Sam, it's, well, look...' She flapped her hands in exasperation, trying to find the right words and failing.

She began again. 'Look, yer know how you said yer'd help me? Putting stuff on the slate for me and everything. Until I, you know, get meself sorted out.'

Sammy's smile disappeared. 'Didn't Lil give you that box of groceries I fetched over this morning?'

'Yeah, course she did.' Cissie dropped her chin. 'Sorry, Sam, I should've remembered to thank yer. It's just that I've had so much on me mind.'

She patted her dress pocket, all too aware that the Craven A packet inside it contained her one and only remaining cigarette, the one she was saving to have with a cup of tea before she went to bed. 'And it was right good of you to think of putting in the fags and all. Ta, Sam. Really.'

'I don't need no thanks, Cis. I just wanna see you and the kids doing all right. I know I can't really understand what yer going through, but I know it can't be easy with them little 'uns to worry about.'

Cissie touched him gently on the arm. 'You're a really good bloke, Sam, d'you know that?'

Sammy shrugged, embarrassed but pleased.

'And that's why,' Cissie went on, 'I thought yer might not mind if I asked you something else.' She screwed up her nose. 'Sorry, but it's not another favour. Well, not exactly, it ain't. I mean, there'd be something in it for both of us.'

'Why don't yer just spit it out, whatever it is?'

She nodded, digging deep into her pocket. 'All right. Someone said this might be worth something.'

She held out her hand to him. On the flat of her palm was her cigarette lighter.

Sammy took the lighter from her, respectfully avoiding brushing her hand with his.

'So, what d'you think?' she asked eagerly.

He went over to the door and, propping it open with his shoulder, he looked closely at the lighter, turning it over and over in the still bright, early evening sunshine.

The examination over, Sammy let the door swing shut again. 'I ain't no expert, Cis, but I think it looks like it could be gold. Probably worth a couple o' quid.'

'Only a couple o' quid?' Cissie shrank with disappointment.

'Well,' Sammy added quickly, 'yer know what Uncle's like. Never gives no one a fair price, does he?'

'I wasn't thinking about pawning it.' Cissie lifted her chin and looked Sammy directly in the eye, willing him to understand what she was hoping for. 'See, the thing is, I couldn't. Just the thought of Ethel or Myrtle, or worse still, that big-mouthed Lena Dunn, seeing me going in there, and having them knowing all me business. I'd really hate that, Sam. Yer know what they're like.'

'I wouldn't mind buying it off yer,' Sammy said, with a nonchalant twitch of his shoulders.

'How much?' she asked, immediately ashamed by her enthusiasm.

'Let's see…' Sammy began slowly, not having the first idea what he should offer her. Buying second-hand goods wasn't something Sammy was in the habit of doing, in fact, it was something he had always carefully avoided. With so many people going through hard times it would have been a dangerous precedent to set. He'd have been inundated with shiny-arsed Sunday suits and grannies' patchwork eiderdowns stinking of mildew and no cash left to run the shop. But this was Cissie asking, and that was an entirely different matter.

'Enough to buy stock for the stall, d'you reckon?'

'Course, yeah,' Sammy agreed readily, relieved that Cissie knew how much she needed and so he wouldn't have to risk upsetting her – and making a fool of himself – by suggesting the wrong amount.

Before she had a chance to think better of it, Cissie threw her arms around Sammy and kissed him smack on the lips.

'Aw, Sam, I'm sorry,' she gasped, springing away from him. She stood there a moment, wide-eyed with shock, then turned on her heel and fled.

Sammy chased her to the door. 'Ain't yer gonna wait for yer money, Cis?' he called after her as she ran across the street.

Cissie skidded to a halt on the cobbles and turned round to face him – just in time to see Lena walking slowly towards her, grinning all over her face.

'Putting it about already are yer, Cissie Flowers?' Lena smirked. 'Nice behaviour for a widow, I don't think. Still, I hope yer give him his money's worth.'

–

It had just gone half past four in the morning; Cissie shook herself like a wet dog and stepped on the brake, bringing the truck to a shuddering halt. She was finding it hard to concentrate on what she was meant to be doing. Her head was so stuffed full of angry thoughts that ideas about what stock she should have on the stall, or even how she should go about buying it, were just about the last things on her mind.

Not only had she had to stand there the night before and watch Lena bowl along the street, knowing she was about to spread her spiteful insinuations to anyone and everyone who would listen – and there were always plenty of those around – but then she'd had to put up with Lil's latest barmy accusations.

According to her mother-in-law, the only reason Cissie was planning to leave the house at the crack of dawn to go to Covent Garden market was not because she was trying to earn them a living, but because she wanted to get out of looking after Matty and Joyce.

Lil wasn't only spiteful, she was stupid. Cissie honestly felt she could murder her at times. As if she wouldn't give the world to be able to stay at home with her children the way she used to, only having the shopping and cleaning and washing to worry about. She could visualise Matty and Joyce as she had left them, tucked up in their beds, not knowing that they were going to wake up to their nanna's miserable face.

Cissie sighed out loud and slapped her hand angrily on the steering wheel. If she was going to do this stall lark properly, she was going to have to sort out something better for them. Not only did they deserve it but Cissie knew she wouldn't be able to settle unless they were happy.

If only she hadn't said all those things to Gladys...

The loud honking of a motor horn brought her back to the present with a jolt.

'Oi! What you up to, yer silly bleeder? You gonna shift that truck or what?'

Cissie stuck her head out of the window to answer him, but he didn't give her the chance.

'It's a bloody tart!' he shouted at no one in particular. 'Your old man should be ashamed of himself letting you out in that thing. This is a bloody wholesale market, darling, not a street full of little dress shops. Now, get that motor out o' the way. Go on, people're trying to do business.'

'So am I,' Cissie said as calmly as she could manage. 'And, if it ain't too much trouble, d'yer think yer could tell me where I can park me truck, please?'

–

Cissie clambered down from the cab and walked towards the bustling complex of elegant buildings, makeshift sheds and surging hordes of people, barrows, baskets and carts. Her first impression of Covent Garden was that she was entering a cross between the biggest street market she had ever seen in her life, and a madhouse.

First of all there was the noise: clanking metal wheels, squeaking trolleys, jarring gears and the crashing of tailboards being lowered, and the constant banter of men being incongruously jolly at such an early hour, all backed up with a just discernible hum – the unmistakable buzz of people making money.

Then there were the smells. She had first noticed the air getting sweeter, heavier somehow, more cloying, as far away as the Strand, but here, in the thick of it, the smell was almost overwhelming: a heady mix of mellow ripeness and sickly overmaturity.

She felt nervous but excited. So many people, so much going on, and here was she, Cissie Flowers, about to plunge into the middle of it. She could hardly take it in.

'Oi! Mind yer back, love!' a man's voice yelled from behind her.

Cissie, still entranced at all this activity that she had, of course, known about but had never expected to witness for herself, stepped silently aside, pressing herself flat against the wall to allow the man, a market porter, to pass.

She watched, fascinated, as he swept past with his barrow, guiding it skilfully over the flagstoned pavement without losing a single strawberry from his piles of brimming baskets. But that trick was nothing compared to the man who dodged round Cissie and then past the man with the barrow: he too was a porter but he was carrying the round wicker baskets of fruit on his head, piled high in a stack like children's bricks about to tumble to the kitchen floor. But somehow they didn't tumble, they stayed there, even when he did a half-turn to get a better look at her.

He flashed her a wink of appreciation. 'Yer like a sailor's dream of home, girl!' He grinned and was gone, sucked into the crowds of men all ferrying their own burdens of boxes, baskets and crates.

'Excuse me,' Cissie called, running to catch up with the man with the barrow. 'Is this the market?'

The man stopped dead. He turned round and looked her up and down. 'No, sweetheart,' he sneered sarcastically, 'it's the Henley sodding regatta, and I'm delivering these here to that bloke over there in his rowing boat. So, if yer don't mind.'

With that, he shook his head, rolled his eyes in exasperation at such stupidity, and shoved his barrow forward with a loud, 'Mind yer backs, there!'

'I meant, is this the *flower* market?'

With a theatrical sigh, the man stopped again, dropped the handles of the barrow and spun round to face her. 'Do these *look* like sodding daisies?' he demanded, pointing angrily at the baskets full of soft fruit. 'No,' he answered himself, 'they don't, cos they're flaming strawberries, ain't they, yer dozy mare.'

Cissie wouldn't let him see how humiliated she felt. She drew herself up to her full height, lifted her chin and looked down her nose at him. 'Well, I'm sure an intelligent man such as yerself would be able to direct a lady to the flower market.'

'Over there,' he said, jerking his thumb over his shoulder. 'Now, if yer don't mind, I'd like to get this fruit moved before it mushes down into jam.'

Nodding in gratitude, Cissie stepped backwards away from the man. She was just about to voice her thanks, when, with no explanation, he lunged forward and grabbed her by the arms.

'What the bloody hell!' Cissie demanded, shaking him off.

'Suit yourself,' the man shrugged, letting go of her. 'But I'd rather be grabbed by the arms,' he went on, gesturing with his chin to something behind her, 'than have to face them old hens if I trod on 'em.'

Cissie turned round to see what he was talking about. Looking up at her was a semicircle of old women sitting by the kerbside on upturned crates. All of them were dressed in black shapeless dresses, coarse aprons and battered hats, and all of them were doing exactly the same thing: with swift, barely discernible hand movements they were shelling massive piles of peas into enamel basins wedged firmly into their broad laps.

'Thanks,' she said sheepishly, stepping carefully around the heaps of discarded husks.

The man tutted and treated her to another roll of his eyes. 'Bloody sightseers. Not fit to be out, some people,' he muttered to himself and went about his business.

As Cissie made her way over to the flower market, she heard the old women laughing raucously.

'Love yer hat, dearie,' one of them jeered after her.

'Yeah,' another one agreed, 'where'd yer get it? From the bootmender's?'

Cissie felt so useless, she could have cried. But the moment she stepped inside the huge glass-and-metal grandeur of the flower market, any thoughts of humiliation, tiredness, her children being at home in bed, even the fact that it was barely five o'clock in the morning, were all forgotten. The sight and scents simply took her breath away. She had had no idea that it would be so beautiful, such a brilliantly coloured, wondrously sweet-smelling kaleidoscope of flowers, plants, shrubs and seeds.

She wandered slowly forward between the wide aisles where the wholesalers exhibited the glories they had on offer that morning, each vying with their displays to catch the eye of the retailers.

She paused by one of the stands.

'I ain't seen you before, dearie,' said a weather-beaten woman sitting at a little wooden clerk's desk. As she spoke she kept her eyes fixed on the roll of notes she was counting.

'I've just started up,' Cissie said proudly.

The woman was immediately on her feet, the cash tucked safely in her money apron. A newcomer. She could smell the scent of easy pickings. 'Just look at these, my

141

lovely,' she said, thrusting a bunch of freesias under Cissie's nose. 'Lovely, ain't they? Fresh in from Guernsey they are. You won't get better than them anywhere in this market. And look at these.' She snatched up a dull, bare-rooted clump of leaves. 'Lovely 'mums, full of bud they'll be.'

Cissie smiled weakly at the woman. 'I'm just looking at the minute, ta.'

'Well don't look too long,' she snapped, 'or you'll get left with all the shit. Good gear like mine always goes first.'

'I'll remember that. Thanks.'

For almost an hour, Cissie walked about the place trying to work out what to do. She watched as men exchanged brass tally tokens, sensing that they were some kind of deposit. But for what? Then she saw a man deliberately knocking over a pile of empty wooden boxes and surreptitiously kicking some behind him to another man who hurriedly bundled them away on a two-wheeled sack trolley. What was that about? And the prices. Were they for a box? A bunch? One of the narrow waxy cartons?

She began to feel the panic rising in her throat. How would she ever know what to do? How would she ever understand all this?

She closed her eyes and took a deep breath. She had to pull herself together. She would just *have* to know what to do – she couldn't afford the luxury of feeling sorry for herself, she had the children to think of.

Slowly, she opened her eyes and, with fists clenched by her sides, she strode purposefully along the aisle towards the woman with the freesias.

–

As she leant against the cast-iron column and toasted her achievements with a thick china cup of dark stewed tea, bought from one of the stalls dotted around the edges of the still-lively business areas, Cissie yawned loudly and lifted her chin to look up at the flower-market clock.

Not quite half past seven. It didn't seem possible; from how tired she felt, she'd been sure it must have been at least midday. But, exhausted or not, she couldn't stop herself from grinning. She'd done it! She, Cissie Flowers, had bought enough flowers to cover her stall in luscious summer colour. She'd spent nearly all her money and she'd probably paid over the odds – especially to the porter who had seemed a bit too delighted to transport her stuff to the truck – but that was all right, she'd soon be as sharp as all the others and would be able to wheel and deal, duck and dive, with the best of them.

Davy would have been so proud of her. And it was knowing this that gave Cissie the energy she needed to get herself moving again and to set about getting the flowers sold.

She climbed back into the truck and drove slowly between the big wire cages being stacked full of empty wooden crates, safe from dishonest hands who, given the chance, would pilfer them and trade them in for the deposits which, she now knew, were represented by the tally tokens.

She grinned yet again. She was learning, learning all the time. And she felt happier than she had for months. She felt in such high spirits that, as the market officer waved her forward, she pitched a handful of coppers out of the truck window to a bent-over old woman scavenging around the cobbles for discarded vegetables.

'Here y'are, Gran,' Cissie called. 'Treat yerself.'

'Good luck to yer, girl,' the old woman called back, pressing the coins to her dry old lips. 'Good luck.'

'Thanks all the same, love,' Cissie replied with a wave, 'but you keep yer luck for yerself, cos I don't reckon I'm gonna be needing any!'

Half an hour later, Cissie was dragging the stall from the lock-up. This time she had a smile on her face. And this time she was not going to make any mistakes. She had remembered exactly where the lock-up was, she knew how to set up the stall, *and* she had flowers to sell. She'd even had the sense to bring a pair of old gloves to save her hands.

She was a bit late for the early trade, she thought to herself as she paused for breath before manipulating the stall round the final corner, but she'd get better at it, quicker. The way she was feeling now, exhilarated by her achievement and knowing it would take just a few more shoves and pushes to get to the pitch, Cissie felt she could do anything.

Just the few more steps past St Botolph's and she'd done it.

But what was going on? There was another stall, another flower stall, on Davy's pitch.

Dropping the handles and leaving the stall where it was, blocking the corner of the street, Cissie ripped off her gloves and sped over to the two tough-looking men who were standing by a sparsely stocked stall.

'Here! What d'you think you're doing?' she demanded, her anger at these men who had dared to dash her dreams yet again making her brave. 'That's *my* bloody pitch.'

The shorter and broader of the two men looked at his companion and sniggered. 'I'm scared, Ron. Don't let her shout at me.'

'Don't worry, Dennis,' Ron answered him with a reassuring pat on the shoulder. 'Uncle Ron'll look after you.' With that, Ron slowly lowered his massive head until his face was just inches from Cissie's, and said quietly, 'I dunno if you've got any sense in that beautiful little loaf of your'n, darling, but if you have, yer'd better use it and bugger off. Now, if yer don't mind, we've got a business to run.' Ron straightened up and adjusted his well-cut jacket around his huge frame.

Cissie didn't move, but she was all too aware of how small she must seem to this great clod of a man. 'I ain't got no idea what yer on about. This is *my* pitch, and I ain't gonna bugger off for you or no one. Yer can ask that bloke on the newspaper stall,' she added by way of proof, jabbing her thumb over her shoulder.

'What bloke would that be then, darling?'

She looked round. 'Bugger it,' she fumed. 'He must have gone to the lav or to get himself some tea or something.' Dennis started laughing, but Ron's face was like stone. He opened his mouth to speak, but when he noticed another man heading towards them, he took Cissie roughly by the arm and marched her to the corner where she'd abandoned her stall.

Cissie was now too scared to complain, she wasn't used to men pushing her around.

'You obviously ain't all the ticket, darling,' he hissed menacingly, 'cos if yer was, yer wouldn't be messing with nothing to do with Mr Plains, now would yer.'

'Who?'

Ron narrowed his eyes. 'Yer really don't know?'

'Know *what*?' Cissie now felt more confused than scared, and the thought of going home yet again, further in debt and without a single penny earned, was more than she could bear. 'What're yer talking about?'

Ron made an elaborate show of checking that no one else could hear him. 'Listen to me, sweetheart. I'm gonna do yer a favour, I ain't gonna tell Mr Plains I've seen yer. So you be a good girl and run along home before I change me mind.' He shook his finger at her as though she were a foolish child. 'When the pitch was left empty we reckoned Turner had seen sense.'

'But this was me husband's stall,' Cissie interrupted. 'What's this got to do with Turner?' She turned her head and looked away from him. 'And now my husband's dead, the stall's mine.'

'Your husband run this pitch? What, Turner got widows working for him now, has he? He must be losing his touch.'

'I don't know why yer keep going on about Turner,' Cissie snapped angrily, 'but if yer reckon I'm gonna stand here and let someone take over my Davy's stall then yer must be an idiot.' Without a thought for how he might react, Cissie poked Ron in the chest. 'And yes, I'm a widow, and I've got two kids and a miserable old cow of a mother-in-law to keep. So if yer think I'm gonna let anyone take this away from me then yer've got another thought coming. This pitch is mine, right? Mine.'

Ron scratched his head distractedly. 'Turner really must be losing his touch if he's got young girls like you doing his dirty work for him.'

Cissie jabbed her finger at him. 'Turner! This is driving me barmy. *Why* bloody Turner all the time? I told yer, this pitch was Davy's.' She pointed at the stall. 'He even owned his own barrow and everything. Look, go on, look. There's his name carved and painted on the side. Not like yours,' she said defiantly. 'I'll bet that's rented.'

The other man, Dennis, appeared by Ron's side. 'Blimey, Ron, ain't yer got rid of her yet? What, yer swapping knitting patterns with her or something?'

'No, I ain't, Den. And, to tell yer the truth, I'm getting the right hump with her.'

Dennis folded his arms and stared menacingly at Cissie. 'Don't let Ron get the hump with yer, girl, cos yer won't like it. Now, if yer know what's good for yer, just clear off and we'll say no more about it.'

'No, I won't clear off, but I think you should. Cos if yer threaten me again, I'm gonna call the police.'

'The rozzers!' sneered Dennis. 'Now that definitely would be a mistake.'

He leant over her, backing her towards the church railings.

'Let me tell yer a little secret, more a warning really. Mr Plains is moving into the area. Got it?'

Cissie swallowed hard. 'What's so special about this pitch? Surely yer can sell flowers anywhere?'

Dennis laughed, a sneering snorting sound like an animal. 'Davy Flowers was no florist, darling. It was all just a front.' He grinned. 'A great big whopping fib. Now wasn't that naughty of him?'

'But if he wasn't a florist—'

Dennis folded his arms again and leant on the struts of Cissie's stall. 'Your old man, Mrs Flowers, was a bookie. He was running this pitch for Turner.'

'That's enough,' Ron warned him.

'No,' Dennis said with a shake of his head. 'Let the mouthy cow know. Let her know what a little, tiny, nomark cog her old man really was. And if she wants to call the coppers then good luck to her, but she'd better be prepared for the consequences.'

Cissie was stunned. Davy was a bookie?

Mechanically she picked up the handles of the stall and started hauling it around the corner and back towards the lock-up.

Could it be true? Had her whole life with Davy been a lie?

No, it couldn't be true. There had to be some other reason why those men said those things. She would have to find Turner somehow. She would go and see him, make him stop people spreading these lies about him and Davy. Tell him about the men and this Plains whoever he was.

Cissie stopped in her tracks, not noticing the cars and bicycles swerving and skidding to avoid her and the stall.

Could this have something to do with what Eileen had been hinting at? Maybe there was some truth in her drunken ramblings.

Eileen. She would know where to find Turner.

Cissie started walking again, oblivious of everything around her. All she could think of was that Turner's name was always there, always lurking somewhere in the background, and she was being drawn closer and closer to his world.

And it scared the life out of her.

Chapter 9

It took some doing, but, by continually pounding on the door, Cissie eventually woke Eileen from her drunken sleep – she knew she was in there, she could hear her bed-rattling snores through the paper-thin walls.

'Whatever's the time?' Eileen groaned, pulling her wrapper round her shoulders and stepping aside to let Cissie in.

'About twelve.'

Eileen tutted miserably. 'I've only been asleep a couple of hours,' she yawned. 'What d'yer want?'

'I want Turner's address.'

Eileen shook her head. 'He don't let no one know where he lives. No one. He keeps his home life very private, does Bill.'

'How about where he works? He must have an office or something.'

Eileen shrugged nonchalantly. 'He might have.'

'And you know where it is, don't you, Eileen?' Cissie cooed. 'Tell me, please.'

'No. I can't. Bill wouldn't like it. He's funny about people knowing things like that.'

Cissie coaxed, pleaded and lied for a solid half-hour. In the end it was her relentlessness that broke Eileen. Her head was throbbing from the drink and she just couldn't take it any more. She got down on her knees and took out a dusty old shoe box from under the bed.

'There, now will yer shut up?' she asked, handing Cissie what she wanted, a battered business card giving Turner's address in the Mile End Road.

'Yeah. Thanks, Eileen. Thanks a lot.'

'Er, hang on, what time d'yer say it was?' Eileen asked, the stupidity of what she had just done had sunk in. She had given a pretty woman, a woman a good ten years younger than her, Turner's address. She'd have no chance of getting him back if he took up with someone like Cissie Flowers.

'It must be about half twelve by now,' Cissie replied. She said it pleasantly enough but she was growing increasingly anxious to get out of there, not only did she have what she wanted, but she had to get away from the stale stench of long-unwashed clothes and of sweaty bodies that permeated the very fabric of the room.

'Half twelve,' repeated Eileen, 'well yer won't find him there then.' She reached out to try to snatch back the card.

'I'll take me chances,' Cissie said coolly, hanging determinedly on to it.

But as she neared her destination, Cissie's determination began to flag. She walked slower and slower, increasingly unsure as to what she thought she was doing going to see someone as infamous as Turner.

She even stopped for a while, when she reached the corner of White Horse Lane, to watch a child of about Matty's age stealing potatoes from a sack outside a fruit and vegetable shop. He was being urged on by a gang of slightly older boys. All the children were dressed in rags, and were wary-eyed and gaunt from hunger, not unlike a lot of other street urchins in the East End.

In the past, Cissie would have ignored such a scene, it having nothing to do with her, and she would certainly have made no connection between their pathetic existence and the life of her own little ones. But now, with her world turned upside down, their predicament held a terrible fascination for her. What would she be prepared to do so that her children wouldn't have to steal to eat?

As she watched the child's practised cunning, she asked herself why she had never questioned why her family should always have done so well while there was so much hardship all around her – there for anyone to see if they cared to look. How had she just carried on as though the easy life was hers by right and would go on for ever? She had been such a selfish fool to presume that everything would always be wonderful. It wasn't easy to admit it, but Gladys had been telling her a very nasty truth when she'd had that go at her.

A woman appeared in the shop doorway and the boy, a picture of guilt, sprang away from the potato sack as though he'd been scalded. The woman cracked him hard – wallop! – right around the ear, and swore loudly, threatening him with all sorts if he didn't clear off out of it and leave her stuff alone. The boy yelped and dodged off around the corner into Ernest Street, followed swiftly by his gang of pals.

Cissie sighed. The poor little sod. What a way to live. She'd go on the game before she'd see her two have to exist like that.

The woman went back inside the shop and, almost immediately, the boy reappeared. He really must have been desperate to risk another smack to that pinched little face of his.

It was while she stood there watching the skinny child darting back and forth from the sack like a nervous bird pecking breadcrumbs from a window ledge that Cissie determined to make it up with Gladys. It wasn't only because she wanted someone looking after her kids properly, someone who'd make sure that they had food in their bellies and that they weren't out raking the streets getting up to all sorts, no, it was also because she missed talking to her friend, she missed laughing with her. There had been so little laughter recently.

She waited until the child had his pockets and his cap stuffed full, and then she moved on.

She found the place. It was a tall, three-storey house, like many others along that stretch of the Mile End Road. It had chipped black railings and a stone stairway leading down to the area.

As she opened the metal gate, making it squeak loudly on its long-unoiled hinges, she noticed the corner of the lace curtain twitch away from the ground-floor window.

She hesitated before knocking on the front door – she didn't only dislike the sensation of being watched by hidden eyes, she was also dubious about what she would find inside. From the state of the outside of the place, rubbish-strewn steps and tall, dusty weeds poking through the black and white tiled path, it looked as though it could well be as bad as Eileen's. And this was no single room, it was a whole big house. She could just imagine the stench inside there.

The curtain twitched again. Then, before she could decide whether to knock or to run away, the door opened.

A skinny, sharp-nosed little man stood there in his shirtsleeves and braces, with a brown trilby hat jammed down to his ears. He jerked his head sideways.

'Come on in, if yer coming,' he said impatiently, scuttling along the hallway. 'I ain't got time to stand here all day.'

Cissie followed him as far as the doorway of the high-ceilinged front room. She was astonished by the scene of frantic activity which confronted her.

Men, nine of them, were sitting at narrow desks set in three rows, for all the world like a room full of over-sized schoolboys. Some were gabbling loudly into the telephones they each had in front of them, and others were scribbling on pads, calling to one another as though they were in another street rather than all lined up next to one another. One man, the one with the hat who'd answered the door, was chalking up names and numbers on a blackboard. A mad parody of a schoolmaster.

The room might have been in tumult, but at least the place was clean, spotless, in fact, and the only smell was that of the cigarette smoke which thickened the air to a hazy blue.

Cissie was suddenly swept into the room by a boy of about twelve pushing past her. He had a pile of evening newspapers under his arm.

'Second edition! Latest results!' he shouted over the din.

The activity became even more frantic as the men leapt from their desks and scrambled around the boy to check the stop press.

'Quiet!' yelled the one man still sitting behind his desk. He had a telephone clamped between his ear and his shoulder. 'I can't hear a sodding thing with you mob all hollering and hooting. You know how Mr Turner likes to look after his special credit customers.' He moved the receiver from his ear and held it to his chest to muffle it. 'Especially the ones what owe him plenty of money,' he added with a broad wink and then returned the phone to his ear. 'Sorry about that, sir. Now, about your account—'

Cissie waited until the man had finished on the telephone, then walked over to his desk and asked politely, 'Are you in charge?'

'I might be,' he said looking up at her. 'Why?'

'I'd like to see Mr Turner.'

'Would yer now?' He craned his neck to get a better view of her legs. 'He expecting you, is he?'

'Yeah, he is, as a matter of fact,' Cissie said haughtily.

'Aw, right. Who shall I say's calling?' the man asked with considerably more courtesy in his voice.

'Cissie Flowers,' she said. Seeing the look on his face, she immediately corrected herself. 'No, not Cissie Flowers, tell him it's Mrs Flowers.'

'Make yer mind up, love,' she heard someone behind her chuckle. 'What's the matter, don't yer like yer fellers calling yer by yer first name till the second date?'

'Shut it!' the man snapped at the joker, a fresh-faced lad of about sixteen, and got up from his desk. 'Wait there a minute, Mrs Flowers, and I'll see if Mr Turner's available.'

Before he left the room, the man pointed at the now straight-faced comedian. 'Get the lady a seat, you.'

The man returned within moments.

'This way, Mrs Flowers,' he said respectfully.

Without so much as a glance at the mouthy youngster, Cissie stuck her chin in the air and followed the man from the room.

He led Cissie along the bare-floored passage, up a small flight of similarly carpetless stairs and stopped outside a freshly painted door with a shining brass handle.

'Mr Turner's private office,' he said by way of polite explanation. He tapped gently on the door, waited a moment, then opened it.

He ushered Cissie inside. 'Mrs Flowers for yer, guv,' he said, before closing the door and leaving Cissie alone with Big Bill Turner.

Turner was sitting in a huge leather chair, behind an enormous desk that was more than four times the size of the ones down in the front room. It was also a lot more expensive-looking, as was everything else in the wood-panelled, thickly carpeted room.

Turner didn't look up at her.

Cissie stood there in silence and watched as he reached out and took a cigar from the ornately carved ivory humidor standing on the corner of his glass-topped desk.

Taking his time, Turner trimmed the end with a silver cutter, lit a match, and then took a long, leisurely puff. As he exhaled his first plume of smoke, he examined the glowing end of the cigar. Only when he was satisfied that it was burning to his liking did he look at her.

'Mrs Flowers,' he said warmly. 'Long time no see. Take a seat. Take a seat.' He used his cigar as a pointer, waving it at the low armchair set at the side of his desk.

'I'd rather stand if yer don't mind. What I've got to say won't take long.'

Not bothering to suppress an amused smile, Turner carefully balanced his cigar in the sparkling crystal ashtray that sat on the desk in front of him, shoved back his chair and stood up. He walked across the room and picked up one of the delicate-looking gilt-and-velvet seats which lined the far wall.

'This'll be more to yer liking maybe,' he said, plonking it down in front of his desk. 'Now sit down, Mrs Flowers,' he commanded. 'Having people standing over me makes me feel uncomfortable.' Gently, but with a touch that was firm enough to demonstrate he wouldn't countenance a refusal, Turner eased her down on to the chair.

'That's better. See, Mrs Flowers, being so tall, I ain't used to looking up to no one. No one.'

He returned to his own seat on the other side of the desk, picked up his cigar and puffed on it contemplatively.

'Strange,' he said eventually, 'I thought yer wanted to see me. Now yer've got nothing to say for yerself. How d'you account for that then, Mrs Flowers? Funny sort o' behaviour, wouldn't yer say?'

Agitated as she was by his sarcasm, Cissie certainly wasn't going to rise to him, nor was she going to let Turner see how nervous she felt. Gathering every bit of dignity, she sat up very straight and looked at him unblinkingly.

'Mr Turner,' she began, angry at the quaver in her voice, 'I've come here to get something sorted out. You see, I tried to set up the stall this morning—'

He jabbed the cigar at her. 'Davy's flower stall?'

Cissie nodded. 'I went to the market, got all the stock and everything.'

'Did you now?'

'Yes, I did. And it weren't easy, believe me. I had a right old time of it.'

'I'm sure yer did. It wouldn't be easy for a lady.' Bugger! Why had she said that? She could have kicked herself for letting him see she was so vulnerable. 'But anyway,' she added hurriedly, 'that's nothing to do with it. It's the pitch. When I got there, there was these two bloody great thugs.'

'Thugs?' Turner no longer looked nor sounded amused.

'Yeah. Cheeky sods. They told me the pitch was theirs.'

'Did they now? And did yer know them, these *thugs?*'

'No, but they said they was working for a Mr Plains.'

'Plains?' Turner ground the barely smoked cigar savagely into the ash-tray.

'Yeah, but...' Cissie rose shakily to her feet. 'Look I don't know what's going on, and I don't really wanna know, to tell you the truth, but from a few things they told me, well, I reckon you owe me an explanation.'

Turner nearly choked. 'I *what?*'

Cissie took a deep breath. Holding on to the edge of the desk for support, she leant forward and said, 'They said Davy worked for you. He didn't, did he?' She could feel the tears of self-pity pricking at her eyes. She wanted to shout at him, tell him to tell her it was all lies. But she didn't. She couldn't. She needed that stall, and, much as she hated it, she needed Turner to help her.

'I dunno what rubbish you've been listening to—'

'Look, Mr Turner, I'm sure the police'd be very interested in your little racket downstairs, but I ain't interested in causing no trouble. If people are stupid enough to gamble away their wages, that's up to them, I reckon. I just wanna mind me own business and make a living. Just have what's due to me and my kids. Fair and square.' The words were coming easier now. 'I've got a stall full of flowers in that lock-up, and they ain't gonna last very long in this weather, now are they? So, if yer don't mind, just send a couple of them blokes o' your'n up to Aldgate, and tell that pair that pitch is mine. Like I said, fair and square. And don't say yer can't, cos I know different.'

'Sit down, Mrs Flowers. Please.'

Cissie sat down. Her outburst had exhausted her.

'For a start, there is nothing illegal in what's going on downstairs. Credit betting is all above board. Got it?' Cissie nodded miserably. Her last card and it was a joker.

'And secondly, you said you don't want no trouble. Just a living.'

She nodded again.

'Right. So why bother with a poxy flower stall?'

Cissie swallowed hard. 'I ain't here to discuss me private affairs,' she said flatly, 'but the long and the short of it is, I ain't got no choice.'

'Now that is where you're wrong. Very wrong.' Turner leant back in his chair and slowly folded his arms. 'I could offer you a choice. A very nice choice. See, Mrs Flowers, you're a very attractive young woman and I don't like to think of you having to work for a living. Well, not on a flower stall anyway.'

She frowned, stunned by this latest turn of events. 'Are you offering me a job?'

He considered for a moment. 'Yer could say that,' he said, apparently absorbed by a speck of dust on his sleeve. 'Yer see, a man in my position, running a big firm like I do, I need to relax.'

He raised his eyes and gazed steadily at her, trying to assess her reaction. She just looked puzzled, so he continued.

'I like to go out of an evening. To nice places. And when I do, I like to have a good-looking young lady on me arm.' He took out another cigar and went through the same drawn-out procedure of trimming and lighting it.

'I thought you was married.'

Turner blew out a stream of smoke and nodded at her through the lavender haze. 'I am. And my Moe was one of the best lookers around. Once. Not as good-looking as you, mind. You're a very good-looking young woman indeed, Mrs Flowers. You'd make any man proud to have you on his arm when he wanted a night out without his wife.' He smiled at her appreciatively. 'I could make your life very easy, Mrs Flowers, very easy indeed.'

Cissie stood up again, even though her legs felt as though they were about to buckle under her. 'Just who'd d'you think you are, Turner? Yer can't buy people, yer know. Yer can't own them, just because yer've got a bit of money.'

'I've not just got a bit of money, Mrs Flowers, I've got a whole lot of the stuff, and that's why I *can* buy people. Just like I bought your Davy.' He sniffed contemptuously. 'Came right cheap he did, and all. Still, he needed the money, didn't he? How else could he have kept you so well, darling? Buy you all them pretty things you ladies like?'

'So he did work for yer?'

Turner grinned his reply.

'Well, yer might have conned him into working for yer, but you ain't gonna con me.'

He held out his hands in surprise. 'Me con people? Yer've got me wrong, Mrs Flowers. I never con no one. People ain't stupid, they just like the good life.' Turner raised a cynical eyebrow and laughed. 'You included. So how about it? I'd make life very good for you. Very good indeed. You could have whatever you wanted. Whatever that pretty little head o' your'n could think up would be yours. Now wouldn't that be nice?'

'I wouldn't take nothing off you, not if I was starving.'

'So yer don't want me to get them geezers off the pitch for yer then?'

Cissie slapped her hand on to the cold smooth glass of the desktop. 'That's different,' she fumed. 'You owe me that.'

'Do I? How d'yer work that one out then?'

'I'll go to the police if yer don't. Tell 'em about you making Davy take bets on the street.'

'What, wanna ruin your poor dead husband's reputation, do yer? And it'd be such a shame to have you took away from them kids o' your'n and all.'

'Eh?'

'Well, everyone knows you used to run a book for me from the house. Ask any of the fellers downstairs, they'll all tell yer. It was common knowledge.'

'You bastard! You wouldn't.'

'Wouldn't I?' Turner pulled his telephone across the desk towards him, looked up at Cissie and smiled. 'Yer know yer look even lovelier when yer've got yer wild up. And yer will think about me offer, won't yer, Mrs Flowers? Now,' he picked up the receiver, 'if yer'll excuse me.'

Cissie spun away from him and stormed over to the door. She wrenched it open and was about to leave, but changed her mind. She twisted back round and yelled at him, 'Yer know where you can shove yer offer, don't yer *Mr Big Bill Turner?*'

Turner blew her a kiss and grinned. 'You just think about it.'

Cissie narrowed her eyes and tugged furiously at her fringe. 'Look, are you gonna get rid of them blokes at the pitch or what?' she demanded.

Turner rubbed his index finger thoughtfully up and down the side of his nose. 'So yer do want me help then?'

'If that's yer attitude, you can go and bugger yerself.'

As she slammed the door behind her, Cissie could hear Turner's raucous laughter.

'It's a long time since anyone's stood up to me like that,' he hollered after her. 'Specially someone as pretty as you, Mrs Flowers. I love it! I look forward to seeing yer again soon.'

He shook his head in amused admiration then, just like turning off a tap, he wiped the smile from his face and set about dialling a number.

His call, through to the chaotic downstairs front room, was answered on the second ring.

'Come up to the office,' he barked. 'That slag Plains reckons he can muscle in on our manor, and I don't like it.'

Chapter 10

While Cissie was making her way home in the truck, in the draining heat of the sultry, June afternoon, still unsure as to whether Turner was planning to help her or not, Lil, who was actually having a far easier time of things, was grumbling irritably to herself.

She had just finished reading the paper and was settling down on her bed in the front room to close her eyes for a little sleep, when someone started tapping on the street door.

'That bleed'n Gladys,' she fumed, hauling herself up on her elbows. 'I only asked the lazy rotten mare to mind 'em for a couple of hours while I had a rest. Won't do nothing for no one, some people. Selfish, that's what it is.'

Stomping along the passage, Lil's temper flared as the knocking grew louder.

'All right, all right,' she hollered, 'why didn't yer just let yerself in?' She grabbed the door and flung it back on its hinges. 'The bloody thing ain't locked yer—'

Lil's mouth was still open, but no words were coming out.

'Hello, Lil,' said the shy middle-aged man who was standing on the step. 'Hope I ain't disturbing yer or nothing.'

Lil bristled and snorted. Her voice restored, she stuck her face close to his and sneered nastily. 'Frank bloody Bentley. What the hell d'you want coming sniffing round here?'

Frank ran his hands through his grey-flecked, but still glossy black hair, tugging nervously at it in just the way that his daughter, Cissie, did whenever she was anxious or worried.

'Me and Ellen want Cissie to have this,' he said, taking a thin roll of notes from his pocket and holding it out to Lil. 'We know things can't be easy for her at the minute.'

Lil's sneer was magically transformed into a look of martyred suffering, as she eyed the money greedily.

'Won't yer step inside a minute, Frank?' she said pulling him into the hall, the desire to keep the visit a secret from the neighbours, rather than good manners or even basic decency, being her motive for doing so. 'And yer right, yer know, Frank. Things ain't easy for none of us nowadays, what with no regular money coming in, like. And what with all the sadness.'

She sighed loudly, and clasped her chest for dramatic good measure. 'It's a terrible thing losing a child, yer know. Really terrible.'

Frank angled his head away from her. 'Yeah, I know it is,' he said quietly. He took a deep breath and then turned back to face her. 'Would Cissie be in, Lil? I'd love to see her.'

Having her sights set on the money in Frank's hand, Lil didn't tell him to bugger off out of it and mind his own business – the first answer that came to mind – instead, she shook her head mournfully. 'No, Frank, she's not. The poor little mare's had to go out and try to earn a few shillings. Anything to put a bit of grub on the table for the little ones. Left first thing she did. Wasn't even properly light. She's a real little trier that one. I'm right proud of her, I am.'

Frank dropped his chin; he couldn't stand the thought of Lil seeing the tears gathering in his eyes.

'This'll help her out,' he said as much to himself as to Lil, waving the roll tantalisingly close to her. 'And how are the kids doing?' He brushed anxiously at the thick fringe of hair that had fallen over his eyes. 'Me and Ellen are always talking about 'em, wondering how they are. P'raps I could see 'em. I'd love that, Lil.'

'I'm sure yer would.' Lil's expression was guarded, wary; the last thing she wanted was to put her own position in jeopardy by helping Cissie make her peace with her mum and dad. She needed to keep control of the situation, not have some sniffling great nancy sticking his nose in and ruining everything. 'But I can't really have yer coming in here while young Cissie's out, now can I, Frank? I mean, it wouldn't be right, now would it? Not with things being the way they are between yers.'

Frank thought for a moment, tapping the roll of notes on the palm of his hand. 'Look, Lil, I know we've never got on—'

'I wouldn't say that,' Lil smarmed, her gaze following the rhythmic motion of the money in his hands.

Frank carried on as though she'd said nothing, '—but I'm gonna ask you a favour.'

Lil had high hopes and a very good idea as to what that favour was going to be, but she kept up her innocent act. 'What's that then, Frank? What can I do for yer? Just you name it, mate.'

'I'd appreciate yer giving this twenty-five pounds to Cissie. And tell her that me and her mum are thinking of her.' He took a deep breath and let it out in a long shuddering sigh. 'And that we was sorry we never got to talk to her at the funeral. And we'll do anything, whatever she wants, to try and get back together again. Anything so's we can see her and the kids. Anything.'

Lil's hand twitched. The money was almost in her grasp. 'Course, Frank, you know me. I'll do whatever I can to make my darling daughter-in-law happy. She's been an angel to me, that girl. A real angel. You ask anyone round here. But then I've been a comfort to her and all at this sad time, ain't I?'

Frank lifted his chin in what could have been interpreted as either acknowledgement of his daughter's virtues or cynicism about Lil's newly acquired decency. 'Just tell her I was here, eh, Lil?' he said, handing the money over.

Putting it straight into her apron pocket, Lil smiled beatifically. 'Yer can depend on me,' she said, easing him out of the door. 'Now, I'll have to be getting on. I've got lots to do. Always plenty o' jobs to keep yer busy when there's kiddies around.'

Frank pulled on his cap. 'I'll call round again, Lil. Try and catch her in next time.'

'When?'

'Sometime,' he shrugged.

Lil could have spat at him as she closed the door. He was coming back! Her plans for the twenty-five pounds melted away like dripping in a roasting pan. If Cissie caught her nicking money off her, she might well turn on her and chuck her out, and Lil had no intention of finding a new meal ticket at her age. No, she thought to herself, as she made her way along the passage to the kitchen, that wouldn't suit her at all. She'd make herself a cup of tea and think up something or other. She couldn't let a chance like this slip out of her hands.

As she filled the kettle, a smile slowly found its way to Lil's lips. She'd think up something all right, after all, didn't she have a real talent for playing around with the truth? Hadn't she taught her boy all the tricks he knew?

Less than a quarter of an hour later, as Lil heard the front door open, and Cissie call out hello, she put her newly hatched plan into action.

–

'Wherever did yer get that?' The sticky heat, Big Bill Turner, and her worries about the two strange men at the pitch temporarily forgotten, Cissie goggled at the sight of her mother-in-law sitting at the kitchen table putting pound notes and ten-shilling notes into two separate piles. Admittedly they were very small piles, but they were piles nonetheless.

'Yer never gonna believe this,' Lil beamed, stroking the ten-shilling pile as though it were a much-loved pet, 'but I found all this lot on the coconut mat in the passage.

'Someone must've stuck it through the street door for us.'

Totally bewildered by this sudden stroke of good fortune, Cissie dropped down on to the chair opposite Lil. 'How much is there?'

'Twenty pounds! Just think what we can do with twenty pounds!'

Cissie shook her head in bewilderment, then suddenly slapped the flat of her hand on the table. 'I know who's done this,' she said, solving the puzzle.

'Who?' Lil demanded.

'It's Sammy Clarke, innit?'

Lil scowled. Not bloody Sammy Clarke again. 'What would he wanna go giving us money for?' she asked suspiciously.

Cissie felt her cheeks burning. 'He's been very good to us lately, Lil. In fact, we wouldn't be getting by without him.'

Lil didn't look very impressed, the last thing she wanted was Sammy Clarke coming on the firm and confusing matters. 'He's a right old woman that one if you ask me. I mean, what sort of life's that for a bloke, serving in a corner shop? He's a right pansy.'

Cissie stood up. 'Well, I think he's a really decent bloke, and I'm gonna go over and thank him.'

Cissie walked over to the kitchen doorway and paused. She swung round, frowning. 'Here, where's the kids?'

'They're all right. They're playing,' said Lil distractedly. This was getting complicated. She needed time to think. 'You get yerself over Clarke's if yer going.'

–

When Elsie Collier – the woman from number six who took in lodgers – finally left the shop with one of her 'gentlemen' in tow to carry all her bags, Cissie was, at last, alone with Sammy.

'Come on, Cis,' Sammy beamed, 'tell me all about it. I've been dying to know all day. How'd yer get on at the market this morning? Get yerself some decent gear, did yer?'

Cissie smiled back at him, touched by his concern and his humility. He'd just given her twenty pounds and he wasn't even going to mention it. Most people would be broadcasting such an act of generosity.

'It was you, wasn't it, Sam?' she said gently. 'Yer knew I'd probably mess it all up at first, and wind up broke again.'

'I never thought yer'd mess up nothing. Yer a clever girl, Cissie Flowers, always have been. Yer used to run rings round the rest of us lot at school. So why should I think that?'

'Yer mean yer really think I've done it?'

Sammy leant on the counter and jerked his head towards the customer's chair. 'Why don't yer sit yerself down and tell me all about it?'

'There ain't much to tell.' Cissie lifted her fringe off her face, brushing it back with her fingers. 'I got the flowers all right, well I reckon I paid a bit over the odds, but at least I got 'em. Trouble was, when I got to the pitch, there was these two blokes there already.'

'What, with a stall?'

She nodded. 'Yeah.'

'That ain't right, surely. Davy had that spot for years.'

'I must have known deep down, yer know, that he was involved with something bad,' she said more to herself than to Sammy. 'We had things too easy.'

'Bad, yer say?'

'Yeah, and now I've gotta start paying for it.'

'But how d'yer mean, *bad*?'

'They was—' Cissie hesitated, considered what she was about to say, then thought better of it. She'd said too much already. She had no business involving Sammy in the world she had glimpsed today. Even talking to him about it could bring him trouble, she wasn't sure how, but she felt it, deep inside.

'They was *what*? You ain't making no sense.'

'No, I ain't, am I? I'm tired out, I reckon, and rambling on like a nutcase. Just ignore me, Sam. Anyway, what I really come over for wasn't to start me moaning again. I come over to thank yer for that twenty quid.'

Sammy scratched his head. 'Are you talking in some sort of code, Cis? Cos honest, love, I ain't following none of this.'

Cissie narrowed her eyes. 'Are you saying you never went over home this afternoon and stuck some money through me letterbox?'

'It weren't me.' Sammy looked put out by the thought that Cissie might have another benefactor. 'But I can let you have more if yer need it, girl,' he added hurriedly, stabbing his finger on the brass till keys and opening the drawer with a loud ring. 'You know that.'

'Thanks all the same, Sam, honest.' Cissie held up her hand to refuse his offer. 'But I owe yer enough already.'

'Don't you worry yerself about that.' He considered for a moment. 'So, who d'you think did it?' he asked, his jaw rigid. Someone was trying to buy their way into Cissie's affections and Sammy didn't like it. He didn't like it one little bit. There wasn't much he could offer Cissie but a bit of financial help, and now it looked as though she didn't even need that.

Cissie lowered her eyes, her voice trembling as she spoke. 'The other day, I went and asked some o' Davy's old mates for help. They was a bit, you know, funny in front of one another. Acting all tough. But I reckon they've come up trumps. He was a popular feller yer see, my Davy. He had a lot of friends. Good friends. I should've known they wouldn't let me down when it come to it.'

Cissie pulled out her hanky and wiped her eyes. 'I'll see yer later, Sam.'

—

Back across the street at number seven, Cissie had another surprise waiting for her. As she stepped inside the front door, there was an envelope addressed to her on the coconut mat.

'When did this come?' she asked Lil, tearing it open, as she went into the kitchen.

Lil, who was standing at the sink washing her hands under the single cold tap, looked over her shoulder. 'I dunno,' she said defensively. *Surely Frank hadn't been back already.* 'I've been out the back in the lav. Show us. Who's it from?'

She wiped her hands hastily on her apron and rushed to Cissie's side as another thought occurred to her. 'Here? It's not more money, is it?'

'No, it's a letter.'

Lil had the horrible taste of bile rise in her throat. That bloody interfering Frank Bentley!

She watched closely as Cissie, her lips moving as she silently read the letter to herself, scanned the page.

'So, who's it from then?'

Cissie looked up. 'It's from some bloke called Jim.'

'Jim? Who the sodding hell's Jim when he's at home?'

Cissie ran her finger through the words, finding the place, then she read:

'I am a wholesale flower seller at Covent Garden who used to have a trade with Davy. I was sorry what happened to him. He was a mate. I want to let you know I will be glad to have a trade with you if you are keeping the stall on. You can find me most mornings in Portelli's cafe having my breakfast. Any time up until half past four or so when we start dealing. I thought a lot of Davy and will do anything I can to help his family.'

Cissie lowered the letter and looked at Lil. 'I bet it was him what put the money through the door,' she said excitedly. 'Yer must've missed the letter, Lil, when yer was picking up the twenty quid. It probably got stuck behind the mat or something.'

'Yeah,' Lil agreed readily. 'That'll be it. Stuck behind the mat. Fancy that eh?' Lil could have kissed this Jim, whoever he was.

Cissie sat down at the table and stared at the letter and the two piles of money. 'D'you know what, Lil? I reckon that after everything I've been through these last couple of months, I really think things are taking a turn for the better at last. And if this Jim is as nice as he sounds, he might be able to help me with another little problem I've got and all.' Lil went across to the overmantel and began applying a thick coat of lipstick to her narrow mouth. 'Problem?' she asked through stretched lips.

'Yeah, with the stall. Yer see—'

'Aw, the stall,' Lil interrupted. 'Right, yeah.' She wasn't the least bit interested in what Cissie had to say, she was too busy patting her hair, studying it in the glass. 'I could do with another perm, yer know, while there's a few quid about.'

Cissie said nothing.

Lil swung around to face her. 'I'd love to stay and listen to yer, girl, but I think I'd better pop down the Sabberton for a drop of something to steady me poor old nerves. All this excitement's fair given me palpitations it has.'

Cissie opened her handbag. 'Here, Lil,' she said handing her a two-shilling piece. 'I don't reckon we can afford money for no hairdos, but go on, take it. Treat yerself to a couple o' drinks.' She put her elbows on the table and rested her chin on her hands. 'I sold the lighter my Davy give me. That's what's left.'

'Well, I hope yer got a good price for it,' sniffed Lil, putting the coin in her pocket with the five one-pound notes already nestling there. 'Don't wait up, will yer?'

Lil unhooked her handbag from the back of the chair, and walked out to the passage.

'Hang on!' Cissie called, rushing after her. 'I dunno what I'm thinking of.' She grabbed Lil's arm. 'You said the kids was playing. So where are they?' She stuck her fists into her waist. 'If you've let them go up the road to play in that dookie Godwins' house…'

'No, I bleed'n ain't.' Lil flapped her hand impatiently. 'They're over Glad's, ain't they.'

'Glad's got them?'

'That's what I said, didn't I?' Lil snapped.

Cissie rubbed her hands over her face, hiding her shame. 'She's a good 'un, that Gladys. Even though we've had words, she ain't taken it out on the kids. Not like some women would.' She dropped her hands to her side and looked at Lil. 'What, did Matty and Joyce ask if they could go over there?'

'No.' Lil shook her head and continued casually, 'I took 'em over after their dinner. Joyce kept being sick and I couldn't settle—'

'You did *what*? Joyce's ill and you've let me stand here...' Cissie barged past Lil and ran frantically along the passage.

'Charming!' Cissie heard Lil snort as she flung open the door and raced across the street.

—

'Glad! Glad! It's me, Cissie, where's Joyce?' Cissie yelled from the street door of number four.

'In here,' Gladys called back.

Cissie skidded into the kitchen, taking the passage runner with her.

In the corner she saw Nipper, Ernie's elderly grandfather, sitting talking to an attentive semicircle of youngsters made up of his younger grandchildren, and Matty. Joyce was curled up on his lap, sucking her thumb, listening intently.

'But Lil said—' As she spoke, it dawned on Cissie that Lil had been up to her old tricks again: telling all sorts of stupid lies just to get herself out of doing anything that might require a bit of effort on her part.

'What did she say?' Gladys asked, looking up from her ironing.

Cissie rolled her eyes. 'She told me some tale about Joyce being sick.'

Gladys chuckled and spat on the iron to test the heat. 'She don't change, that Lil, does she? Joyce's right as rain, ain't yer, darling?'

Joyce looked round. Seeing her mum, she scrambled down from Nipper's lap and launched herself at Cissie. 'Mummy! Look, Matt, Mummy!'

Matty gave his mum a wave and a smile, but didn't move from Nipper's feet.

Gladys jerked her thumb at her grandfather-in-law. 'He's had the lot of 'em spellbound all afternoon. Telling 'em tales about when he was in the army out in Africa of all things. And there's all that lovely sunshine out there and all. They should have been out getting their little knees brown. But he could've been talking double Dutch and they'd all still be sitting there, I reckon. The kids all love him. We're lucky yer know having him living here with us.'

Cissie shifted Joyce on to her hip, reached out and took Gladys's hand. 'And I'm lucky to have such a good friend, Glad, even if I ain't always been clever enough to realise it.'

And, Cissie thought to herself, as she carried Joyce back across the street to number seven, I'm lucky that Davy had friends as decent as this Jim, whoever he was. There weren't a lot of fellers who'd take the time to write letters and send money to a mate's widow. But Davy was the sort of bloke who'd inspire that sort of loyalty in a friend. Davy was a good 'un all right.

She smiled wistfully to herself as she stepped inside the passage. She knew it, she'd been right all along. Davy would never have been involved in anything crooked. He wasn't the sort. And as if he wouldn't have told her all about it if he had been. They'd never kept secrets from one another. Never.

All that talk, the hints and suggestions, about things Davy'd been involved in, it was all just spiteful-minded gossip and jealousy. Big Bill Turner was just trying to take advantage of her. And the blokes at the pitch were just trying to scare her so they could take it over. After all, Davy had proved what a good little earner it could be.

But she'd show them all, she didn't need help from the likes of Turner, not with friends like Gladys and Jim on her side.

Chapter 11

First thing the next morning, Cissie climbed into the truck and headed back to Covent Garden market. She was going to find Jim Phillips, the man who, since she had first read his letter the previous afternoon, Cissie had come to see as her hope and benefactor. She couldn't stop herself from putting all her trust and hope in this person she had never met, and, she had decided, the more she thought about it, the more reasonable it seemed for her to do so.

Firstly, she'd never been in a position before where she had had to make the decisions and pay the bills, as there had always been a man there to do that in Cissie's life. Her dad, then her husband. And that, if she was honest, was one of the things she had missed most since Davy had been killed – someone being around who would take on all those things that she had never in the past had to worry about, the things that now tormented her in the early hours when she couldn't sleep, or when she woke up sweating, in a complete panic about how she would pay Brownlow when he came sniffing around and she still hadn't figured out how to sell the stupid flowers off the rotten stall. Jim would, she sincerely believed, be able to fill that role for her.

Secondly, Cissie liked the feeling she had when she read Jim's letter. Even though she'd not so much as clapped eyes on him yet, she just knew that he was decent, and he'd be kind – a man who was genuinely concerned to do the right thing by his friend's widow, rather than acting the big, flash man who was more interested in what she would look like hanging on his arm like an ornament as he walked into a bar.

Sammy Clarke had been kind to her of course, and she'd never forget that, but, much as she hated to agree with Lil, he was a bloke who ran a corner shop. A grocer. Hardly the sort of man to set a woman's heart racing by sweeping her off her feet and by making her feel that everything would be all right just because he was there.

Davy had been that sort of man. A real man. Strong, able to sort anything out. And that's what Cissie wanted again, that kind of strength and support. And Jim sounded as though he might just fit the bill.

She smiled happily to herself as she eased the truck on to the East India Dock Road and joined the sparse early morning traffic heading towards the City and the West End. She knew she had every good reason to feel optimistic.

And things were looking up at home too. Last night, Gladys had promised Cissie that as soon as she got home from her early morning cleaning jobs she would go straight over to number seven and take the children back to hers, leaving Lil to 'rest'. As for the children, they were only too pleased to hear about the new arrangements. Joyce – who wasn't even sickening for something, let alone ill – was looking forward to playing with Gladys's youngest; and as for Matty, he had gone to bed thrilled by the idea of hearing more of old Nipper's wartime exploits.

She was still smiling as she manoeuvred the truck off of the Strand and into the outer edges of the market.

Everything was going to be all right.

When she found Portelli's cafe – the place where Jim had said she could find him – Cissie's run of luck seemed to be continuing. Although, even at such an early hour, the place was crowded with men eating enormous fried breakfasts, the very first person she asked was able to point Jim Phillips out to her. Nothing was going to spoil Cissie's day, she just knew it.

'Oi, Jim! There's someone over here to see yer,' the helpful man yelled over the din of noisy chatter, clashing cutlery and hissing urns. He stabbed his fork, complete with dripping egg yolk, towards Cissie. 'I hope your Iris don't find out. Look at her, right little beauty, ain't she?'

With her cheeks flushed pink from a combination of embarrassment, the heat of the cafe, and the already warm morning air, Cissie edged her way through the maze of chairs to a table near the counter, where a fair-haired man in his thirties was beckoning to her.

He looked nice, she thought, as he waved a friendly, warning fist at the source of one of the more ribald remarks as she squeezed past a table full of leering breakfasters.

'Mrs Flowers innit?' Jim asked her, bobbing up in welcome.

Cissie nodded. 'That's right. But call me Cissie.'

Jim waved his fork in triumph. 'Never forget a face. I recognised you straightaway, from the funeral like.'

Immediately realising how clumsy his remark had been – fancy mentioning the funeral! – Jim began flapping about, throwing down his cutlery, pulling out a chair for

Cissie, beckoning to the cafe owner, anything to try to cover up his stupidity. The comments and loud laughter continued as Jim managed to toss both his knife and fork and the mustard pot crashing to the floor, and his chair careering into the narrow alleyway between the tables.

Cissie felt sorry for him; he was only trying to make her feel welcome. She helped him pick everything up, flinching with coyness as their hands touched.

'Hark at them,' Jim said, rolling his eyes, as he finally settled back into his chair. 'Anyone'd think they'd never seen a young lady before.'

'They're all right, I'm not taking any notice,' Cissie said shyly, sitting down opposite him. She pulled her dress firmly down over her legs and set her handbag primly on her knees. 'And thanks for the compliment. The way I've been feeling lately, I never expected no one to call me a young lady ever again.' She giggled in an unconvincing show of happy-go-lucky casualness. 'Well, not in such a nice way I didn't.'

'No fear of no one not complimenting you, darling,' said the aproned cafe owner, leaning over the counter and treating her to a broad wink as he shoved a brimming mug full of tea towards her. 'Come round here and I'll call you a young lady any time you like.'

Cissie looked at Jim, trying to get a clue as to how she should respond. He shook his head, warning her not to rise to the bait, then leant back in his chair, rocking it on to its back legs, and reached behind him for the tea.

As Jim handed it to Cissie, he gave the owner a matey ticking off. 'You just behave yourself, Bob. Honestly,' he tutted loudly, 'you're just like the rest of this lot in here.

Let you outta the sight of yer old woman for five minutes and yer go stark raving mad.'

'Yer can't blame a chap now, can yer, Jim,' Bob said, levering himself away from the counter and getting on with the business of running his cafe. 'She's a right little smasher yer've got there.'

Cissie picked up her tea and sipped the scalding, stewed brown liquid. 'Yer married then, Jim?' Cissie peered at him across the rim of her mug. 'Iris, did they say?'

'Er, yeah,' he answered, the muscles in his face tensing. 'That's right, I'm married to Iris.'

'Kids? You got any, have yer?'

'Yeah, I have.' He pushed his half-finished breakfast to one side, took his cigarettes from his jacket pocket and offered them to Cissie.

'Please, don't let me stop yer eating.' Cissie took one of the cigarettes and narrowed her eyes against the flare of the match as he lit it for her. 'I like to see a man enjoying his food.'

She could have kicked herself as she saw his hand shaking as he tried to close the packet of Players. Here was this kind man, a friend of Davy's, taking the time to help her out, giving her that twenty pounds, and spending his time with her when he could be relaxing with his mates before work, and what had she done in return? She'd opened her big mouth and put her foot right in it. Because from the way he was acting, he was obviously having some kind of trouble with his wife. Maybe they were separated or something. Why had she opened her big mouth? She could have slapped herself, she really could.

'I was finished anyway,' Jim said, flicking the spent match on to his discarded plate. 'And we might as well get right down to it anyway.'

He flashed a look at Bob who was still hovering in the background, warning him not even to think about making any crude remarks. 'Cos if yer gonna run that stall, there's plenty yer gonna have to learn, Mrs Flowers.'

'Cissie. Please.'

'Cissie.'

'And yer right, Jim, there is plenty I've gotta learn. I've never seen nothing like this market in all of my life. It's a right old turn-out, innit? All the noise and confusion, I didn't know what way to turn when I came here yesterday.' Cissie lowered her voice and bent her head towards him. 'But, to be honest, that's not all. I was wondering if I could ask yer to help me, or just advise me like, with this other little problem I've got. See, there's these two blokes who reckon they've taken over the pitch. I'm really worried about 'em. Can they just do that? Take it over? Cos—'

Jim held up his hand to silence her. 'One thing at a time, eh? Let's talk about the market first. Then we'll start worrying ourselves about blokes and pitches.'

Cissie slumped back into her seat. 'It won't be any use me knowing the market inside out and back to front and getting the flowers for free,' she said dejectedly, 'not if I ain't got nowhere to sell the bloody things.'

She leant forward again, urging him to understand. 'I *need* that pitch, Jim. It's close to the lock-up. It's got good passing trade from the station and the factories, and there's all them offices just up the road. And there's no other competition. I've really thought about it. That's how Davy earnt so much, see. I need it.'

Jim dragged agitatedly on his cigarette, 'Look, let me say something. And I want yer to listen. Yer've gotta get the market side sorted first. Right? Just trust me.'

'All right,' she said, but she didn't look convinced. This wasn't going the way she'd planned at all.

'I'll show you all the little tricks and wrinkles. Then what I'll do is ask around about these blokes. Find out who they are. Where they're from. That sort o' thing. You can bet they'll just be a pair o' chancers trying to muscle in.'

'I reckon it'll take a bit more than asking round.'

'Just listen to me, will yer?' Jim began, stubbing out his cigarette with unnecessary force as he spoke. 'There's plenty of handy sorts round the market what owe me favours – plenty of favours, if you understand what I mean. So, like I said, trust me. I'll sort them blokes out for yer. Don't you worry yerself about that.'

Cissie thought of Jim's kind-hearted letter and the money on the mat, and nodded. 'Thanks, but will yer tell me something first?'

'What?'

'It was you what gave me that twenty quid, weren't it?'

Seeing from the look on his face that he had no idea what she was talking about, Cissie planted her elbows on the table and buried her face in her hands.

'I'm not making a very good job of all this, Jim,' she murmured.

She raised her head until her eyes met his. It was a while since she'd willingly met a man's gaze in that way. 'Since my Davy died, I've been in a right state. Like a bad dream, it's been. I've got two kids and Davy's mum to keep, and even though I'm nearly twenty-six years old, I ain't done a single day's work for no one in the whole of me life. Never earnt a penny. But I've got this chance, Davy's stall. I thought it was gonna be easy, so I just went stumbling into it. But it wasn't. It was awful. Sodding, rotten, bloody awful.'

'It's hard work all right, even for a feller.'

'But it ain't just that, there's something else. People have been saying things to me. Bad things.'

'I don't know nothing about—'

'No, Jim, I ain't saying yer do. What I'm saying is that I'm gonna work really hard. I'm gonna make that stall work. I'm gonna show 'em all that yer can earn plenty from that sort o' work. And I just wanna say how really grateful I am to yer for offering to help me. But them fellers on Davy's pitch. I dunno, but I reckon they're real hard men. I'd hate to get yer involved in something like that.' She swallowed the last of her now cold tea. 'Specially as yer've got yer kids to think about.'

Jim stood up and flashed Cissie a warm, easy smile. 'You've been watching too many of them gangster films, ain't yer? Who d'yer think's after yer, Little Caesar?'

'I know yer probably think I'm just being a silly cow,' Cissie shrugged, embarrassed, 'and I'm sorry for going on, but since I lost my Davy everything feels like it's just getting on top of me. It's all been really getting me down.'

'I understand, love,' Jim reassured her, placing a comforting hand on her shoulder. 'Come on, let's get stuck in, eh?'

He ushered her out of the cafe and into the bright sunshine of the early morning. It promised to be yet another baking-hot day with not a sprinkle of rain to relieve the heat and humidity.

'You, Cissie,' he said with an encouraging smile, 'are about to learn the mysteries of the flower market.'

This time, as Cissie walked across the cobbles to the great cast-iron-and-glass hall, her reception was very different. She still got a few whistles and smart remarks, but at least she was shown respect by the sellers, taken seriously as a buyer rather than as a fool to be duped by the sharp-witted wholesalers. She could have kissed Jim with the relief of it all.

–

'Honestly, Jim, I can't tell you how grateful I am for all yer've done for me.' Cissie leant out of the truck window, reached down and touched him gently on the arm. 'Yer one of the good 'uns, d'you know that?'

'Don't worry about it, love.' Jim stepped away from her, back on to the pavement. 'Now go on. You get off home and I'll see yer in the morning bright and early to see how yer buy yer first lot of *proper* stock at the right prices. You remember what I told yer, yer don't have to take no old nonsense from none of this lot round here.'

'I won't have no trouble now I've got you looking out for me.' Cissie released the handbrake and pulled away.

Jim watched until the truck was out of sight, then he sprinted back into the market hall.

'Oi, Ginge!' he bellowed at a red-haired lad resting against a pile of crates. 'Get off yer lazy bleed'n arse and see to them customers. I'm gonna be gone for a couple of hours on a bit of business, and when I get back I don't wanna hear you've been slacking, right?'

–

As she made her way home in the truck, Cissie had the wonderful feeling that Jim really would be her saviour; he'd help her sort out all her problems, just as he had promised. He was going to take some of his friends round to the pitch right away, and explain to the two men that they should go elsewhere. The pitch would be cleared and she would be able to go there tomorrow morning, straight after she'd been to the market; she'd set up her stall, and everything would be fine. She just knew it.

After all, Jim was a decent feller. Just like her Davy.

–

Pausing only to get his breath, Jim pushed open the creaking cast-iron gate set in the chipped black railings and walked along the tiled path which led to the shabby street door of the tall three-storey house on the Mile End Road.

The net curtain at the ground-floor window twitched. Jim nodded almost imperceptibly. He stood there just a moment before the street door was opened.

A skinny, elderly man with a trilby hat jammed down firmly to his ears let him in. They didn't exchange a single word. Jim walked straight past him, along the passage and up a narrow flight of uncarpeted stairs. He knocked on the freshly painted door at the top, paused briefly, then went inside.

The room couldn't have presented a more unlikely contrast to the austere hall and stairway. With its sumptuous wood-panelled walls decorated with dark-hued sporting prints in heavy gilt frames, its thick carpets and heavy brocade curtains, it gave the impression more of the smoking room of a gentlemen's club in St James's than of the upstairs back room of a house in the East End.

A man was sitting behind a huge glass-topped walnut partners' desk, studying a newspaper. He took his time finishing what he was reading, slowly folded the paper, then looked up.

'Jim. So, how'd it go then?'

'Good, Mr Turner,' Jim said nervously. 'Good. She'll be all right with me sorting her out down the market. There won't be no problems there.'

'She'd better be all right.' Big Bill Turner took a leisurely puff from the cigar that had been balancing on the edge of a heavy crystal ash-tray. 'But it ain't only the market what interests me. Yer gonna make sure she's all right at the pitch and all. See, I'm interested in that little lady.'

'She mentioned something about some strange blokes getting down there. I said I'd go round today with some of me mates and see 'em off.'

'Strange? Is that what she called 'em?' Turner leant forward, folding his massive arms on the desk in front of him. 'I'll give 'em strange if they turn up again. They're working for that slag Plains.'

Jim gulped. Plains. Bloody hell. He had as bad a reputation as Turner. This was even worse than he'd thought. Why, out of all the blokes in the market, had Turner had to pick on him? It was just his luck he'd been having a beer with that arsehole Bernie Denham when this had all blown up. He didn't even like bloody Bernie. He was just a neighbour whose old woman, Queenie – a right dirty old sort, a moneylender who most people hated

– sometimes talked to his wife, Iris. Typical bloody Iris. She'd talk to anyone.

Turner laughed, a low, throaty rumble. 'Yer look like yer gonna shit yer pants, Jim,' he cackled, 'but there's no need. I've already sent some of the chaps round to speak to 'em this morning. See, your job is to keep an eye on Mrs Flowers for me. Make sure that little stall of her'n runs like clockwork. I'm intrigued by that pretty little widow, see. She's got guts. And I like that.'

He took another unhurried puff at his cigar. 'Makes a change,' he added, looking Jim up and down with unconcealed contempt, 'someone standing up for 'emselves. Anyway, you're gonna make sure she's all right, on the business side, and you're gonna make sure she don't know yer doing this for me. Is that clear?'

Jim nodded in reply. It was no use him trying to speak, his mouth was so dry it would have been pointless.

'I like it when people see things my way.' Turner leant back in his chair and linked his hands across his stomach.

'Your old woman ain't had no more trouble with broken windows, has she, Jim?'

Jim shook his head.

'Good. Cos I hate to see women getting upset, don't you?'

Chapter 12

'Jim. What can I say?' Cissie stood there, feeling like a spare, if grateful, part, as she watched Jim expertly manoeuvre the stall into place and then set about organising the flowers for her.

'All yer help at the market yesterday and today, and now yer helping me like this with the stall. Honest, I just dunno how to thank yer, showing me the ropes like this. Yer a really good bloke, d'you know that?'

'Someone wants to tell my old woman,' puffed Jim, as he started hauling the stacks of display vases from the storage compartment between the wheels.

Cissie flinched at the mention of Jim's wife. She didn't like to think of him as being a married man. Even though as far as Cissie could gather, based on the little he'd actually said about his wife, there didn't seem much love lost between them. In fact, Cissie had noticed that he could hardly bare to mention her name. But, all that apart, the realisation that she even thought about whether Jim had a wife or not still came as a surprise to Cissie. More than a surprise really. It was hard to admit, a bit shocking actually, but she cared about it a lot.

That terrible day, when Cissie had heard that Davy had been killed, she had just felt numb. If anyone had told her that she would ever expect to feel attracted to another man, ever again – never mind a scarce three months after her husband's death – she would have laughed in their face.

Perhaps it was because Jim was making it possible for her to begin her life again, she wondered. Perhaps. Or maybe it was nearer the truth to say that his fair-haired good looks and his gentle strength reminded her so much of Davy.

Jim straightened up, kneading his fists into his back. 'That's it then. Yer all set and ready to go.'

'Sorry, Jim, what did yer say? I was miles away for the minute.' Cissie could feel her cheeks flushing, as though he had the power to read her thoughts as clearly as if they had been printed on her forehead like the headlines on the evening paper.

'Well, yer'd better wake up, love, cos here comes yer first customer by the look of it.'

Jim began to walk away, as the young woman who had paused by the stall sniffed at a bunch of pale pink rosebuds.

'Say them blokes come back?' Cissie called after him, ignoring the potential sale in her sudden panic at being left alone.

'They won't,' Jim called without turning round. Then, thinking better of it, he stopped. He had been told to keep Cissie Flowers happy. If she started getting all worked up and upsetting herself, Turner might find out. Bloody Turner.

Looking at Cissie over his shoulder, Jim smiled and winked. 'I promise yer they won't, all right. And see that big bloke along there by the station? The one with the newspaper stand—'

'Yer mean Fat Stan?'

'Yer know him, do yer?' Jim asked, surprised. He hadn't expected that. Turner had said she'd no idea what had been going on at the pitch. And Stan hadn't said a thing when he'd had a word with him yesterday afternoon. This was all getting too much for Jim. Just who knew what and whom? It was all a bloody mix-up and he was in the sodding middle of it, and he didn't like it one little bit.

'I've met him before. Sort of,' she said with a throw-away little shrug. She didn't want Jim getting the wrong impression. Stan might have been fat and getting on for fifty, but she'd only been a widow for a few months after all.

'You know,' she went on with a self-deprecating smile, 'when I tried to do the stall by meself and mucked it all up. He was kind to me.'

Jim could feel the relief loosening his muscles. Perhaps she was as innocent as she made out. He hoped so, other-wise he feared he would find himself being drawn further and further into this whole rotten mess. And then who knew what he might get involved in? But, whatever he felt, Jim knew that Turner had given him instructions and, if he had any sense at all, he had better carry them out.

'Tell yer what, it looks like yer've lost yer customer anyway,' he said, lifting his chin towards the departing woman, 'so how about if we go along and have a quick word with Fat Stan? Make sure he keeps an eye out for any trouble?'

Cissie nodded, delighted that Jim was looking out for her.

As they neared the station entrance where Stan was pitched, a big, burly man came up and stood alongside the paper stand. But Cissie wasn't interested in him, she was interested in Fat Stan, or rather the state of Fat Stan's face.

Both of his eyes were blackened and swollen and he had a jagged cut running from one cheek to the other, right across his nose. He looked terrible, in a really bad way. 'Stan! Whatever's happened to yer?'

'This? This ain't nothing.' Fat Stan rolled what little could be seen of his eyes and tutted, dismissing her concern as completely uncalled for. 'I had a stupid accident on me way home from work last night, didn't I?'

Cissie moved closer, she went to reach out and run her finger along the distended contours beneath his eyes, to rub and kiss the pain better just as she would have done with the kids, but she didn't. It looked too horrible, and it would take more than a mother's touch to make that lot heal up.

She dropped her hand back to her side. 'How on earth did it happen?'

'Fell over, didn't I?'

'Yeah,' agreed his burly companion. 'Lucky I was there to save yer, weren't it, Stan?'

'Yeah, Bernie,' he agreed matily, 'right lucky.'

'It must have been some fall.' This time Cissie did reach out to him, but instead of his face, she laid her hand softly on his arm. 'And there was me being all selfish, I was calling you all sorts yesterday morning cos yer weren't here, d'you know that? All I could think of was why yer wasn't here to help me when I needed yer.'

She lent forward and said in a whisper, 'There was these two right horrible blokes here see, they thought they could take the pitch away from me.'

Cissie dropped her chin in shame. 'I'm sorry, I can be such a selfish cow at times.'

With her head bowed, Cissie didn't notice Jim mouthing a question to Fat Stan about what had happened, nor the aggressive look of warning that Bernie flashed at Jim in return.

When she looked up again, Fat Stan was smiling encouragingly at her, his puffy eyes reduced to slits. 'Yer don't wanna worry about a big ol' lump like me, girl. I'm all right. And it'd take more than a few bruises to put old Stan off his stroke. You just concentrate on running that stall o' your'n.'

'Talking of which, Cissie,' Jim interrupted, jerking his thumb back towards the stall. 'Yer never gonna make a living if yer don't start serving some of them customers.'

–

It was late Friday afternoon, the end of another relentlessly humid day.

'So,' Fat Stan called along to her. 'How's things?'

'All right, Stan. Yeah. Ta.' Cissie zipped her takings securely into her money apron, and walked over to him. 'And how are you? Yer face still healing up all right, is it? Sorry I ain't been along to see yer today, but I've been that run off me feet, I ain't had a chance.'

'Me boat's doing just fine, sweetheart,' Fat Stan answered, gingerly touching his cheek with his great pudgy fingers. 'But I tell yer what, this bleed'n heat's getting me down. I wasn't built for this sort o' weather, was I?'

'It could be snowing for all I care,' Cissie grinned. 'Cos I've done it, ain't I? I've run the stall for me first whole, complete week. All by meself!'

'Well done, girl,' Fat Stan congratulated her.

'Yeah, well done,' growled Bernie.

Cissie smiled her thanks at them both, but she really had to make the effort to act pleasantly towards Bernie. She couldn't put her finger on it but there was something about him that gave Cissie the creeps, and it wasn't just the fact that his big, bull's neck was wider than his head, it was his manner. He was over-confident, swaggering, vain. Horrible. And the way she caught him looking at her sometimes... She shuddered.

Still, it wasn't her business being worried about the likes of him, he was Fat Stan's friend, not hers, and she had better things to think about.

She'd done it. Cissie Flowers, with help from some very kind people, was making a living for her family!

–

Fat Stan hesitated at the top of the stairs, but Bernie ushered him forward with a wordless grunt. As he stepped tentatively into the office, he could sense Bernie right on his tail.

Sweat was beading on Fat Stan's forehead and upper lip, stinging his still-sore face. His shirt was soaked, and he felt like a damp dish-rag. But it wasn't just the almost unbearable humidity from the gathering storm clouds that was getting to him – Fat Stan was terrified.

'Yer wanted to see me, Mr Turner,' he mumbled, head lowered respectfully. He could feel Bernie's breath, hot on the back of his neck. He wished he'd just step back a little, give him a bit of space. He felt suffocated, knowing he was there behind him, looming over him, ready with those bastard fists of his.

Turner slowly propelled his chair around until he was facing Fat Stan. He took a long, unhurried puff on his cigar. 'That's right,' he said eventually. 'I did wanna see yer.'

He sniffed and looked Fat Stan up and down, appraising him slowly. 'I've been a bit busy this last week, but I just wanted yer in to say how I'm right disappointed in yer, Stan.'

'Disappointed?' Fat Stan didn't look round at them, but he was very aware of the two large men who, he could see at the edge of his vision, had come to stand on either side of him. He was surrounded. Neither they nor Bernie spoke, but he could sense that they were waiting attentively for instructions.

'How's that then, Mr Turner?' he asked, when the silence had grown too uncomfortable.

'Let me say, Stanley,' Turner went on, 'that I don't just mean disappointed, I mean *very* disappointed. Disappointed that yer left yer stand the other day, especially when yer knew that Mrs Flowers was gonna be there. She had a nasty shock, yer know, when she come across them two slags standing there on her pitch. I didn't like that. It got on me nerves.'

'But I had to go to the lav, Mr Turner. I had to—' Turner slammed back his chair and was on his feet, leaning across the desk. His finger was in Fat Stan's face. 'You had to do *nothing*. You *are* nothing. Not unless I tell yer. Right?'

He nodded feebly. 'Right, Mr Turner.'

'Good.' Turner sat back down. 'Now, if yer don't want another slap, you just remember that. And don't you let me catch yer leaving that little lady alone again. Right?'

'Right, Mr Turner.'

Turner smiled easily. 'Good. Good. And now, yer've got Bernie here and his mates to help yer, there should be no more trouble. Am I right?'

'Yer right, Mr Turner. Dead right.'

'Good, now bugger off, fat man.'

Stan turned to go.

'Wait.' Turner called him back. 'Here.'

Stan looked round, half expecting another chiv in the face or a fist in the guts, but instead Turner held out a thin roll of notes. 'Take yer missus out for a bit o' supper,' he said with a wink. 'I like to see the ladies kept happy, don't you, Stan? It makes life so much more pleasant.'

Fat Stan took the money and left the office as fast his bulging legs would carry him, muttering his thanks and apologies.

'So, Bernie, tell me, how's it going down there at Aldgate?'

'Good, Mr Turner. She's had plenty of customers all this week, I've seen to that.'

'Have yer?' Turner inclined his head in a gesture of. 'I like that.' He pointed his cigar at Bernie. 'You've got the right idea. You know how much that little lady means to me. Good.'

He considered for a moment, thoughtfully tapping the ashes from the end of his cigar. 'No more sign of Plains or his pet monkeys then?'

'I, er, bumped into one of 'em outside a boozer in Houndsditch on Tuesday, if yer get me meaning, Mr Turner. And I give him a little message for his guv'nor.'

Turner grinned. 'Did yer?' He sighed wistfully. 'I miss the old days, yer know, when I was out in the streets keeping order. It's all sodding bits o' paper and telephone calls nowadays.' He flicked idly at the tray full of letters and bills in front of him, then stubbed out the remains of his cigar. 'I'll have to come out with you chaps one night, keep me hand in, eh?'

Without waiting for a reply, Turner closed his eyes, leant back in his seat, folded his arms across his chest, and said, 'Now, before Mrs Turner picks me up, I've got a bit of business to see to with Bernie here, so clear off you two, and tell that mob downstairs to keep their noise down.'

The two silent heavies who had flanked Fat Stan so menacingly did as Turner told them without question, leaving the room surprisingly quietly for such big men.

It wasn't until they were at the bottom of the stairs that either of them spoke.

'I don't understand it, yer know,' said one of them, his voice a low rumble. 'That Turner's got himself obsessed with this Flowers woman. He does it every time. All right, this one's a looker, a real looker, but there's women round here what'd drop their drawers and fall flat on their backs if he so much as lifted his little finger at 'em.'

'It's the challenge, ain't it?' his big mate snarled philosophically. 'See, if yer've got girls ready to throw 'emselves at yer all the time, when one comes along what's a bit prim and proper like, it drives yer mad, dunnit. 'Specially when yer always used to having whatever takes yer fancy whenever yer fancy it. Taking no for an answer ain't something Turner understands, see.'

'Prim and proper,' the first man sneered sceptically. 'I reckon she's just playing games. Seeing how far she can push him. Keeping him panting for it, cos she knows she'll get more out of him in the long run. Tarts're like that.'

'I think it's a bigger mystery what keeps him with that old woman of his,' the other one sniggered.

'You telling me yer really don't know?' his companion asked, with a surprised lift in his voice.

'Know what?'

The other man looked over his shoulder, checking that they couldn't be overheard. 'Now that Moe is a lady who definitely enjoys playing games. Right peculiar sort o' games and all if yer get me drift. Games that the guv'nor really loves to play.'

'What sort o' games would they be then?'

'For Gawd sake, you fresh off the boat or something?' He leant close to him and whispered something in his ear.

The loud rumble of the other man's lewd laughter echoed through the uncarpeted passageway.

–

Back upstairs, Turner was making Bernie sweat buckets, asking him all sorts of questions about Cissie Flowers and what she'd been doing during the last week and a half.

Bernie had always been a willing worker in the past, a man who would use a chiv or a set of brass knuckles on his boss's orders without a second thought, but all this stuff about what some bloody tart was getting up to on a sodding flower stall, well, it was enough to shame a man. He had just about had enough of being a rotten nursemaid.

–

'Hello, Glad,' Cissie called as she stepped into number four. 'It's only me.'

'Hello, Cis.' Gladys was at the stove, stirring a big pot of stew – not the right sort of food for such muggy weather, but the sort of food that could be stretched to feed a hungry, growing family.

'Where's me babies then?'

'They're all right,' Gladys said, resting the dripping wooden spoon across the top of the pan, 'they're out the backyard with Nipper and Ernie. Having a right old time they are, messing about with them rotten pigeons. Leave 'em for a minute and sit yerself down. I'll make us a quick cuppa before I call 'em in.'

'I could certainly murder a drop o' tea.' Cissie sat at the table, kicked off her shoes and, very tenderly, she massaged her calves and ankles. 'Gimme a chance to catch me breath before I have to go over and look at Lil's smiling face.'

'Feet aching?' Gladys asked over her shoulder as she filled the kettle.

'You ain't wrong there.' Cissie laughed mockingly at herself. 'I ain't used to hard work, that's my trouble.'

'Don't go knocking yerself, Cissie Flowers,' said Gladys, busying herself getting the tea things ready, 'yer've done yerself proud this week, I reckon.'

'Do yer?' Cissie was chuffed with her friend's praise.

'Yes, I do. Well done, girl.'

'I've earnt a bit and all, yer know.'

'Good luck to yer. You deserve it.'

'And you deserve this.' Cissie stood up and dug into her pocket. 'Here, Glad,' she said going over to the stove. 'It's just to show me appreciation for all yer've done for me.'

'Thirty bob!'

'I know it won't go far with a family your size,' Cissie apologised. 'But—'

'Yer daft mare,' Gladys interrupted her. 'I ain't gonna take no money off yer. I'm helping yer with the kids cos I'm yer mate.'

'But I really have done all right.' Cissie shrugged. 'I ain't sure how, or why, but they've been buying flowers off me like I was giving 'em away or something. I ain't never seen so many buggers buying flowers. I've earnt enough to get plenty of new stock, make ends meet indoors and, honestly Glad, that thirty bob's for you.'

'Listen to me, Cissie,' Gladys said, pouring them both some tea. 'I'll take money off you when yer've got a chain o' flower stalls right across the East End, all right? But until then, you keep it where it belongs, in yer purse. You've got enough to do.'

'Well, yer'll have to let me bring some food in then. Yer can't keep feeding my two for nothing.'

'I'll be truthful, I wouldn't say no to that, Cis.'

'Good, and how about if yer let me treat us both to the flicks tonight? I'll have to ask old happy cods first, but if I buy her a few bottles of light ale—'

'Don't worry about asking Lil,' said Ernie who had just appeared in the back doorway. 'Gladys could do with getting out for a few hours. Me and Nipper'll see to the kids.'

'Would you, Ern? Smashing!' Cissie, her tiredness forgotten, was now looking forward to her evening out. 'How about that new Paul Muni film?'

'Bloody hell, Cis, do us a favour. That's the last thing I wanna do. Can't we see a nice musical? Something cheerful?'

'It'll have to be down the fleapit then, Glad.'

'We've done worse,' smiled Gladys.

'And better! Remember when me and Davy and you two went up West to that supper club? Me and Davy'd only been married about six months. All cased up we was. They was the days, eh?'

'This sounds like girls' talk to me,' said Ernie, stepping back out into the yard. 'I'll go and finish out there while you two drink yer tea.'

–

Cissie was back over at Gladys's within the hour, washed, changed and excited. It was the first time she had been out in months. Lil had been appeased with a few bob to see her through another evening at the Sabberton Arms, so there was no worry there. And Matty and Joyce, who had had their tea and been changed into their night things so they could bunk in with their little friends, were both lookingto this new adventure.

As for Gladys, she had cleared up after her mob had demolished their stew, had combed her hair, and had swiped a lick of lipstick across her full, smiling mouth.

Cissie and Gladys were as ready as they'd ever be for their night out together.

'See yer, girls,' Ernie called to them from the front door of number four, as they swung away along the street, 'and don't do nothing I wouldn't do.'

'Well,' Gladys called back over her shoulder, 'that gives us plenty of choices, don't it!' Then she leant close to Cissie and whispered something.

As one, they both stopped, turned round and called out, 'Night-night, Lena!'

'Don't wait up for us tonight, will yer?' Cissie added with a saucy grin. 'Cos we all know yer need yer beauty sleep. We'll report to yer in the morning with all the details.'

They were both still giggling at the look on Lena's face as they turned out of Upper North Street into the East India Dock Road.

'We've had some good times, ain't we, Glad?'

'We have that, Cis.'

'But who'd have thought we'd have wound up like this, eh?' she asked wistfully.

'Hark at you. You're doing all right for yerself, ain't yer?' Gladys could have bitten her tongue. 'Sorry, Cis, I didn't mean to say that. It's just that I still forget sometimes.'

'Don't worry, Glad. I'm the same. I still can't believe Davy ain't gonna stick his head round that kitchen door, start teasing the kids and pinching me bum and messing.' She looked away. 'I don't half miss him.'

'I know, love.'

She turned back to face her friend. 'And I know yer do, Glad, and that's why I'm so pleased we're mates again. It was like losing another one of me family when we wasn't talking.'

Gladys squeezed her arm.

'I'm sorry about the way I've behaved, Gladys, right sorry.'

'Daft, what've you gotta be sorry for?'

'Being a selfish cow? Only thinking about meself? Not seeing that other people have worries of their own? How about them to start with?'

Gladys shrugged. 'You never *had* to worry about nothing before. So why should yer? And anyway, I wouldn't have wished my worries on no one. And, let's face it, Cis, you're the one who's really gone through it lately.'

'But I ain't a kid, am I? I should have realised. I could've been a bit more, I dunno, understanding about how other people was having to get by.'

'I'd have been the same if I was in your position.'

'No yer wouldn't, Glad, and you know it. Still, all that's gonna change. I know what it's like now, having to earn me living, don't I?' She laughed happily to herself. 'Makes yer sodding knackered, don't it!'

Before Gladys had the chance to agree, a sudden, violent clap of thunder had them clasping wildly at each other. 'Bloody hell, Glad, that's God after me for bloody swearing!'

The rain started coming down in big fat drops, drying on to the baking-hot paving stones almost the instant it fell.

'Come on, Cissie, run!' Gladys shouted, dragging her along by the elbow. 'We're gonna get soaked.'

'Tell yer what,' puffed Cissie, jerking her friend to a halt outside the Star of the East, 'let's sod the pictures, eh? Let's go in here and have a drink.'

Gladys, eyes wide at the thought of going into a pub without Ernie, and in the Eastern of all places, held her hand up to her mouth. 'We can't, Cis.'

'Go on. Course we can.'

Casting caution to the wind, Gladys grinned. 'All right. Why not? But not this near home. Let's find another one, eh?'

'Yeah, come on then.' Cissie grabbed her hand. 'Here, wouldn't Lena love to see this? Us roaming the streets looking for a boozer!'

As though they hadn't a care in the world between them, Cissie and Gladys started running along in the pouring rain, laughing and giggling like a pair of school-girls.

–

The door to Turner's office opened. No one had knocked. It was Moe, Bill Turner's wife. She eyed Bill and Bernie suspiciously.

'Don't let me stop yer talking. And don't pretend yer wasn't neither. I could hear the pair of yers chatting away nine to the dozen when I was coming up them stairs.'

Bernie shuffled backwards towards the door, not fancying the idea of waiting around for Moe's reaction if she had actually heard that they were talking about Turner's latest bit of stuff. She was a woman with a spiteful reputation. And while Bernie played away as much as any other feller, more than most when he came to think of it, he didn't hold with broadcasting it when his wife could hear. In fact, it wasn't the sort of thing he thought a feller should talk about at all. That was women's business, talking.

'What's the matter with yer, Bernie?' Turner snapped. 'Take Mrs Turner's coat for her. Can't yer see she's wet through?'

Bernie moved across the room to do as he was told. Either Turner was convinced Moe hadn't heard them, or he was playing it very casual. He must be barmy either way. Everyone knew what Moe Turner could do when she got the mood on her, and no one would dare even defend themselves, let alone retaliate. It was a real mystery to most people – discussed only when Turner was well out of earshot, of course – why he put up with the old cow. Suggestions ranged from the practical, to do with money and the like, to the downright obscene stories about his and Moe's little 'games' which circulated amongst some of the more loose-tongued members of Turner's workforce.

But Bernie had never got involved with that sort of talk. It wasn't his concern. Thank goodness. And right now he was too busy, trying to take her coat off her without offending her, even to be bothered wondering what attractions she held for Turner. But taking the coat wasn't an easy task. Moe Turner could be upset very easily, and she wouldn't stand still; she was pacing about like a caged cat.

'It's coming down out there like it's the sodding Flood,' she fumed, waving her arms about and spraying the desk with raindrops. 'I only walked up the path from the motor and look at me.' Moe glared accusingly at Turner. 'Them blokes of your'n ain't got a brain between them, Bill. Not one of 'em had a sodding umbrella ready for me. What do they do down there all day? Pick their teeth?'

Bernie dodged around behind her, eventually managing to slip her coat from her shoulders without too much fuss.

Moe didn't thank him, she just sat herself down by Turner's desk, took a cigarette from the silver art deco box standing next to the ivory humidor, and waited for Bernie to light it.

She took a long drag and blew a plume of lavender smoke up towards the ceiling. 'Right,' she said, staring up after it, 'piss off, you, I wanna talk to me husband. And mind you hang that coat o' mine up properly. Cashmere that is, not some old bit of schmutter from down the Lane.'

As Bernie quietly closed the door and crept off down the stairs, the thunder cracked as though the sky were about to split open, so he didn't hear Moe come over and lock the door behind him. Even if he had, he couldn't possibly have envisioned the strangeness of the scene that was about to take place inside the office.

Without a word, Moe came round and took Turner's place at his desk, lowering her bulky frame into the big leather chair, while he went round the other side and stood, head bowed, in front of her.

The hard-headed, violent-tempered Big Bill Turner lifted his chin a little and spoke, in a high, faltering voice, the opening lines of his confession about his desire for Cissie Flowers.

Moe rose slowly to her feet again, keeping her eyes fixed on his.

Turner's whole body began to shudder with anticipation; he was now ready, ready to begin the game, ready to be punished for misbehaving...

Chapter 13

During the next couple of months, Cissie not only found herself getting better at running the stall, but she also found herself beginning to find a real pleasure in being able to do something positive and useful for her family. And she was proud of herself, proud of what she had learnt and what she had achieved. It hadn't been easy, but she had done it.

She'd learnt which flowers her customers preferred; that Thursday and Friday, with their wage packets and bonuses, were good days with plenty of custom, but that it wasn't even worth setting up on a Monday; and she'd learnt that Saturdays could be really variable, because the offices and local sweat shops were mostly closed, and even with the passing trade, it still didn't amount to enough to merit her being apart from the children for another day.

Cissie had even tried setting up on a couple of Sundays, but had soon found out that there was too much cut-price competition from the wide boys in the nearby Lane, selling off their bright, if overblown, blooms, to warrant even thinking about it as a sensible proposition.

And then there was the Covent Garden market. The lesson Cissie had learnt there was that it was important not only to put up with the banter and ribbing she was nearly always subjected to – even if at such an early hour she felt more like yawning and scratching than chatting and having a ready smile – but that she might as well look forward to having a laugh with the other flower sellers and wholesalers, and even enjoy a bit of a flirt with them. Because that was what made the world of the market turn around, and her taking part in it helped her to be accepted as 'one of the lads' rather than as a 'snooty cow' who couldn't take a joke.

Her new-found wisdom about joining in with the wisecracking wasn't always a complete success, however. There was one morning when she could have kicked herself for being quite so quick with her witty answers. Jim had turned up unexpectedly, leaving his stand to see how she was getting on; she would normally have been delighted to see him, but he had appeared at the very moment when she was exchanging a particularly saucy bit of backchat with one of the porters. When Jim tapped her on the shoulder and she turned round to see that it was him standing there, she'd blushed like a schoolgirl on a first date and had started stammering out some old nonsense about what she thought she was up to, her explanations only serving to make matters worse.

She really hated the idea of Jim seeing her fooling around like that. She wanted him to take her seriously, to like her as a person, not as a loud-mouthed tart, chatting up barrow-boys.

Her feelings towards Jim made her so unsettled. There they all were, all the old feelings, buzzing around her head and her body, all coming bubbling back to the surface. Feelings that told her, and warned her, that she could really get to like Jim, like him in an even stronger sense than her initial physical attraction to him had warned her of. But, she constantly had to remind herself, Jim was married, out of bounds. And even if he didn't get on with his wife, he still wasn't single. And he had kids.

But it wasn't as straightforward as that, things never were. The trouble was, she was beginning to miss having a husband in many more ways than one. In ways that made her blush to think of.

Such awkward moments apart, Cissie was really beginning to act like her old self again. Even with autumn taking hold, and the mornings growing darker and damper by the day, she still leapt out of bed, raring to go. Some mornings she actually found herself throwing off the eiderdown and looking forward to what the day had in store for her, before she even remembered what had happened and felt the familiar pain of seeing the empty pillow beside her.

Gladys had been right. It was getting better, day by day. She would never lose the pain, Cissie was sure of that, but she *would* find it easier to deal with. Just as she was sure that no matter what another man had to offer, he would never ever be able to replace what she felt for Davy.

Cissie had a lot to be grateful for. Particularly for being lucky enough to have a friend like Gladys, who had played such an important part in her making so much headway in getting her life sorted out. She had proved to be an invaluable help, having really come up trumps with the children, and now Matty had started school, and Gladys's older ones could escort him back and forth, the arrangements were even simpler.

Lil, never a woman who could be described as having a sunny disposition, was still a bit of a fly in the ointment, usually managing to find something or other to complain about when Cissie came home in the afternoons, but Cissie now felt strong enough just to put that down to Lil being Lil, and to accept that there was nothing she, or anyone else, could do about it.

Cissie's only concern, as far as she was concerned, was the matter of the occasional visit from the two men who had tried to take over the pitch on behalf of Mr Plains – a man she had since heard from one of the porters was definitely not someone to be messed with.

But even they seemed to present no real problem, not with Fat Stan and Bernie being there. Also, Stan seemed to have a group of friends, all built like Bernie and just as scary-looking, who appeared as if by magic whenever things looked as though they might prove a bit tricky. That way, any threats or skirmishes were soon dealt with and Cissie was left to sell her flowers and get on with her life, safe in the knowledge that she had good friends looking out for her.

Cissie was a fortunate woman, and she knew it. She'd got herself some high-spending regular customers and was now bringing home enough to pay herself almost as much as Davy had given her for the weekly housekeeping. She was not only making ends meet, but was now in a position where she could insist that Gladys should take something for her help.

Gladys had, of course, refused point-blank when she had tried to give her the envelope with the three pound notes in it, just as she had refused the thirty shillings Cissie had tried to give her before. But Cissie knew that things in the Mills' household weren't improving – if anything, they were getting worse. Gladys had even talked about following Elsie Collier's example and taking in lodgers, but what with having five children and old Nipper living with them, there was barely enough room to sleep the family let alone to make room for strangers.

So Cissie had insisted on paying Gladys what she genuinely saw as her debts – just as she had insisted that Sammy Clarke should start taking a weekly amount from her so that she could pay back what she owed him as well.

Sammy had been as adamant as Gladys that Cissie had no reason to pay him anything, but Cissie, in her newly found role as a working woman, had become someone who didn't relish being in debt to anybody. She would take help, and be grateful for it, but she would pay her way.

She had taken particular pleasure in paying Brownlow every single copper she owed him, and had just stared down her nose contemptuously at him when he had made more of his filthy remarks and suggestions.

Over the weeks, Cissie had done her best to try to find out who had given her the twenty pounds that she still believed had appeared anonymously on the doormat, wanting to pay them back too, but no one would admit to knowing anything about it.

It had probably been Sammy after all, she had decided, no matter how he protested that it wasn't, and so had added the twenty pounds to the total that she was gradually repaying him as she slowly got herself back on her feet.

It still would have been nice, she couldn't help thinking, to have earnt just a little bit more. She knew she *shouldn't* have thought like that, especially when she compared her life to that of so many others who were having to scrape by. But it wasn't for luxuries. Both the children were growing fast and clothes and shoes didn't come cheap. And what with winter on the way, there were winter coats and coal to be bought. Then there was Christmas to start thinking about, and, although trade was more than reasonable for the time of year, flowers were getting expensive, even at wholesale prices.

It was with all that in the back of her mind that Cissie could, at first, hardly believe her latest bit of luck when, one chilly October morning, a big, shiny car drove slowly past and then pulled in at the kerbside outside St Botolph's Church. The driver got out and came over to speak to her.

'How much for everything yer've got?' he asked, pointing carelessly in the general direction of the stall.

Cissie hesitated. But even after thinking for a moment, all she managed to say was: 'What, everything?'

The man repeated himself.

Raising her hands in a gesture of total bewilderment, Cissie swung round and surveyed her stock. 'What, *everything*?'

'Blimey, you a bit slow or something?'

She turned back to face him again. 'I'd have to add it all up.'

'Well go on then,' he snapped impatiently.

'You sure you mean everything?'

'For Gawd sake, woman.' The man stepped round her and jabbed his finger at a bucket of mop-headed bronze chrysanthemums. 'Start with them. How much for that lot?'

Cissie Was so flustered, she couldn't think straight. 'I'd only ever sold 'em by the bunch before.'

The man slapped his forehead with his palm. 'Well how many bunches are in the sodding bucket?' His voice was growing louder.

Cissie was beginning to feel alarmed. Why was this man shouting at her?

She glanced sideways, checking that Fat Stan was there by the station entrance. Relieved to see that he was, and that he had Bernie with him, Cissie flashed a thin smile at her potential customer; he might be strange, but she couldn't turn her nose up at the sort of money he was talking about. And if she did flog him everything, she could get off home early and save Gladys having to cook tea for the kids.

'If yer don't mind waiting a minute,' she said politely, 'I'll get some paper. I'll write it down, and work it all out proper like. Would that be all right for yer?'

'Yeah.' The man snatched a quick look in the direction of the car. 'But yer'd better make sure it is only a minute. I'm in a hurry.'

'One minute,' Cissie assured him and dashed across to Stan.

'Stan,' she whispered urgently. 'Quick, give us a bit of paper to write on. Anything'll do. I've got a real live one over there. Only wants to buy all me flowers, don't he!'

'Good for you, sweetheart,' Stan congratulated her, tearing a sheet of paper from a small note-pad and handing it over.

'Ta, Stan, you're a mate,' she said, practically snatching it from him. She was in so much of a hurry that she didn't notice the surreptitious look that Fat Stan and Bernie flashed at one another then at the car.

As she rushed back to her customer – surely, the customer of all time? – Cissie was sure she heard Bernie laugh and call after her something about betting slips, but she was too concerned with keeping the big spender happy to stop to ask him what he meant.

'Right,' she smiled, puffing as much from excitement as from the effort of running the few yards between her and Fat Stan's pitches. 'Let's get this written down.'

She rested the paper on the edge of the flower stall and smoothed it out, ready to begin her reckoning. Her smile vanished. 'Here, you ain't got a pencil, have yer?'

'What's going on over there?' someone called from behind them. 'Can't you even run a little errand? I only wanted the bleed'n flowers.'

Cissie and the man both spun round.

It was Big Bill Turner. He was standing by the open rear door of the big black car, leaning on the wing. His arms were folded and he looked fed up and angry.

'We was, er, having a bit of trouble like, working out the price,' the man explained.

'Just get yerself back in that motor, Jack,' Turner said, jerking his thumb over his shoulder as he walked over to the stall. 'Go on, move yerself. Before I lose me temper. And send Chalkie over here.'

Jack seemed only too pleased to do as he was told. He quickly disappeared into the driver's seat and slammed the door firmly behind him.

Another man slipped out of the front passenger door, and went to stand silently by Turner's side.

Turner took his wallet from the inside pocket of his overcoat without even acknowledging the man's presence.

He counted out fifteen large white notes. 'Seventy-five quid fair, d'yer reckon?'

'I don't understand.' Cissie instinctively backed away from him until she was pressed hard against the stall. 'Why're yer doing this?'

'Are these flowers for sale or ain't they?'

'Yeah, but why d'yer want 'em? Why d'yer want so many?'

Turner slapped the money down beside Cissie. 'Seventy-five quid.'

He raised his chin at the man by his side. 'Chalkie, help the lady wrap 'em up. And don't take too long about it. Yer know how I get if I'm kept waiting.'

With that, he turned on his heel and headed back to the car. He ducked his head as though he were about to get in, then, thinking better of it, he straightened up again. 'I'll be round to pick you up at about eight,' he said matter-of-factly.

'You talking to me?' Cissie asked, tapping herself on the chest.

'Sod me,' Turner gasped, 'no wonder Jack was taking so long. I ain't never heard a bird ask so many bloody questions. Yes, I mean you. I'm taking yer to a supper club. Up West. So make sure yer wear something nice. I like a bird to look classy.'

He pointed at the pile of notes. 'Buy yerself something outta that if you ain't got nothing decent.'

Cissie shook her head at him as though he were mad. 'I ain't going to no club with no one. And especially not with the likes o' you, I ain't.'

'Eh?' Turner walked slowly back to the stall. 'I don't think I heard yer right.'

'Yes yer did. You heard all right.'

Turner's face flared the colour of port. 'Chalkie. In.' He stabbed his finger at the car.

'How about the flowers, guv?'

'In,' Turner repeated savagely.

Chalkie did as he was told.

'Is this cos I ain't been around for a few weeks?' he asked. 'You showing off or something?'

'Are you mad?' Cissie shook her head in wonder at the man's arrogance.

'I've been busy,' Turner went on. 'Doing some big deals. Important business. Sorting a few things out.'

'Why should I care what you've been up to?'

'You saying you ain't noticed I ain't been around?'

'That's right.'

Turner looked at Cissie with a final indignant frown, then without saying another word, he followed Chalkie back to the car.

'Yer forgot yer money,' Cissie called, snatching up the pile of fivers and dashing after him.

'Keep the sodding money,' snapped Turner and slammed the car door in her face.

Cissie stood and watched as the car sped away in the direction of Mile End, then walked slowly back to the stall.

'Everything all right?' Fat Stan shouted across to her.

'Yeah,' said Cissie absently, as she shoved the notes deep into her money apron. 'I'm fine thanks, Stan.'

But she wasn't fine, her mind was in turmoil as she thought of all the things she could do with seventy-five pounds. She tried to weigh them against what the cost of taking it would actually be; Turner had made it quite clear the price he had in mind.

'Stan,' she called across to the news-vendor, 'I'm packing up early today. Something's come up.'

'You sure everything's all right?'

'Yeah. Just a bit of business. I've gotta go and see someone.'

Cissie had the stall back at the lock-up in record time, and within an hour of saying goodbye to Fat Stan, she was standing at the door to Eileen's grubby room.

'Please, Eileen, it's too much to put in the post. Please, take it round there for me. So's I can be sure he's got it. I don't want him thinking I've kept it, or he'll be able to hold it over me.'

Eileen shook her head even more determinedly. 'No. I told yer. I'll help anyone if they're in trouble, but I ain't gonna humiliate meself.'

'Humiliate yerself?' Cissie frowned. 'I don't under-stand.'

'No, your sort never do. Yer've still got the sort of looks that mean yer don't have to understand no one but yerself.' Eileen stepped on to the little landing and pulled the door to behind her. She stared at Cissie with a booze-blurred glare. 'How would it be, eh, just you think about it, me going round there looking like this, running errands for you? I'd look a right pissing idiot. Make it look like that was all I was fit for.'

She lit herself a cigarette without offering one to Cissie, and started laughing, which soon degenerated into a raw smoker's cough. 'I reckon being selfish goes with being pretty, d'you know that? I was the same meself once, when

I first went with Bill. Couldn't give a monkey's about no one, I couldn't.'

Cissie had the good grace to look ashamed. She'd done it again, thinking only of herself. When would she ever learn?

'Now,' Eileen said, 'if yer don't mind, yer'll have to shift yerself. I've got a friend in there waiting for me, and I ain't in the position to say no to a few bob.'

–

Cissie stood by the black chipped railings, knowing she was being watched from behind the net curtains.

She stuck her chin defiantly in the air and strode purposefully up to the door.

This time no one waited to be asked, she was shown straight to Turner's office.

'Aw, yer've brought me flowers round, have yer?' Turner asked, with a sarcastic lift in his voice. 'I didn't know yer did a delivery service.'

'I've brought you yer money back,' Cissie said levelly, laying seventy pounds on the desk in front of him. 'I kept back a fiver to cover the earnings yer've lost me this afternoon.'

Turner grinned appreciatively. 'I meant what I said about liking the idea of having a pretty woman on me arm when I go out of a night. But I like the idea of having a clever one who ain't afraid to use her brains even more. Makes things more interesting don't it, having something to talk about afterwards?'

'What would yer wife have to say if she could hear the filth you talk?' asked Cissie, shaking her head in disgust.

'Mrs Turner don't enjoy the social life like she used to.'

Cissie leant across the desk at him. 'What, and I suppose she don't understand yer any more either, does she?'

'That's where you're wrong, sweetheart. She understands me very well. Very well indeed, actually. In fact, it was something she said to me the other day, in this very office if yer wanna know, what's convinced me I should improve me offer to yer.'

Cissie straightened up. 'What d'yer mean?' she asked suspiciously.

Turner leant back in his chair, folded his arms and stared directly into her eyes. 'I've just completed a very nice deal, got a good few quid going spare I have. So Mrs Turner thought we could invest it in a bit o' property like. That's why I'm gonna set you up in a little flat, Mrs Flowers.' Cissie's mouth dropped open. It took her a moment before she could speak. 'You're out of your head,' she finally managed to say. With that, she turned round and strode over to the door, using every bit of her strength to stop herself screaming abuse at this vile man.

'You'll come round to my way of thinking, you just see,' Turner said to her back, as she grasped the brass door handle. 'People always do. And a clever girl like you wouldn't waste your special type of assets running a poxy little flower stall. Not unless you was a fool, of course.' She didn't even look round at him.

–

Cissie parked the truck on the waste ground at the end of Linman Street, and climbed down from the cab. She was worn out. The traffic back from Mile End had been murder, then she'd had to stop to fill up at the petrol

station, and had got her dress covered in grease after struggling with the starting handle – much to the amusement
of the young lad who was working the pump.

Then, as she locked the truck door, just to put the
final touch to a rotten afternoon, she heard them: Ethel
and Myrtle, standing on Myrtle's street doorstep, were
gossiping loudly about her. That was all she needed, that
pair running her down.

Ethel nudged Myrtle. 'My Lena's Reg heard from
someone that that Cissie Flowers has been to see that Big
Bill Turner again, yer know.'

'She never has!'

'True as I'm standing here.'

'The brazen trollop.'

'I'd love to see that Moe Turner get hold of her if she
found out that her old man was sniffing around her. Little
whore. It's about time she was brought down a peg or two.
Walking about like a painted doll. Her old man's barely
cold in the ground.'

Cissie put her keys in her pocket, took a deep breath,
and took the few steps from the waste ground to Myrtle's
street door.

She stood in front of the pair of them, hands on hips
and said, in a quiet, controlled voice, 'Has your Lena
thought about asking her Reg where he heard that, Ethel?'

'Eh?' Ethel's face was like stone.

'Well, I reckon the answer might interest her. See,' she
said turning to Myrtle, 'as far as I know, the only one who
knew where I was going was an old brass.'

Cissie turned back to Ethel. 'She wants to be careful,
that big-mouthed daughter o' your'n, or she'll wind up
with a dose.'

'You filthy-minded little—'

'Just shut yer trap for once, can't yer, Ethel?' Cissie sneered.

'Don't you talk to her like that,' put in Myrtle, torn between standing up for her friend and having the chance to hear a bit more dirt about Reg Dunn. 'If anyone should've found out what her husband was up to, it should've been *you*, Cissie Flowers.'

'What?'

'You heard. She said you,' chipped in Ethel. 'I mean, he earnt a lot o' money from being a so-called flower seller, that old man o' your'n, didn't he? Ain't you ever wondered how?'

Cissie shook her head contemptuously. 'You make me sick, d'you know that? Don't think I ain't heard all the nasty little rumours and stories your sort put around, cos I have. And that's all they are, rumours and bloody stupid stories. And all cos the likes of you are jealous. Jealous cos my Davy did so well for himself and his family. And now jealous cos I'm doing it too. So don't think you can get me at it with all your old shit.' She held up her head and stabbed her finger at them. 'You hate it, don't yer, me showing you all that I can do it and all. That's what's wrong with yers. I know. Yer can't stand it, can yer? Any of yer.'

Cissie turned her back on the pair of them and marched along the street towards Gladys's. She was determined not to cry in front of the two old bags, but that didn't stop the pain their words were causing her. Why did they have to be so spiteful?

'I'm doing well on the stall,' she said to herself, 'I am. I'm doing well enough to be able to give that pig Turner his seventy pounds back. And to be able to tell him what he can do with his so-called "offer".'

The first angry tear spilt on to Cissie's cheek just as she stepped inside Gladys's street door. But although she was crying, Cissie Flowers was also smiling.

She was doing it. She was making a success of caring for her family. And Davy would be proud of her. She had shown them all. Even if they couldn't stand it.

Chapter 14

'Ta, love.' Cissie handed the man his bunch of flowers and a rattle of loose change. 'See yer next week,' she added with a confident, happy smile.

'You're looking pleased with yerself, girl,' said Fat Stan as he strolled over to her and then leant back against the wall, all the while concentrating on the cigarette he was rolling in his great, sausagey fingers.

'Why shouldn't I look pleased on a smashing day like this, eh, Stan? Friday dinner-time's always good for business. The sun's shining more like it's the middle of June rather than the end of October. And I'm getting more and more customers what're coming back regular.'

She jerked her head at the man who was filtering his way back into the busy lunch-time crowds. 'Blokes like him. He's back twice every week.'

She lowered her eyes and giggled girlishly. 'Must have a wife *and* a bit on the side. What d'yer reckon?'

Fat Stan sealed his cigarette with a lick along the paper and joined in with the amusement, his deep bear's growl of a laugh making his chins wobble.

'Yer know,' Cissie sighed contentedly, 'I never thought I'd be doing this well, Stan. 'Specially not at this time o' the year.'

She turned round and appraised the stall. 'Good stock, I suppose. That Jim Phillips does me right proud at the market. I dunno what I'd have done without him. Really looks after me, he does.'

'Good. I'm glad to hear it, girl.' And he was. Fat Stan nodded approvingly, more than relieved that things were, at last, going along so nicely. Because if Cissie Flowers was happy, then so was Turner, and – at the end of that little line – so was he.

He flicked his spent match into the gutter and left Cissie to deal with two men who had paused to look over the stall.

They were youngish, but not too young, and smartly dressed; City-looking types, good for spending a few bob at the end of the week, Cissie judged.

'How can I help you, gentlemen?' she asked pleasantly. 'These camellias are lovely. Not cheap, mind,' she added. She'd learnt a fair bit about how to sell, and expensively rigged-out fellers like these two wouldn't want to be seen looking mean in front of one another. 'Fancy one do yer? I could put it in a nice little box, if it's for someone special like.'

'We ain't interested in no flowers, darling,' said one of them in a surprisingly rough, East End drawl. 'We're here as representatives. For a firm of property developers. And we've got a bit of news for yer. News you might not like very much, but I'd advise yer to listen all the same.'

Cissie pulled her brows together in a puzzled frown. Property developers? What was this all about?

'This here factory's gonna be pulled down, and they're gonna build offices on the site. Right *modern* offices they'll be.' As he said the word 'modern' the man's voice took on a loving, cooing sort of tone. 'With *smart* little shops on the ground floor.'

'But what about me pitch?' Cissie turned her head and looked at the soot-blackened factory wall, the velvet backdrop to the jewelled colours of her flowers.

'Selling flowers off o' barrows is a thing of the past, darling,' he said with a sniff. 'Like all the slums what they're ripping down. People want smart, modern things nowadays, not street rubbish.'

Smart, modern. He was saying those words again. And what did he mean by 'rubbish'?

'There won't be no places for the likes of you and your stall, sweetheart,' he said as though reading the question in her mind. 'That's the way o' the world, I'm afraid.'

He shrugged his broad shoulders down into his expensively warm overcoat. 'These might be hard times for some,' he went on, with the combined cockiness of youth and power, 'but there's still plenty what're doing well for 'emselves. Very well. People who can buy up land *nice and cheap* at a time like this.'

Cissie hated the way he kept emphasising the words, there was such menace in his horribly assured tone, and she hated the way his companion stood there next to him, smiling feebly in what looked like slightly scared silence.

She looked along the street towards Fat Stan, but he and Bernie were both busy, their heads bent low as they talked to two other men.

She licked her lips, her mouth was parched. 'You said you was representing someone.'

'Yeah.'

'So, who's yer boss then?' She had intended to sound forceful, in control, but her voice had come out squeaking and trembling like a frightened child's.

Trying to recover at least a bit of dignity, she added with an impetuosity she immediately regretted, 'Whoever he is, he'd better watch out for himself, cos I've got friends, yer see, powerful friends. And you can tell him, whoever he is, that that come straight from me.'

The man who had done all the talking appeared amused by her pathetic attempt at bravado, but the quiet one just dug into the inside pocket of his overcoat and handed Cissie a card.

'That's our boss,' said the chatty one, 'on that card he's given yer. But I dunno what good knowing that's gonna do yer. I'd just get used to the idea if I was you, darling. Cos all this is gonna be settled by the New Year, no matter how *powerful* your little friends are.'

He smiled again, almost politely this time, then they both raised their hats and left her standing, gawping after them.

She stood there in shocked silence until Fat Stan hollered across to her.

'You all right, girl?' he shouted. 'Yer look like yer've just lost a tanner and found a farthing.'

'Fancy asking Bernie to mind the stalls for a bit and coming over to the Tuns for a drink, Stan?' Cissie asked, keeping her eyes on the two men as they dodged across the road towards Mansell Street, the noisy one slowing an oncoming truck almost to a halt with an arrogant lift of his hand.

'It's a bit early ain't it, girl?' he called back with a good-natured grin. 'The old church ain't even bonged half twelve yet.'

'Please, Stan.'

Hearing the urgency in her voice, Fat Stan said something to Bernie, handed him his money apron and hauled his great bulk over to the flower stall.

'Come on, I'll treat yer,' he said ushering her along the road in the direction of the Aldgate Pump.

—

'Now,' he growled, handing Cissie a gin and orange. 'What's all this about?'

'I had to talk to someone, Stan.' Cissie's hand shook as she raised the glass to her lips.

She sipped at the burning, sticky liquid and shuddered, then fumbled around in her bag for her cigarettes, managing only to scatter its contents all over the floor of the busy pub.

'Blimey, Cis, calm down, girl.' He patted her shoulder with his huge hand. 'It might never happen yer know.'

'Sorry, Stan.' Gratefully, she sat there while he lowered his huge frame to his knees and collected all her bits and pieces for her. Then she let him light her cigarette, took a deep drag and finally settled back into her chair.

'Them two blokes,' she began nervously. 'Did yer see 'em?'

'Can't say I noticed anyone in particular,' he said warily, his lack of breath after scrabbling about on the sticky, beer-sprinkled floorboards forgotten.

The young girl was worried. Really concerned about something, and Fat Stan was sure that he wasn't going to like what she had to say. His wife had warned him enough times lately: he wasn't getting any younger, or any fitter, and all this villainy lark was a young man's game. And she was right.

'I can't believe what's just happened, Stan.'

Cissie swallowed a hefty gulp of her gin, the unaccustomed strength of so much liquor making her nose sting. She narrowed her eyes and shook her head free of the tingling. 'It's my fault, I suppose,' she went on, in a slightly strangulated voice. 'I was getting so conceited. So bloody smug. Going on about how well everything was going; how lucky I was. I suppose I was just asking for it all to go wrong, wasn't I?' She dropped her chin and buried her face in her hands.

'Look, love,' Fat Stan said in an uncharacteristically gentle voice. 'You drink that up while I go and get us both another one. Then you can tell yer Uncle Stan all about it.'

Fat Stan took as long as he could up at the bar, anything to give him a bit of thinking time. What was he supposed to do? He was taking bets he didn't wanna take for Turner. There was getting on for a bloody hundred pound in that money apron at times. He was keeping an eye on a girl he wanted nothing to do with. And now he was expected to give her a bleed'n shoulder to cry on into the bargain. She was a good enough kid, but he didn't need all this aggravation, he really didn't, not at his time of life.

When he could spin out his time at the bar no longer, he returned to the table with their drinks, prepared, at least, to let her tell him what was upsetting her. He felt he owed her that.

'So, like I say,' Cissie continued, 'it was only one of 'em what spoke. He said they was...' She made a little fluttering gesture with her hand as she tried to remember his exact words. 'Representatives. That's it, representatives.'

All the while she was talking, Stan listened attentively, nodding and taking note. Then, when he was sure she had finished, he swallowed the last of his pint and stood up.

'Look, Cis,' he said, as though he was humouring a fretful child, 'it ain't no good you getting yourself all wound up, now is it? If they're gonna knock the place down, they're gonna knock it down. What can you, or me, or anyone else for that matter, do about it?'

'But it's me living, Stan,' she wailed.

'Tell me,' he said, sitting down again, 'd'yer really wanna stand outside a poxy factory flogging daisies for the rest of yer natural?' He leant towards her and rested his massive arms on the table in front of him. 'Just you think about it. A pretty young girl like you's gonna hate it out there in the winter. I'm telling yer, bloody murder it is. Yer can't imagine what it's like on a dark January morning when yer fingers stick to the metal rods of the stall while yer trying to put it up, and the pipes are frozen and yer can't get no water for yer vases. And the cost of the flowers! It'd break yer heart it would.'

Cissie stared down unseeingly at the tabletop. 'I thought you'd be on my side, Stan. I thought you was me friend.'

'I am, sweetheart. Course I am.' He reached out and took her hand, covering it completely with just three of his fingers. 'Now come on, why don't yer just make hay while the sun shines? Yer've got a stall full o' flowers out

228

there to shift, and there's all them punters just waiting for yer to part 'em from their wage packets.'

Cissie didn't move. 'But if I lose that pitch, how am I gonna pay Brownlow?' she whispered, as much to herself as to Stan.

Fat Stan sighed inwardly. He hadn't even heard of this one, whoever he was. Not another one on the firm to deal with, surely? A moneylender, maybe? Protection of some kind? Aw, well, in for a penny...

'So, who's this Brownlow?' he asked, not really wanting to know.

'He's me landlord,' sniffled Cissie.

'So, he's yer landlord, is he?' Fat Stan handed Cissie his handkerchief, a cloth of such huge proportions it could have passed muster as a cot sheet. 'Don't cry, love, it's only money, innit?'

Fat Stan really hated all this women's business, all this crying and wailing, but at least it seemed as though Brownlow wouldn't be causing him any problems. Turner had never mentioned landlords as being any concern of his.

But Fat Stan was wrong. As Cissie continued – telling him not only about her worries as to how she could possibly pay the rent if she couldn't run the stall, but also about the stroke Brownlow had tried to pull when she couldn't pay him just after Davy had died, when he'd suggested she should pay him in kind instead – then Stan knew that Brownlow was very much his concern. Turner would do his crust if he thought something like that was going on without him being told.

Retirement, despite its associated day-long enforced proximity to his wife and his nit-picking mother-in-law, was seeming a more and more attractive prospect to Fat Stan as he sat in the Three Tuns pub and wondered how Turner would react to this latest little titbit, that he knew, unfortunately, he had no other choice than to pass on to him.

–

The rest of the day passed in a haze for Cissie; all she could think about was the two men and what would happen if she lost the pitch. But it couldn't happen, she kept telling herself. It couldn't. Not after all she had gone through.

But the man had seemed so certain that it would. So what would happen to her in, when was it, ten weeks or so, when the developers moved in?

Cissie needed help now more than she had needed it at any time since the day Davy had been killed. If only Davy was still with her. He would have known what to do. He always did.

She felt so useless; so stupid; so scared, like a lost child who knew she would never see her parents again.

Her parents. If only she could speak to them. That would be something. But they wouldn't want her now. Not after the way she had treated them.

'I think you've given me too much, my dear,' a softly spoken middle-aged man said to her, holding out a ten-shilling note. 'You've given me change of a pound.'

Most of her other customers were also honest enough to tell her when, in her distracted state, she gave them too much change, but losing a few shillings of her day's takings was the very least of Cissie's worries. What concerned her above all was the thought of how she would take care of her two little ones if her living really was taken away from her. She'd been selfish, she knew that, but she'd never been a really bad person. Surely she didn't deserve this. And Matty and Joyce certainly didn't.

As she stood, wide-eyed and staring by her stall, nightmare visions of children's homes and workhouses filled her mind with horrors she had never thought would ever come to haunt her, not pretty Cissie Flowers, a woman for whom something had always turned up. A woman whose life had been blessed with a wonderful husband and children.

Maybe everyone only got so much luck in their life, she thought, and she had used up all her allowance in a single go when she had met Davy. But she didn't have Davy any more. So who could she turn to now? Jim Phillips?

He was certainly kind enough to help her, and he might know all about flowers, but she didn't suppose for one minute that he had the first idea about property developers. That was something out of the league of anyone she had ever known or was ever likely to know. The most powerful person she would ever be likely to come across was Big Bill Turner.

Turner.

Cissie bit the inside of her cheek and stared down at the pavement, she didn't even like the idea entering her mind. And anyway, even if she felt she could turn to the likes of him, she had to be realistic, what would a crook know about property?

But Turner had offered her another way out.

For the first time, Cissie seriously contemplated what it would be like if she accepted Turner's proposition. Maybe life as a rich man's mistress wouldn't be so bad after all – not when compared to the workhouse.

Cissie was no fool, she could guess that no woman would last very long with a man like Turner. He would no doubt soon become bored and move on to the next one. She only had to look at Eileen if she needed proof of that. But surely, if she used her loaf, she could get enough out of him to be able to take care of her family, enough to make the brief humiliation worthwhile?

It took a lot of effort, but Cissie made sure she had a smile on her face when she went to collect Matty and Joyce from Gladys's. Everything she was doing was for the kids, after all, so she wasn't going to let them see she was upset yet again. The poor little devils had seen enough tears since they had lost their father, they didn't need her making things worse.

As she stepped into the passage of number four, Gladys came flying out of the kitchen and almost threw herself at Cissie.

'You'll never guess what's happened, Cis,' she gasped.

'What? It ain't the kids, is it?'

Gladys shook her head, making her hair bounce about her shoulders. 'No, they're fine, they're in the kitchen with Ernie and Nipper. It's Brownlow.'

'Brownlow?'

'Yeah. He's only in hospital, ain't he. The law found him. Down by the Cut, he was. On the towpath. In a right old state. He'd been beaten up good and proper. And, yer'll never believe this bit, his hair had all been cut off.'

'His hair?'

'Yeah, his hair!'

'Who did it?'

Gladys shrugged. 'Who knows? He definitely ain't telling. Too scared I suppose. But, like everyone's saying,

232

there'd be a bloody long queue o' suspects if they lined up everyone what had it in for the bastard. But that ain't all. He only had this card thing hanging around his neck, didn't he.'

Gladys leant forward and whispered behind her hand, her eyes wide. 'And yer'll never guess what it said.'

Cissie swallowed hard. 'No. What?'

'It said: Next time it'll be yer...' Gladys looked over her shoulder along the passage, checking that none of the children had wandered out of the kitchen.

'Yer what?'

Gladys gulped. 'It said: Next time it'll be yer, you know.' She lowered her eyes and pointed in the region of her apron pockets. 'Yer dick!'

Chapter 15

'Look, I know you ain't had yer tea yet, Matt, but I promise, I'll be as quick as I can.'

Matty looked up at Cissie with his big, pale eyes. 'I'll be all right, Mum.'

It almost broke Cissie's heart, how grown-up Matty sounded. It *wasn't* all right. How could it be right for her little boy to be taking on so much at his age? Only five years old and he was acting more like a grown-up than she herself ever had, until a few months ago that is, when she had been forced to grow up. Cissie only wished she could do more to protect him.

But although it hurt her badly to see him that way, it also gave her the strength she needed to go over to see Sammy Clarke, cap in hand, yet again. Because when she saw Matty's anxious little face, she certainly didn't have to remind herself why she was going over there.

It wasn't money, or even tick, she was after this time, however, it was advice. Cissie needed someone to tell her what to do about those men and their boss, this property developer, whoever he was. She needed someone to make everything all right again, to put the world back into some sort of order that she could understand.

After her initial rejection of going to Jim for help, Cissie had reconsidered the idea. She had thought long and hard about it, but had, in the end, finally decided that it wasn't very sensible after all. And it wasn't anything to do with his trade being in flowers rather than property. Business was business after all, and he was definitely no fool in that area, he made a very good living for himself. No, it was more to do with Cissie not wanting to become even more involved with him. Seeing him about work was difficult enough for her.

Every time Cissie set eyes on Jim she had to remind herself that he wasn't available, she had to deny the feelings she had about him so that she didn't make a fool of herself. So she couldn't even begin to think what would happen to their already confusing relationship – on her part at least – if she went to him with her fears about the property developer. Cissie would have been asking him, a married man with children, for something that could so easily mean that their association would become far too intimate.

It wasn't until Cissie had been dragging the stall wearily back to the lock-up, in the by then chilly late afternoon air, that the idea of going to Sammy Clarke about her problem had come to her. She was a bit surprised that she hadn't thought of him sooner: he was sensible, reliable, he was in business, and, most important of all, she could depend on him wanting to help her.

But she shouldn't really have been surprised. She'd realised months ago that that was the trouble with being worried: your head got muddled, you couldn't think straight, and your energy just disappeared. Every little thing became almost too difficult even to contemplate tackling.

Once Cissie had reminded herself of that, she'd secured the lock-up for the night, had given herself a good shake and had climbed up into the truck ready to set off for home and to start sorting things out. It was no good wallowing in despair, she had told herself yet again, she had responsibilities, and, exhausted by her worries or not, she had to do something to ensure that she met them.

And that was why she was about to go over to see good old dependable Sammy Clarke.

Cissie bent down and kissed Matty tenderly on the top of his head. 'Play nicely with yer soldiers for me, Matt. And try not to wake Nanna and Joycie from their nap, eh? Then when I get back from Sam's, I'll do us all something nice for our teas.'

Cissie was about to step out of her front door, when she saw Lena coming out of her house across the street.

The miserable-faced woman looked over at Cissie and sneered loudly, 'Blimey, look who it ain't! Don't say yer actually at home with yer kids for once? What, couldn't yer find no mug to mind 'em for yer?'

Cissie felt like going over there and slapping Lena's cocky, rotten face for her, but she wouldn't lower herself. Instead, she kept her mouth shut and just stood there on her doorstep, watching Lena striding jauntily along the street towards the corner shop, pulling her shopping bag primly up her arm as she paused to have a leisurely nose first into Elsie Collier's, and then into Gladys Mills's front windows as she passed their houses.

Cissie shook her head at the woman's bare-faced cheek. She really was a cow.

She sighed loudly, knowing she couldn't face the idea of going into the shop, not with Lena in there, and especially not with the way she was feeling – so fragile that the slightest thing could tip her, yet again, into weeping tears of self-pitying frustration. So she would, Cissie decided, let Lena finish her business in there first, and she would go over there afterwards. There, she'd decided.

But her pleasure at her decisiveness soon melted away. It was all very well thinking things, but doing them was a whole different matter. She was so tired.

She turned round slowly, stepped back into the passage and walked back along towards the kitchen as though she were in a dream. Why were all these things happening to her? And worse, why were they happening to her poor babies? What had they ever done to harm anyone?

She got no further than the kitchen doorway, and stood there, for a long time, watching Matty play. He looked so serious, so intent, with his little fair head bent over his toys, just like a miniature version of Davy.

With legs that felt as if they'd been weighted with lead, Cissie eventually walked over to him.

Hearing someone behind him, Matty looked round, startled.

'Mum? You was quick.'

'I ain't been yet, babe,' she said softly.

Crouching down on her haunches, Cissie gently took her son's face in her hands and looked deep into his eyes; the eyes that should have been full of laughter and mischief, but were instead clouded with worry and fear.

'Yer know, Matt,' she said, 'people are so quick to make judgements about me. But they don't know what's inside me head, or me heart. Do they?'

Matty frowned, his expression more frightened than ever.

'Yer dunno what I'm going on about, do yer, darling? But me, I know.'

She kissed him again, and brushed his floppy fair hair away from his face.

'Five minutes, yeah,' she promised, standing up.

Matty nodded solemnly, and returned to his soldiers.

–

Inside the shop, Elsie Collier, from number six, and Gladys were waiting with increasing impatience, while Lena put Sammy Clarke through his paces, objecting to every rasher of streaky as being either too fatty or too thickly cut; rejecting the wedge of cheese as being half an ounce heavier than she had asked for – even though Sammy had told her he'd only charge her for the quarter of a pound she'd wanted; and, finally, almost too much for the usually mild-mannered shopkeeper, she was now insisting on going through the tub of broken biscuits to pick out all the cream-filled bits.

'Come on, Lena,' Sammy coaxed her, 'there's only two hours till I close, yer know.'

'Yeah, come on,' Elsie chipped in, 'I've got me gentlemen waiting.'

'And I ain't got all night, neither,' added Gladys. She didn't explain that her kids were famished as she'd not had any money to buy anything for their tea – her wages having gone to buy the two eldest second-hand boots from the market and to pay to keep the gas on for a few more hours – and had to wait on Cissie coming along with the envelope she now regularly gave her on a Friday evening.

Lena didn't bat an eyelid of concern for either of the two women, instead she turned on Sammy. 'Yer mum and dad would be ashamed if they could see the way yer running this place, Samuel Clarke,' she said, discarding another handful of biscuits back into the drum and digging out a fresh lot. 'They would never have been so rude to a good customer like me. They valued trade, they did. Knew what side their bread was buttered.'

The bell over the door tinkled and Cissie walked into the shop, unaware that Lena was still in there and had been doing a very good job of raising the tension between herself and the other customers to steadily bubble up towards boiling point.

Cissie didn't notice Gladys and Elsie either, as they stood in the shadows of the shelf-lined walls, and she walked straight over to the counter as though there was no one else in the place except her and Sammy.

'D'yer think I could have a word, Sam?' she asked him urgently.

'Course yer can, Cis.'

'Hold on.' Lena straightened up from her biscuit-sorting in the corner and bowled over to Cissie. 'I was here before you.'

'It's all right, Lena, keep yer hair on. I didn't see yer there. But I ain't pushing in, cos I ain't come to buy anything anyway.' Cissie could have kicked herself; why hadn't she thought to peep through the door to see whether the interfering cow had gone home? 'I just want a quick word with Sam.'

'Aw, so that excuses yer for shoving up the front then, does it?' Lena demanded.

Cissie sighed edgily. 'Look, Lena, I've got kids indoors waiting for me.'

'And *I've* got me gentlemen waiting, Cissie Flowers,' Elsie bristled, stepping forward like a surprise witness for the prosecution, 'so don't get no ideas about pushing in front of me neither, yer cheeky mare.'

It was as though Elsie's words – very mild by the standards of Linman Street – had slapped Cissie around the face. She burst into an uncontrollable flood of tears. 'Why don't no one understand?' she wailed pitifully. 'I'm all by meself. I've got no one. I'm a widow. I'm alone. I'm—'

'For Christ's sake,' Lena snapped. 'You ain't the only one in the world with bloody worries.'

'That's right,' agreed Elsie. 'You wanna have three gentlemen demanding their teas on time. And clean sheets every three weeks regardless of rain, wind or snow.'

Lena spun round. 'Who asked you for yer two penn'orth, Elsie Collier? You and yer so-called gentlemen. Everyone knows what goes on in that house o' your'n. You're as bad as her.' Lena jerked her head towards Cissie. 'Funny how it's always blokes what seem so keen to help your sort, ain't it?'

Cissie wiped her eyes roughly on her sleeve and stuck her fists angrily into her waist. 'D'you wanna say that again, Lena Dunn?' she asked, unable to keep the sob from her voice. 'And this time, yer can spell out exactly what yer mean, and all. Come on. If yer dare.'

'What I mean—' Lena began, but she got no further. Sammy had lifted the flap in the counter and had stepped between her and Cissie.

'That's enough, Lena,' he said firmly, holding up his hand and making little skipping movements, back and forth, like a referee in a boxing match. 'We don't want no rows in here, thank you.'

'Aw, that's nice, Sammy. Very nice. Yer on her side, are yer?' Elsie crowed triumphantly, offering a sudden allegiance to Lena. She pointed dramatically at Cissie. '*She's* the one what's causing all the row.'

Sammy scratched his head, totally bewildered. How had he got involved in this little lot? 'Look, I ain't on no one's side, Elsie. I just don't want no trouble in me shop, that's all.'

With that, he whisked Lena's bacon and cheese off the counter and shoved them haphazardly into her basket, then took her by the arm and steered her spluttering in protest towards the door.

'Now, if yer don't mind,' he said, more pink-faced than usual with suppressed fury at such uncalled-for and stupid behaviour – not to mention embarrassment at being seen to favour Cissie, 'I'm gonna shut up early tonight. So, anything else any of yer want'll have to wait till tomorrow morning.'

Astonished by Sammy's uncharacteristic show of determination, Gladys, Elsie and Cissie filed silently over to the door, and stood there alongside Lena, their open-mouthed neighbour.

'I didn't mean you, Cis.' Sammy flashed her a brief smile of encouragement as he stepped to one side to let the others out into the street. They had obviously seen through him and made up their minds about how he felt about Cissie, so what did he have to lose? 'I thought we could have that little chat. In private.'

The other women didn't move. They stood there, enraged by such cavalier treatment. They were his customers. Who did he think he was? And who did Cissie Flowers think *she* was?

Completely unexpectedly, it was Gladys – who up until then had said nothing – who dashed her bag to the floor and twisted round to confront Cissie.

'Here we go again,' she fumed. 'I really thought yer'd got over all this *me, me, me* lark, Cissie. How can you even think of asking Sam for tick again when there's others, like *me* for instance, what could really do with it, but are too proud to bloody well ask? D'you know how I'm having to scrimp and scrape? D'you know there's nothing in that cupboard o' mine? Not a single crust o' dry bread, and not a single scrape o' marge.' Gladys dropped her chin and said in a voice full of quiet shame, 'That's why I never give Matty and Joyce their tea. I didn't have nothing to give 'em.'

Cissie felt her lip tremble. 'I ain't come over to Sammy for no tick, Glad. And I do know how hard things are for yer. Honest.'

Much to Lena's delight, Gladys didn't fall into Cissie's arms in a flurry of reconciliation, instead she took a step closer to Cissie, her finger raised in anger. She looked incensed.

'Well, what have you come over for then?' Gladys demanded. 'Tell me that, if yer can.'

She stood there looking at Cissie, her chest rising and falling as she struggled to control her tears. Her tears that had, all too often lately, been coming closer and closer to the surface, and which now threatened to spill from her eyes and send her into a screaming fit of panic and despair.

Cissie swallowed hard. 'Don't let's row again, Glad. Please,' she breathed.

'I don't wanna row, Cis. I just wanna...' Gladys clapped her hands over her eyes. Then, slowly dragging them down her cheeks, she stared at her friend. 'It don't matter what I want. I'll see yer later. I've just got meself a bit upset, that's all. I dunno what I'm doing.'

With that, Gladys twisted away from her and ran out of the shop as though she were being pursued by the evil-looking rent man who, it had been rumoured, was to replace Brownlow while he recovered from his still-unexplained beating. Cissie snatched Gladys's bag off the ground and went to chase after her, but Sammy put himself between her and the door. Lena and Elsie watched in dumbstruck delight at such a show, as Sammy took the bag from Cissie and pushed her gently backwards towards the counter.

'Don't worry about Gladys's bag now,' he said, 'I'll drop it in to her later on. And I'll make sure she gets her shopping. You just sit yerself down, Cissie. Go on. Sit down. I won't be a minute.'

'What's up with Gladys?' asked Ethel Bennett, stepping into the shop doorway. 'It was like her drawers was on fire, how fast she was moving. Never seen nothing like it. Nearly had me over on me arse she did.'

As Ethel spoke, her hair bristled with the curlers that stuck out all around her head in a metallic halo, and she had a horrible, mean little smile playing around her lips, making her usually not very attractive appearance look even less appealing than ever. She was enjoying herself.

Lena slipped her arm through Ethel's and drew her into the shop. 'There's been a bit of a row, Mum,' she said, a look of sly pleasure twisting her lips, narrow and dry just like her mother's, into her own hideous parody of a smile. 'Cissie here's upset poor old Gladys Mills again.' She tutted and rolled her eyes in an exaggerated travesty of concern. 'They've had another row. That's why she took off like that. Poor bugger. Right upset she was. Yer should have heard her. Break yer heart it would. And what with all her bad luck and everything, that's all she needs, her supposed best mate turning on her.'

'I never meant nothing,' Cissie protested, immediately wishing she hadn't when she saw the victorious expression on Ethel's face. 'No, what I meant—'

'That's it. That's enough,' Sammy interrupted. 'Go on, you three, out. I'm closing.'

Ethel, Lena and Elsie, seething with indignation, but relishing the drama of it all, allowed themselves to be ushered out on to the pavement. There were plenty of compensations for such treatment. The three of them were almost bursting with glee at the juicy bit of gossip they had just witnessed first-hand, and were, in their minds, already embroidering the incident into a full-scale fight between Cissie and Gladys, the two presumed best friends in Linman Street.

And there was a wonderful added bonus, and further fuel for their fevered imaginations, when Sammy Clarke not only shut the door firmly behind them – shutting him and Cissie in the shop alone – but also pulled down the blinds and put up the closed sign.

'Here we go again!' gloated Lena.

'Almost broad daylight still, if yer don't mind!' gasped Elsie.

'Dirty little whore!' concluded Ethel gleefully.

'So, these two men, yer sure yer've never seen 'em before?' Sammy had listened to Cissie trying to relate her story through her tears for almost a quarter of an hour, and they were the first words, apart from little noises of comfort, he had spoken.

'Never. I'm sure.'

'And yer sure they was genuine?'

Cissie nodded miserably. 'Positive. Look.'

She dug into her pocket and pulled out the card the man had given her. 'They wasn't playing no games, Sam,' she said, handing it to him. 'They meant it all right. They're gonna knock that factory down and I'm gonna be ruined. And how am I meant to feed the kids and pay the sodding rent then, eh? You tell me that if yer can.'

She brushed her eyes roughly with her fists, angry at the all too familiar sensation of tears running down her cheeks again. 'And that's another thing. That bastard Brownlow.'

'What about him?'

She thought for a moment, sniffed and then shook her head. 'Nothing. I'm just rambling.' She was in enough trouble as it was, without voicing the terrible fears she had about that little episode, that it was her telling Fat Stan about him that had somehow led to his beating. Speaking those fears out loud might lead to who knew what further complications?

'All right,' said Sammy, frowning. 'Take yer time.' He wouldn't push her. If there was something she wanted him to know, he'd listen when she was ready. 'Let's just sort this out a bit at a time, eh, Cis?'

Cissie said nothing. She just buried her face in her hands and sobbed. Sammy so wanted to take her in his arms. But suddenly she was on her feet, throwing up her hands in despair.

'What am I gonna do, Sam? What am I gonna do if I lose that pitch?'

Sammy put the business card carefully on the counter, reached out and took her gently by the hands.

'I ain't sure yet, Cis,' he said, his voice cracking with the effort of having to resist pulling her to him and crushing her against his chest, where he could keep her safe from everyone and everything. 'But I'm gonna think about it. I'm gonna work something out. I promise. Cos I'm not gonna let anything else bad happen to yer, not ever again.'

Sammy's whole body felt as though it was on fire. All he could focus on was her mouth. Her soft, beautiful mouth. The thought of it made him dizzy.

He dropped her hands and took a step away from her, and fiddled distractedly with the strings of his starched white apron. 'Yer do trust me, don't yer, Cis? Cos I mean it, I'll do anything I can. Yer do know that, don't yer? Anything.'

Cissie nodded. 'Course I do, Sam. But I need more than you being kind to me. I need a bloody miracle.'

'*I know.*' *Sammy stared down at the floor. Why couldn't he just say it? Why couldn't he just say:* Everything'll be all right, Cissie. Yer've just gotta marry me and come and live here with me and the kids, and yer won't have to worry about nothing ever again. I'll wrap you up like a little doll and love yer and cherish yer. Treat yer like that flash Davy Flowers never knew how.

But how could he? He was dull, boring Sammy Clarke. Pink-faced and about as exciting as a slab of cold bacon. Why would she want him, a grocer who wore an apron and talked to old women all day?

Maybe she could somehow grow to think something of him. But what was the point of day-dreaming? She'd only been a widow for six months. So, no matter how or what he felt, Sammy knew that decency had to prevail.

'I promise, Cis,' he said softly, 'I'll think of something.'

'Will yer, Sam?' Cissie lifted her chin and looked at him, a glimmer of hope flickering dimly in her eyes. 'Will yer really?'

Chapter 16

Later that evening, when Cissie had cooked the tea, had cleared up, had had the same old words with Lil about not wasting money, and had finally put Matty and Joyce up to bed, she sat at the kitchen table, more tired than ever, with a piece of paper and a pencil and tried to come up with a plan.

What on earth could she do?

Sammy Clarke had been kind to her when she'd been over there. He'd been nice, gentle, interested. But he hadn't actually been much help.

And that was what Cissie needed: help.

She didn't want to seem ungrateful. Sammy had done so much for her since Davy had died, far more than she had any right to expect a neighbour to do, but, she now had to admit, it didn't seem very likely that Sammy, a corner grocer, would really be able to come up with any useful answers to her sort of problems. Hers were the sort of problems that involved dealing with proper businessmen, property developers who could change people's lives just because they felt like buying an old factory building and knocking it down and putting up offices in its place. Men with power.

No, Sammy was well-meaning but he was a dead loss when it came to it. So she had no other choice, she had to sit down and do some serious thinking of her own. She'd come this far and she would not give up. She had to see a way through this, a way that would mean her children didn't have to suffer.

–

Cissie had been sitting at the table for over an hour and had got as far as writing down two lists. One was a frighteningly long list, itemising all the things that had to be paid for if she and her family were going to survive. The second was much shorter, showing what she could do to earn money if she lost the pitch. All that was written there was: *find another pitch*. But she knew it wasn't that easy. Pitches that brought in any sort of money were jealously guarded. She knew that all too well from her own experience.

She sighed miserably and rubbed her hands over her face.

The sound of Lil, who had been sitting glowering opposite her, suddenly slamming down her cup into her saucer made Cissie start as though she'd been shot.

'It's like the bloody cemetery in here,' Lil barked. 'I don't see no one all morning while I'm stuck in here with bloody Joyce until that Gladys gets home – while you're out enjoying yerself, I might add – and then, when yer do get in, I get the sodding silent treatment. I can't stand it. I'm telling yer, it's driving me round the flaming bend. I'll wind up in Banstead at this rate. I'm telling yer, I will.'

'Have you finished?' asked Cissie, very calmly, setting down her pencil.

Lil scowled angrily in reply.

'Good, cos I wanna get a few things straight round here. First, I don't spend all day out enjoying meself, and you know I don't. I work bloody hard to put food on that table and to keep you in beer money to throw away down the pub. And second, I've got more on me mind than bothering to play games like giving you the silent treatment.'

Lil snorted contemptuously.

'And if yer must know,' Cissie continued, tapping the paper with her finger, 'what I'm doing here is trying to figure out a way to keep our heads above water. Trying to find a way of sorting things out so we don't have to wind up in the bleed'n workhouse. So, if yer don't mind, I'd better get back to me writing.' She picked up her pencil and stared at the lists again. 'Mind you, perhaps yer'd prefer the workhouse. At least yer'd have a bit o' company there. Wouldn't have to spend all that time on yer own, now would yer?'

'Charming.' Lil tugged her cardigan primly round her shoulders. 'That's a fine way for a girl to talk to her dead husband's mother, I don't think. If my Davy was here now—'

'If Davy was here now, Lil,' Cissie cut in, 'we wouldn't be in this sodding mess, would we?'

'May God forgive yer!' Lil slapped her hands against her cheeks, and rolled her eyes in horrified indignation as she flashed a plea for absolution at the ceiling. 'Talking about my angel of a boy like that. Gawd rest his soul. Anyone'd think he got himself killed deliberately the way you're going on.'

Cissie rose to her feet, walked around the table and stood over Lil. She was shaking with temper, but she wasn't going to let the old bag see she was upsetting her. That was a victory Cissie wouldn't allow.

'If you wanna listen for once, Lil,' she said in a determinedly even tone, 'instead of keeping that great moaning
gob of your'n open all the time, perhaps yer'll learn something.'

'Aw yeah?' Lil came back pugnaciously.

'Yeah. I'll tell yer a few stories I've been told about
that so-called angel o' your'n, shall I? Things what'll make
your frizzy, rotten hair stand right up on end.'

'I don't have to put up with this from the likes o' you!'
Now Lil was also on her feet, jabbing her finger at Cissie's
chest. 'In fact, I'll tell *you* a few home truths, you stuck-up
little madam—'

'Go on then. Tell me.' Cissie folded her arms and leant
back, daring her mother-in-law to continue. 'Come on,
I'm listening.'

The two women stood there, glaring accusingly at one
another, both all too aware that they were dangerously
close to saying things that could change their relationship
for ever, things that could all too easily put them on the
first steps of a very slippery slope that led to an even worse
mire than that in which they were already floundering.

So intent were they both on controlling the situation,
because despite their show of boldness, neither of them
could face the choice which presented itself – the end
of the last bit of family security that either of them felt
they had, namely each other – that they were genuinely
shocked when the next voice they heard wasn't either of
theirs but Sammy Clarke's.

'Cis? Cissie?' they heard him call along the passage.
'Can I come in? I think I've come up with an idea for
yer.'

'It was obvious all along really. I dunno why I never thought of it before. Profit and loss,' Sammy concluded, with a lift of his hand. 'It's what all businessmen understand. Money.'

Cissie glanced nervously at Lil, who, not wanting to miss anything had sat herself, still grimacing angrily, in the corner like a bulldog with a wasp sting on its nose.

'So you reckon I'd really be able to convince 'em?' Cissie asked doubtfully. 'I mean, why should they care about what the likes of me's got to say for meself?'

'Don't start knocking yerself again, Cis.' Sammy smiled reassuringly. He really wanted to reach out and take her hand, cover it with tender kisses and tell her everything would be fine, but with Lil sitting there like the bad fairy at the christening, it was even more out of the question than usual. 'And anyway, it's a good business proposition,' he continued. 'They'd be mad not to listen. And with a clever girl like you explaining it to 'em, why wouldn't they?' He leant across the table and looked directly into her eyes. 'Yer'll be able to convince 'em. You'd be able to convince anyone of anything, you would.'

'Huh!' exploded Lil. 'If she was so flaming clever, she wouldn't be sitting here listening to your old nonsense, Sammy Clarke. She'd have her best frock on, a bit o' lipstick, and she'd be round that Big Bill Turner's gaff like sticks o' cracking. She'd be fluttering her bloody eyelashes and holding out her hand, waiting for him to pay all the bleed'n bills. But what is she doing, this *clever girl*? She's sitting in a back kitchen in Linman Street listening to a sodding grocer talking a load o' shit.'

Sam felt his already pink cheeks flare scarlet with embarrassment. 'Maybe I should get going, eh, Cis?'

'No,' Cissie said, staring steadily over his shoulder at Lil. 'You don't have to go, Sam. But I think if Lil's so obviously overtired, maybe she should go to bed. I mean, when you get to her age, it's like being a kid, ain't it? Yer get all bad-tempered when yer need yer sleep and start saying all sorts o' stupid things yer don't mean.'

–

'So, yer gonna tell me what yer've been up to then?'

Moe Turner stood there in the office towering over Turner. It was late at night and there was no one else in the building in the Mile End Road except her and her husband.

She was dressed expensively in a neat charcoal-grey costume, a narrow-brimmed black hat with a spotted veil, and matching kid gloves. Her arms were folded tightly across her broad, matronly bosom, and she was tapping her foot impatiently.

She was actually a good foot shorter than her husband when they were both standing, but when he was pressed down into his big leather chair as he was now, it was as if he were a child with an adult looming over him.

'Well?' she demanded. 'I'm waiting.'

Turner spoke in a strange quavering falsetto. 'After this deal goes through, there's gonna be plenty o' spare dough about. So I've definitely thought about setting her up in the flat.'

'You've what? You've *thought*?' Moe bellowed, her eyes flashing with fury. 'I don't think I'm hearing you right, am I?'

Turner shrunk even further into the chair; his body trembled with anticipation of what, if the game went the way he hoped, the way it always did, would come next. 'No,' he corrected himself, looking up at her through deferentially half-lowered lids, 'I *don't* think. I'm sorry. What I meant to say was I took your advice and did as you said.'

Moe lifted her chin and stared down her heavily powdered nose at him. 'I don't like it when I have to remind you to show me respect,' she said. 'It was my idea. Right?'

Turner nodded, the movement of his head barely perceptible.

'You know how I like to have you tell me all them little stories. And you know I like to choose the girls you're gonna tell me about. But I really don't like having to remind you to show me respect.'

She began peeling off her gloves, and walking slowly around the desk towards him. 'It makes me angry when that happens,' she breathed. 'Very angry indeed.'

Chapter 17

Following Sammy's advice, not so much because she thought it was good advice, but more out of desperation, because, when all was said and done, it was all she had, Cissie set out early on Monday morning to set up the stall.

She didn't usually bother working on a Monday, trade at the beginning of the week hardly made it worthwhile, but part of Sammy's suggested plan was that she should do everything she could to make the stall seem as viable a business proposition as possible. And every little helped, every penny she could show the stall earning would help her to state her case more convincingly.

After making sure that Fat Stan was keeping an eye on her stock – thieving hands didn't only come attached to the arms of ragged street urchins, City gents were just as liable to let bunches of roses slip up the sleeves of their expensive, cashmere overcoats – Cissie put the next stage of the plan into action.

Taking her courage in her hands, she went along to the telephone box by the station entrance and dialled the number on the business card that the silent man had given her on the previous Friday. As she waited for someone to answer, Cissie's hands shook, but not nearly as much as her voice shook when she had to speak.

'Hello,' she stammered. 'Is that Mr Clayborne? Mr Peter Clayborne?'

It was.

'Aw...' She paused, closed her eyes and swallowed hard. Remember what Sammy had said, she told herself. Come on. Remember.

'Are you still there?' the voice on the other end asked.

'Me name's Cissie Flowers,' she blurted in reply. 'I wanna come and see yer. Please. If yer've got the time, like. I wanna talk to yer about me pitch outside the factory. In Aldgate.'

That wasn't how she had meant it to go at all, but, astonishingly, Clayborne didn't seem to mind that she sounded like a jibbering idiot. He was actually agreeing, without any question, to see her in his office that very afternoon.

As she replaced the receiver, Cissie didn't know whether to laugh or cry.

'Yer look like yer've been pole-axed, girl,' Fat Stan kidded her good-naturedly, as she stepped out of the telephone box. He had grown almost fond of young Cissie Flowers in a funny sort of way. She was a bloody nuisance to him, but he had come to accept her as being the innocent party in all this. After all, he didn't suppose it was her fault that Turner had taken a shine to her – she certainly hadn't thrown herself at him, not like most of the silly little tarts he took up with.

When Cissie didn't respond quick as a flash with a saucy bit of backchat, Fat Stan frowned. 'Everything all right?' he asked solicitously.

'Yeah. I think so.'

She wandered along from the kiosk to the newspaper stall, a vague expression clouding her face, and, taking Stan by the arm, she pulled him out of earshot of Bernie, whom, although she wasn't sure why, she still didn't trust.

'Stan,' she whispered, pulling him down closer to her. 'Guess what? I've got an appointment to go and see that property developer bloke this afternoon.'

Fat Stan raised a single furry eyebrow. 'Have yer now?' he said, flashing a look over her head towards Bernie. 'The property developer, eh?'

Cissie was so nervous about the impending meeting that, for the rest of the morning, she scarcely took any notice of the few customers who stopped at the stall. What she did notice, all too plainly, was how the time dragged. She could have sworn that the church bells had been deliberately slowed down, just to make her feel worse. All she wanted to do was go and see this Clayborne bloke, say her two penn'orth, and get out of there. She wasn't feeling very optimistic about her chances of persuading him of the value of Sammy Clarke's plan, and so she just wanted the bad news over and done with.

The only thing which distracted Cissie from her clock-watching was practising the little speech which Sammy had written for her to recite to Clayborne. She went over and over the words in her head, repeating them as though they were a prayer of supplication. Sammy had insisted on her being word-perfect, explaining how important it was for her to know exactly what she was going to say, so that she wouldn't get herself all confused and wind up wasting the opportunity by failing to make her point.

Cissie had agreed with him about that, she had agreed with him about all of it. Not because she thought it was all such a great idea, but, as she had already acknowledged, she hadn't been able to come up with a better one.

This really was her last chance.

Sammy had printed the speech, neatly and clearly for her, on a sheet of lined paper torn from the back of one of his ledgers, and, by nine o' clock Friday evening, Cissie had it off pat, she knew the speech by heart. But Sammy had said he wanted to be really certain and, much to Lil's loudly voiced disgust, he had been in and out of number seven to practise it with her, reappearing in their kitchen at all sorts of inconvenient times during the weekend, even snatching the odd five minutes whenever the shop was quiet.

Lil had fumed and spluttered, tutted and sighed, while she watched Sammy coaching and encouraging Cissie as though she were a schoolgirl learning verse for a recital competition. In Lil's opinion, Sammy Clarke had nothing of any interest or use to offer anyone in their household, and she would have preferred it if he had kept away from all of them.

By Sunday evening, Cissie felt she could have repeated the words in her sleep. But, with her nerves in such a state, she had to make really sure there would be no mistakes, and that was why she was going over it, time and again, as she stood at the stall, counting the long hours until her appointment with Clayborne.

In the end, she became so mesmerised by the sound and rhythm of the words that, if it hadn't been for Fat Stan hollering along to her to get her skates on, she would have missed the meeting altogether.

Less than ten minutes after Stan's reminder, Cissie found herself hovering shakily in the doorway of a sparsely furnished, windowless office situated above a printer's shop in a dank, cobbled courtyard close to Fenchurch Street station.

When she had first pushed open the door, Cissie had been shocked to find that there was no one else in the room except the silent one of the pair who had so upset her on the previous Friday.

'Come in, Mrs Flowers. Sit down. Or do you prefer to be called Prentice?'

The man had a surprisingly cultured voice; nothing like his roughly spoken companion who had done all the talking on Friday.

'Flowers'll be fine,' she said, warily. 'And you're… ?'

'Clayborne. Peter Clayborne. Now won't you sit down? Please.'

He was so polite. It didn't make sense. Not after the way the other man, who had had so much to say for himself at the stall, had spoken to her.

And why wasn't he there? Or even some sort of assistant, or secretary, or someone? And him mentioning her actual married name, rather than Davy's nickname; it all had the effect of further unsettling Cissie, as if she wasn't nervous enough as it was.

She hesitated, then feeling ashamed of her childish reticence, she hurried across the office, aiming for the single vacant chair set at the side of Clayborne's desk. But before she could reach her goal, she tripped over the mean square of mat that provided the only floor covering in the entire room, and went crashing into the side of his desk.

Clayborne shot out a steadying hand, but it was too late. As if in slow motion, Cissie slipped gracelessly to the floor.

She cursed herself under her breath. She had to compose herself, present herself as someone with a good business idea, an idea that was so good, he would feel he was really losing out if he passed it up. But here she was, acting like a gawky twelve-year-old, having to be helped to her feet after falling arse over elbow, and flashing her stocking tops at him into the bargain.

With a strained little smile, Cissie let go of his hand, noting, even in her confusion, how soft and smooth it felt against her wrist – more like a woman's than a man's – straightened her hat, and lowered herself demurely on to the chair.

'Are you all right?'

Cissie nodded dumbly. Her cheeks were burning.

Clayborne eyed her quizzically. 'You seem quite flustered, Mrs Flowers. I hope I'm not the reason.'

'No. No,' she insisted, shifting herself forward to the very edge of the chair. 'I ain't flustered.'

'Make yourself comfortable, please,' he said, his expression turning to one of barely concealed embarrassment as she wriggled around, pulling her skirt decorously over her knees.

'So,' he continued, with a gulp, 'you wanted to see me.'

Cissie said nothing, the words just wouldn't come. What had Sammy told her? Seem shrewd, positive. That's it. That's what she had to do.

She nodded enthusiastically, demonstrating the cheerful ease that Sammy had suggested would present a good impression for the meeting. In fact, she nodded very enthusiastically indeed, far more so than she'd actually intended. Her head wagged up and down like a demented chicken pecking for com. God she felt a fool.

Why couldn't she just do it like they'd planned? The way Sammy had told her to?

'And it was about... ?' Clayborne prompted her. He now looked almost as alarmed as she felt.

She nibbled the inside of her cheek and tugged anxiously at her fringe. She had to stop nodding.

'About the stall,' she eventually managed to mumble.

It was as though saying those three words triggered something in Cissie and prompted her into action. Quite suddenly she was transformed from being a bumbling idiot into a jabbering one. She just couldn't stop the words pouring out of her mouth.

'It's like this, yer see,' she began, waving and flapping her hands to emphasise her babbling. 'Flowers are never gonna be a thing of the past, are they? I mean, people are always gonna want beauty in their lives. They always have and always will do. Even when they've got almost nothing in their purses, they'll always find a few coppers for a little bunch o' sweet violets. But I know what yer said, well what yer mate said, about things being modern and smart and that, so I've thought about that. And I reckon I could be a real credit to yer outside that place. I could go for the posher sort o' trade, see. Where there's plenty o' money, even in these hard times.'

She laughed wildly. 'Who ever heard of a poor posh person, eh?'

As she spoke, Cissie shifted even further on to the edge of her chair – it was a wonder she hadn't slipped off altogether.

'I get some good regular orders already, yer know.' She had now bent forward, and was pointing at him. 'And I could do orders for all sorts of places. Offices, hotels even.

I'm full of ideas. There's loads o' ways I could make that stall look really classy. And flowers! I know more about flowers than—'

Cissie stopped as suddenly as she had begun. She had run out of words.

So, that was it. The best she could do. Now it was up to him.

She sat bolt upright and waited, staring at Clayborne, willing him to tell her that everything would be all right after all. And that even if she had made a complete fool of herself, he knew it was only because she was so nervous, and that he didn't know why he hadn't realised before what a brilliant asset to his offices it would be if he let her keep her flower stall pitched outside.

But Cissie wasn't stupid, even if she had just acted as though she was. She knew it wasn't going to be like that. It was all over. She'd had her chance to say her piece and she'd messed it up. She could see from the look on his face that Clayborne thought she was barmy. Why hadn't she just said the words she'd practised? The words about profit and costs and overheads. The words that Sammy had explained to her and helped her with.

Clayborne shook his head, he had a grim, sorrowful expression on his thin, pallid face. 'I'm sorry to disappoint you, Mrs Flowers. Very sorry. The stall obviously means a lot to you—'

'Not just to me, Mr Clayborne,' she cut in urgently. 'It's what I do to earn me living. For me family. I've got two little kiddies at home. They depend on me. I'm a widow. Then there's Lil, that's Davy's mum...'

Clayborne pushed back his chair and stood up. He walked to the far end of the long, narrow room and stood by a door in the back wall that faced the door through which Cissie had entered.

He leant against the door-frame and began speaking in a slow, firm voice. 'I would like you to listen to me, Mrs Flowers.'

'What?' Cissie demanded angrily. 'Listen to you telling me yer gonna take away the only chance I've got of feeding me kids? Listen to you telling me yer gonna ruin me?'

'No,' Clayborne said bluntly. 'Not ruin you.' He shifted slightly to one side as though he were making himself more comfortable against the door jamb.

'What *are* you saying then? Tell me that, eh?'

He raised his hand authoritatively. 'If you'll just hear me out, Mrs Flowers. Please.'

Cissie shrugged feebly, she was tight-lipped with help-lessness. 'What choice have I got?'

'Maybe more than you think.'

Cissie listened, stunned, as Peter Clayborne outlined an offer which, had anyone told her he would be making, would have had her laughing in their face. But here she was, listening to him with her very own ears.

'Let's get this right,' she said, leaning forward as though she was having difficulty understanding him. 'You're telling me that when yer knock down that old factory and put up this new office place, yer gonna let me rent one of the shops on the ground floor?'

'That's right, Mrs Flowers.' Clayborne looked and sounded relieved, as though he'd managed to get some-thing off his chest that had been stuck there like a fishbone. 'And very fine shops they'll be too. Curved plate-glass windows. Bronze handles on the doors. All the latest fitments. Very attractive. More like Paris than London.'

'Well,' Cissie snorted derisively, 'that's all right then, ain't it? So long as they're flaming attractive.'

She shook her head disbelievingly as her final glimmer of hope fell away as surely as petals from a dead rose.

'Can yer tell me, Mr Clayborne,' she went on, stifling back the tears of disappointment and rage, 'how exactly yer reckon I'm supposed to afford the rent on some posh shop with curved sodding windows and bronze bloody handles?'

'I'm sure we can come to some sort of arrangement, Mrs Flowers.'

'Some sort of arrangement?' she repeated, stressing each word as though it were in a foreign language. 'Some sort of bloody arrangement?'

As she rose to her feet and strode towards him, Cissie was in too much of a temper to notice how he hurriedly grasped the door handle behind his back as though blocking the way to the room beyond.

'What would *you* wanna come to some sort of arrangement with the likes o' me for?' she demanded, jabbing her finger at his face.

Clayborne now looked as terrified as she had felt when she had first entered the office.

'Because I think a woman like you could go far,' he burbled, his chin tucked so close to his chest that he could barely speak.

'Aw, do you now? And what'd be in it for you if I did *go far* as you so bloody well charmingly put it?'

Clayborne frowned as though the answer had, for the moment, escaped him. He thought for a bit then nodded;

something had come to him. 'It's my age,' he said as though that were a plausible explanation.

'Your age?' Cissie now sounded more confused than angry. 'What the hell's that gotta do with the price of cod?'

'Let's just say it's a whim.' He smiled weakly. 'You remind me of myself when I first started out as a raw young man with hardly a button to my name.'

Clayborne tipped his head to one side, and raised his eyebrows in what he intended to be an appealingly friendly gesture, but which only served to further infuriate Cissie.

'For a start,' she yelled, 'from the state of this dump it don't look like yer exactly rolling in it. So what would you know about *going far*?' She began jabbing her finger at him again. 'And as for yer age, you ain't exactly no granddad, now are yer? Yer can't be no more than bloody thirty years old.'

Cissie moved even closer, and her finger was now making contact with his chest. 'I wouldn't trust you, Mr Clayborne, as far as I could flaming well throw yer, and that wouldn't be very far, yer great long streak of nothing.'

Clayborne responded to her insult with another feeble attempt at a charming smile. 'You're a young woman after my own heart,' he beamed manically. 'Full of spirit. I like that.'

Cissie could feel herself twitching with temper at his audacity. What was wrong with some men? 'Are you married, Mr Clayborne?' she asked, staring up into his watery hazel eyes.

'I am, as a matter of fact, but I don't see what that has to do with anything.'

'Aw, but I think you do, Mr Clayborne. And d'yer know what? Yer don't have to say another word, cos I know exactly what yer gonna say next. Ain't that strange?'

Claybome frowned anxiously. He'd been cornered by a madwoman.

'Yer gonna tell me how you and yer wife don't get on like yer used to. Am I right?'

Cissie was now very close to him, so close that she could see the sweat beading on his forehead.

'No. No. You're not right,' he said hurriedly. 'In fact, you have entirely the wrong impression of me, Mrs Flowers. Absolutely entirely wrong. I never intended you to get that impression, I assure you.'

Cissie stepped away from Clayborne and looked him up and down. She didn't bother even to try to hide her contempt. 'You ain't the only one who's ever made me that sort of offer, yer know, and yer probably won't be the last, but I'm telling yer this for nothing, Mr Peter Clayborne, I ain't gonna say yes to no one what makes me that sort of offer. Not ever. Got it?'

'I really must insist,' Clayborne said, darting a nervous glance over his shoulder at the door. 'You've completely misunderstood me. And,' he added, his voice rising to a frantic whine, 'I would like you to know, that this offer has a time limit.' He was speaking quicker and quicker as though he were being timed against the clock. 'And I need to have your answer tomorrow as to whether you will be taking up the offer of the shop lease.'

'Yer don't give up easy,' she sneered. 'I'll give yer that.' With a final flick of her eyes up and down his tall, besuited body, Cissie turned on her heel and walked purposefully over to the door by which she'd entered.

'So, I'll expect to hear from you tomorrow then?'

'I wouldn't put no money on it if I was you, mate.'

She grasped the handle, pulled open the door and looked round at Clayborne, who was still jammed up tight against the door opposite.

'There's just one thing I'd like to know.'

'Yes?' he replied eagerly, in the desperate hope that she had changed her mind.

'Why are yer guarding that door like that? You got yer bleed'n old woman in there or something?'

When Clayborne, dry-mouthed and sweating profusely, was absolutely certain that the sound of Cissie's footsteps on the stone stairs leading down to the street had really stopped, he ran over to the open doorway and peered down into the gloom to make sure that she wasn't hiding in the shadows of the stairwell, lurking there, ready to catch him out. He waited a moment, then a moment longer, and then, carefully closing the door behind him, he went back into the office and opened the interior door he had defended so resolutely.

'She's gone,' he said stepping into the much bigger and more elaborately furnished room which lay beyond the outer office.

'So I heard,' Big Bill Turner replied.

Turner was sitting there in a studded, leather wing armchair, his feet propped up on the polished brass fender which surrounded the veined marble fireplace. He was staring into the flames, his eyes narrowed against the bright heat.

Jim Phillips, the wholesaler from the flower market, was standing on one side of him, and Bernie and Chalkie, another of Turner's bullet-headed minders, were on the other. Each of the four men had a glass in his hand.

Jim seemed far less at ease than the other three, and sipped nervously at his drink, peering watchfully at the rest of them across the rim of his glass as he raised it to his lips.

'Did you hear everything else all right, Mr Turner?' Clayborne asked.

Turner tapped his finger along the length of his cigar, knocking a shower of grey ash and sparks into the blazing hearth. 'Aw, I heard all right.' He turned his head slowly until he was facing Clayborne.

From the redness of his eyes and his slurred speech, Clayborne guessed that Turner had been responsible for drinking the lion's share of the now almost empty bottle of scotch that was standing on the little side table.

'And I have to say,' Turner mumbled, 'that I weren't very impressed by it.'

'No?' Clayborne's voice was quavering.

'No. I pay you good money, Clayborne. Very good money. And, after that little performance out there, I'd like yer to tell me why I should.'

'You pay me to be your accountant, Mr Turner, and—' Clayborne had begun surprisingly confidently, thinking himself to be on safe ground, but having seen Turner's expression change to one of almost apoplectic fury, he immediately thought better of it and shut his mouth again.

'No, Clayborne, I don't pay yer to be me accountant.' Turner rose unsteadily to his feet, gripping the arms of his chair until his knuckles stood out white against his skin. 'I pay yer to be loyal to me. Bastard loyal.'

Clayborne took a step backwards. 'I did my best, Mr Turner.'

'Your best?' Turner stared at him in disbelief. 'Your bloody best?'

He snatched up his crystal tumbler from the side table and smashed it into the hearth, sending up shards of glittering glass and beads of amber whisky sparkling and dancing in the firelight.

He wasn't shouting, but his ominously low tone, made garbled and faltering by the drink, was enough to terrify the now quaking accountant as Turner moved closer and closer towards him.

Chalkie dodged round both Turner and Clayborne and planted himself in the doorway, blocking the only way out of the room.

'I pay people like them over there,' Turner said, jerking his thumb over his shoulder towards Jim and Bernie, 'so that they can do their job. So they can make my life easier. So that I don't have to worry meself about little details. And that takes loyalty. Understand? Any sodding trained monkey can add up a row of figures but loyalty, that takes bastard brains.'

Jim gulped down the rest of his drink and watched, transfixed by the sordid scene of fear and menace unfolding in front of him. This wasn't a world he was used to.

Clayborne nodded. 'Yes, Mr Turner,' he agreed readily, 'I understand.' Seeing the expression on Turner's face, he'd have said that black was white if he'd have told him to.

But Clayborne's agreement wasn't enough for Turner, it wasn't even what he really wanted. It was Cissie Flowers. Cissie, the bloody woman who was making him so angry. He was furious at the way she had, yet again, slipped out of his reach. And someone was going to pay.

He walked forward, backing Clayborne against the wall, and leant over him. The accountant was tall, but Big Bill Turner dwarfed the man's skinny frame with his own massive bulk.

'I don't get it,' Turner said, spreading his hands to show his sadness. 'I'm putting me neck on the line, making deals with Plains, one of the hardest men in the East End. Buying up property so we can both cut our losses and go into a bit of legitimate business together. And d'yer know why I'm doing all this?'

Clayborne shook his head.

'I'm doing it so I can look after them what work for me. Save 'em having to go out on the streets and doing one another in. And what do I get in return?'

Turner twisted round to see if Jim or Bernie cared to give him the answer. Very wisely, they didn't. This was Turner's show.

'I'll tell yer,' Turner said, shaking his head sorrowfully. 'Disloyalty, that's what I get.'

He slammed his hand hard against the wall, sending the vibrations running through Clayborne's gangly body.

'And I don't like it. I don't like it at all. And know what I don't like even more?'

Claybome shook his head again, he was going to wet his trousers, he just knew he was.

'I don't like you messing it up for me with Davy Flowers' old woman.'

Turner sighed and rubbed the balls of his thumbs hard into his eyes. He was tired, angry. Why did he have to do everything? Why couldn't he trust anyone to do their job properly? Even the simplest thing and he couldn't trust a single one of the prats to do things right for once. His head ached.

He wished Moe was there with him.

'That little tart was begging for it. Ready for the picking,' he said, slowly opening his eyes to stare at Clayborne. 'And you messed it up for me. I really ain't very happy about that.'

Turner's fist moved at such a speed that Clayborne didn't even realise he'd been punched until he felt as though his left kidney had exploded. He slumped forward, and rolled on to the floor, a stream of hot urine running down his leg and puddling out beneath him.

As Turner threw himself upon him, Clayborne felt the first ten or so blows, but after that, as the blood began to flow from his mouth, his nose, and then from his ears and, by the feel of it, from whatever internal organ it was that enabled him to breathe, Clayborne fell into the blissful oblivion of unconsciousness.

All the while that Turner kicked and punched and pummelled, in a blind frenzy of hate and vengefulness that had very little, if anything, to do with the man who had become the object of his rage, Chalkie stood, arms folded, covering the doorway, watching on with a blank, disinterested stare as Clayborne was pounded to a pulp before him. And Bernie stood against the wall opposite, calmly sipping at his scotch.

Jim wasn't made of such strong stuff, he wasn't used to seeing such violence; the worst he had seen were the fights in the pub after work between drunken porters who would more often than not leave as the best of mates, with their arms around one another's shoulders.

He felt the vomit rise in his throat and, rushing to the hearth, Jim spewed into the coal scuttle, the only possible receptacle in the room he could see as appropriate. Even in such a state of nausea and disgust, he didn't dare risk spoiling Turner's rugs.

He then dropped down into the leather armchair, plugged his thumbs into his ears and covered his face with his hands. Anything to try to block out the terrible sight of someone being kicked around like a broken toy by a man who had obviously lost all sense of reason.

Bending down to wipe the blood from the toes of his highly polished shoes with the handkerchief Chalkie had handed to him, Turner smiled with the serenity of satiation. 'He'll know better next time,' he said pleasantly.

With that, he stood up, took a cigar from his inside pocket, stuck it between his lips, and stood there, with his arms outstretched for Bernie to help him on with his overcoat.

'You, Phillips,' he said, shrugging down into the heavy camel-haired Crombie, 'get this mess cleared up. And you, Chalkie, you nip across and get the takings off o' Fat Stan and get 'em down to Mile End. I've gotta be off. Mrs Turner's expecting me in for me tea.'

Turner rolled his eyes and smiled fondly, as though he was dealing with slightly slow children. 'And what's the matter with you, Bernie? Go on, don't just stand there. Go and get that motor started. Yer know how she hates it when I'm late.'

Bemie left without a word, quickly followed by Chalkie.

Turner walked slowly over to the fire and, crouching forward, he took a spill from the box, lit it in the flames and then touched it to the end of his cigar. 'And don't forget to clean out this coal scuttle, will yer, Phillips?' he added amiably.

Turner stayed there for the moment, staring down at Clayborne who was laying beside him on the fireside rug. Apart from the blood and urine, he looked for all the world as though he was curled up for an early evening nap in front of the fire. He looked almost cosy.

With his head cocked to one side, Turner considered the unconscious man. Then he stood up, aimed a final kick hard into Clayborne's kidneys, shook his head sadly at the man's failings, and sauntered over to the door, leaving the room, and a grey-faced Jim Phillips to his tidying up.

Chapter 18

'You're back early, Cis.' Ernie Mills peered over his news-paper at his neighbour as she came into his kitchen. 'What, Monday turn out as bad for business as yer thought it would?'

'No, I just fancied packing the stall away early that's all.'

Ernie nodded approvingly. 'So business was good then, eh?'

Cissie managed a thin smile. 'Something like that, Ern.'

'Well, good luck to yer, girl, that's what I reckon.'

Cissie looked around the jumbled but cosy little room with a frown. 'Gladys and the kids not here?'

Ernie folded his paper and shoved it down between his leg and the side of the chair. 'No. It was such a nice afternoon, as soon as the older ones got in from school, Gladys thought she'd make the most of it. Take 'em all off for a bit of a walk like.'

'Where'd they go?'

'Down Chris Street, to have a look on the stalls.'

'She's brave, taking that little mob.'

'Well, it's like Gladys said, before yer know where we, Cis, the dark nights'll be drawing in again and the kids won't see a bit of sun on their knees for months. I'd have gone with 'em, but Nipper wasn't feeling too bright.'

'Is he all right?' Cissie asked, concerned as much for Ernie and Gladys as for the old man. She knew that if a doctor's visit was called for, it would mean the pair of them going without proper meals for the rest of the week to pay for it.

'He's just a bit worn out, that's all. Not getting any younger, is he? Like the rest of us.' Ernie raised his eyes towards the ceiling. 'He's up having a bit of a lay down before he has his tea.'

Ernie stood up. 'Here, talking about tea. What am I thinking of? Make yerself at home, Cis, and I'll put the kettle on.'

'No, yer all right, Ern.' Cissie held up her hand to stop him going over to the stove. She couldn't let him go wasting their tea on her. 'You sit yerself back down. I don't want nothing, thanks. I'll just have a walk along and meet Gladys.'

'Sure?'

'Yeah, thanks all the same, Ern.' Cissie bowed her head to hide her embarrassment. 'I ain't daft, I realise Glad's just trying to give old Nipper a bit of a blow from all the noise. Me and the kids've been a right nuisance to yer all, ain't we? I just wish there was some way I—'

'Don't even *start* thinking like that,' Ernie reassured her.

'I can't help it, Ern, I feel a right liberty-taker at times the way I've used you lot.'

'Look, Gladys took the chavvies out cos she wanted to. You know what she's like.'

Cissie shook her head in wonder and sighed. 'Yeah, I do, and I dunno how she does it to be honest. She works all them hours scrubbing and cleaning, and she still has time to think about the kids getting out for a bit o' fresh

275

air. Now me, if I was to be truthful with yer, Ern, I catch meself forgetting I've even got my pair at times. 'Specially when I'm dragging that bleed'n stall in and out o' the lock-up.'

'Well who can blame yer for that, girl? I mean, it's flipping hard work running a stall. 'Specially for a woman.'

Cissie nodded in heartfelt agreement. 'Yer can say that again. But yer've gotta earn a living, ain't yer?'

'Yeah,' he said flatly. 'If yer lucky enough to have the chance.'

Cissie felt her cheeks flare. 'Aw, sorry, Ern, me and my big gob. I wasn't thinking. I didn't mean nothing.'

Ernie shrugged resignedly. 'S'all right. I'm getting used to it after all this time. Yer wind up giving up hope after a while, don't yer?'

'Still no sign of no jobs then?'

'Nah, there's nothing going nowhere, Cis.' He pulled out the paper and waved it at her. 'This is a waste o' time, and I've been from one end of the East End to the other knocking on doors, and all I get is insults about me age. They know they can pay women and kids a quarter of a man's earnings, see. But, to be honest, girl, I'd take any sort o' wage if they'd have me. Anything to make Glad's life a bit easier.'

Cissie stood there in embarrassed silence, watching Ernie as he stared down unseeingly at the ragged but spotlessly clean lino.

'Something'll turn up,' she said, not managing to sound very convincing. 'It always does, don't it?'

Slowly, Ernie raised his head and looked at her. 'For some people maybe, Cis. But not for the likes of me I don't reckon.'

Cissie backed away towards the door, a thin smile just managing to bend her lips. 'I'll be getting off now,' she said, knowing she would have nothing else to say to him if she stayed any longer. 'Gladys'll be doing her nut what with your young 'uns and my two nippers hanging round her skirts.'

She was doing her best to sound and look cheerful, but the effort was beginning to make her jaw ache. 'And I'll bet my Joyce'll be moaning for a carry. She hates walking too far, that one.'

With a little wave, Cissie turned on her heel and fled along the passage.

–

As she stepped out into the warm, October afternoon, Cissie gave an involuntary shudder all over her body. Ernie Mills had the very smell of despair and hopelessness about him. And it was making him look like an old man.

It made her think that maybe she should be counting her blessings instead of moaning. There she was, being offered a nice little shop under a block of smart offices in a prime site; and she had two blokes, Turner and Clayborne, who both seemed only too keen to 'look after her' if the shop idea didn't appeal. And that was apart from Sammy Clarke, who was ready to do the slightest little thing for her the second she even mentioned it.

And then there was Ernie, and millions of others just like him, who had lost all hope of getting even a rubbishy sort of job, never mind the sorts of offers she had waiting for her on a plate. She could just imagine what plenty of other women in her position would be saying. She should stop thinking so much of herself and start thinking seriously about her children. All right, she was working her guts out, but she had their future to consider. Maybe that fleeting idea she'd had about it not being so bad being someone's bit on the side for a while was the right one after all.

The trouble was, even the thought of Clayborne or Turner touching her made Cissie feel sick. No. She was sure, that would never ever be her choice.

But then again, maybe she no longer had a choice.

Cissie stood there on Ernie's step, undecided as to whether she should nip across the street to number seven first, to let Lil know she was home, or whether she should go and meet Gladys and the kids straightaway.

It didn't take much consideration. After the day she'd had, the thought of having Lil whining on about Gawd knows what wasn't exactly an attractive proposition, whereas seeing her children most definitely was. So Cissie turned right and walked past the shop, with the intention of going a few yards along Upper North Street and then doubling back along Brabazon Street towards the market. That way she wouldn't have to go past the house and risk getting collared by Lil.

She had just reached the corner of Linman Street and was about to turn left into Upper North Street, when the shop door was flung back on its hinges and Sammy Clarke stepped out, calling after her with loud urgency.

'Cis! Cissie! Hold on. Wait for me.'

She turned round and saw him struggling to untie his apron strings.

'Hello, Sam,' she answered with a lift of her chin. 'Where you off to in such a rush then?'

Sammy, winning his battle with his apron, pitched it over his shoulder into the shop, slammed the door behind him and locked it, leaving the display of goods on the pavement to the mercy of passing children.

'I was just, er, nipping out,' he said, trotting up to her, 'and when I saw yer going by, I thought I could walk along with yer. Bit o' company for yer, like.'

'How about the shop? And how about the, you know, the Godwins?' Cissie jerked her head sideways, indicating number one Linman Street, the end terrace house that stood on the opposite corner to the shop.

'It'll be all right,' he said with an easy-going smile. 'Anyway, how much would a crew even as bad as the Godwins try and nick in broad daylight, eh?'

Cissie's eyes opened wide at Sammy's saintly trust in the innate common sense of the Godwin tribe. 'I don't think the time of day's gonna bother that little lot very much.'

'It'll be all right,' he insisted.

Cissie cocked her head on one side and looked at him. 'You always look on the bright side o' things, don't yer, Sam?'

'I try to,' he shrugged. 'Anyway, why shouldn't I? It's better than always walking about with the blimmin hump, innit? Now, which way are we going?'

Cissie pulled in her chin and studied his face. 'Hang on, Sam, what's going on here? You wasn't going nowhere, was yer?'

Sammy smiled sheepishly. 'I thought yer might wanna have a bit of a talk, that's all. When I saw yer coming out of Gladys and Ernie's just now, yer looked a bit, yer know, worried about something. And when I noticed yer never had the kids with yer, I wondered if yer was upset cos yer'd had a knock back from that Clayborne bloke.'

'Yer notice a lot, don't yer?'

Sammy looked mortified. 'Aw, look, Cis. I don't want yer getting the wrong idea or nothing. I wasn't being nosy. Honest. I was just wondering whether yer managed to set up a meeting with that property bloke.'

Cissie ran her fingers through her hair, pulling her fringe back off her forehead. 'I'm sorry, Sam. I know I'm being a bit touchy. I've got a lot on me mind, ain't I?'

She smiled gently and nudged him matily on the arm. 'I'm really sorry.'

'So, can I walk along with yer then?'

'Course yer can. But I ain't going nowhere exciting. I'm just gonna go and meet Gladys and the kids. But come on, it'll give me the chance to tell you all about what happened this afternoon.' She glanced sideways at him. 'I went to see him, didn't I?'

Sammy and Cissie waited on the corner of Upper North Street for a raucous rag-and-bone-man to pass by on his way towards Bow Common Lane; the clattering and rattling and ringing from his horse, his cart and his handbell all competing with the racket he was making with his strangulated cries for custom.

'So he saw yer right away then, this Clayborne feller?' Sammy called over the din. 'That's gotta be a good sign.'

Cissie said nothing.

'Did he see sense?' he asked.

They stepped down from the pavement into the road, Sammy reaching for Cissie's arm to guide her round a steaming pile of droppings left by the ragman's shaggy-legged pony.

'Not exactly, Sam,' she replied, daintily avoiding both the dung and Sammy's touch. 'In fact,' she went on, 'I think I'm in right schtuck, if yer really wanna know.'

Not wishing to risk offending her further, Sammy hastily shoved his hands into his trouser pockets – it was all too tempting to reach out to touch her.

'It can't be that bad,' he said, as they turned into Brabazon Street to cut through to the market.

'Sam,' she sighed, 'I reckon it's just about as bad as it can get, mate. See, I reckon I've just about messed it up as far as it can be messed up. I'm in real trouble now. Going to see Clayborne was me last hope, I know that.'

'What, wouldn't he even listen to yer?'

'He listened all right, but then he did some talking of his own.'

'Yeah?'

'Yeah.' Cissie hesitated a moment, working out how much to tell him. 'He offered me the lease,' she eventually went on, 'on one of the new shops they're gonna build when they pull down the factory.'

'Aw,' Sammy said flatly, 'a shop. And what did you say to that?'

'I said I probably wouldn't be able to afford the sort of rent he had in mind.'

'A lot was it?' Sammy hated it in himself, but he felt immediately relieved; Cissie leasing a shop was the last thing he wanted, it would have ruined his plans, the plans that he had been secretly hatching for months.

Cissie turned her head slightly to one side so that Sammy couldn't see her face. 'Yeah, it was,' she said, picturing Clayborne's watery hazel eyes as he made his offer about coming to 'an arrangement'.

'A lot more than you could afford by the sound of it.'

'Yer right there, Sam,' she said, and added, almost inaudibly, 'Well, let's just say it was a lot more than I'd be prepared to pay.'

She turned her head to face him again. 'So, like I say, I reckon I'm in schtuck.'

They reached the end of Brabazon Street, and were just about to turn into Chrisp Street when Sammy pulled his hands from his pockets and took hold of her arm. 'It don't have to be like that, Cis,' he said.

Cissie frowned as she stared down at his hand grasping her sleeve.

'Like what?' she said, raising her eyes to look at him.

Sammy let go of her and tapped the back of one hand rhythmically into the palm of the other. 'It don't have to be a problem. I mean, maybe it's all for the best in the long run.'

'I don't understand.'

'Look,' he said standing there facing her on the corner, blocking her way into Chrisp Street. 'I want yer to hear what I've gotta say.'

Cissie frowned, not understanding what he was going on about, but she didn't try to get past him.

'Yer've got me sympathy, Cis, you know that,' he began. 'There's a lot o' things that have happened to you in these past six months, things that'd make anyone feel desperate. But you've managed, you've coped. And yer should be proud o' yerself for that. But maybe losing the stall like this is for the best after all.'

Cissie stuck her fists into her waist. 'I think yer've taken leave o' your senses Sammy Clarke, ain't yer.'

'No, I've not. Please, just listen. I've thought about it, thought about it a lot and it all makes sense.'

'It might make sense to you, mate—'

'Please, Cis, just hear me out.' Sammy exhaled loudly and tapped his pockets, looking for something. 'You ain't got a fag on yer, have yer, Cis? I'm gasping for one.'

Without a word, Cissie opened her bag and took out her packet of Craven A. They both took one and lit them from Cissie's match.

'See, the way I see it is yer don't have to worry about all that any more.'

'All what?'

'Earning a living. Getting up at all hours. Worrying about leaving the kids.'

'What, live off me fortune, shall I?' she snapped sarcastically. 'Grow up, Sam, this is the world where kids need grub and new boots, not the world where pretty princesses get saved by marrying blokes on big white horses.'

'I'd save yer. If yer married me.'

Cissie's eyebrows shot up and her mouth fell open. 'Do *what*?'

'I know it's come as a bit of a surprise to yer—'

'Surprise? Yer can say that again. I'm bloody stunned.' Cissie looked frantically about her.

She reached out and grabbed Sammy by the braces, yanking him towards her, pulling him back into Brabazon Street. The street was full of kids tearing up and down playing some sort of racing game, but at least they weren't in full view of the market there. Mind you, it was bad enough, all Cissie needed was a few of the children's mothers to come out and start rounding them up for their teas, and stories about her and Sammy Clarke would be all round the neighbourhood before bedtime.

'But it makes so much sense,' Sammy went on, growing more confident as he spoke of the familiar ideas, which, he would have been ashamed to have admitted, had been in his head since the moment he had heard of Davy Flowers' death. 'I know yer've only been widowed a while.'

'Yeah, six months,' said Cissie, agitatedly, blowing a stream of smoke over her shoulder.

'But Lil's never seemed too bothered about the idea of you getting yourself another chap, has she? I mean, the way she went on about you and Big Bill Turner. And she's Davy's own mother.'

'Lil don't seem bothered?' Cissie said, transfixed by the madness of what she was hearing. 'How about what bothers me?'

'Look, Cis, I know I'm no oil painting, and I know yer could have the pick of any feller yer fancied, what with your looks and how clever you are and everything.' He dropped his half-smoked cigarette to the pavement and watched it as he ground it out beneath the heel of his boot. 'But just think what a help we could be to one another,' he said, lifting his head.

He looked at her with a smile of luminous yearning. 'You could work in the shop and keep the house for me. And I'd make a good home for the little ones and for Lil. It would be a really practical solution for both of us. I've never had much opportunity to meet anyone else, what with looking after Mum and Dad and running the place all these years—'

'But how about love?' Cissie interrupted him in a voice so small it could barely get past her lips.

Sammy's smile became less convincing. 'I know yer don't love me, Cis,' he said, tapping his chest, 'but, honest, I've got love enough in here for the two of us. I've always loved you, Cissie. Always.' He scratched his head shyly. 'And who knows how these things come to happen. Maybe one day yer might come to think something o' me and all.'

'But I already think a lot of yer, Sam. A real lot. But I don't—'

'I know, but please, will yer just think about it?'

'I don't know if I—'

'Please?'

'Mum!'

Hearing the familiar voice, Cissie looked past Sammy and saw Matty launching himself around the corner at her.

She held out her arms and ran along the street towards him. 'Hello, darling.'

Matty clasped his arms round her legs and buried his head into her coat.

Sammy stepped back and leant against the wall, watching the two of them hugging, and knew that Cissie and her child were sharing more warmth, standing there on that street corner, than he had ever experienced in his whole life.

His head told him that he had probably just made the worst mistake possible and that he had put Cissie, beautiful, gentle Cissie, off him for good. But his heart was skipping like a sixteen-year-old's as visions of him being included in such a family embrace filled his mind with hope.

'Hello, Cis. This is a surprise. What you doing here?'

Cissie and Sammy both looked up to see Gladys appearing from around the comer with children bouncing around her like eager puppies.

Gladys looked puzzled. 'And you, Sammy Clarke...'

'I'll see yer later, ladies,' Sammy said, chucking Matty under the chin. 'I'd better be off before the Godwins clear me out. Don't forget what I said though, Cis, will yer?'

Cissie nodded. 'I'll think about it,' she said, bending down to scoop Joyce into her arms.

'Good,' he replied simply, and with that Sammy treated them all to a brief smile and set off back along Brabazon Street.

Gladys stood next to Cissie and watched, bursting with questions but silent, until Sammy had disappeared into Upper North Street.

'Well, what was all that about then?' she asked. 'We come back this way so's we didn't have to put up with seeing Myrtle and that mob. But we didn't expect—'

'Can yer keep a secret?' Cissie interrupted her.

'You know me, Cissie, course I can.' Gladys thought for a moment. 'Hang on.' She clapped her hands loudly. 'Right you lot!' she hollered authoritatively, beckoning to the children who were involved in trying to construct a sort of human pyramid against the wall of the house on the comer, with Gladys's youngest serving as its wobbly, crowning peak.

As they hurried to obey – there were never any tantrums, refusals or questions when Gladys clapped her hands and spoke in that particular voice – the children tumbled to the ground in a heap, picked themselves up without a murmur and scampered over to her.

'Right, I want the lot of yers to listen to me. Right?'

286

A row of little heads nodded.

'And I don't want no arguments,' she began, counting off her points on her fingers. 'I want all of yer to stay on the pavement *all the time*. And I don't want no roads being crossed on the way.'

'Where we going then, Mum?' asked Terry, at nine, Gladys's and Ernie's eldest child.

'Yer gonna ran all the way home to the corner of Linman Street and yer gonna see who can run the fastest,' she said with a surreptitious wink at him, acknowledging the fact that both she and Terry knew that he could outrun the lot of them but would let the little ones have a good time thinking they were in with a chance. 'And you, Terry, I want you to hold Joyce's hand every step o' the way. Understand?'

Terry nodded eagerly. He reached out and grabbed Joyce almost before Cissie had set her down on the pavement beside him. He was being put in charge – well, as good as – and he liked the feeling.

'We'll all be all right, Mum,' he reassured Gladys, getting Joyce in a grip firm enough to have held a dog chasing a rabbit. 'And don't worry,' he added in a whisper, 'I'll keep an eye on 'em all.'

'And no collecting up no strays on the way,' Gladys called after them.

With much hooting and hollering, the children sped off along the pavement in the direction of home.

'Right, that's them taken care of,' puffed Gladys, linking arms with Cissie. 'Now we've got a bit o' privacy, yer can tell me all about this secret o' your'n.'

Cissie licked her lips and began. 'Yer know I've been running the stall, Glad?'

'No!' Gladys exclaimed. 'You never have! And there was me thinking yer was going out at the crack o' dawn every morning to pick up sailors down the docks.'

'Cheeky mare!' grinned Cissie, elbowing her friend in the side. 'I just don't know where to start, do I? It's sort of, well, difficult.'

'Well, I know quite a lot about yer already, girl, so I reckon yer could start straight in with this secret, whatever it is, and,' she added, laying her hand dramatically on her chest, 'I promise yer, I won't be shocked.'

'Yer might be actually, Glad.' Cissie halted, pulling Gladys to a stop beside her. 'Sammy Clarke's only asked me to marry him.'

"He's done what?'

Cissie looked round anxiously. 'All right, Glad, don't go shouting it so's everyone can hear.'

'Sammy Clarke.' Gladys shook her head in amazement. 'Here, is that what was going on just now? You two walking along all cosy together and him proposing!'

'Yeah.' Cissie nodded. 'Yer know I couldn't believe it. I thought I was hearing things at first.'

'He's always fancied you though, Cis. Everyone knows that.'

Cissie frowned. 'Do they?'

'Course they do.' Gladys rolled her eyes at her friend's naivety. 'So how did he, you know, ask yer then?'

Instead of answering straightaway, Cissie pulled out her cigarettes and she and Gladys both lit one as they began to move slowly along the street.

'Well?' Gladys prompted her.

'It's all gotta do with the stall.' She flicked a sideways glance at Gladys. 'That's what I was trying to explain. Anyway, it looks like I'm gonna lose the pitch.'

'Aw, Cis, no, that's terrible.'

'I know. They're pulling down the factory, see, and putting up offices with poncey little shops under 'em. The bloke what's doing it offered me one. But there was strings attached, if yer know what I mean.'

'I know what yer mean, all right, dirty bastard. They want it chopping off, some fellers.'

'Yer right there, Glad. Anyway, so I told Sammy and he said maybe losing the pitch wasn't such bad news, and that I could marry him instead.'

'He never!' This time it was Gladys who pulled them to a halt. 'That's gotta be the most unromantic, rotten way of proposing I've ever heard in the whole o' my life.'

Cissie snatched a nervous drag on her cigarette. 'I'm making it sound horrible, it wasn't like that at all, it was… Anyway, I've only been a widow for six months, haven't I? What does he expect?' Cissie tugged anxiously at her fringe. 'I dunno, Glad. What do you think?'

'D'yer wanna know the truth? The honest to God, on my Ernie's life truth?'

'Course I do.'

'Well, I think, Cissie Flowers, that you would be stark, staring, raving, flipping bonkers if yer didn't jump at the chance. Say yes, girl! Don't let this chance get away from yer.'

Gladys closed her eyes and threw back her head. 'Being married to a grocer! It's a sodding dream come true. Never having to worry about where the next meal's gonna come from, or if yer can afford to make another pot o' tea.' She moaned ecstatically. 'Bleed'n bliss! Marry him girl, and yer'll never have to worry again.'

Cissie sighed wearily and blew a stream of smoke through her pursed lips, narrowing her eyes as she tried desperately to put her confused thoughts and churning feelings into words.

But all she could come up with was, 'Yeah, Glad, but *Sammy Clarke?*'

Chapter 19

While Cissie and Gladys walked along slowly behind them – each deep in thought as to what marriage to Sammy Clarke would mean – the children got on with their much speedier and far more erratic journey home. Authorised bursts of running ahead of their mothers were interspersed with sudden halts, predetermined by Terry, at street corners where they were not only in danger from any passing traffic, but where they might also disappear from sight and get up to no good, meaning that Terry would be in trouble with his mum for letting them.

But once they'd turned into Linman Street the younger ones, apart from Joyce, all raced on ahead of him, heedless of his shouted instructions, warnings and threats, and threw themselves into the boisterous game of British Bulldog which the Godwins, and assorted other children from the surrounding neighbourhood, already had well underway. And which, despite her living at the other end of the street, Myrtle Payne had found reason to complain about, and was voicing her displeasure at a volume that was causing far more disturbance than all of the kids could manage between them.

It was this scene – Myrtle bellowing at the heap of sprawling children, including Terry, whose efforts at containment and order had been abandoned to the seductive thrills of knocking his mates flying across the rough surface of the tarry blocks and into the middle of the road – which confronted Cissie and Gladys as they turned into Linman Street.

Matty was the first to spot them coming round the corner, and was up on his feet and running towards them before they had even passed the shop.

'All right if Terry comes indoors and sees me soldiers, Mum?' he yelled, intent on cementing his alliance with such a grown-up kid as Terry Mills, a move that would definitely bring him honour in the playground. 'I said he could but I had to ask you first.'

Relieved to see her son, who had been so serious lately, in such carefree high spirits, and determined to demonstrate to Myrtle that some adults actually approved of children having a harmless bit of fun, Cissie ruffled Matty's hair and smiled down at him. 'Course it is, babe, and tell yer what, why don't yer take the rest of 'em indoors and all, and I'll see if Sammy's got a farthing's worth of odds to share out between yers and all, shall I?'

Whoops of pleasure from the gang of kids disappearing into number seven were Cissie's only answer, as she watched, with a sinking heart, as the Godwins, and a couple of other youngsters she knew by sight but not by name, all presumed that the invitation had been extended to them as well. She made a mental note to get out the nit comb before she put her two to bed that night – the Godwins being notoriously cooty – but refused to call them all back out as Myrtle was still standing there as though she was on guard duty.

'I like to see kids having a good time,' Cissie said loudly and pointedly, for Myrtle's benefit, then added under her breath to Gladys as she pushed open the door to the shop, 'Might as well try and keep the poor little so-and-sos happy while I can, eh, Glad? Cos I ain't gonna be able to afford no luxuries like sweets when the stall's finished.'

'Blimey, Cis,' Gladys whispered, as she followed her friend into the shop doorway, 'you're a bit bold coming in here so soon, ain't yer? You ain't made yer mind up already surely, have yer?'

Cissie's eyes opened wide with realisation. 'Aw Christ! I wasn't thinking,' she hissed back. 'Mind.' Cissie went to turn round to escape, but Gladys blocked her way.

'Too late now,' Gladys grinned, pushing her right inside. She followed her friend in and looked around the shop, shaking her head in wonder at such riches. 'All this. Just look at it, Cis. All of it. You can have every single thing. A farthing's worth of odds'll be nothing. Yer'll be able to have a quarter o' pear drops or half a pound o' barley sugars whenever yer feel like 'em. How can yer even think about turning him down?'

'Gladys!' Cissie spluttered, all too aware of Sammy's chubby pink face beaming at her from across the counter, and of Ethel, arms akimbo, glaring at this interruption to her shopping. 'Will you be quiet?'

'Hello, Cissie. Glad,' Sammy greeted them, keeping his eyes fixed on Cissie.

'Oi!' the elderly woman exclaimed, slapping her hand on the counter. 'D'you want me custom or not, Samuel Clarke? Cos if yer don't, there's plenty of other shop-keepers round here what do.'

Very calmly, Sammy folded his arms across his aproned chest and addressed Ethel in a slow, unflustered way. 'Well, Ethel,' he began, 'of course I do. In fact, I value your custom very highly indeed. I mean, I can't think what I'd do to get by if I was to lose the price of a quarter o' tea, a stale loaf, and a slab o' marge every couple o' days. But,' and here, he gave a low, gentlemanly bow, 'the choice of where you shop is, madam, entirely yours.'

Gladys didn't quite register Sammy's meaning for a moment, but then it clicked, and she threw back her head and burst out into loud, uninhibited laughter. 'That told her, Sam!'

Ethel was fuming. 'I've never in all my life—'

'Aw, ain't yer?' squealed Gladys, now almost uncontrollable with laughter. 'So where did your Lena come from then? Out o' the cabbage patch?'

'That's it, I don't have to come in here to get insulted.'

'So where d'yer usually go for your insults then, Ett?' Gladys snorted.

Catching Cissie's stony expression out of the corner of her eye, Gladys thought that maybe she'd pushed things too far, so she bit her lip and did her best to stop herself from saying anything more, although her shoulders still shook with suppressed laughter.

Sammy, on the other hand, still had the devil in him and, knowing how Cissie had always enjoyed a lark, he carried on the joke. Eyes twinkling, he made a great show of wrapping Ethel's purchases and then presenting them to her with a flourish as though they were the finest provisions from an exclusive West End emporium. 'Madam,' he pronounced solemnly, 'your groceries.'

Gladys squeezed her lips tightly together as Ethel snatched up her things and strode across the shop to the door, with her chin in the air, and an angry, 'I'll pay you later, Samuel Clarke.' Then she stood there in the doorway, waiting for any further cracks from any of them, muttering darkly about what Sammy's mother and father would have had to say about such carryings on.

'He did all that just to make you laugh, Cis, you do know that, don't yer?' Gladys whispered to Cissie behind her hand. 'Yer know, I reckon he'd do anything to impress you. Give you anything yer wanted, he would.'

'I dunno what's got into you, Gladys, but I wish yer'd keep yer trap shut,' Cissie spat back at her.

From her position in the doorway, Ethel narrowed her eyes at the two women whispering animatedly behind their hands. Going by her own standards they would be saying bad things about her, and she didn't like it, but, as she had no allies there in the shop to support her, she stepped backwards to leave them to it. She would repay them later – with interest.

However, to add to her indignation, Ethel's supposedly dignified withdrawal from the shop was ruined. Her exit was blocked by the sudden explosion of a bundle of youngsters all cannoning through the doorway at once, sending Ethel stumbling back into the shop.

'Matty! What d'yer think you're doing?' Cissie demanded. She might not have had any time for the likes of Ethel Bennett but Cissie wouldn't put up with that sort of behaviour from her children. 'Now, you let Mrs Bennett out o' that door at once!'

The sound of such determined authority in an adult's voice was enough to chasten all of the children to a silent, respectful halt. They stepped to one side and let the now puce-faced Ethel leave with what little dignity she had left.

When the shop door was closed behind her and the little bell had stopped its jangling, Cissie spoke to Matty again. 'Whatever's got into you, child? Pushing past an adult like that. And I don't know if I'm going to get them sweets I promised yer now. Not after that show-up,' she added, wagging her finger at him. 'And how about yer soldiers? I thought yer was all gonna play nicely together.'

Shamefaced at being the cause of his mother's displeasure, Matty swung his shoulders from side to side and stared down at the sawdust-strewn floor. 'Nanna Lil's talking funny, and she told us all to get out.'

Cissie swallowed hard and flashed a sharp look at Gladys. Talking funny. They both knew what that meant. Lil was pissed again. Cissie felt like going straight over to number seven and wrapping her hands around Lil's bloody throat and shaking her till she sobered up.

'Glad, would you mind keeping an eye—'

Gladys didn't let her finish. 'We never finished that story that Uncle Ernie started earlier, did we?' she said, taking Joyce by the hand.

'He's not Uncle Ernie,' chipped in Gladys's youngest. 'He's our dad.'

'That's enough of that, thank you very much.' Gladys opened her eyes wide in warning, silencing him immediately.

'Here, Sam,' Cissie said, putting down a thru'penny piece on the counter, 'weigh 'em out some sweets, will yer?'

'Course I will,' Sammy replied, reaching down and chucking Matty under the chin. 'But I don't need no money. This is my treat.'

With that, he flipped the coin back to her in a glittering arc, right across the shop.

As Cissie caught it, she also caught Gladys's 'I-told-you-so' expression. The sight of her friend winking so knowingly had her fleeing from the shop faster than if she'd had Old Nick himself on her tail.

'D'yer mind telling me how yer got the money to pay for this?' Cissie asked.

She walked over to the kitchen table, snatched up the half-empty bottle of gin and weighed it in her hand.

Lil peered up at her through bloodshot, unfocused eyes. 'It was another little surprise, weren't it?' she mumbled happily.

'A surprise?' Cissie asked, backing away from the blast of Lil's alcohol-tainted breath. 'How d'yer mean, a surprise?'

Lil smiled wonkily. 'Money. Found it on the mat, didn't I? Shoved through the letterbox it was, just like that other lot.'

Cissie dropped down on to the chair opposite Lil's. 'Give it here,' she said slowly and deliberately.

'What?' asked Lil, her mind befuddled with the drink.

'The rest o' the money.'

Lil shrugged non-committally. 'Don't know if there is any more.'

'Stop sodding around, Lil, or I'm gonna get the hump. Now, just hand it over.'

Cissie pocketed the two five-pound notes that Lil eventually surrendered to her, and then went over to put on the kettle, to start the process of sobering up her mother-in-law before the children came back from Gladys's.

She sighed wearily to herself as she took down the tea caddy from the dresser. Lil was such a bloody nuisance. If only she hadn't been Davy's mum she would have booted her out of the house so fast her feet wouldn't have touched the ground. But she *was* Davy's mum and so she had to put up with her.

Anyway, she was lucky in other ways. She hadn't even given Sammy his answer, but he'd still come straight back from walking along with her and had put the money through her door, just because he knew she was worried about losing the stall. He probably wouldn't admit it though, just like last time, but Cissie knew it was him. There was no one else it could be.

He was a good feller. Really kind. But if only she could think of him as a man rather than as good old Sammy Clarke. If only he was a bit more like Jim Phillips…

–

By the time Cissie had managed to get her mother-in-law to swallow almost the whole contents of the teapot and to coax several slices of buttered toast down her throat, Lil was considerably less incoherent, and was even looking reasonably presentable. Not wonderful, but she would do for when the children returned from Gladys's.

Cissie topped up the empty pot with a couple of spoons of tea leaves and some freshly boiled water and poured them both another cup.

'There's something I wanna talk to yer about before the kids get back,' Cissie said carefully.

'Aw yeah,' Lil replied, stirring a heap of sugar into her tea. 'Gonna tell me off for trying to forget me pain, are yer? That's why I do it, yer know, to forget.'

'Yeah, yeah, all right.' Cissie rubbed her hands over her face. 'But that ain't what I wanna talk about – not this time anyway,' she added bluntly. 'I wanna talk to yer about something that's gonna affect us all. Me, you, and the kids.'

Lil tore her gaze away from the gin bottle that Cissie had stood on the draining board, so tantalisingly close to her grasp, and looked across at her. 'What yer talking about? Affect us all?'

'Sammy Clarke's asked me to marry him.'

'He's *what*?' Lil screeched.

'Calm down, Lil, I ain't said I will or nothing.'

'I should bloody well think you ain't,' she fumed.

'I know it must hurt, Lil,' Cissie said, staring down at the tabletop. 'Davy being yer only son. But I'm a young woman. I don't like even to think about it, but I'm probably gonna get married again one day, and so—'

'This ain't nothing to do with Davy,' Lil snapped.

Cissie raised her eyes and looked at Lil who was almost vibrating with temper. 'How d'yer mean?' Cissie asked carefully.

'I couldn't give a bugger who yer marry, or when yer marry for that matter,' she sputtered. 'In fact, the sooner the better for my part. I'm fed up skivvying round here while you swan about all day. But what the hell does a good looker like you wanna waste yer time with a no-hope, sodding grocer like Sammy Clarke for?'

Lil's face twisted in a contemptuous sneer. 'You could do better for us both than the likes of *him*.'

Cissie felt sick. 'What's wrong with you, Lil? You're no mother. Yer son's been dead for six months and how many times have you even been to the cemetery? Yer've never had any time for me, I know that, but you ain't gonna treat me the way yer treated Davy. If you don't watch that mouth o' your'n, yer gonna come in for quite a shock, cos I ain't got no reason to be your meal ticket if I don't wanna. Got it? You ain't gonna take liberties with me the way yer did with Davy.'

Cissie raked her hands roughly through her hair, pulling it back off her face.

Lil, the drink still sloshing around in her veins, was trembling with fury. She leant across the table and jabbed her finger at Cissie's chest. 'You ain't got a clue. D'you *really* wanna know the truth about Davy?'

Cissie blinked warily. 'Don't say nothing yer gonna regret, Lil. Yer pissed. You dunno what yer talking about.'

'Aw, don't I?' Lil taunted Cissie. 'Well, let me tell you, if you hadn't have been so bastard greedy, Davy would never have done what he did, and you wouldn't be a widow with two little kids to bring up on yer own.'

Cissie shook her head. 'No. I ain't gonna listen. I've heard all sorts of shit about him before. All that stuff about him running a book and I don't believe none of it. And nor should you.'

'Running a book!' Lil snorted. 'That's all you know. Betting ain't the half of it.'

Cissie went to stand up, to get away, but Lil reached out and grabbed her arm, pulling her back down.

'Not the half of it by a long chalk, yer silly cow.'

Cissie dragged her arm from Lil's grasp and rose unsteadily to her feet. She shook her head and backed away towards the door. 'You're just saying all this to hurt me. You're just a spiteful, wicked old woman who don't know how else to get at me.'

'Am I?' Lil stood up too and began walking slowly towards her. 'And what are you? A moaning, lazy—'

Cissie lunged at Lil. Lil stumbled sideways, and fell against the dresser, sending a shower of cups and plates crashing to the floor.

'That's it,' she screamed, 'attack a defenceless old woman.'

'Attack yer?' Cissie yelled back. 'Yer lucky I ain't throttled yer!'

The two women stared at one another across the room, neither of them moving, until Cissie suddenly turned her back on Lil, went over to the sink and turned on the tap.

She let the water run until it was icy-cold and then splashed it over her face.

She turned round and faced her mother-in-law. 'You and me had better get a few things straight,' Cissie breathed. 'So I reckon you'd better sit down at that table and get ready to answer one or two questions. Like whether Davy really was involved in street betting, and whether there really is something else to tell me.'

Lil sat back down at the table and fiddled with her empty cup, turning it round and round in the saucer. Almost stone-cold sober now, she was regretting the price she was having to pay for her moment of drunken glory over her daughter-in-law.

Just watching her sit there made Cissie feel like running out of the house, but she had the terrible feeling that she was about to discover some very unpleasant truths, or rather, some very uncomfortable lies that she had been living.

'So, come on then. What are yer gonna tell me?'

'Not much,' Lil said flatly, shifting her weight on her chair.

'You'd better tell me what yer mean, Lil, when yer say "not much".' Cissie's voice was not raised, but it was obvious that she would brook no more evasions.

'I told him yer was gonna leave him,' Lil said bluntly.

'You did *what*?'

'When he first started seeing yer, I told him that if he had any ideas about marrying a pretty girl like you, he'd better buck his ideas up and find a way of bringing in a bit more dough. I said that yer'd told me, in confidence like, that there was all these other blokes with loads o' money sloshing about, and cos yer wouldn't be able to manage to keep yerself looking nice on the sort of money he was fetching in from his dad's old stall, you'd probably wind up going off with one of 'em. But it was all a terrible shame cos you was desperate to stay with him, cos he was the one yer really liked.'

Cissie rolled her eyes at the ceiling. 'I don't believe I'm hearing this.'

Lil shrugged. 'It worked out all right, didn't it? He was already taking the bets like for himself, just like his dad used to, but he earnt a whole lot more once he started up for Turner—'

'You mean he really was running a book for him?'

'Course he was.'

'And you knew all along?'

'Blimey, Cissie. Course I did. I was his bleed'n mother, wasn't I?'

Cissie was too dumbfounded to answer.

'Well, it was nice, wasn't it, having the extra money?' Lil smiled, a sly, slow smile. ''Specially when everyone else

302

round here was doing so bad. It made me feel proud, being able to flash a few quid about.'

She drained the last of the tea into her cup and lit herself another cigarette without offering one to Cissie.

'But you know what it's like.' She was speaking as though Cissie was someone she was chatting to in the bus queue, rather than her son's widow. 'I had this feeling, deep down like, that having a little bit more would be even nicer. That's when I put the idea in his head.'

'What idea?' Cissie asked flatly.

Lil smiled again, obviously pleased with the memory. 'I told him he better watch himself, cos it was obvious, wasn't it? Even though yer was married, a nice-looking girl like you, a girl what'd had plenty o' blokes hanging around her in the past. Well, the first rich feller what showed a bit of interest, you'd be off with him, wouldn't yer?'

'You told him *what*?' gasped Cissie, sending her chair flying as she sprang to her feet. 'I ain't never been with no one except Davy. No one!'

'I didn't think you had,' she shrugged casually. 'But what did that matter? He started doing other little jobs for Turner, and then a bit more besides – for himself like, and it all worked out all right, didn't it?'

Calmly, Lil took a drag on her cigarette. 'Well, at first it did. But it sort of got a bit out of hand. I must've pushed it too far. Saying how you was gonna leave him and that.' Cissie was gripping the edge of the table. 'Go on.'

'Well, he sort o' got carried away with the idea, didn't he? And one night, when he got in right late, he come into me room, before he went upstairs to you, and he was crying his bloody eyes out. Like a right big baby he was.'

'When? When was this?'

Lil thought for a moment. 'Dunno. Ages ago. Matty could only have been a couple o' months old, cos I'd just moved into that bloody front parlour, hadn't I? I hate it in—'

'Don't even think o' starting on that, Lil.'

'Anyway,' Lil wisely decided to continue, 'it must have been about then. Well, he was moaning and groaning and carrying on.' She shook her head fondly. 'Silly sod. Anyone would have thought he'd committed a bloody murder, the way he was leading off.'

'So what had he done?' Cissie asked quietly. She was shaking all over.

'He'd knocked off some little tart he'd picked up in a boozer near the market,' Lil answered lightly. 'He'd been feeling a bit sorry for himself, see? Wanted to prove he still had it in him. Yer know what fellers are like? Anyway, after that, it didn't seem to worry him so much. He just got on with it. But he always told his old mum about his latest girls, and there was enough of 'em.'

Before Lil realised what was happening, Cissie had smacked the cigarette from her grasp with one hand and had caught her a stinging wallop across the cheek with the other.

'You vicious, spiteful...' Cissie couldn't go on, words failed her.

Lil rose to her feet. 'Yer'll be sorry you ever raised yer hand to me,' she seethed.

'Aw no, Lil, you've got that wrong,' Cissie breathed. 'I ain't the one who's gonna be sorry.'

Chapter 20

'You said yer wanted yer answer today. About the shop lease.'

Having refused a seat, Cissie was standing in front of Clayborne's desk. Her mouth was dry and her legs felt as though they might buckle under her at any moment, but she was determined to keep her chin in the air and her voice steady.

If she hadn't been in such a state of raw-nerved anxiety, Cissie would have realised that Clayborne was in a far worse state than she was. In fact, if she had just looked at him, rather than stood before him addressing him as though he were a public meeting, she would have realised that there was something very wrong with Clayborne indeed.

'That's right ain't it?' she went on, with a superior flick of her eyebrow. 'Yer wanted it today? Well, I've come to give it to yer.'

'I'm very glad, Mrs Flowers,' Clayborne replied weakly. 'Delighted.'

Every word Clayborne uttered made his chest hurt like hell. Turner had done his usual skilful job when he'd worked him over the day before. He'd hurt him good and proper without leaving a single visible mark on him. To all intents and purposes, Clayborne didn't even have so much as a cat scratch. Unlike some of his less refined henchmen, Turner was a real professional when it came to beating people up.

'Me name ain't Flowers,' Cissie snapped back, the pain of Lil's words from the night before hurting her, did Clayborne only but know it, far more than his bruises were hurting him. 'It's Prentice.'

Cissie spelt out the name for him so that there would be no further mistakes. 'And I can't say as I even like Prentice very much, to tell yer the truth,' she added, dragging her handbag further up her arm.

She could hardly keep still, it was as though she was standing barefoot on broken glass. She fiddled with her gloves, then stuffed them into her swagger coat pocket, tugged at her fringe, then tucked her hair behind her ears.

It was so claustrophobic standing there in Clayborne's dismal, rotten office, with him staring up at her, appraising her, through his watery hazel eyes. It was like being some clapped-out, cheap old brass standing on a street corner while a dithering punter tried to make up his mind whether she was worth the ten bob he had left in his pocket.

That might have been how Clayborne made her feel, but Cissie didn't look like some low-cost streetwalker. Far from it. She looked good, and she had every right to. She had taken so much care over her appearance that morning; she had dressed as though she was attending a wedding, had put on her powder and lipstick as though she was the bride herself, and had polished her shoes until they shone like mirrors. Cissie had decided that if she was to keep any sort of control of the situation where she would be dealing with a man who spoke as though he had swallowed a mouthful of prunes, then she would have to feel good about herself, and for her that meant looking good too.

But it hadn't been easy. As she'd woken that morning, after what had seemed like a night spent wide awake and staring up at the ceiling with tears streaming down her cheeks and into her ears, the thought of Davy going with other women had stabbed into her mind as surely and as viciously as a kick in the kidneys or a stiletto blade across the cheek could ever have done.

Davy and other women. It was enough to kill her.

She'd rolled herself out of bed, had snatched the photograph of her, Matty and Davy at Southend off the side, and had shoved it roughly into the bottom drawer of the tallboy, where it could stay for ever for all she cared. Lil and her heartless, ugly words had ripped the very soul out of what Cissie had most cherished, and she would never, ever forgive her.

'So, Mrs Prentice.' Clayborne pronounced her name with great care. 'You're ready to sign the lease. I'm very pleased to hear that.'

Sticking her chin even further in the air, and looking down her nose at him, Cissie said calmly, 'I said I've come to give yer me answer, Mr Clayborne. But I didn't say what me answer was gonna be. And, if yer must know, you can stick yer lease, cos me answer's no. I wouldn't sign that bloody lease if it had flaming bells dangling off it.'

Clayborne bent forward across the desk. He was propped on the very edge of his seat. His body blazed with fresh agony every time he moved, but he knew he had to persuade her. He had to. He had to make her see sense.

'But I don't think you fully understand the implications, Mrs Prentice,' he wheezed urgently.

Cissie frowned. Clayborne sounded odd, sort of fidgety. Why should he give a toss about whether it was her or one of a million other flower sellers who rented his poncey shop? She'd already made it quite clear that she wasn't interested in having any of his funny business. He could have offered her a double-fronted property, wrapped in red ribbons, right in the middle of bloody Regent Street and she still wouldn't have changed her mind.

All right, she had her price, Cissie knew that now, and would have to come to terms with the fact that she had, over the years, chosen to turn a blind eye to the question of how Davy had managed to provide so well for them during such hard times. But her price would never be the sort that Clayborne or Big Bill Turner had in mind. That was a price she would never pay. Not ever.

'I dunno if yer've got something stuck in yer lug'oles, Mr Clayborne, but I told yer, me answer's no,' she said firmly. She rocked back on her heels and folded her arms challengingly across her chest. 'I think it's you what don't understand. *I ain't interested*. And that's final.'

'But you can't mean—' he breathed, his eyes closing with the effort of speaking.

'Aw yes I can. I can mean anything I bloody well like. But if yer too stupid to get what I'm on about, I'll spell it out for yer, shall I? You, Mr Clayborne, can take yer offer and stick it right up yer jacksie with both hands. Understand that all right, do yer? Clear enough for yer? Cos I'm telling yer, I don't need the likes of you, or yer nasty, snide little offers of help. I'm gonna manage just fine. And without your sweaty little mitt going up me skirt for a feel whenever yer fancy a bit on the side from Mrs Clayborne, whoever she is the poor cow.'

Clayborne was feeling hysterical. He let out a strangulated giggle, an anxious titter more suited to an elderly aunt at a tea party than to a supposedly powerful property developer. 'And how exactly do you think someone in your position, Mrs Prentice, will be able to manage?' he gasped, clutching at any straw that might save him from another kicking.

Infuriated by such a personal question from such a disgustingly sordid, horrible man, Cissie stabbed her finger at him across the desk. 'I'll tell you how, Mr Clayborne,' she yelled, the force of her anger making him shrink back in his seat – a sudden move that he, and his pain-wracked body, immediately regretted. 'I'm going into the grocery business, that's how.'

'The grocery business?' he stammered, smacked in the face by this latest twist of madness.

He cast a hasty glance over his shoulder and then lowered his voice to a barely audible rasp. 'May I ask how you intend doing so?'

'I dunno why yer whispering, Mr Clayborne. The way you're acting, anyone'd think being a grocer's something to be ashamed of. But let me tell you, I'm proud I'm gonna do it. Proud. D'you hear me? You're the one who should be sodding ashamed. Thinking yer can buy people with a sodding shop lease. I'm worth more than that. And I've made the right decision. A decent decision. The sort of decision what the likes of you wouldn't even begin to know nothing about.'

Cissie was shouting angrily, but from her expression and her tone of voice, it should have been more than obvious to Clayborne, had he not been in such a state of shock, that she was trying harder to convince herself than him by what she was saying.

'And it's gonna make my life better than it's ever been,' she went on. 'Better than...' Her words trailed away. 'Ever.'

'But surely, Mrs Prentice, you must see that you should at least reconsider.' Clayborne was pleading with her, his voice rising to a pitiable whine. 'You have no experience of that type of business.'

'No, yer right. I ain't. But the bloke what I'm gonna marry has.'

While Cissie was standing there, stunned at the words she had just spoken, the words that she'd actually said out loud as though she really meant them, the door behind Clayborne flew open and Big Bill Turner burst into the room.

As Turner pushed past Clayborne's desk and loomed over Cissie, Jim Phillips followed him into the room at a far slower pace, a pace that had more to do with nerves than with dignity.

'You stupid little tart!' Turner spat each word at her as though he were a reptile ejecting venom at his victim, his face an ugly mask of twisted hatred. From the look of him he'd been up all night, his clothes were creased, he needed a shave, and his oiled hair had flopped forward over his eyes.

'Yer gonna chuck yerself away on some bastard grocer? Throw away the one decent chance yer'll ever have to better yerself?'

Cissie was so overcome by the anger, the stench of stale booze and the wafts of cigar smoke that Turner had brought with him – and the sight of the trail of saliva that was dribbling disgustingly from the corner of his slack red mouth – that it took her a while to register what she was actually seeing: Turner was somehow associated with Clayborne.

And Jim Phillips. What was he doing here? None of it made sense.

Cissie ran her hands through her hair, staring wildly about her.

When the realisation of what was happening finally dawned on her, Cissie was almost too incensed to speak. Her mouth opened and closed, but no words, no fully formed words that is, came out. It took a few moments of real effort for her even to begin to make herself coherent.

'You! You bastard!' she hollered, clenching her hands in tight fists by her side, for fear that she would snatch the chair which stood beside her and crack it across Turner's head, shattering his skull like a boiled egg. 'You. You're behind all this, ain't yer? There's no use you denying it.'

Shaking visibly with the effort of controlling herself, Cissie turned to Jim, who at least had the decency to be staring, shamefaced, down at the floor. 'And you, Jim Phillips. As for you. I really thought you was me friend.'

She dropped her chin and laughed self-mockingly. 'D'yer know what?' she said, raising her eyes to meet his. 'And this is a joke, this is. For a while, I even fancied you, Jim. You was so kind to me, so gentle when yer was helping me.'

She pressed her lips tightly together in an effort to stop the tears from coming.

'Or when I thought yer was helping me,' she went on. 'And if you hadn't been married, d'you know that I'd have...'

She dropped her chin again, unable to face him any longer. 'But now I realise what a bloody, stupid, idiot, silly, sodding fool I was. Yer just as bad as him.'

She took a deep breath and twisted round to confront Turner. 'Just as bad as Mr Big Man. *Mr Big Bill Turner.*' She sneered sarcastically. 'No, worse, cos I don't suppose the likes of him can help it. The likes of him don't know no better.'

Turner's eyes bulged. He grabbed the telephone from Clayborne's desk and smashed it to the ground at Cissie's feet. It shattered into a hundred pieces; bits flying from the case like shrapnel from an exploding bomb.

Instinctively, Cissie held up her hands to shield her face.

'Yeah,' breathed Turner, 'that's right, darling, you wanna protect yerself. You wanna watch yer don't get that pretty little face o' your'n cut.'

Cissie immediately and defiantly dropped her hands to her sides and stepped forward. She was just inches from Turner's great barrel of a chest.

'Just tell me one thing,' she demanded, staring up at him. 'Why me? Why pick on me?'

'I'll tell yer why.' Turner's jaw was so rigid, he could barely open his mouth to get out the words, to fling them in Cissie's face. 'Because,' he snarled through his teeth, 'I can have anyone I want.'

He raised his hand and crooked his little finger. 'Just by doing that. I can own 'em.' He snorted horribly. 'Just like I owned your old man. Belonged to me he did. D'you know that?'

312

Something occurred to him and he chuckled happily to himself. 'Actually, someone suggested yer to me, if yer must know. Said yer was my type, and anyway, might as well keep it in the family now he's gone, eh?'

Cissie shook her head sadly. 'You're pathetic, d'you know that? Really, totally pathetic.'

With that, she flashed a final, melancholy smile at Jim Phillips, turned on her heel and started walking from the room.

'You wanna be careful, darling,' Turner shouted after her. 'Accidents happen yer know. 'Specially round that market. Crates and all sorts o' things can fall on yer if yer go round upsetting people. Especially if you upset people what've tried to be good to yer.'

Cissie spun round and stared at him. 'Accidents? Upsetting people?'

'Yeah, that's right. If someone upsets me, they suffer.'

Cissie swallowed hard. 'Like Davy suffered?'

Turner looked at Jim and laughed knowingly, then he turned back to Cissie. 'Yeah,' he snorted. 'That's right, sweetheart. And if yer know what's good for yer, you just wanna remember it.'

Cissie ran from the room and took the stairs down to the street two at a time, not caring that her feet were slipping and sliding on the uncarpeted surface.

As she threw herself but of the narrow front door and into the street, she leant against the rough brick wall trying to catch her breath, trying to make sense of the nightmare that was closing in on her.

She could hear Turner's laughter echoing from high above her.

Chapter 21

Cissie lay awake listening to her mother-in-law's snores reverberating through the house. How could Lil even think of sleep after what she'd said to Cissie about Davy going with all those other women? Surely even Lil, hard-nosed, tough-talking, selfish, bloody Lil, must have realised how much she had hurt Cissie by saying those things?

Although Cissie didn't have money to throw around, it had been more than worth giving her mother-in-law the five shillings out of the emergency tea caddy to see her off to the Sabberton Arms and out of her sight for the evening. Because after those agonising revelations, and then after what she'd been through in Clayborne's office – *if* his name was Clayborne and *if* the office was his – the last thing Cissie could have stood was Lil going on and on about what a good idea leasing the flower shop would be.

As soon as Cissie had stepped into the house, Lil had started on about the shop again: when was Cissie going to open it; how much more than the stall would it earn for them? Them! Lil never lifted so much as a finger to help and yet she considered she had the right to a share in every single penny that Cissie brought into the house. But then, money was Lil's god; Cissie knew that now.

Lil had been so busy going on at her about what money they could earn, that she hadn't even noticed the state Cissie was in, pale and trembling, shaken to the very core, after the latest blow Turner had dealt her over Davy's death.

Cissie turned on to her side and pulled the eiderdown up over her shoulders. She had all these terrible things on her mind, all these things driving her closer and closer to despair and to her eventual breaking point, and all Lil was interested in was knowing that she wouldn't lose out in any way when the stall had to close.

Cissie could have kicked herself for ever having mentioned the sodding shop. And mention it was all she had done. Nothing more than that. But Lil's eyes had lit up as she'd immediately grabbed at the idea of Cissie bringing home plenty of drinking money. She hadn't bothered, as usual, to give a toss about what Cissie thought or wanted. With Lil it was always me, me, me.

Cissie sighed loudly to herself. She'd been selfish too, once upon a time. A time when she was like an innocent child with no knowledge of the wicked world and all the horrors it held in wait for her.

It made Cissie feel so ashamed when she thought about the way she'd treated poor Gladys. But at least she'd learnt. She doubted that Lil would ever learn anything except the price of booze and the opening hours of the Sabberton Arms.

Another floor-vibrating snore came from the front parlour. Cissie had a blissful vision of going down there and shoving a pillow over the old cow's face. But she had to be fair, it wasn't just the row from downstairs that was making her wakeful; she had a whole lot more on her plate than her mother-in-law's whistling and snorting.

Her husband had been murdered. She was sure of that now. Just as she was sure, as she had looked into Lil's spiteful, mean-mouthed face, as she had oh-so-casually told her about his other women, that Davy, the love of her life, had been unfaithful to her. And, worse, that Davy was a man she had never really known.

Cissie really felt as if she was losing touch with reality.

She tried closing her eyes again, but it was no good. She rolled on to her back and stared up at the shadows on the ceiling.

The next thing Cissie was aware of was the sound of a car pulling up in the street, right outside the house.

She must have fallen asleep. But for how long? There was no light seeping through the cracks in the curtains, so it was still dark out.

Who could it be out there at such an hour? And in a car? No one in Linman Street even had a car.

Maybe it was one of Elsie Collier's 'gentlemen' coming home in a cab from somewhere? No, that wasn't very likely, they were being far too noisy. Elsie would never have put up with that, she always insisted on what she snootily called 'a bit of poise' from her lodgers.

There was more racket from below. It sounded to Cissie as though someone had fallen out on to the pavement, let off a string of foul language, and then slammed the car door in anger.

Cissie hauled herself up on her elbows. If they didn't shut up, they'd disturb the kids, and she wasn't having that.

With a weary sigh, she threw back the eiderdown and swung her legs on to the bedside rug. She straightened her nightdress, and ran her fingers through her hair, raking her fringe off her forehead.

She peered blearily through the gloom at the clock on the bedside cabinet. Half past four! Christ, she must have forgotten to set the alarm. She should be down the market by now.

But maybe, she half laughed to herself, more from hysteria than from amusement, what with Sammy proposing to her she didn't have to worry about going to the market any more.

Sammy Clarke.

Cissie buried her face in her hands. What the hell was she going to do about Sammy Clarke?

But all thoughts of the pink-faced grocer were hurriedly pushed to the back of Cissie's mind as the sound of another round of loudly abusive cursing came screaming up from the pavement below, further shattering the still of the early morning. The row he was making, whoever he was, would have carried right down to the docks. What on earth was wrong with him? Nobody had any reason to be in Linman Street at that hour.

Her hand flew to her mouth, not unless... A horrible thought occurred to her. Not unless they were planning to turn over the houses. But no, she reassured herself, no one in Linman Street had anything worth nicking, and a burglar would hardly be making all that racket, now would he?

But say he was drunk?

And, now she thought of it, of course someone had something to steal. The shop had cigarettes and the money in the till. There was all sorts of gear to pinch over there.

Say whoever it was broke into the shop and attacked Sammy? Say they hurt him?

Cissie was on her feet, ready for action, but not sure what to do next.

And how about the truck?

Say they were desperate? Say they broke into the houses anyway?

The children. Say they hurt the children?

Cissie crept over to the window and peered round the edge of the curtain, her hands trembling as she pulled back the edge of the net.

Her mouth fell open.

Bloody Bill Turner! What the hell was he doing out there?

She looked up and down the street, careful not to let Turner see her. He seemed to be alone, unless there was someone waiting for him in his big, flashy car.

Which there probably was, she decided, because from the way he was slumped against the lamp-post, he certainly didn't look capable of driving a car. In fact, he looked completely incapable of most things. The man was, what Davy would have called, totally rat-arsed.

Cissie ducked back behind the safety of the curtain as Turner lurched towards the street door, *her* street door, and began furiously rattling the letterbox. She flattened herself against the bedroom wall as she listened to him yelling.

'Open this bastard door, before I kick it off its bastard hinges!'

There was a brief pause.

'If that's how yer want it,' he hollered, 'then that's how yer gonna have it. You've had yer chance. This door is coming down. Now!'

And from the sound of it, Turner was acting on his word.

'Mum?' Cissie heard Matty call out to her.

That was it. Cissie was taking no more of this. Turner might have been a big man, a man who talked so easily about accidents happening to people, but no one, not even him, was going to scare her babies.

'All right, darling,' Cissie called. 'Mummy's coming.'

It took her a moment, fumbling around in the dark, to find her dressing-gown, but when she did, she grabbed it from the bedpost, rushed into the back bedroom to reassure her son that it was just a silly man having a game outside with his friends, gave him a kiss, pulled the covers up over him, and then flew down the stairs.

Cissie was only halfway down, when she saw she was too late. She stood clutching at the banister in disbelief.

Lil hadn't only gone to the street door and answered it, but – stupid woman! – she had let Turner into the house.

He was standing there, or rather swaying there, practically blocking the passageway. And beside him was Lil, looking as small as a child next to him.

As Cissie slowly focused in the dim light leaking into the passage from the streetlamp outside the house, she could hardly believe her eyes. Lil was actually smiling adoringly up into the big gorilla's face.

It was lucky for Lil that Cissie was now more scared for her children than angry. Her little ones were in bed upstairs, right above their heads, and there was this man, who had as good as admitted he'd murdered Davy, standing in their house, and he was blind-drunk.

Cissie thought quickly. Her only hope was that there was someone in the car who was a bit more sober than Turner and whom she could shame into helping a terrified widow with two little kids.

She took a deep breath and pointed accusingly at Lil. 'Get him in the kitchen,' she ordered her.

Amazingly, Lil did as she was told; she jerked her head sideways and began walking along the passage. Even more amazingly Turner followed her, stumbling along behind like a great lumbering bear.

Cissie closed her eyes in a silent prayer of thanks and then ran out into the street, pulling her dressing-gown tightly to her throat. She just knew that Ethel, Myrtle, Lena – all the usual suspects – would be almost wetting themselves with pleasure as, undoubtedly, they stared down at the spectacle from behind their bedroom curtains. They'd be loving every minute of it.

Cissie rapped her knuckles on the car window. 'Oi! You!'

A man was sitting behind the steering wheel. He was very low in the seat as though he was asleep. He had his trilby pulled well down over his eyes and his overcoat collar turned up.

'Oi!' she hissed again, this time rapping much harder. 'I'm talking to you.'

This time the man responded; he shoved his hat to the back of his head and looked round.

'Bernie!' Cissie's legs almost gave way under her. 'You!'

What was happening to her? If even the man who had helped Fat Stan look after her was one of Turner's men, then probably Fat Stan himself was in on it in some way. She had always known there was something dodgy about Bernie. But Fat Stan… ?

Who could she trust any more? Who was left?

Bernie Denham puffed out his cheeks with a resigned sigh, stretched across the passenger seat and wound down the window.

'Yeah?' He sounded bored. 'Wad'yer want?'

It took Cissie a moment to compose herself, then she said very calmly, 'If you've got even a streak o' decency in that bleed'n great big lump of a body o' your'n, Bernie, then yer'll get into that house and make sure that that bastard don't do me no harm while I explain a few things to him. Right?'

Bernie let out a sarcastic gasp at her stupidity and shook his head. 'Don't look at me, darling. You find yerself another mug.'

'Don't look at you, eh?' she said evenly. 'Well, I wonder what the law'd have to say if I went round and explained how it was you what was involved in the "accident" down the market what killed Davy Flowers?' She narrowed her eyes, weighing up his reaction. 'Cos I know all about it, see.'

'Now you listen to me,' he began, sitting bolt upright. 'I never had nothing to do with—'

'No, you shut up and listen to me. I need help. And if I don't get it and I do go to the law, just think about it. Who are they gonna believe? Me, a poor, grieving widow, or you, a bloke with a cauliflower ear'ole and a bent nose what's mixed up with Turner?' With that, Cissie flicked her dressing-gown to one side and strode back into the house. She paused on the step and said over her shoulder, 'It's up to you.'

She only began breathing again when she heard Bernie, muttering furiously to himself, get out of the car and follow her along the passage.

'Right,' Cissie said, stepping into the kitchen.

She almost laughed as Turner looked round to face her. He and Lil were sitting at the kitchen table as though it was all perfectly normal, drinking the remains of Lil's bottle of gin from the pretty, spotted cocktail glasses that Davy had bought home for her one day from down the Lane. She had a passing thought that he had probably bought them, and all the other little presents he used to turn up with, out of guilt.

Turner rose unsteadily to his feet, then slumped back down on the chair that Lil hastily shoved behind him.

'I will give that woman,' he said, waving his hand at Cissie, but looking past her at Bernie, 'anything she wants if she'll go to bed with me. Anything. All I want is a quick—'

'Shut your filthy mouth!' Cissie demanded. She glared at him. She hated giving such foul-mouthed rubbish the dignity of a reply, but her children were upstairs and she couldn't bear the thought that they might hear him.

'Cissie,' Lil smarmed, all mealy-mouthed charm. 'Don't you go being so rude to our guest.'

'Our *guest*? Have you taken leave o' your sodding senses, Lil?'

'No,' she said, primly, 'I ain't, but I think you must have. You've got the chance of—'

'A nice little shop,' Turner cut in, as though Lil wasn't even there. He stared down at the floor, and mumbled into

322

his chest, his words running drunkenly into one another. 'That's what I'll give her. Full o' the best flowers what money can buy. Loads o' flowers.' He raised his head and looked sorrowfully about him, as though not quite sure where he was. 'Them offices and shops. They're mine see. Not Clayborne's.' He laughed softly to himself. 'That dozy bleeder ain't in no state to run nothing let alone no shops. Me and Plains, we—'

'I ain't stupid,' Cissie sneered, 'I managed to work that out for meself. You should have realised that. Just like yer should have realised what me answer was gonna be.'

Lil smiled greedily. 'Yer gonna take the flower shop then!' she said triumphantly.

'Are you stark raving mad, Lil? How many times do I have to say it? I can't afford Bill Turner's prices.'

Turner lifted his head, and closed one eye in his efforts to focus on her face. 'No money involved,' he said holding out his hands by way of proof. 'Not a single brass farthing.'

'D'you still think I'm talking about money?' Cissie shook her head in wonder. 'You really must be stupid, d'you know that?'

She took a step towards him, pulling her dressing-gown closer round her. 'My kids're gonna be brought up decent. Nothing to do with you, or anyone like yer.'

'You wanna remember how your Davy made his living,' Lil said sharply.

Cissie rounded on her. 'If it hadn't have been for you, you wicked old bastard, he would never have got mixed up in all that in the first place.'

Lil shrugged nonchalantly. 'Someone had to push him. But who cares? That's all in the past now.'

'That's right, darling,' Turner grinned at Lil. 'I don't care about him for a start.'

He turned back to Cissie, leant back in the little wooden kitchen chair and stabbed his finger at her for emphasis. 'But I care about you, sweetheart, and that's why I'm gonna look after yer, now yer old man ain't around no more.'

That was the final straw. Cissie flew across the room at him. She was just about to slap the smug smirk from his great, beaming face, when Bernie grabbed her arm from behind.

'That wouldn't be such a good idea, now would it, love?' he growled, twisting her arm up behind her back.

'You no-good cowson!' she sobbed, her chin dropping to her chest. 'Let me go. Just let me go. And get out o' my house. The pair of yer.'

Turner dragged himself to his feet and stumbled drunkenly towards her and Bernie. He could barely stand.

Suddenly, his hand shot out and he grabbed Cissie's face. She squirmed as his fingers dug painfully into her cheeks. But Turner wasn't letting go, and Bernie now had both her arms behind her back. There was nothing she could do.

As her eyes widened with fear, Turner lowered his head and kissed her hard on the mouth, his hand gripping her face like a vice as he forced his tongue between her lips. She felt his other hand pull open her dressing-gown and paw roughly at her breasts through the thin material of her nightdress. Then he pulled his head back and, still holding on to her face, he wiped his lips on the back of his other hand.

After a long, terrifying moment, Turner let go of her as suddenly as he had grabbed her.

'Out,' he snapped at Bernie and stumbled his way out of the room.

'I'll be back for a bit more o' that,' he called from the passageway with an obscene laugh. 'You can depend on that, darling.' With that he slammed the street door behind him.

Cissie was still shaking as she heard the car roar away. She staggered over to the back door and threw it open, taking great gulps of air to get rid of the stink and taste of him.

The dawn had broken. It was a lovely autumn morning, but there was a harsh chill in the air.

Soon it would be winter.

Cissie closed her eyes and tried to calm herself by thinking of the children upstairs in their bedroom. They were safe, that was all that mattered.

Slowly she turned round to face Lil who was standing wide-eyed by the stove, her empty glass still clutched in her hand.

'You. Sit down,' Cissie commanded. 'And just keep yer gob shut for once. I'm gonna say something, and this time I want yer to listen to me.'

Lil opened her mouth to protest but Cissie would have none of it. 'Just sit down, Lil.'

With a defiant little shrug, Lil did as she was told.

'Now,' said Cissie, sitting down opposite her. 'I've decided. I'm definitely... Definitely...'

She paused, rubbing her hands over her face. She felt sick, she still had the taste of him in her mouth. 'I realise that there's plenty about Davy I never knew and, to be honest, I don't ever wanna know, and that's why I'm gonna make a new start. I'm definitely thinking of marrying Sammy Clarke.'

'That lump o' lard?' Lil sneered.

'I thought I told you to be quiet.' Cissie raked her fingers through her hair. 'This going into the grocery business,' she continued wearily, the vision of Turner looming over her, crowding out her thoughts. She shook her head, angry that she was letting him get to her. '... is an opportunity,' she went on determinedly, 'what I don't reckon I can let go. And, if I do, and I mean *if* I marry him, and you wanna come and live with us, then I'll think about it. I'll see how we get on. But I'm warning you, Lil, you'd better watch it.

After the way you behaved in here tonight—'

'I don't believe this,' Lil interrupted. She was quivering with indignation. 'I thought you'd got all that rubbish out o' yer head. That it was just some stupid idea. How can yer even think of marrying Sammy Clarke when yer could have Turner keeping yer?'

Cissie felt an hysterical giggle bubbling in her throat. 'You ain't got a clue, have yer? The bloke was ready to rip me clothes off, right here in front of yer and that animal with him would have—'

'You take things too much to heart, girl,' Lil dismissed her. 'But Sammy Clarke? Yer've just gotta look at him. How could you even think of going with someone what looks like him? That great pink baby face.' Lil shuddered, disgustedly.

'It don't all come down to "going with" someone, Lil. And, anyway, I ain't saying I'm in love with the bloke, am I? I dunno if I'll ever be able to love anyone ever again, not after what yer told me about Davy. But Sammy's decent. If it hadn't have been for him, I don't know how we would've managed. It's like that money. He wouldn't hear a single word o' thanks for it.'

'What money?' Lil was worried she might be missing out.

'You should know. You spent enough of it on gin.' Seeing she still wasn't getting through to Lil, Cissie spelt it out. 'The money what he stuck through the door.'

Lil rolled her eyes. 'That weren't from him, yer dozy mare,' she shouted, flinging up her hands at her daughter-in-law's simple-mindedness. 'That weren't from Sammy. It was from yer mum and dad.'

Lil's mouth snapped shut like a letterbox. Shit! She hadn't meant to say that.

Cissie blinked as though trying to clear something from her eyes. 'Me mum and dad?'

Lil said nothing, she just poured another drink and lit herself a cigarette.

'It couldn't have been them. And anyway, where would they have got that sort o' money from?'

When Lil still didn't answer, Cissie snatched the glass from Lil's hand. 'I'm warning you, Lil, if you wanna keep a roof over your head…'

Lil snorted contemptuously and took a long drag on her cigarette. 'When the stupid sods heard that their dear little daughter had been widowed they worried about yer, didn't they? So they went without so that you could have all their dough. Silly bleeders.'

It took every ounce of Cissie's willpower not to wrap her hands around Lil's throat and choke the life out of the vicious, wicked old bag.

She ran from the room and started up the stairs. 'Matty. Joyce. You awake, kids?' she called. 'Come on, up yer get, we're going out.'

–

Within five minutes, Cissie and her two children were at the street door.

'I know it's early,' she whispered gently to them, as she tied the strings of Joyce's hat under her chin, 'but this is like a big adventure, ain't it?'

'How about school, Mum?' Matty asked, his little face contorted with concern as to what new problem might be facing him.

'Don't you worry yerself,' Cissie answered him, planting a soft kiss on the top of his little fair head. 'Now, you two stand there for me. Mummy won't be a minute.'

As Cissie stepped back in the kitchen, Lil hurriedly shoved the tea caddy back on to the top shelf of the dresser.

'It's all right, Lil, yer might as well take the lot, cos yer've taken everything else off o' me. Well, nearly everything. At least I've still got the kids, thank Gawd. But before I go out, as one mother to another, I just wanted yer to know what getting your son involved with Turner really meant.'

Lil shrugged dismissively.

'Have you got even the first clue about what Davy really got himself involved in, Lil? And have you got even a tiny little idea about what happened to him cos o' your stinking, rotten greed?'

The crepey skin on Lil's left cheek began to twitch convulsively. 'What you going on about now?'

Cissie closed her eyes, took a deep breath and then let it out in a long slow sigh. 'Nothing, Lil,' she said with a weary shake of her head. 'Well, nothing that'd make you see any sort o' sense anyway.'

Chapter 22

Matty clambered up into the truck. He was hollow-eyed with tiredness; it was barely six o'clock in the morning and he had hardly slept. He'd been woken up when all the noise had started downstairs and hadn't been able to go back to sleep again.

There'd been the man shouting, and his nanna telling off his mum. And then he'd heard what sounded like his mum's own voice, but that was much quieter so he couldn't really tell, and then another man had said something, and then one of them had started laughing. Horrible laughing. Just like the bogey-man that Tommy Godwin had told him about.

Then his mum had told him and Joycie to get up. And Matty didn't understand any of it, but he knew it scared him. And he knew that because he was only five years old people wouldn't explain to him what was going on. But he really wanted to know, not for himself – he had been taught that it was rude to be nosy – but so that he could help his mum. He wanted to help her because he hated her looking unhappy.

It was just like when his dad had gone away. It was so much better when his mum had told him all about it. He was still sad after she told him, but he was also glad when she explained that his dad hadn't left them because of anything naughty that he or Joyce had done. That had really worried him for a while.

It was hard being little. He really wished he was a grownup.

He slid his bottom along the bench seat to make room for Joyce. 'Where we going, Mum?' he asked. If he at least knew that then he would know what to expect.

Cissie set her daughter carefully next to Matty and put her finger to her lips to warn her son to keep his voice down. Joyce had gone back to sleep as Cissie had carried her the short walk from number seven to the waste ground where the truck was parked, and she didn't want her to wake up in strange, cold surroundings that might frighten her.

'We're gonna see Nanny and Granddad,' Cissie whispered, taking off her coat and draping it across Joyce and Matty's legs.

'What, the nanny and granddad what you've got?'

Cissie nodded. 'That's right, babe. My mummy and daddy.'

That satisfied Matty for the moment and he settled back in his seat to think about what these people he had never seen before might be like. He hoped they weren't like Nanna Lil.

Cissie was also thinking about what they might be like, not as people, but how they might have changed physically during the six and a half years since she had last seen them. But even though Cissie had not so much as set eyes on her parents since she had decided to marry Davy, she had never said anything bad about either of them to her children, and had actually made a point of referring to them occasionally. She had not gone so far as talking about the happy times she'd had with them when she'd been a girl, but had done her best to establish them as people who existed, a way of keeping them alive in her own mind, and for her children. Matty and Joyce had, after all, a right to know that they had two other grandparents whom they might, one day, want to visit. She'd always felt that it was important to know those sort of things and not to keep secrets from your family.

She nibbled nervously at the inside of her cheek. Secrets. The trouble they had caused. And not just the big, terrible, cruel secrets that Davy had kept from her, but the other type of secrets, the ones you even kept from yourself. The ones that you daren't even think about. Ones such as whether you really did have any idea as to why your family was doing so well while all the others around you, decent families like the Millses, were struggling just to survive.

And secrets that you kept locked away, secrets such as the way Cissie really felt about her mum and dad. And how, apart from on the day of the funeral, she had never, ever admitted to herself, let alone to anyone else, that, at times, she missed her parents so badly it was like a physical pain in her guts.

She had never got used to not having them around. And now Cissie was beginning to admit it – along with all those things she didn't much like about herself. If she had been more honest with herself, maybe the story of her life might have been very different.

She sighed wistfully, but it was no good feeling sorry for herself, that wouldn't get the engine cranked.

She shivered in the cold, early morning air and rubbed her hands together, trying to warm them through before she set about starting up the truck.

–

As Cissie eased off the brake and pulled the truck off the waste ground on to Linman Street, net curtains twitched and sharp tongues began to wag.

–

'Back home then, guv?' Bernie asked optimistically.

Bernie Denham had finally plucked up the courage to ask Turner what he wanted to do next. Well, he had more hinted at what they *should* be doing rather than asked, because Bernie knew exactly what his thoughts on the matter were.

He flashed a hopeful glance in the rear view mirror to gauge his boss's reaction to the idea of going home. But it was difficult to tell whether he was capable of thinking at all, the state he was in. He looked barely conscious. And it was no wonder, the amount of booze he'd put away. Bernie ran through the previous eighteen hours with a resigned sort of disbelief at the drink the man had actually consumed.

It had started when Davy's missus had said no to the shop lease and had buggered off, and Turner had called him and Chalkie in to give that idiot Clayborne another hiding.

Turner always had to blame someone if he failed in any way, and this time it was the luckless accountant who

Turner decided should take the blame for the fact that Cissie Flowers had dared to turn him down again.

After that, Turner, already a bit the worse for wear from the night before, had swallowed a few large measures of scotch by way of a typically unpleasant sort of celebration of Clayborne's punishment, and then they had left the office in Fenchurch Street, and had taken the short drive to the Grave Maurice pub in Whitechapel. The idea of going there was that Turner would collect his cut from one of the spielers – the illicit gambling clubs – he 'looked after', they'd have a few more drinks, and then they'd all go home.

At first it was fine: a few beers had been bought – beating blokes up was thirsty work, Turner had joked – laughs had been had, and dues had been paid. Within the rules of their world, it was all very civilised. But then a big winner had turned up, he'd made a packet on whist of all things, and he was flashing his wad like a right bloody idiot, buying round after round for everyone, and loving the idea of mixing with the likes of a notorious hard man such as Big Bill Turner. Turner had gone back on to the scotch. And his mood, as it so often did, had suddenly switched from back-slapping, hand-shaking camaraderie to vicious- tongued anger.

His mood deteriorated further and he became nastier and nastier; ever more convinced that Flowers' old woman was just playing hard to get, jerking him around like a spiteful kid with a runt-of-the-litter puppy on a bit of old string, thinking she was getting one over on him.

Bernie had almost cheered with relief when they'd finally left the pub at about midnight – no landlord would ever call time when Bill Turner was drinking – but his hopes of getting home even then had been dashed when Turner announced that they were moving on to a drinking club in Bethnal Green.

More hard drinking had gone on. And on.

At about four o'clock, Turner had got it in his head that if he went to see Davy's missus, there and then, she wouldn't be able to resist him; she'd throw herself into his arms and he'd have her in bed before either of them knew what was happening. Although it was the last thing he felt like doing, Bernie had had to drive Turner to the little terraced house in Poplar where she lived with her kids and Davy's mum.

He'd waited outside in the car, glad at least for the opportunity to close his eyes for five minutes – he felt like an overused dish-cloth that had been wrung out once too often – but even his few moments of shut-eye had been snatched from him. He'd been woken up and dragged inside the house by Flowers' silly cow of an old woman. It was beyond Bernie why the dopey mare didn't just drop her drawers and get on with it. All right she was good-looking and probably had plenty of other offers to consider, and, yes, she was playing it very clever acting all uninterested – that was always a sure bet to get Turner going – but why Turner didn't just give the cocky, big-mouthed sort a slap, as he would have done, was something Bernie could definitely not understand.

He'd stood there in the stuck-up tart's back kitchen like an idiot, while Turner hollered and hooted and the old lady, Davy's mum, had carried on, and while Davy's missus acted like she was the bloody queen of the May. And the way she'd had the cheek to threaten him, Bernie Denham! If she wasn't careful, she'd wind up like her stupid old man.

Then they'd got back in the car and Turner had told Bernie to start driving. Again. He'd been driving for bloody hours, and he was just about sick of it.

It must have been getting on for half past six by now and all Bernie wanted to do was go home and get his head down for a bit. And that was another thing, he could just imagine the rucking he'd get when he pitched up on his street doorstep. His old woman, Queenie, had a worse tongue on her than that Flowers bird. He didn't know why he was bothering with all this old nonsense. Queenie was doing very nicely with the moneylending, he had a good little line in taking side bets, and he was also earning more than a fair screw from the dog-flapping over on the Marshes. He had every reason to get away from Turner, not least of which was the fact that being around the bloke was doing his head in.

But leaving someone like Turner to set up for yourself wasn't exactly straightforward, Davy'd found that out when he'd started all his little sidelines and had tried going it alone. But who was to know, maybe before his son Albie was much older, perhaps something'd happen to the drunken bastard – like him blacking out and falling down a flight o' stairs and breaking his thick bull's neck – and then Bernie and his boy could set up a nice little family firm of their own. It was what Bernie had dreamt of.

His son was still really only a kid at the minute, barely fourteen years old, but he was built like the side of a bloody tram and could already handle himself with blokes twice his age. They would take on a patch together over Poplar, or Bow way even; Hackney maybe. Anywhere that wasn't bloody Aldgate.

Thinking of Queenie waiting at home for him, ready to bend his last night's tea over his head because she'd thought – wrongly this time as it happened – that he'd been out birding it, prompted Bernie to try speaking to Turner again, louder this time in case he'd nodded off: 'Back home then, boss?'

Turner heaved himself up to a sitting position. His eyes were puffy slits. 'I can have anyone I like,' he mumbled. 'Anyone.'

'Yes, guv,' Bernie said, rolling his eyes. 'I know yer can.'

'Loyalty, that's all I want.'

'Right.'

'My Moe's loyal.'

'Yes, guv.'

'And Eileen. She's been a good girl to me over the years, has Eileen.'

Without a word of warning, Turner lunged forward from the back seat and grabbed Bernie's arm. It took all Bernie's strength to keep the car from going out of control and hitting the kerb.

'I wanna see Eileen,' Turner demanded, like a petulant child suddenly discovering he needed to go to the lavatory.

'Yes, guv,' sighed Bernie, doing a swerving u-turn through the early morning traffic on the Mile End Road.

'No, wait.' Turner slapped Bernie on the shoulder. 'I want me breakfast first, and a quick wash. I wanna look me best. I'm gonna take her out.'

'Home then?' Bernie asked hopefully. With a bit of luck he'd get home, collapse on the bed and forget all about Eileen.

'No. Over there.' Turner stuck his hand right across Bernie's face, oblivious of the fact that he was obscuring his vision. 'Stop at that cafe opposite Mile End station.' Bernie took a deep breath. He was really getting to hate Turner. If something didn't happen to the bastard soon, he might seriously have to think about taking matters into his own hands.

–

Cissie drew the truck to a halt outside the house in Charles Street where her parents, Ellen and Frank, had a couple of rooms in the run-down-looking terrace. She had never actually been in there but knew the address and the look of the outside of the place by heart. Her parents had moved to Stepney, from the nice little house in Devons Road where Cissie had been born, to this miserable-looking dump, just two weeks before her wedding.

Cissie had already moved out of the house in Devons Road the week before they had – as soon as Davy had got the house in Linman Street. Cissie had originally intended to keep it all above board and to go to Linman Street on their wedding day, but when she had started rowing with her parents over and over again about Davy, he had persuaded her to move in two weeks before the ceremony. Despite having been brought up to be the sort of girl who thought seriously about whether she would even let a feller kiss her, let alone anything else, before she had a ring on her finger, Cissie had readily agreed. She was only a kid, and Davy had turned her head. She had taken completely against her mum and dad for even daring to criticise the man she loved.

The one thing Cissie hadn't banked on, however, was the fact that Lil had planned on settling into number seven at the same time. But she hadn't liked to say anything about it at the time, as Davy had seemed so fond of his old mum.

So, not having spoken to her parents since then, Cissie had never seen inside their new home, but she had, over the years, made regular, secret trips – more secrets, she thought to herself with a sigh – to the far end of Charles Street where she could look at their place without being seen. She had never thought too much about why she did it. She just had. And even though she knew they had moved away because they hated Davy and everything to do with him, it had always puzzled her why they should move to such an awful place.

Ellen, her mum, had always been so particular indoors, and, even when times were hard, had always kept their home lovely, spotlessly clean and tidy. In fact, Cissie could never remember them having much money at any time, even though Frank, her dad, had always worked hard in his job at the sugar factory in Silvertown, and her mum had always done piece-work, machining at home for a sweatshop owner from Brady Street. But they had always been respectable.

Jumpers were darned, windows were washed, holes patched and steps polished. Cissie's little ankle socks had been the whitest in the street and her plaits were always neatly tied with ribbons that might have come off the toot stall down Chrisp Street but were always freshly ironed.

And now they were living here. They must have been having really hard times to put up with such a place. And then they had gone and given all that money to her and the kids. It made Cissie feel so guilty as she stepped down from the truck and went round to open the passenger door for her children.

'Come on, you two, out yer come.' Cissie helped the sleepy pair down on to the narrow pavement. 'Now,' she said, brushing Matty's floppy golden fringe from his eyes, 'I want you two to be extra 'specially good for me, all right?'

Matty nodded, looking up at her with the heartbreaking seriousness that seemed to cloud his pale little face all too often nowadays.

Joyce just yawned, rubbed her knuckles hard against her eyes, and then lifted up her arms for a carry. 'I'm cold, Mummy.'

'I know, sweetie-pie.' Cissie scooped her up with one arm and held on to Matty with the other. 'Ready?' she said, wondering what she was letting herself in for, and whether she had any right to be putting her children through this.

–

'All right, Frank, I'll get it. It'll be Mrs O'Brien with her key,' they heard a woman's voice call from the other side of the closed street door. 'I said I'd let the bloke what's looking for a room in for her while she's at work.'

The woman's voice was as familiar to Cissie as her own.

It was her mother's, the voice she hadn't heard for more than six years.

As Ellen opened the door she was holding out her hand ready to take something, but instead of receiving a key, her hand flew to her mouth. Tears filled her eyes as she stood there, unable to take in what she was seeing.

'Blimey, Ellen!' came a voice from inside. 'Hurry up and close that door, girl, it's freezing in here, and I'm trying to have me wash.'

Ellen reached out and folded her daughter and her grandchildren in her arms.

–

'You've got the place looking lovely,' Cissie said, admiring the cosy little back kitchen that served all Ellen and Frank's purposes bar sleeping.

Ellen smiled easily over her shoulder at her daughter as she bent forward to shoot another scoop of coal on to the fire. It was so strange. Six and a half years and it was as though they had been chatting away only yesterday.

'Yer mean yer wouldn't think it was as nice as this from the look o' the outside?' she said, straightening up from the hearth.

'I didn't—'

'It's all right, girl. Don't you go fretting.' Frank laid his hand gently on his daughter's shoulder, then crouched down to his two grandchildren who were clinging close to their mother's knees. 'You two a bit warmer now?'

Matty nodded but Joyce turned her head into her mother's lap.

Frank smiled tenderly as he reached out and stroked the back of her glossy dark hair that was as black as her mother's, as black as his had once been before he had started going grey.

'Mummy!' Joyce grizzled.

'She's shy, ain't she,' Cissie said, embarrassed, then added, almost shyly herself, 'but she'll soon come round, Dad. In time. When she gets used to yer.'

There, she'd said the words that retied the severed bonds of their relationship. The words that admitted they all had a future together.

'Right,' Frank agreed. 'That's what's the matter with her. Shy. Just like you was, love, when you was a nipper.'

'Kettle's boiled,' Ellen said, filling the pot. 'We'll soon have this brewed, and then I'll make both you little 'uns a cup o' nice milky tea. How about that? D'you like milky tea?' she continued, taking cups and saucers down from the dresser.

None of the china matched, and there were more than a few chips and cracks in it, but it was all spotlessly clean. 'Your mum used to drink her tea so milky that granddad here used to say yer might as well just give her a cup o' milk with sugar in it.'

'I like milky tea,' Matty said warily. 'Don't I, Mum?'

'Yes, darling, yer do.'

'And me,' Joyce whispered.

Cissie squeezed her children to her. 'And you.'

–

'Look, Mum, Dad,' Cissie said, taking her cup over to the gleaming white butler's sink. 'I've gotta go now, cos I've got a lot of things to do. But I'll be back soon. I promise.' She set the cup gently in the blue and white enamel washing- up bowl on the scrubbed wooden draining board and turned round to face her parents. 'But before I go, I've gotta say what I came here to say. I'm really sorry. About everything. And I wanna say thanks.'

'I won't hear no sorries,' Ellen said firmly. 'We all make mistakes. And we don't need no thanks neither, we're your mum and dad. And we've only done what's right.'

'But that money. It really helped me out. Yer can't imagine, Mum. Honest, I dunno what I'd have done without it.'

She paused, and signalled at them with her eyes that she didn't want the children understanding what she was about to say next, then added quietly, 'I'd have thanked yer sooner, but someone kept it all a little secret, didn't she?'

'I ain't surprised, love,' Frank said with a shrug, 'but we mustn't let ourselves get bitter, eh? That never did no one no good.'

Cissie walked back across the tiny room and took her coat from the back of her chair. 'You're good people, d'you know that? It's something I don't reckon we appreciate most of the time, people being good to us. And decent.'

'She's a daft thing, ain't she, Frank?' Ellen said, beaming with pleasure.

'I mean it. Now, before I go,' Cissie began carefully, 'can I ask yer something, Dad?'

'Course yer can.'

'When you and Mum moved from Devons Road, why did yer move here?'

'To this dump, yer mean?' Ellen asked, saving her husband the embarrassment.

Cissie rolled her eyes heavenwards. 'Me and my big mouth. I've done it again, ain't I? I honestly didn't mean to say it like that.'

Frank and Ellen smiled lovingly at their daughter. 'Don't be silly,' Ellen reassured her. 'We know what yer mean.'

'Well, why did yer?'

'We did it to save money,' Frank said matter-of-factly. 'We reckoned that, you know, that if yer married...' He paused. 'Him. Then yer might need our help one day.'

'And I did, didn't I?'

Ellen reached out and touched her daughter's cheek. 'Don't upset yerself, darling, that's all in the past.'

'All in the past,' echoed her husband. 'It can't hurt yer now, love.'

'Yeah,' Cissie nodded as she buttoned up her coat. She felt like bursting into tears, they were being so kind, so understanding, and she had been such a cow, such a prize bitch to the pair of them. She wondered if she would be so understanding, so all-forgiving, with her children. She hoped so. She really hoped she had learnt her lesson. It had been her way for too long, taking people for granted. It was about time she did something about it.

'Look, I really had better shift meself,' she said, with a little sniff. 'I've got ever such a lot of things to get sorted out.'

'Well, if yer busy, love,' Frank said warily, not wanting to overstep the mark so soon, when old wounds were still being healed between them, 'you could leave the little ones with us, yer know.'

He smiled down at the two children who were now sitting contentedly on the hearth rug eating a slab of toast and dripping each. 'They seem happy enough with us now.'

'But how about work?'

'It won't hurt if I miss one day shifting bloody sugar.' He grinned happily at the thought. 'And anyway, I'm getting old, I could do with a bit of a rest.'

Cissie nibbled her lip. The tears were moving closer. 'Yer'll never get old, Dad. Not to me.'

Matty scurried over to his mother's side. 'Can we stay, Mum?' he asked in a whisper.

'Would yer like to?'

'Yeah,' he said, solemnly. Part of him was scared by the thought, but he sensed deep down, young as he was, that this was something his mum really wanted.

'I could show him all the old photos,' said Frank flashing a look of excitement at Ellen. 'And how about me getting out me medals to show yer, Matt?' he asked, turning to his grandson.

Matty's face lit up. 'Was you really in a war, Granddad?'

'I was.' Frank nodded proudly, not so much for his brave war record in the trenches of Flanders, but for the fact that his little grandson had just called him Granddad for the very first time.

'So was my friend Terry's granddad. He was in a war in Africa. And I'm gonna tell 'em both all about yer,' Matty added triumphantly.

'And I'll tell yer what,' said Ellen, now as excited as Matty, 'I could get out that little doll's pram of Cissie's. I bet young Joyce'd love it.'

'What, yer've still got me old doll's pram?' Cissie could hardly believe it. 'Not the one I got that Christmas from the posh ladies down the mission?'

'Yeah, the very same.' Ellen nodded. 'I mean, how could I get rid of it? It was part o' yer, darling. Yer wouldn't let that thing out o' yer sight, would yer?'

Ellen looked away and blew her nose noisily. 'And I've still got the little knitted rabbit what old Nellie Tillson made yer to push around in it and all,' she sniffled into her hankie.

'Aw, Mum.' Cissie threw herself into Ellen's arms and let herself be cradled just like any other lost child who had found her mother.

Chapter 23

'Oi, come on! Move yerself, Bernie.' Turner rapped his knuckles hard on the driver's side window and beckoned impatiently.

Bernie groaned quietly to himself. What now? His eyelids felt as though they'd been weighed down with lead shot; he hadn't slept since God alone knew when; he had a greasy breakfast wedged up behind his ribs, and now Turner – still half-cut but with a second wind after his wash and brush-up in the back of the cafe – was telling him to get out of the car. Surely Turner didn't expect him to go upstairs with him to Eileen's flat? What did he want him to do, stand there and hold his trousers for him?

Those might have been the thoughts going through Bernie Denham's mind, but he knew better than to voice them. Instead, he rolled down the window and stuck out his head. The cool autumn air hit him like a wall. Bernie's bulky frame shivered.

'What's that yer say, guv?' he asked, the perfect picture of a respectful employee.

Turner shrugged down into his overcoat. 'I said to move, we're going up to see Eileen.'

'Right.' Bernie wound up the window again, and heaved himself out of the car and on to the pavement. Just what he needed, going up to see some old tom.

A huddle of ragged-arsed youngsters, boys of about ten years old, suddenly appeared from the slimy-looking alley that ran alongside the tumbledown house in which Eileen lodged on the top floor.

'Nice motor, mister,' one of them piped, giving his nose a quick swipe on the filth-encrusted sleeve of his hole-ridden jersey.

Turner reached out and grabbed the skinny kid by the ear. 'And it'd better stay nice,' he snarled, 'or I'll know who to blame, now won't I?'

The child, too well-trained in the ways of the street to complain, nodded his head in urgent agreement and waited for the man to release him. 'I'll keep an eye on it for yer.'

'See, Bern,' Turner said with a grin, tipping his head towards the boy. 'That's what I like to see: loyalty. Someone who does what I want without question.'

Turner opened his camel-hair coat and searched his trouser pocket for change, but he had none.

'Bernie, give the chavvies here a few bob,' he said, walking away from them towards the house.

Bernie waited until Turner had stepped inside the chipped and peeling street door and then clouted the kid, hard, round the back of the head with the flat of his hand. 'Go on,' he roared, 'piss off out of it.'

–

By the time Bernie joined Turner at the top of the stairs, Turner was smacking the flat of his hand against Eileen's door.

'Wha'd'yer want?' Eileen mumbled from the other side of the door. Her voice was thick with sleep despite it now being almost ten o'clock in the morning. 'Who is it?'

'It's me, yer dozy tan,' Turner shouted at the keyhole. 'Now get this door open.'

'Bill!' she exclaimed. 'Is that really you?'

'Who d'yer reckon it is, the sodding Prince o' Wales? Now get this door open.'

There was the sound of urgent whispering and then a sudden thump as if something heavy had hit the ground.

'What's going on in there?' Turner demanded.

'Nothing, Bill. Nothing.'

'Are you gonna open this door, Eileen,' Turner's voice had dropped to a low, menacing growl, 'or do I have to open it for yer?'

The door opened just a crack. Eileen, her face caked with the remains of last night's make-up and her hair a wild, matted halo of unnaturally ferocious red, peered out at him.

'I didn't know he was still here, Bill,' she mouthed. 'Honest.'

'Who yer talking about?'

'One of me friends,' she said with a bleak shrug. 'He must have fell asleep last night. I woke up when yer knocked just now, and there he was.'

Turner shoved the door open, sending Eileen stumbling backwards into the room. As he strode in after her, he made no attempt to help or to steady her.

Bernie, despite his anger at Turner, was suddenly on the alert. From years of practice in assessing such situations, Bernie could sniff the scent of impending trouble as readily as a bloodhound tracking an escaped convict. He squared up his shoulders and stood there on the landing, blocking the escape route down the grimy stairway.

'Oi! You!' Turner barked through gritted teeth. He stabbed a finger at a wide-eyed man, who was in the compromising and powerless position of trying to pull up his trousers whilst lying prostrate on the filthy bedside rug. 'Out!'

The man tried to rise to his feet, but he wasn't quick enough for Turner's liking. He landed a kick in the man's back and sent him rolling across the narrow stretch of floor towards the door. He came to a halt at Bernie's feet.

'Now!' Turner hollered.

Bernie reached down with one of his great beefy hands and dragged the man to his feet.

'Do as the gentleman says, eh?' Bernie suggested with a broad, sarcastic wink. 'And it wouldn't be a bad idea to pull yer strides up neither, moosh.'

The man stared up at Bernie; his mind working overtime wondering what the hell was going on, as he hitched up his trousers. Neither of the two men – both of whom looked as though they would kill him as soon as say goodmorning to him – could have been the brass's husband. They were too prosperous-looking for that. She might have been in their league a few years back, but, from the state of her now, she definitely wasn't any more. Maybe they were her pimps? Maybe they'd found out she'd been working a foreigner on the pair of them and was keeping the extra takings, and they'd come round to put the frighteners on her. But whatever and whoever they were, he knew he didn't like the look of either of them. It came to something when a man couldn't come off the ships and do an honest, straightforward bit of business with a tart without getting himself a kicking.

He did up his final button and took a tentative step towards the door that Bernie was still guarding like a dog ready to break its leash. Bemie stepped aside to let him pass, but the man stopped and turned round. Bernie immediately returned to blocking the doorway.

'Er, can I get me jacket, mate?' he asked Turner nervously, pointing at the armchair piled high with clothes and taking care to avoid any eye contact with Eileen, who had firmly stated her allegiance by positioning herself next to Turner.

Turner slowly took off his trilby, placed it just so on the bed and then turned his attention to the armchair. With a delicately poised finger and thumb he lifted a dark blue seaman's reefer-jacket from the heap. 'This it?' he asked, holding it out to the man as though it were covered in something very unpleasant.

He nodded. 'Yeah. That's it.'

Turner, still staring at the man, patted the pockets until he found what he was looking for – a roll of money. 'Just home from a trip are yer?'

'That's right.'

'I thought so. Yer face is all brown from the sea air. It's good for yer, yer know, the sea air.' He flung the now empty-pocketed coat at the man's feet. 'And it's a good, keeping healthy. Yer wanna bear that in mind when yer go spending the night with birds what yer don't know.'

Turner let the roll of money drop from his fingers to the floor as though it was so much rubbish, and then, without shifting his gaze from the now sweating man, he grabbed Eileen by the top of her arm, his huge fingers digging into her skinny flesh. 'Say goodbye to the sailor boy, Eileen,' he commanded her. 'And let him know if yer wanna see him again.'

'Goodbye,' Eileen gasped – her arm was really hurting. 'Yer've gotta go now and I don't wanna see yer round here no more. Right?'

The sailor desperately wanted to do as she asked, but no one seemed to notice that he couldn't get past the man blocking the doorway. Why on earth hadn't he stuck with the sorts down Chinatown like he usually did? He'd kill that bloke he'd met in the pub who'd told him he could get this bird on the cheap. What was the idiot's name again? Reg Dunn, that was it. He'd find the bastard before he had to go back on board. And he'd have him. The silly bleeder had wound up costing him the whole of his wages and, by the feel of it, a cracked rib for good measure. Some cheap night this had turned out to be.

'I liked how yer said that, Eileen,' said Turner, grinning with pleasure. 'Cos I appreciate a bit o' respect from a woman. A bit of loyalty. I was saying that to Bernie here, just a minute or so ago, wasn't I, Bern?'

Bernie nodded his agreement.

'I mean,' Turner continued, 'what more could a man want than a woman what wants to please him?' He let go of her arm and clapped his hands together with a loud crack. 'Tell yer what, you get yerself all dollied up, girl, and I'll take yer out to celebrate. Now, how'd yer like that?'

'That's a smashing idea!' Eileen was glowing with pleasure and excitement; she'd been right, Bill did still love her.

Bernie, on the other hand, wasn't nearly so impressed with the idea of another outing. He'd just about had his bellyful of driving Turner round the streets. And Turner hadn't mentioned where he wanted to go on this particular little jaunt. But from Bernie's experience it probably wasn't going to involve a trip over to the boating lake in Vicky Park for a bit of a row around, or even an early matinee at the Poplar Hippodrome. If Turner's usual form was anything to go on, it would probably mean that they were going to spend the rest of the day in one of the twenty-four hour drinking dives that catered for the big-time gamblers.

Bernie closed his eyes. He could just see it coming. They'd be in for the bloody duration.

'Guv,' Bernie began, as gently as he could, shoving the sailor to one side as though he were a parcel. 'All right if I nip off home? Cos Queenie, you know...'

Turner reached out to Bernie who, half expecting a slap for even suggesting such a thing, flinched and stuck up his guard to protect his face. But Turner, his mood having returned to one of sentimental camaraderie, was only interested in being best pals.

'You get yerself off home, Bern,' he said magnanimously. 'And here—' he stooped down and picked up the seaman's roll of notes '—you take this for yer trouble. Leave the motor for me, get yerself a cab, and something nice for the old woman. Cos I like to see the ladies kept happy, don't you, Bern?'

Bernie took the wad gratefully. Not so much for the money, although by the weight of it, he guessed there was a good forty or so quid there, but for the chance, at last, to escape.

His mind was made up this time, he would not be working for Big Bill Turner's firm very much longer, not if he had anything to do with it.

He turned on his heel, grabbed the sailor by the shoulder and started to steer him towards the grimy narrow stairway. His nose twitched at the stench. His Queenie was definitely not the proudest of housekeepers but this place smelt like a rat-hole.

'Bernie!'

He froze. Turner was on his case again. What was the matter with the man? Bernie slowly turned round to face him.

'Yes, guv?'

'I've changed me mind. I'm feeling a bit tired, you'd better drive us.' He chucked Eileen roughly under the chin. 'Then me and you can have a little cuddle in the back seat, eh, babe?'

Eileen beamed back at him in a state of near ecstasy.

'Now,' he went on, 'you take jolly Jack Tar here downstairs and explain to him, nice and clear mind, how he ain't welcome round here no more, and we'll be down in a couple o' minutes.' He leered lecherously at Eileen. 'As soon as madam here's said hello nicely to me.'

Bernie nodded. Now he really had the hump. He was gonna be sitting downstairs like a little kid waiting outside the public bar for his old man to drink away his wages, while Turner was up here shtupping Eileen. Great. Just what he wanted.

Yanking the hapless merchant seaman out on to the landing and pinning him against the rickety washstand, Bemie pulled the door to and left Turner and Eileen to it. That was a sight that he definitely would not like to see.

But while those two were getting on with their bit of fun, Bemie intended having a bit of his own. He'd take Eileen's 'friend' down the side alley and explain to him – nice and clear, just as Turner wanted – not to stray on to another feller's pitch. Because not only was Bernie now in a very bad mood indeed, but he'd never liked sailors.

Their stupid trousers got on his nerves.

–

'You got any booze in here?' Turner swept all the clothes off the armchair with a single swipe of his arm and settled down to wait for Eileen to get ready.

'Under the bed,' Eileen's reflection answered him from the little mirror on the chest that doubled as a dressing-table. 'The sailor boy fetched me a couple of bottles.'

It was only because she was leaning forward to examine her face in the mirror – in an effort to decide whether to scrape off last night's make-up and begin again or to try to plaster over the cracks – that Eileen didn't notice Turner looming up behind her.

'Good was he?' Turner hissed into her ear.

She twisted round, her hands clasping her throat.

'Blimey, Bill, yer frightened the life out o' me, creeping up on me like that.'

'Did I?' He was standing right over her, breathing very hard. 'D'you like being frightened?'

'What?'

'I do.'

'Bill?' Eileen swallowed hard. 'Don't talk like that. Yer know I—'

'Not all the time.' He had closed his eyes, and tipped back his head. He began gently smoothing her hair. 'But sometimes...'

Suddenly he grabbed a handful of her hair and dragged her on to the filthy carpet.

'My Moe'd be interested in hearing all about you and your sailor boy,' he said, straddling her now shaking body. 'What was he like?'

'Look, Bill, yer know I don't like it when yer want me to—' Eileen began nervously.

Turner nodded, deep in thought, and continued as though he hadn't heard her. 'She likes me to tell her stories. About what I've been up to. And about—'

'Look, Bill, I really don't—'

Turner raised his hand, slapped Eileen hard across the face and then smiled down at her. 'Get yer things off, Eileen.'

–

As he buttoned up his trousers, Turner looked around the room as though seeing it for the first time.

'How comes you wound up living like this?'

Eileen, still naked, stared up at him from the mound of covers on the unmade bed. She propped herself up on one elbow and half-heartedly pulled the stained and torn sheet over herself to cover the booze-aged and sagging body that she knew was no longer the great asset it had once been. 'It was when you said I had to leave the flat,' she said quietly. 'I didn't have nowhere else to go, did I?'

'Bernie's old woman's as bad. And she's a piece o' shit like you and all. It proper suits the pair o' yer living in dosshouses like this.'

As he tucked his shirt tails in and looped his braces on to his shoulders, Eileen climbed unsteadily off the bed and went over to him. 'Yer can't mean that, Bill,' she whined. 'Not after what we've just done.'

'*After what we've just done*? Do me a favour. Don't remind me, or yer'll have me fetching me breakfast up again.' He curled his lip at her in disgust. 'I'm gonna have to go down the baths and get meself cleaned up before I go home as it is. My Moe'd never let me in the house if I tried going in with this stink on me.'

She shook her head. 'You don't mean that. You don't.'

'Don't I?' Turner started laughing at her and then bent over to tie his laces.

Eileen backed slowly away from him towards the door, keeping her eye on his every move.

She opened the door, slipped, still naked, on to the landing and snatched the long-bladed bread knife from the side of the grease-encrusted stove.

–

Bernie was just about fed up with waiting. 'A couple o' minutes' Turner had reckoned. Well, that must have been a good half-hour ago. Bernie wasn't taking any more of it. He got out of the car, slung the keys on to the driver's seat, and slammed the door.

He paused to flash a just-about-interested glance along the alley towards the slumped heap of clothes that was the unconscious seaman, then began to walk off in search of a cab, when he heard a gurgling scream coming from the top window.

His instinct for bother immediately aroused, Bernie was up the stairs and had put his boot to Eileen's already half-rotten door before he had stopped even to think about what he was doing. As the door crashed off its single hinge, he was through the doorway and barging into the room like a train at full steam.

He pulled up as quickly as if he'd hit a brick wall.

The room looked as though someone had gone mad with a can of red paint. There was blood everywhere.

Turner was sitting astride Eileen on the big, unmade bed. He was fully clothed but Eileen was naked. Her eyes stared sightlessly up at him as her head lolled over the edge of the mattress, her frizzy red hair tumbling down on to the filth-and-blood-darkened bedside rug. Her throat had been slit, and the blood was still pumping from the wound like a fountain, gushing in rhythmic spurts.

A long-bladed knife glinted up at Bernie from the floor. It took him a very short time to decide what to do.

–

Cissie hauled on the brake and closed her eyes. She had decided. Once she had got out of the truck and had started walking along the street, then that would be that – she would go and give Sammy his answer.

She covered her face with her hands and groaned. She had put it off for as long as she could. She hadn't even driven straight back from her parents' house, but had cruised around the streets, stretching out the time, taking every moment to consider what she should do. But now the time had come.

She rubbed her eyes, and then dragged her fingertips hard down her cheeks. So much had happened to her in the seven months since Davy had died – no, not since

Davy had died, since Davy had been *murdered* by that bastard Turner – that she should have been craving the safety and stability that Sammy Clarke could offer her. But were safety and stability what she really wanted?

She leant her arms on the steering wheel and peered over them at the corner shop at the far end of the street.

The wife of a pink-faced grocer.

It certainly wasn't how she had ever seen herself.

–

'Hello, Sam,' she greeted him, immediately lifting her hand to silence Lena, Myrtle and Ethel, who were standing by the counter like a set of Toby-jugs. 'It's all right, you three, I ain't gonna try and push in. I just come in to ask Sammy something.'

'Hhhhmmmph!' snorted Ethel for the three of them.

'What is it, Cis?' Sammy asked with his usual eager affability.

'Can we have a word when yer've got a minute?'

'Course we can.'

'A word eh?' Myrtle said, her chins quivering with hostility. 'Wouldn't have nothing to do with them terrible goings-on in Whitechapel, I don't suppose?'

'As usual, I ain't got a clue what yer going on about, Myrtle,' Cissie responded wearily.

'D'you mean you ain't heard?' Lena asked, delighted as always whenever she found herself with the opportunity to be the bearer of bad news.

'How can I tell yer if I have, if I dunno what yer talking about?'

'Cis,' Sammy said, with a warning flash of his eyes, 'it ain't a very nice—'

'Big Bill Turner's been stabbed to death,' Lena interrupted him. 'Found with the old whore what did it. She killed him, then slit her own throat. Blood-bath it was.'

'Whitechapel?' Cissie breathed. She blinked rapidly. Eileen…

It couldn't be.

'Queenie Denham, you know, that moneylender from over Bow Common,' Ethel chipped in, 'her old man found 'em. He said he heard the screams as he was just passing by and went up to help. But if yer believe that, yer'll believe anything. Bloody load of old toffee. I reckon he'd gone round to do a bit o' business with the old brass, if the truth was known, and he come across that little lot instead.' She grinned nastily at her daughter. 'I bet that put him off his stroke, eh, Lena?'

Lena sniggered back at her mother. 'It will do when that Queenie has his balls off him for going with a tom!'

Cissie stared incredulously at Lena. 'You must feel the same about your Reg then, Lena,' she snapped. 'Cos he favours working girls, don't he?'

Lena's eyes glinted with fury; she'd never liked *that* side of things since they'd first got married and was only all too pleased when Reg did his business elsewhere and didn't bother her with it, but she hated the thought that a stuck-up bitch like Cissie Flowers knew about it. She'd have her, the cocky cow.

'Turner was a bit of a friend o' your'n, weren't he, Cissie?' Lena looked knowingly at Sammy. 'There's talk going around that he come down Linman Street to see yer. In the early hours of this morning, as a matter of fact. It surely can't be true, can it? I mean, that ain't a very nice thing to go saying about a young widow woman, now is it? People might say she's putting it about to earn herself a few quid, to buy all them nice things what everyone says she has to have, while there's others having to go without even a loaf o' stale bread and a screw o' tea. No, it really ain't a nice thing to say.'

'No, Lena, it ain't nice. And d'yer know what, that's why I ain't surprised that it's the likes of you what's been saying it. And that's why I'm gonna smack yer stupid, bigmouthed, ugly boat for yer, to teach yer some manners.' Cissie stepped towards Lena, slowly pushing her coat sleeves above her elbows.

Lena backed away. 'Don't you threaten me!'

'All right, Cis,' Sammy said, lifting the flap in the counter. 'There's no need to upset yerself. You go outside in the fresh air for a smoke, eh, and calm down. And I'll be out as soon as I've finished serving these…' He paused. 'Ladies.'

'Yeah, good idea, Sam,' Cissie said, sticking her chin in the air and glaring down her nose at Lena. 'I could do with some fresh air, cos I don't like the stink that these three have fetched in with 'em. And,' she added with loud emphasis, 'what I've gotta discuss with yer is private anyway. So while the kids are at me mum and dad's it'll be a good opportunity, won't it? I'll have a walk up towards the Cut and I'll see yer there, by the bridge.'

As Cissie walked towards the door to leave the shop, she left her three flabbergasted neighbours momentarily dumbstruck by her revelations. But as Cissie stepped out on to the pavement, Lena had obviously made at least a partial recovery, because she heard her gasp incredulously, 'Private talks with you, Sammy Clarke? And she reckons she's left her kids at her mum and dad's?'

Cissie leant against the bridge and took her cigarettes from her pocket; her hand was trembling. She couldn't get the thought out of her mind about how poor Eileen must have suffered. Eileen, a woman who had been used and abused most of her short and brutal life. She sighed loudly. Poor Eileen. It certainly made her own problems seem insignificant by comparison.

'Want a light for that?' It was Sammy.

Cissie looked down at the unlit cigarette still dangling from her fingers and nodded. 'Please.'

Sammy dug into his apron. 'I've left the three witches back in Linman Street brewing up all sorts o' lies about yer. Yer've really got 'em going, yer know, about yer mum and dad.'

'Mind if we talk about that later?' she asked, turning away from him and staring down at the oily grey-brown water. 'There's something else I wanna say.'

'Look, Cis, I wasn't trying to pump yer about yer mum and dad or nothing. You know me.'

She looked over her shoulder and smiled at him. At pink-faced, kind Sammy Clarke. 'Yeah, Sam, I know you, and I know what a good, decent man you are.'

Sammy felt his face burn scarlet. 'I still ain't lit yer fag,' he muttered, fumbling with clumsy embarrassment with the lighter he'd produced from the pocket of the apron that, he had only just realised to his even greater shame, he was still wearing.

'Here, let me,' she said, reaching out and taking it from him.

'You might as well keep it,' he said softly, as he watched her study the familiar gold casing.

She looked up at him. 'Aw, Sam, it's my one, ain't it? You give me that money for it, then yer never sold it.' Sammy shrugged self-deprecatingly, whilst wishing desperately that it was dark and that Cissie couldn't see the now deep shade of beetroot his face had gone: 'I wanted to keep it for yer.'

'I dunno what to say.'

He dropped his chin and stared down at his shiny brown boots. 'How about this thing yer said yer wanted to talk about?' he asked quietly.

Cissie took a long drag on her cigarette. 'Lena wasn't making things up for once, yer know, Sam. Turner did come to see me early this morning. I'm surprised yer never heard all the row. He was pissed as a sack and shouting the odds like a madman.'

'I was getting me fruit and veg down the wholesalers' in Stratford. But I'd have been over like a shot if I'd been there, Cis. I wouldn't have let him bother yer.'

'I know, Sam,' said Cissie gratefully, knowing that Sammy would have come to help her, but glad he hadn't. Turner would have squashed the likes of Sammy like a fly. 'He come to make me an offer. Offered to set me up in business. Gimme a flat. Everything. You name it and it was mine. I reckon I could've just about named me price.' Sammy looked away. 'Now it's me what don't know what to say,' he breathed.

'I said *no* to him, Sam.' She weighed the gold lighter in her hand, staring at it through half-closed eyes. 'And I'm glad he's dead. D'you know that? He thought he could own me, see. Just like he owned Davy.' She hesitated. 'Yer do know what Davy was involved in, don't yer, Sam?'

'There was talk, but there always is. And you know me, Cis, I don't take no notice o' things like that.'

'Did everyone know?'

'A lot thought they did. There was all sorts of rumours. You know what they're like.'

'No wonder so many of 'em had it in for me round here; why they reckoned I was a selfish, stuck-up mare.' Cissie frowned thoughtfully, threw her cigarette to the ground and crushed it under her heel. 'I wonder how many of 'em was in debt to him. How many couldn't put grub on the table cos their old man had lost all their money trying to win a few bob to stretch out his dole?' She raked her fingers through her hair, dragging it off her face. 'And it weren't just the gambling yer know. From what I can gather, from the sort of people he was involved with, and from what happened to him, Davy was tangled up in all sorts.'

'I know, Cis,' he said softly.

She handed the lighter back to Sammy. 'You have it, Sam, please. I don't want it no more.'

'No, Cis. Nor do I.'

Sammy leant all his weight on to his back foot, extended his arm behind him and then, with every ounce of effort he could summon, he threw the lighter in a high arc up into the sky.

The pair of them stood on the bridge, side by side, watching it as it fell – plop! – into the Limehouse Cut.

Chapter 24

April 1934

Cissie, puffing from the exertion of bending over, cocked her head on one side and narrowed her eyes, assessing the display the flowers made in the two enamel buckets either side of the door.

'They'll never sell,' a woman's voice barked.

'Yes they will, Myrtle,' Cissie replied. She didn't need to turn round to see who was speaking. 'Cos I reckon early daffs like these are like little bits o' sunshine after all the dark winter days we've had.'

'What at that bloody price?'

'People always have a few coppers for something beautiful.'

Myrtle snorted derisively. 'D'yer reckon?'

'Yes, Myrtle, I really do.'

'Them greens fresh, are they?'

'Sammy got 'em fresh from Stratford yesterday morning.'

'Well, they wanna be,' she grumbled, 'or they'll be off for Arthur's Sunday dinner tomorrow. And he gets in a right old mood if his veg ain't just right.'

'D'you want some then?'

'Gimme about half a pound – I can't afford no more at your prices – and make sure yer finger ain't on them scales when yer weighing 'em up and all.'

Cissie threw a handful of greens on to the scales that were set on a little table in the middle of the vegetable boxes outside the shopfront, and started changing the little metal weights on the other side until they balanced.

'So yer working here full-time now then?' Myrtle snapped as she peered suspiciously at the scales.

'That's right, Myrt,' said Cissie, stuffing the leafy greens into Myrtle's string bag. 'They've weighed a bit over, but, go on, I'll just charge yer the three ha'pence. Now, what else can I get yer?'

'Nothing thanks,' she said spitefully, handing over two ha'pennies and two farthings. 'Like I said, I can't afford these prices. I should have gone down Chris Street, but I had to come over here for this ceremony thing what Sammy's been going on about. I must be the first to show up, eh?'

'Ceremony?' asked Cissie, slipping the money into her money apron. 'What's that yer going on about now?'

'Aw, ain't he mentioned it to yer?' Myrtle asked with a delighted sneer. 'Well, he can't think much of yer as a worker if he ain't even told yer about the ceremony, now can he?'

'I honestly ain't got a clue what yer talking about, Myrtle, but I think yer must have got it wrong, whatever it is.'

'We'll see,' Myrtle said, hoiking the string bag up her arm. 'So, is it true what they're saying about yer mum and dad then?' she went on.

'What would that be then, Myrtle?' Cissie asked wearily.

'That they're moving into your place?'

'Blimey, your ear'oles must be flapping night and day.'

'There's no need to be so bloody rude.' Myrtle sniffed haughtily and poked dubiously at a display of onions. 'So, are they moving into number seven or what? I mean, I have every right to know who me neighbours're gonna be, yer know.'

'Yer right, Myrtle. Yer do. And they are. Satisfied?'

'Ain't gonna be much room in there then, is there? Cos Lil already has to sleep down in the front parlour, don't she?'

'All right, love?' a woman's voice asked from behind them.

'Hello, Mum, Dad,' said Cissie, turning round with a relieved smile. Not only was she pleased to see her parents, but it was a chance to escape any more of Myrtle's awkward questions.

Cissie kissed them both on the cheek. 'This is a nice surprise, I wasn't expecting yers till this afternoon.'

'Sammy asked us over,' said Frank.

'That'll be for the ceremony, I suppose,' said Ethel as she and Lena parked themselves next to Myrtle.

'That's right, Ett,' said Ellen pleasantly. 'Now, where's them grandchildren o' mine, Cissie, cos I can't wait to give 'em a great big cuddle.'

'What's all this about, Dad?' Cissie whispered behind her hand, as they followed her mum into the shop. 'What ceremony?'

'Don't ask me, darling,' Frank whispered back with a happy shrug. 'You know what I'm like. I'm just here cos yer mum said I had to be.'

Cissie squeezed his arm. 'She's a lucky woman having a man like you, Dad.'

'I think so,' he said with a wink, 'but don't tell her I said so, will yer?'

'Where's Lil?' Ellen asked, looking round the empty shop. 'I thought she'd be here.'

'She reckons she's having one of her turns,' Cissie said with a roll of her eyes, 'and, knowing her, she won't be up till at least dinner-time.'

'Took it bad, did she?' Ellen asked with a sigh.

'No worse than she takes anything, Mum. You know her. Look, why don't you go through the back to the kids. They're in the storeroom with Sammy and Ernie. Been in there all morning they have. Up to some mischief or other. I don't like to think the state they'll be in, the pair of 'em.'

'They get on well with Sammy, don't they, babe?'

'They certainly do, Dad.' Cissie cocked her head on one side and looked at her dad, her kind, decent, gentle dad who had only ever done what he thought was best. 'He reminds me a lot of you, yer know.'

'That's a very nice thing to hear, Cissie. Thank you.' Ellen took hold of the handle to the door that led through to the back rooms, but it was snatched from her grasp as it was opened inwards from the other side.

'You made me jump, Sam!' Ellen grinned at Sammy standing there framed in the doorway. 'How are yer, love?'

'Covered in paint,' he said, grinning back at her. 'Don't let me get none on yer frock.'

Ellen backed away, making room for him and Ernie to step through into the shop. Between them they were carrying what looked like a short plank of wood covered with sacking.

Cissie frowned. What was all this about?

Joyce and Matty came trotting through behind the two men, with the sort of easy smiles on their faces that Cissie was so pleased to have come to expect. The moment the children spied their grandparents, the pair of them launched themselves across the shop with whoops of pleasure.

'Guess what, Nan?' yelped Matty. 'Guess what we've been doing?'

Ellen scooped him up into her arms. 'Remember what Nanny told yer?'

Matty nodded. 'It's a surprise?'

'That's right. Good boy.'

'You sure you don't know what's going on, Dad?'

Frank smiled and shook his head unconvincingly. 'I never know nothing, me.'

'Come on, everyone,' Sammy said, with a gesture of his head towards the doorway. 'Out we go.'

Outside, Cissie could hardly believe her eyes. Where had all these people come from? Practically everyone from the street was standing there, and they all had expectant looks on their faces, as though something special was about to happen. There were even a couple of Elsie Collier's gentlemen, as well as quite a few women, plus their noisy broods of children, from the surrounding neighbourhoods, whom Cissie knew from their visits to the shop, although she couldn't have put a name to most of them.

'What's going on, Sam?' she asked with a frown.

'Yer'll see,' he said happily, and with that he clapped his hands loudly. 'If I could just have yer attention ladies and gentlemen.'

'Ladies and gentlemen,' sneered Lena Dunn, 'who the hell does he think he is, the bleed'n Lord Mayor o' London?'

'Thank you, Lena,' Sammy said patiently. 'I won't be keeping yer for very long.'

'Bloody good job and all, the Sabberton'll be open soon,' Ethel's husband muttered darkly.

'Yer might be offered a little drop o' something in here in a minute, Dick,' Sammy encouraged him, 'if yer can just bear with me.'

'Well,' beamed Dick, hooking his thumbs into his waistcoat. 'That's a different matter, son. You carry on.'

'Thanks. Now I've invited you all here this morning,' Sammy began, 'and a very nice morning it is too—'

'Get on with it!' a voice growled from the crowd.

'To unveil me new sign. The sign that Ernie,' he said turning to Ernie Mills, 'is gonna help me screw above the door later on.'

'What, had to sell the shop, have yer?' Ethel sniped. 'I knew it'd come to this. It's all that credit what he's been giving to the likes of her, that Cissie Flowers,' she added knowingly, pulling in her chin and jerking her head sideways. 'She could work here till doomsday and she still wouldn't be able to pay off that slate of her'n.'

'Actually Ethel, I'm glad to say that I ain't had to sell the shop, but things are gonna be a little bit different round here. And that's why I invited all of yers here today to see the new sign.'

With that, Sammy pulled the sacking covering from the board that he and Ernie had carried out on to the pavement, with a dramatic flourish.

It read 'Cissie and Samuel Clarke'.

The unity with which the onlookers gasped made it sound as though they had all been practising.

'Yesterday afternoon, Cissie did me the honour of becoming my wife.'

There was new gasping, more ragged this time, and a flurry of whispers.

'You and her?' Lena asked incredulously. 'Married?'

'It's a bit of a surprise to me and all, to tell yer the truth, Lena,' Sammy said, smiling shyly across at Cissie, who was clasping her mum's arm as though she would never let her go again. 'I never thought I'd be lucky enough to be this happy.'

Increasingly loud whispers and mutters passed around the now astonished neighbours.

Sammy held up his hand to silence them. 'There's a lot of other things about to change that yer might as well all know about and all.'

'I'll bet there is,' a wag shouted from the back of the crowd.

Sammy ignored him. 'Gladys'll be helping Cissie in the shop,' he went on, his smile growing broader by the minute. 'Cos Cissie's running it from now on. And she's a clever girl, so don't worry, yer'll all be well looked after.'

'She's a clever girl all right,' hissed Ethel into Lena's ear. 'Got the bleed'n shop off him, ain't she? He must be barmy.'

'And me and Ernie are gonna be busy and all,' Sammy went on, all the jibes and heckles unable to dent his happiness. 'We're setting up a new fruit and veg stall down Chris Street. We've got the pitch all sorted, so, if yer down the market and yer want the right gear at the best prices, yer know who to come to, don't yer? Clarke and Mills, Quality Greengrocers.'

Mouths dropped open like trapdoors. Now Sammy really had taken leave of his senses this time. Everyone knew what a useless lump Ernie Mills was, the man hadn't worked for years. He didn't want to work. It was a well-known fact.

'That shut yer up, didn't it?' Gladys beamed at Ethel.

'Now,' Sammy concluded, 'if yer'd all like to come inside and join us in a toast, I've got a few bottles out the back that might just need opening. Including some lemonade for all you little chavvies!'

The Godwin kids beat everyone to the door, leaving Sammy and Ernie waiting for their turn to go through and start pouring the drinks.

'Maybe yer'll change that sign again one day,' Ernie said, punching Sammy matily in the shoulder, 'to Clarke and Family. If you and Cissie have a nipper of yer own, like.'

'I've got all the family I need already,' Sammy replied, smiling proudly over his shoulder at Cissie and her children. 'Come on, Ern, let's get inside before them Godwins pinch the lot.'

—

As the drink flowed and the people who packed into the shop joined in toast after toast, their benevolence towards the happy couple and the new arrangements increased with every glass of free drink they swallowed.

Cissie pushed her way through the now congratulatory crowd to go over and speak to Ellen.

'I'd better nip over and tell Lil, Mum. She'll go barmy if she thinks she's missing a drink.'

'It's all right, darling, I'll go over.'

'You sure?'

'Yeah, cos if me and her are gonna be sharing that house, I reckon there's a few things we're gonna have to get straight between us. And me not appreciating having to get up and do all the jobs while she stays in bed till dinner-time cos she's got another bloody hangover is one of 'em.'

'Well, I'll just step outside with yer for a bit of air anyway.'

–

While Ellen went over to speak to Lil, Cissie stood outside on the pavement, staring at the freshly painted sign that Sammy had propped against the vegetable boxes.

'Cissie and Samuel Clarke'.

Cissie Clarke.

She didn't know if she'd ever get used to not being known as Cissie Flowers, it had been her identity for so long. And even though it was a name she had chosen to reject long before she had accepted Sammy's proposal, it still seemed strange to her. But not nearly as strange as being married again. A little over a year ago, who would have thought that all this – marriage to Sammy Clarke, working for a living, seeing her mum and dad again – would all be happening to her?

But Cissie was now grown-up enough to know that life was never as simple as you thought it was going to be.

And that marrying Sammy Clarke was definitely not just a simple matter of loving him. Cissie didn't know if she would ever be able to love a man again. Not in the way she had loved Davy.

She put a cigarette in her mouth and lit it with the pretty engraved silver lighter that Sammy had given her instead of the engagement ring that she had refused. She had had one of those once, and that was enough for her.

She blew out a stream of smoke and whispered the words to herself, 'Cissie Clarke.'

Was this really what she wanted? Or was it more to do with having a bit of security for her kids? And a bit of safety for herself with a decent man for once? Or was it the fact that Sam had just been there at the right time and she didn't know what else to do?

With Davy she had no choice in the matter. She had seen him, and that had been that. She had fallen in love with him and nothing anybody could have done would have stood in her way.

It shamed her to admit it to herself even now, but she had had a similar sort of feeling when she had first known Jim Phillips, although he had been different to Davy. But he had been kind to her, or so she had thought, at a time when she had really needed it.

But then so had Sam. Kinder than she had ever deserved.

She thought of the lies she'd been told and the lies she'd told herself.

And she thought about how things might have been.

No one could ever know how their lives were going to turn out. She knew that. And she knew that no one in her life would ever be like Davy. Funny, romantic, unpredictable Davy.

But wasn't that a good thing?

Cissie stared unseeingly through her cigarette smoke at the sign.

Probably.

She'd been hit with a lot of hard lessons in the year since Davy had been killed. Lessons that, if she had any brain at all, she would make sure she would learn from.

'You look miles away, love.' It was Sammy. 'I just came out to see if everything was all right.'

Cissie nodded; unable to face him. 'Course it is, Sam. Why wouldn't it be? I've got everything a woman could ever want, haven't I? Two lovely kids who are smiling again, me mum and dad back with me, and a man who loves me.'

'A man who loves yer more than you can ever know,' he said, his voice catching with emotion. 'And I'll give yer time, Cis,' he added, looking down at the sign through tear- glazed eyes. 'I promise yer that. As much time as yer want.' He scrubbed roughly at his cheeks with the back of his hand. 'For ever, if that's how it's gotta be.'

'Time?' she asked, dropping the cigarette to the floor and grinding it beneath her heel. 'What for?'

'I understand, yer know, Cis. I know I ain't what yer wanted. But I love yer enough for the both of us. Honest I do.'

Cissie turned to Sammy, took his pink-cheeked face in her hands, and kissed him gently on the mouth. 'If she had any brains, Sammy Clarke, any woman in the world would tell yer that you're all she could ever want. And ain't you always telling me what a clever girl I am?'